BELMONT COUNTY LIBRARY
3 3667 00481 7
P9-DFM-591

Vengeance Road

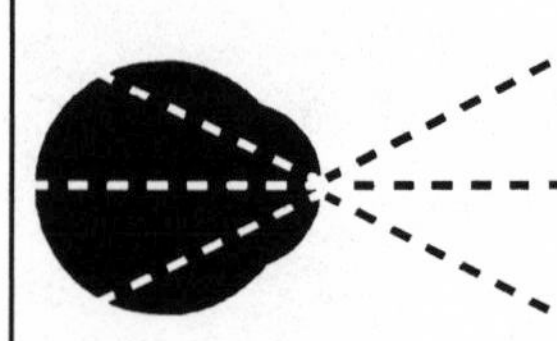

This Large Print Book carries the
Seal of Approval of N.A.V.H.

Vengeance Road

Christine Feehan

THORNDIKE PRESS
A part of Gale, a Cengage Company

Farmington Hills, Mich • San Francisco • New York • Waterville, Maine
Meriden, Conn • Mason, Ohio • Chicago

Topeko Ink.
Thorndike Press, a part of Gale, a Cengage Company.

This is a work of fiction. Names, characters, places, and incidents are either the product of the author's imagination or are used fictitiously, and any resemblance to actual persons, living or dead, business establishments, events, or locales is entirely coincidental.

Thorndike Press® Large Print Romance.
The text of this Large Print edition is unabridged.
Other aspects of the book may vary from the original edition.
Set in 16 pt. Plantin.

**LIBRARY OF CONGRESS CIP DATA ON FILE.
CATALOGUING IN PUBLICATION FOR THIS BOOK
IS AVAILABLE FROM THE LIBRARY OF CONGRESS**

ISBN-13: 978-1-4328-6089-9 (hardcover)

Published in 2019 by arrangement with Berkley, an imprint of Penguin Publishing Group, a division of Penguin Random House LLC

Printed in Mexico
1 2 3 4 5 6 7 23 22 21 20 19

For all the women brave enough
to take on the wild ones

FOR MY READERS

Be sure to go to http://www.christinefeehan.com/members/ to sign up for my PRIVATE book announcement list and download the FREE ebook of *Dark Desserts.* Join my community and get firsthand news, enter the book discussions, ask your questions and chat with me. Please feel free to email me at Christine@christinefeehan.com. I would love to hear from you.

ACKNOWLEDGMENTS

I would very much like to thank the men and women who contributed, sharing information generously when I asked them. Anne Roffe Tann, I appreciate your letter so much. Ed and Ruth, thank you for answering questions, even late at night when I'm getting crazy. A huge shout-out to Patrick J. Mears from Spread Eagle Tattoo for working so closely with me to create my vision and concept of the Torpedo Ink graphics. Sheila, you helped me very much, letting me talk things out endlessly. Domini, Brian and Denise, thank you for your help with everything from research to edits to pushing me to work faster.

TORPEDO INK MEMBERS

Viktor Prakenskii aka *Czar* — President
Lyov Russak aka *Steele* — Vice President
Savva Pajari aka *Reaper* — Sergeant at Arms
Savin Pajari aka *Savage* — Sergeant at Arms
Isaak Koval aka *Ice* — Secretary
Dmitry Koval aka *Storm*
Alena Koval aka *Torch*
Luca Litvin aka *Code* — Treasurer
Maksimos Korsak aka *Ink*
Kasimir Popov aka *Preacher*
Lana Popov aka *Widow*
Nikolaos Bolotan aka *Mechanic*
Pytor Bolotan aka *Transporter*
Andrii Federoff aka *Maestro*
Gedeon Lazaroff aka *Player*
Kir Vasiliev aka *Master*
Lazar Alexeev aka *Keys*
Aleksei Solokov aka *Absinthe*

Newer Patched Members

Gavriil Prakenskii
Casimir Prakenskii

Prospects

Fatei
Glitch
Hyde

One

Breezy Simmons leaned against her pickup for a moment, staring at the large building that housed the Torpedo Ink Motorcycle Club. Her heart beat so hard in her chest she was afraid she might vomit. The world spun uncontrollably, and she quickly leaned down, putting her head between her legs, drawing in great gulps of air. She caught a glimpse of two men on the other side of the compound as her head went toward the asphalt, and she didn't recognize either of them. That made her pounding heart sink.

She couldn't possibly have the wrong club. This *had* to be them. She was running out of time and options. She slowly righted herself and took another cautious look around. The two men stared at her from across the parking lot. She was careful not to look at them too long. She didn't want them coming anywhere near her. She needed to get in and out very fast.

The Torpedo Ink compound was extremely large and had a high chain-link fence surrounding it. There was even razor wire up on top of the fence, making the place look like a fortress. The rolling gates were wide open, and she'd driven her truck right inside, parking as close to the clubhouse as possible. She'd deliberately left the door to her beat-up pickup open and the engine running. Hopefully, no one recognized her, and she could get in and out of the building quickly, once she asserted these were the right people, the ones she was looking for.

In the early morning hours, the club was just beginning to stir. Clearly, they'd partied hard over the weekend. In the enormous side yard, the one with the beautiful ocean view, she could see embers in fire pits glowing as the breeze stirred them up. A man with his back to her watered them down with a hose. He wore a tight tee and jeans, but no colors. Still, she knew this was the home of the club that called itself Torpedo Ink. She sent up a silent prayer that this was the one she'd been looking for.

There were empty bottles strewn around the grass and on the ground to the side of the building in the wide expanse of open field. Cars, motorcycles and trucks were scattered around the parking lot, although no one parked where the club did. Their motorcycles were lined up neatly and a prospect watched over them. He sat on the curb looking at her. She was parked too close to the precious bikes, but she didn't care — other than that it had drawn the attention of the prospect.

Another long line of motorcycles was parked a short distance down from the clubhouse and a prospect watched over those bikes as well. He looked at her without much interest, which indicated to her that those bikes belonged to a visiting club. He wasn't as interested in protecting the grounds as the one closest to the clubhouse.

She had to get this over with. Just being in such close proximity to an MC made her sick. The fact that she knew what went on at the party made her even sicker. That this might be *his* club, and she had to risk running into him, made all that far worse.

Breezy squared her shoulders, dragged the envelope off the seat and turned all in one motion. The prospect was on his feet. If she knew for certain this was the right club, she would have thrust the letter into his hands and left, but she was guessing from a process of elimination.

She purposely hadn't kept track of him,

especially when she'd heard, a year after she'd left, that eighteen members of the Swords had set up the international president for assassination and had, allegedly, wiped out a number of members and then disappeared. She knew who those eighteen members were immediately, and knowing them, she knew it was possible when others said it wasn't. She'd run as far from the life as she could, and now she was being pulled right back in.

The parties. The violence. The utter disregard and disdain for women. She shut that down fast and walked with brisk, purposeful steps to the club. She yanked open the door and went right in. It smelled just the way she remembered. Booze. Sex. Weed. Her stomach lurched. God. *God.* She couldn't stand walking into the clubhouse, let alone anything else.

The common room was enormous. One side held a long, curving bar, in the center of the room were tables and chairs, and the other side had several couches and armchairs. Sleeping bodies were everywhere. A woman picked up bottles and put them into a garbage bag, dumping paper plates in along with the other trash as she moved through the mostly naked bodies strewn around the floor. She glanced at Breezy but didn't say anything. She kept picking up trash as if on automatic pilot. Breezy remembered what that was like. She could have been that woman.

She didn't recognize any of the men that she could see lying on the floor or slumped in the chairs, and her heart sank. She paused by the bar, her gaze going from one face to the next. Half-naked or naked men and women were draped in chairs around the room or on the floor. Most snored softly, but one woman was busy going down on a man with wild blond hair and ice-blue eyes. Three teardrops were tattooed at the corner of his eye like ice drops dripping down his face.

He slumped in a chair looking almost bored, his eyes at half-mast as the woman knelt at his feet, her mouth busy, while another woman kissed her way up his chest. Across from him, a second man who looked exactly like the blond, obviously his twin, watched, his fist around his impressive and somewhat intimidating cock. With a jerk of his chin, the one with the teardrop tattoos indicated to the woman kissing his chest to go to his watching brother. She immediately dropped to her hands and knees and crawled between the thighs of the other twin.

It was them. The right club. The men she had searched for. She'd found them. She recognized the twins and her heart kicked into overdrive. How could she *not* recognize them? They were gorgeous men. As cold as ice, but beautiful. The one with the tattoos, Ice had been his name, suddenly lifted his gaze and met hers. Her heart stuttered at the recognition she saw in his eyes.

She slapped the envelope onto the bar. "Give that to Steele." She turned to go, her gaze sliding around the room once more.

At the sound of her voice, three women stirred in the far corner of the room, their sleeping bodies pushed aside by the man who lay under them. The movement drew her eye. He half sat, shoving at the dark hair spilling onto his forehead. It was thick and wild, a little out of control. He blinked drowsily at her. Her heart faltered. Stopped. They stared at each other, her stomach lurching.

Breezy threw dignity to the wind. She ran. Fast. She heard the sharp whistle following her, but she had already flung herself into her pickup and thrown it into reverse, foot stomping on the gas pedal. She pressed down hard, and the truck roared as it backed all the way through the rapidly closing gates. Men poured out of the clubhouse, she could see them through her windshield when she glanced at them, but they were mostly naked, and the gates had closed behind her with a loud clang. She was on one side, the side of freedom; they were on the other, those gates holding them in. For once, luck was on her side.

She backed straight into the street, thankful it was so early and there was no traffic. Throwing the pickup into drive, she nearly spun out of control as she overcorrected before straightening out and taking off toward Highway 1. She had a plan, just in case, and she was grateful she'd made it. Her entire body trembled, so much so that it was difficult holding on to the steering wheel. She did though, her knuckles turning white.

Why did it hurt? He'd made it very, very clear she was nothing to him. Another club girl. No, lower than that. A whore. One her family had pimped out. A drug mule. Nothing. She was nothing. She'd thought he was her world, and all the while, he'd been plotting to take down her family's club. She'd loved him. He'd used her and then thrown her away, shattering every dream, every hope she'd ever had.

Her vision blurred, and she swiped at her eyes, furious that he'd made her cry again.

That he *could* make her cry again. She'd cried enough tears over him. The liar. He was just like all the others in the clubs. Women were nothing to them. Nothing. They used them. Humiliated them. She'd been born into that life, but she didn't have to stay there. She wasn't that girl. Not anymore. Not ever again.

She pulled off onto the little narrow dirt road she'd scouted earlier, just in case she was recognized. She knew they'd come after her; after all, she was the daughter of their mortal enemy. She drove the truck as far down as the narrow road allowed, right into a thick grove of trees. The track had long since been abandoned and it was overgrown with shrubbery, vines and trees. She parked, hastily got out and covered the pickup with the branches and vines she'd cut earlier in preparation.

When she was positive the truck couldn't be seen from any angle, Breezy crawled through the driver's window, reached into the back and pulled a blanket around her. She couldn't stop shivering. Even her teeth chattered. She let herself cry, but she did so silently, and she told herself she wasn't crying for lost dreams or heartache. She had so little chance of being successful and yet she *had* to be. There was no room for failure. None.

She closed her burning eyes and leaned her head back against the seat, trying not to think about Steele. She didn't know any other name for him. She'd only known him as Steele. She should have realized that if you'd been with a man for a year and he hadn't told you his given name, he wasn't into you. But she'd been young and desperate, and he'd been the white knight. She'd been so stupid. She hit her head on the back of the seat multiple times wishing she'd been smarter. Wishing she'd been born into another family. Another life. Wishing time hadn't run out on her.

It took only a few minutes before she heard the roar of pipes as motorcycles moved in force down the highway. It sounded like an army was coming after her. Out of stark fear, she slid down farther on the seat. It was going to be a long wait until night. She'd had no choice. She knew clubs. She knew on a Sunday morning, after partying all night, they would be sleepy, and she'd have her best chance at getting away if she was recognized. She also knew she didn't dare go out on the highway until nightfall. She hadn't slept in nearly forty-eight hours, and this would be her only chance for a long while. She closed her eyes and willed herself to stop thinking about anything she couldn't control and go to sleep. It didn't work, but she tried.

Lyov Russak — Steele, the vice president of Torpedo Ink — whistled loud and long, raising his hand high, pushing his way through the soft flesh of women to spin his finger in a circle, indicating to Absinthe, who manned the monitors, to close the gates fast. He shoved his way to the surface, cursing in his native language as he got to his feet.

Her voice. He'd never forget that voice. Breezy Simmons. *His* Breezy Simmons. The girl that had forever made him a sick fuck who still, to this day, thought of her, dreamt of her and pretended every woman he tried to be with was her. That was how truly fucked up he was.

He had never confessed to his brothers that he had somehow, inadvertently or not, become the very thing they despised. The thing they hunted. He was ashamed of that. Ashamed, not because of the terrible mistake, but because he couldn't get the way she felt wrapped around him — and his cock — out of his mind. It was nearly all he thought about, and that made him the sickest fuck out there.

She was even more beautiful than he remembered. She'd matured. Her figure had matured. He'd just caught a glimpse of her, one small glimpse, but his body had recognized her almost before his brain had. All that thick, tawny hair, those large green eyes. So green it was like looking into an emerald sea. His entire body clenched, and he pushed aside the women lying sprawled over top of him.

The Demons had come for the weekend, bringing their women with them, and the two clubs had partied hard. He'd drunk too much, the way he usually did at these events. He'd indulged far too much in his attempt to be with women, the way he also did at the events. The endless cycle that got him nowhere because he fucking lived in hell. The woman who could have changed all that was leaving. Walking away from him — again. No, make that *running* away from him. It wasn't happening, and he didn't care how much of a monster that made him. She wasn't getting away from him twice.

Across the room, Ice and Storm were pushing women off their cocks and rising to their feet. Keys and Player untangled from the women they'd been with and rushed the door with the twins. Steele was right behind them, practically shoving them out of the way just in time to see the gates slam shut, effectively stopping pursuit as her truck backed out onto the street in a furious rush.

"No. *Fuck* no." He swung his head toward the prospects. "Get after her. Don't fuckin' lose her. I mean it. You stay on her."

It was definitely Breezy. She was older. Three years older now, but it was her. She'd stared at him in absolute horror, and he couldn't blame her. What the *fuck*? He'd looked for her covertly, after Torpedo Ink had completed their mission and taken down the Swords president and weakened their club, but she'd dropped off the face of the earth. That had been the plan — for her to disappear — but he always thought he'd be able to find her. And he'd tried — God, but he'd tried.

When he'd driven her away, he'd told himself he wouldn't look for her, that he'd let her go. He'd lost that battle with himself, not that it had done him any good. He had searched, over and over, but he hadn't found her. Now she'd walked right into his lair and he wasn't about to let her get away.

"She left something for you, Steele," Ice said, shoving his hand through his hair. He shook his head absently at the woman who tried to drape herself over him. "Sorry, babe. Time to leave."

"I could stay with you," she whispered, her hand sliding down his belly toward his cock.

He gave her a friendly slap on the ass as he expertly avoided her hand. "Sorry, babe. Need you to get on home, wherever the fuck that is."

Ice turned away from her, striding across the room to the bar where he'd seen Breezy put something. He picked up the envelope and turned it over. It was plain white. No writing on the outside.

Steele took it out of his hand and went striding out of the common room to the hall where their private rooms were. He needed to get dressed fast and get on his bike. Find her. He had to find her. He hesitated as he grabbed a pair of jeans. He couldn't go to her stinking of other women. She'd know. She'd smell them on his skin. Urgency made him yank up his jeans and drag a shirt over his head. She already knew. She'd seen the women piled on top of him. He could explain later. Right now, the most important thing was to make certain she didn't get away. He grabbed his colors and slid into them, feeling whole the moment he put them on.

Ice, Storm, Maestro, Keys and most of his other brothers joined him as he half ran out of the clubhouse to his bike. The Demons had rallied, news sweeping through the compound that something was up, and they were supportive of their new allies, immediately offering help. Player was already directing the search, sending bikes in various directions. The prospects had said they'd seen her truck turning south, toward the Bay Area, so that was the direction he was going. Absinthe had gotten her license plate number off the camera continually sweeping their parking lot.

Steele threw his leg over his bike and had it roaring within seconds. Then the wind was in his face and his brothers were at his back as he tore down the highway looking for his woman. He'd been the one to end things, and it had been ugly. Really ugly. Deliberately ugly. He'd said things to drive her away — and she'd gone. She'd managed to take pieces of him with her. She'd stolen those pieces from him, and he'd known when she left, he wasn't going to get them back.

He'd been angry. He'd been afraid for her. He'd been so shocked that just by being with her he'd become everything he most despised in the world — a predator. It hadn't mattered how it had happened; he'd only known it couldn't continue and he'd sent her away. No, he'd driven her away.

He increased his speed, straightening out curves and hurtling down the highway as fast as he could travel without putting himself in the ocean. He was risking doing just that, but to find her, to see her again, was worth anything. Then Keys and Maestro slid up next to him, moving in perfect unison with him, and he realized he wasn't risking just his life — he wasn't alone. His brothers were with him every step of the way. Lately, he'd come to realize, Keys and Maestro guarded him the way Reaper and Savage protected Czar. He didn't need or want it, but they stuck to him like glue. He slowed a fraction, just enough to be safe as they searched for the one woman he knew had cut out his heart and kept it.

Breezy slept fitfully, waking at the least little sound, such as a branch scraping across her rust bucket of a pickup. It sounded like a saw rasping over the paint and yanked her out of her dozing over and over. She climbed out of the truck only when it was absolutely necessary and she had to use the bushes. Each time, she forced herself to drink more water. She'd given up eating, but that only made her feel slightly faint. She wasn't hungry anymore, but thirst persisted in spite of her desire to ignore it. She drank water, and that meant more trips outside the truck, which meant she was at risk.

She watched the fiery ball of the sun begin its drop into the sea. The sky turned all shades of golden, and then orange spread through the low clouds drifting overhead. She had to admit, as sunsets went, it was pretty spectacular. She could have settled here in Northern California. She didn't like big cities, and this area was far from that. Truthfully, she needed to be in a city, to disappear. There, no one cared or noticed a waitress working in a diner. In a smaller town, like Caspar or Sea Haven, everyone would notice.

She had been so careful, keeping her head down, working, nothing else. Just staying off the radar and as far from the club life as possible. Still, she'd been pulled back despite everything she'd tried to do to prevent that from happening. The life was insidious, and once in, it seemed there was no way out.

She was crying again, and that always gave her a vicious headache and annoyed her. She had stopped crying three years earlier after she'd spent weeks giving herself a headache and little else. She'd stopped, gotten on her feet and taken care of business.

She'd been proud of herself for every accomplishment. Then her world had fallen apart and she'd had no choice but to make certain Steele got that letter. Everything depended on him getting it and following the instructions. That was important and yet she knew following instructions was very unlike Steele. She didn't even know for certain if it would matter enough to him that he'd do it for her.

The sun plunged into the sea and she immediately began preparations for leaving. It was nearly time. She climbed out of the window and began removing the branches and vines from around her pickup. She had to back the truck straight along the road for a good thirty feet before there was a wide enough area for her to turn around.

She made it the thirty feet without using lights as the darkness was only just beginning, inky streaks running through the very dim light. As she started up the road, heading away from the ocean and toward the main highway, she saw that a small tree had fallen across the dirt track. It didn't surprise her, given the wind. Fortunately, the round trunk looked more like a sapling than a mature tree, one she could handle by herself.

Sighing, she turned on her headlights to

illuminate the area, so it would be easier to shift the fallen tree. Pulling gloves out of her glove compartment, she pushed open her door with the soles of her boots and slid out. She was tired, afraid and anxious to be gone from Torpedo Ink territory. Just the thought of that dangerous ride along the highway was terrifying. She planned to take the Comptche-Ukiah road leading away from the coast. It would take her off the highway. They probably thought she hadn't done any research or planned ahead — after all, she was a stupid female to be used for carrying drugs or weapons or prostituted out on behalf of the club. She couldn't actually *think.*

Bitterness nearly choked her. She detested MCs and all they stood for. She crouched, took a breath and reached down for the trunk. The moment she had her hands on the tree, arms reached around her, caught her wrists and yanked them behind her back. She rose up fast, throwing her head back to try to make contact with her attacker's head. He grunted when she smashed into his chest, but he had already secured her wrists with zip ties.

"How many times did I tell you to look around? You forgot all my training, babe."

Furious, and more than a little scared, she

spun around and tried to kick him the moment he let her go. She *had* forgotten, damn him. He blocked the kick hard, numbing her leg when he defended himself by striking down on her shin to deflect the blow. She tried again, and he blocked a second time with equal power.

The breath hissed out of her lungs and she bent forward as far as she could, drawing her hands up as high as possible, intending to slam them back down as she came upright fast in order to break the zip ties. He'd taught her that as well. Before she could straighten, his hand was on her back, holding her down.

"Breezy, you'd better calm down before you get hurt."

Her breath hissed out of her lungs. "Go to hell, Steele. You have no right to lay one finger on me."

"That's not exactly true, sweetheart, and you know it," he said.

"I'm not part of your club. I'm not part of your life in any way. Just get the hell away from me."

He didn't let her up, his palm pressing her down while he texted one-handed. "You always were a smart little thing. I looked at the tapes we had of your ride." He sounded derisive. "Babe. Really. You're driving a shit truck. It's a rust bucket if I ever saw one. There was no way it could have gotten that far ahead of us, even if we were a minute or two behind, which the prospects were. That meant it was a process of elimination on which road you'd turned off onto. I also remembered you as being extremely patient when you needed to be. That meant you were going to hide out until nightfall. It gave me plenty of time to track you down."

"Let me up."

"Ask nice."

For one moment, she was afraid she might spontaneously combust — and not in a good way. She stayed quiet. He had to let her up sometime.

"I'm not real happy with you."

Staying quiet went right out the window at the bite in his voice. "I really don't care whether you're happy or not. Let. Me. *Up.*"

"You ask nice. You don't want to play hardball with me, Breezy, because you won't win. Not when I'm this pissed. Didn't have much to do when I found the truck but wait for you to wake up, so I read the fuckin' letter."

Her heart jerked hard. Fear shot through her and she went very still, no longer resisting or struggling to get free. If anything, she tried to make herself smaller, frozen like a little mouse with a big predator about to pounce.

"I read that fuckin' letter eighteen times, Breezy. *Eighteen.* I showed some restraint by not going near the truck because I might have strangled you. I still might."

His palm moved up her back to settle slowly around the nape of her neck, his long fingers curling around either side of her throat. "You get how really fuckin' pissed I am with you?"

"You get how I really fucking don't care?" she spat back. Let him kill her. She was dead anyway. "You threw me out, Steele. I begged you to let me stay with you. It was humiliating, and I still did it. Then I begged you to go with me when it was obvious you wanted me gone. You made it abundantly clear that I was nothing to you. A whore for the club that kept you warm at night. I can repeat verbatim what you said to me, if you'd like. So don't get all self-righteous on me."

The fingers tightened, digging into her throat. The thumb pressed into her chin. His other hand bunched her hair in his fist and slowly pulled her to a standing position. She stared up at his set features. He was even more gorgeous than she remembered, and she dreamt of him every night.

Every night. That made her a masochist.

Unlike most of the others he rode with, he had few scars on his face. They were mostly on his body, covered with ink. She knew every scar, every tattoo. She had traced every one of those scars and tattoos with her tongue. With her fingertips. She'd memorized them until they were etched so deeply in her brain, she could have drawn them and gotten every detail perfect.

She wore his tattoo on her skin. He'd had his friend ink her for him, a tattoo of his design, right across the top curve of her butt, an intricate pattern that she always thought was beautiful. She had a love/hate relationship with that tattoo. The ink beads dripped down onto her buttocks, both cheeks, but high up, the intertwining lace wove his name there, declaring her his property. His. She'd loved that. It had meant something back then. Now, not so much.

She'd been shaking, and he'd held her hand and whispered to her, beautiful, loving things, things that had made her laugh or want to cry with happiness. All the while his friend Ink had tattooed the custom design on her. It had felt intimate. Loving. She often thought of that day and the way, for the first time in her life, she'd felt important and loved by someone.

"Untie me."

He shook his head slowly. "You're coming back to the clubhouse with me."

She flinched. She couldn't help it. She didn't want to go anywhere near that place again. "Once was enough, Steele." There was sarcasm in her voice. Maybe bitterness. "One look, one smell, and I knew I was so finished with that life. You managed to fall right back into it once I was gone, or were you still participating while we were together? I should have known it would take more than one woman to satisfy you. You always had such an appetite." She made that as nasty as she could manage.

She didn't look away from his glittering midnight-blue eyes. She'd always thought he had the most beautiful eyes, ringed with all those dark lashes. The color of his eyes was unusual, in that they were so dark one had to stare at them a long while before realizing they were actually blue. His hair was wild and always out of control. When it was longish, it was decidedly unruly, falling into his face, but it didn't make him look young. Nothing took the cold from his eyes.

She found that his friends, the ones he mostly ran with in the club — and at that time they'd all been riding with the Swords

— had eyes that were flat and deadly. She'd been young enough and stupid enough to get a thrill from that. Now, she just knew they weren't good people and she didn't want any part of them.

"Did you come here to kill me? To kill Czar?"

If her hands hadn't been tied, she would have slapped him right across the face. She'd risked everything to warn him. To warn Czar. And some man named Jackson Deveau she'd never even met. She'd risked *everything* just to do the right thing. "Screw you, Steele. Yeah, that's exactly what I did. I came here and left you a letter detailing how I planned to kill you all." Sarcasm dripped from her voice.

In the distance she heard the sound of pipes as two Harleys approached. She saw their lights once they rounded the bend. There would be no escaping from this if Steele didn't let her go. She raised her gaze to his once more. "You know what the stakes are. Let me get out of here. If I can't —"

He shook his head. "You aren't going anywhere, Breezy. We're going to put this before the others and take a vote."

Horror swept through her. "We're not something to *vote* on, Steele. What's wrong with you? Just let me go. I warned you. I warned Czar. It's up to you to warn this Deveau."

Steele transferred his hold to her elbow, and she closed her eyes and took several deep breaths. Her only hope was to convince Czar she was no threat to anyone. The others had always followed Czar's lead, even within the Swords club, much to the chagrin of the president of their chapter. Czar had been the enforcer and very trusted. No one suspected, not for one moment, that he — and the others — were plotting to assassinate the international president and bring the club to its knees. Of course, she was gone by then. Long gone.

The motorcycles reached them. She recognized Maestro on one, with Keys riding behind him. Ink was on the second bike. Her heart sank. She shook her head, trying not to feel desperate. A few hours could cost her everything. She looked up at Steele again, to catch him watching her. She should have known. Steele could be so completely still, it felt like he could disappear. His energy would get so low that you could forget he was in your space. He never missed anything when he was like that. He took in the smallest detail.

He wasn't a particularly small man either.

He was a good six feet, all muscle, but not bulky about it. The definition was there, and not an ounce of fat. When she'd been with him, she'd been self-conscious about the softness around her tummy, but he had assured her time and again that he loved every inch of her body. She remembered how he'd looked at her with those cold eyes, just watching as if any second something would happen and he didn't want to miss it. He wasn't looking at her that way now. Now, it was more like he was about to shred her to pieces. He didn't have to; he'd already done it long ago.

She remained silent when he nodded toward the truck. What was there to say? She started toward it, Steele pacing along beside her, one hand on her arm as if he feared she would bolt for the cliff and toss herself over it. That wasn't likely, but she clearly had made a mistake. She should have just shot him and then made her run.

He yanked open the passenger door, put his hands on her waist, lifted her and tossed her easily onto the seat. Slamming the door again, he indicated his bike, telling Keys without words the keys were in the ignition. His Harley was big. It was powerful. It was hidden in the brush just as cleverly as her truck had been. He'd been the one to teach her self-defense moves. How to break out of zip ties. How to hide her vehicle if there was need. Always to have a plan. He'd warned her repeatedly that she had to pay attention to her surroundings.

She pressed her head against the seat and closed her eyes, keeping them that way even when he shoved the seat back and took the driver's position. "You should have told me."

Breezy glanced at him. Steele. He could always make her heart flutter and butterflies take off in her stomach. Always. He did so now in spite of everything, and she hated herself for that. For being weak.

"Let's just get this over with. Is Czar waiting? Because I want out of there as fast as possible."

"He's waiting, but you aren't going anywhere. You may as well understand that right now. The Demons are already gone. They cleared out this afternoon. We're all set to deal with this as soon as we get you back to the clubhouse."

"The Demons take all your women with them?"

"Breezy —"

She cut him off. "We aren't together. We never really were. You made that very clear, Steele, so there's no need to explain yourself. You like sex. I get that. You like all kinds of sex. I get that too. I was one of the ones serving your needs; I certainly know your . . . appetites."

His expression hardened. "Don't fucking pretend we weren't on fire together, baby. Right now, hating me the way you do, you still want me. You think I can't tell when a woman wants me?"

"I'm certain you know everything there is to know about sex and women wanting you, Steele. You make an art of it. All of you do. My body may remember what it was like with you, but so does my brain. You're bad news. I thought the Swords were bad, but you were worse. Far, far worse. At least they were up front in the way they treated me. My father turned me into a whore when I was fourteen. He told me straight up it was the only way I was worth anything to him or the club. He made me carry drugs and service other clubs to cement deals. I was so low, he let them beat the shit out of me right in front of him, but at least I knew what I was to him — to my brother and every other member of that club. You made me think I was worth more than that to you."

She couldn't stand looking at him, so she turned her head away and stared out the window into the night. She'd gone over and over every single detail of her life with him, looking for signs that she should have caught along the way that it had been a charade. A complete sham. She'd just been so young and stupid.

"Breezy, come on, baby, it wasn't like that and you know it."

"Don't. Don't, Steele. I'm not that same girl. You saw to that. I'm not naïve anymore. It may take hard lessons, but they get through. You made yourself clear and I heard every word. I made a life for myself and . . ." She broke off, her lungs seizing. It took a few minutes to find a way to breathe again. "Did you really assassinate the international president of the Swords? That's what the rumor mill is saying. The Swords hate you more than any other enemy and there's a price on every one of you."

"He had the biggest human trafficking ring in the world, Breezy. He was even allowing his clients to use and kill men, women and children on his designated freighters and bury the bodies in the ocean. He had to go."

"Czar joined first. And then one by one, the rest of you." She made it a statement. They'd joined the chapter in Louisiana, the one her family belonged to. Czar had risen to power fast. He was that scary, and Habit, the president of the chapter, had relied on him heavily. Whenever Czar had recommended a prospect, Habit had been more than happy to oblige him. Each man had been as cold as ice and equally as deadly. They'd made the chapter extremely strong.

"That was the plan."

"You rode with them for three years before you sent me away." One of those had been as a prospect, and he'd just watched her. A year of them dancing around each other. Another had been with her as his old lady. His woman. No one else had dared to touch her or try to use her for anything in that year. She'd been safe for the first time in her life. And then . . . he'd told her the truth. He didn't want her anymore. He'd never wanted her in the first place. She'd known all along her father had given her to him with the idea of currying favors from Czar and his very strong companions. Her father had wanted to be part of that.

"Five years Czar was with them. I rode with the Swords for four years." He turned off Highway 1 to Caspar. "A fucking lifetime."

"You spent four years with them, another year after you sent me away, and yet you could so easily betray them?" She knew he could. He'd spent a year with her and she hadn't meant anything to him.

"They're all scum, Breezy. Every last one of them."

She couldn't help it. She glared at him. "And you aren't? You rode with those men, pretended to be their brother and then put a bullet in them? You killed a bunch of them, didn't you? You and your friends."

"Yes, we did," Steele replied evenly, without one iota of remorse. "I'd do it again in a heartbeat. Believe me, baby, I don't lose any sleep over it."

"I'm sure you don't." She was equally as sure he didn't lose any sleep over her either. There was evidence of that when she found him lying naked under three women.

"You're avoiding every subject but the one we need to talk about."

The lash of anger in his voice sparked her own. She wanted to swing around on the seat, put her boots up and slam them right into his chest. Drive them right through his black heart. She sat very still, blood thundering in her ears.

"You need to let me go. I've worked this all out. All I asked from you was to follow the plan. That's it. In all this time, that's all I've asked. I know you're busy with your parties, Steele. That's clear. But maybe this once, for a few days, you can skip getting drunk in order to be ready in case you're needed. I'm going in first and taking all the risk. Maybe your three women can take turns giving you blow jobs and keep you happy while you wait to see if I get killed or not."

He slammed on the brakes, gave her a hard look and jumped out of the cab. She watched him round the hood, toss the keys to one of the prospects and then he was yanking open her door. He caught her chin in hard fingers, forcing her head up so she was looking into eyes glittering with sheer anger. "If you think I'll let you go into that hornet's nest you've got another think coming. He's *my* son. I'll be the one going to get him."

Two

He had a son. Just saying it tore at Steele's heart. More, he'd had a son with Breezy. His woman. The woman that he'd taken a thousand times in a thousand ways and still hadn't gotten enough of. He knew he would never have enough of her. Touching her was always a mistake. Just now, with her face turned up to his, he wanted to slam his mouth down on hers and kiss her until neither of them could breathe.

That was the problem. That was the way he was. He liked certain things. He'd learned to like them from a very early age. He liked things his way. Always. He'd learned that as well from an early age. He'd been programmed, and as much as he knew, that was what it was; there was no going back from that programming, nor did he want to. He was used to deference and control. He was used to others doing what he said. As a doctor, his word was law. As a

VP of the club, it was the same.

To say he'd been shocked when he read that letter was an understatement. Few things ever threw him, but that had. That had made him crazy. She'd been all alone. She'd never been away from the club or learned how to make decisions on her own. She hadn't been able to, not with every order coming from her father or brother. Being out on her own for the first time, alone and pregnant, had to have been a nightmare for her.

Fear for her. For his son. Anger at himself. At the situation. Emotions boiled together, and Steele let go of Breezy's face, caught her around the waist and pulled her out of the truck, easily tossing her over his shoulder like she was a sack of potatoes. She cried out, the sound like music to his ears when he'd wanted to shake some sense into her. He wanted to put her over his knee and spank the living daylights out of her, and not in an erotic way. Things tended to go down that road fast with the two of them. They burned long and hot. He felt her nipples pressing tightly against his back, two hard buds, telling him she was as aroused as he was just by being in close proximity. That and how aggressive he was with her. Her body responded to aggression whether she liked it or not. At least he wasn't alone in his hell.

He stomped into the clubhouse, kicked the door closed behind him and put her down in the center of the common room. Savage tossed him a knife and Steele cut through the zip ties. Savage was one of the two Torpedo Ink enforcers. He had the sergeant at arms patch on the front of his vest. His head was shaved, he had blue eyes, cold as a glacier, and he looked every bit as dangerous as he was. He nodded at their prisoner but didn't smile.

Breezy brought her arms in front of her and began massaging her wrists. Steele took her hands, using force when she tried to pull away, and examined both wrists for bruising or marks. Both were good, and he let her go.

"Breezy," Czar greeted.

This was the president of Torpedo Ink, and she wasn't at all surprised. She remembered him as the enforcer for her father's chapter. He'd been scary then; he was even more so now. She remained very still, motionless, frozen like that mouse she often thought of herself as. From the time she was a toddler and her mother had run off after too many beatings and being passed around, or her father had sold her off,

Breezy had been beaten for getting underfoot. She'd learned to stay out of her father's way. Her brother had treated her with the same contempt. The other club members had followed their example.

Silence reduced the chances of beatings. The less she was noticed, the better for her. She kept her eyes as downcast as possible, when she was really looking around at her surroundings. Without all the men and women covering the floor, the place looked huge. Someone had thoroughly cleaned it. The floor gleamed and the room smelled fresh, completely different from what she'd found earlier.

"Steele shared the letter you left him with me," Czar continued, waving her toward a chair. "I want you to tell us, step by step, everything that happened. Absinthe is going to sit next to you and hold your wrist."

Her gaze jumped to Absinthe and then she stumbled toward the chair Czar had indicated. They had all the exits blocked. It was casually done, a man near each door, all watching her. She raised her gaze to Steele as she sank into the chair. It was high-backed, not uncomfortable, but she thought it rather telling that she wasn't offered one of the really nice armchairs on the other side of the room.

Absinthe sank into a chair beside her. Her gaze jumped to him. He was like the rest of them, all muscle. He had one scar that curved along his jaw on the left side of his face, and his nose might have been broken more than once. His hair was blond and spilled across his forehead. That should have made him look young, but it didn't. His eyes were different. Light. Almost like two crystals.

Breezy stretched her arm out and concentrated on the floor. She just wanted them to get the questions over with, so she could leave. Absinthe's touch was very gentle. He circled her wrist with his hands, his fingers over her pulse. She knew her heart was racing and that scared her; she was afraid he would tell them she was lying when she wasn't.

"You want to tell me the truth," Absinthe said, his voice as gentle as his touch.

She thought that was an odd way to put it, but she had no intentions of lying to him. What would be the point?

"Breezy, do you have a son?"

She heard a gasp and looked up. The room went electric. Lana was there. Alena. They had ridden with the sixteen men during their time with the Swords and were always protected. Always. Their faces showed shock as did those of most of the men in the room. They'd all looked down on her because she was Swords. She'd also been a whore and a mule, lower than some of the other patch chasers. Now, she was the mother of Steele's son. That must make them all a little sick, Steele included.

"Yes."

She saw their gazes all switch to Absinthe. He nodded. "Is he Steele's son?"

"Yes." She looked up at Steele. "You're such a son of a bitch. I would *never* have come here if I didn't need you to back me up. I didn't ask for anything from you. Not one damn thing. You know I didn't sleep with anyone else once we were together. That was you being the slut, not me." She spat the accusation at him, furious that he would question her word that her son was his as well. Steele, as usual, wore an expressionless mask, making it impossible to see what he was thinking, but the question told her everything.

"Breezy," Absinthe directed her attention back to him.

"Get it over with," she snapped, clenching her teeth.

"Did your brother and father kidnap your son?"

"Yes. They did."

"Had you had contact with them prior to that?"

"No." She swallowed the lump growing in her throat and told herself to keep it together. Zane would be so frightened, and her father believed in hitting children until they couldn't cry anymore. She knew from experience. "I worked in a diner in New Mexico. Someone spotted me there, at least that's what Braden — you know him as Junk — told me." She was so upset she couldn't remember if they knew given names of club members. They were rarely used.

"You spoke to your brother?"

"They came in the middle of the night, broke in and took him." Her voice cracked, and she pressed two shaky fingers to her mouth. She thought leaving Steele after the ugly things he'd said to her had been the worst that could happen. She'd been wrong. She turned her head to the right, toward Absinthe, and swept back her hair so he couldn't fail to see the bruising beneath the makeup she'd applied. "There's more. A lot more."

"You fought them?"

"Of course I did. Did you think I'd meekly hand my baby over to them? I lived through a nightmare childhood with them." She closed her eyes and forced herself to breathe. She was feeling faint again. "I just want him back. I need to leave. To go get him."

"How much damage did they do to you?"

She hadn't expected that question. "Not much. It wasn't bad." The moment she lied, something stabbed deep into her head, like a punch to her brain. She cried out.

Absinthe let her go immediately and the pain subsided. Steele made a move toward them, but Czar caught his arm and shook his head.

"Finish this, Absinthe, but gently," Czar cautioned.

"I'm trying. I wasn't expecting her to lie. She hasn't until right then. I wasn't ready for that," Absinthe explained.

Breezy didn't understand what they meant, but when Absinthe reached for her wrist again, he seemed more reluctant than she was.

"You want to tell me the truth, Breezy." Absinthe repeated what he'd first said to her. "We all know your father and brother and what they're like. They beat up women. We need to know how much damage they did to you."

His question actually gave her hope that they might help her get Zane back. Why bother asking otherwise? "Bruises mainly. My ribs hurt when I take a breath. My stomach. I bleed some when I go to the bathroom, and there's a huge bruise on my thigh. No broken bones."

"Damn those fuckers," Steele snapped. "I'm going to kill them both."

"Not if you let me out of here," Breezy said. "I'll do it myself."

"That's the truth as well," Absinthe told the others. "Why didn't you send the letter to Steele through the mail?"

"I didn't know if Torpedo Ink was the right club. I had to see for myself. I don't expect that I'll succeed in getting him back, so I wanted Steele to know where he is. I had hoped it would matter to him that he had a son, but then I forgot that he believes me to be a whore."

She ignored Steele's low growl and kept going. "I also felt it was important for all of you to know they're after blood. Czar." She refused to look at Steele, instead deliberately regarding the man wearing the patch declaring he was the president. "I *have* to go. You can see I'm not a threat to you. I didn't even bring a gun into the clubhouse. I left the warning. What more do you want from me?"

"Are you setting the club up for retaliation by the Swords?" Absinthe persisted.

"No."

"Why didn't the Swords tell you where we were?"

"They don't know you're Torpedo Ink. They don't know much of anything that happened to the members who came here to kill Deveau. They only know they didn't return, that they're all dead along with the international president and that all the money is gone along with their ability to set up lines to traffic. They suspect all of you, because you were capable of it, I guess, but they don't really know anything."

"So, they wanted you to find us and kill us for them."

She nodded. "I started in California because this is where the members were all headed. They came from various chapters. I heard a newer club was set up in Caspar, and I checked it out. There were eighteen members. I did check out a few other clubs first, but when I heard there were eighteen of you, I was fairly certain this would be the right club."

"Once you found us, did you tell them where we're located?" Absinthe asked.

She wanted to pull her hair out. "Of course I didn't. What would be the point of warning all of you if I told them where you are?" Exasperation warred with exhaustion.

She had tried to sleep throughout the day but hadn't been successful. What little sleep she'd gotten didn't make up for the nights of frenzied hunting for the Torpedo Ink members after her baby was taken.

"When was the last time you ate something?" Alena asked.

Breezy pulled back, tugging at her arm to try to get away from Absinthe. She understood the need for them to protect their club. She did. She understood self-preservation, but that was a personal question and one she didn't want to answer. She pressed her lips together and shrugged.

"Breezy."

Steele's voice bit through her. It was cold, the voice he used when he was displeased with something she'd done. Before it had made her curl up into a little ball and withdraw. She hated it when he was upset with her. Now, he could go to hell. Her eyes met his in a storm of defiance. They locked together in some weird combat that tied her stomach in knots and made little tremors move through her body.

"I'm not doing this," Absinthe said and let go of her wrist. "It's clear she hasn't eaten in a while. She's pale, shaky and close to fainting."

"Some very bad people have taken my

son," she snapped and rubbed at her wrist as if she could remove Absinthe's touch. "I need to go. Now that you've got what you wanted, and you know you're all safe, I have to get out of here." She poured venom into her scathing comment hoping to shame him. Shame all of them. Zane was a toddler. They were adults.

"You're not leaving," Steele said. "Don't waste time arguing. I'm not about to let you anywhere near your father and brother and the rest of those assholes. We'll get our son back, but *we'll* be going, not you, Breezy."

"Like hell I won't be going. He's my child, Steele. I took care of him. I raised him. You weren't there, and you made it clear you didn't want to be there."

"I gave you money . . ."

She surged to her feet as adrenaline coursed through her. Adrenaline, anger and pure hurt. "As if I'd spend your money. I'm not a whore. I wasn't a whore when we were together, and I refuse to let you make me into one by clearing your conscience and giving me money. I told you that. Every penny I used to get us started I replaced and will send back to you the minute I have him and can get home."

"Damn it, Breezy. I gave you that money so you would be safe."

She took a step toward the door. The man they had always called Savage stood in front of it, and he scared the crap out of her. She wasn't about to fight him to get out. She appealed to the president of the club.

"I have to go get my baby, Czar. I would appreciate it if you would ask everyone to let me leave."

Czar studied her face for what seemed an eternity. Finally, he shook his head, and her heart sank.

"Honey, you know you aren't going to get out of there alive with him. You know you'd just be throwing your life away. This is what we do, and for one of our own, there's no question we'll go. We have a better chance of getting him back than you do. The moment you tell your father we're dead, he would kill that boy and then you. If he didn't kill you, he'd sell you."

She hated that everything he said was true. She didn't want to feel helpless again. Or without hope. She had left all that behind and become so much more. Tears burned behind her eyes, but she wasn't about to shed them in front of these people. All she could do was listen to the pounding of her heart and feel terror overwhelming her. Zane was with them. Her beautiful little boy with her mop of tawny hair and Steele's unusual midnight-colored eyes. Dark blue would have been rare enough, but Steele's eyes were so dark they often looked like a midnight sky. That was how she thought of them, and her son had those same eyes.

"He'll be so afraid." It escaped before she could hold it back.

"I've got soup made," Alena said. "Let me get that for you."

Breezy glanced at her. Alena had always ridden with Czar as his old lady. He'd been so protective of her. None of the Swords dared look at her for fear of his retaliation. She'd kept to herself unless Lana was around. Lana was always on the back of Ice's bike. She didn't remember either woman saying much to her. In fact, it was possible it was the first nice thing Alena had *ever* said to her.

She tried not to allow hurt to rule her. She'd promised herself she would be a better person. She wouldn't be judgmental or nasty to other women if she could help it. That had been done to her almost from the day she was born, others snubbing her both inside the club and outside it.

Breezy nodded. "Thank you." She practically choked on the words, so she couldn't get anything else out. Alena didn't seem to mind that she was brief because she left the room through the door on the far side, away from the entrance. Breezy had noted that door. If it led to all the bedrooms, it was possible there was another exit.

"Baby, stop looking for an escape route. Your ride is gone."

That jerked her head up. Her gaze clashed with Steele's and then she ran to the window to look out. Her truck wasn't there. She whirled around to find him close. He was so silent he could walk like a cat across a room, not making a sound. That had always freaked her out a little.

"Get it back, Steele."

"Not happening, Breezy. You're not running out on me in the middle of the night. You have every right to be angry. And hurt. But you also have to admit, you should have told me you were pregnant . . ."

"You didn't give me the chance when you were throwing my ass out. You couldn't get rid of me fast enough. You made it very clear I was nothing to you . . ."

"Damn it. I had no choice."

"Step back." He was too close, and she was still intimidated by the biker world and those in it. She'd been trained to obey the members or get beaten. Three years, most of it trying to learn to survive on her own, hadn't been enough time to block out that programming. He was a threat to her, and her body reacted with those years of conditioning. She detested that she froze, holding her breath. Waiting.

Steele immediately took two steps back, giving her room. "Breezy, we have to talk. You know we do."

"I know we need to talk about getting Zane out of their hands. If that's what you want to talk about, let's do it. I'm ready. Anything else, there's no reason."

"Zane? You named him Zane?"

There was a note in his voice, possessive maybe, that scared her. He couldn't have her son. He *couldn't.* "The moment I have him safe, I'm taking him home."

"The home they stole him from?" Steele shook his head. "What's to say they won't take him back?"

"They'll be dead. If you don't kill them, I will."

"Breezy, you know the life. Baby, come on. You were born into that club. They'll come after you. Chapter after chapter. Brother after brother. You won't survive. Neither will Zane."

He was right. He was *so* right. She pressed her fingers to her throbbing head. She was so terrified for her child she was almost numb. From the moment she'd rolled over onto her hands and knees, vomiting blood and hurting so badly, she'd been panicked for Zane in the hands of men who were capable of great cruelties.

She looked up at Steele. He'd been the man she believed in. The one she thought she could count on. His betrayal was far worse than the club's. She wanted to collapse into his arms and let him take care of everything, but she couldn't. She wasn't that girl anymore and she refused to be, even when she desperately needed someone. It had been a hard-won fight, but she'd made it. She'd learned to stand on her own and she wasn't going back.

"He's so little, Steele. He's just so little." Her voice broke and she pressed her fingers over her mouth, knowing her lips were trembling and he could see that telltale sign that she was about to fall apart.

"We'll bring him back to you, Breezy," he promised.

She wished she could believe him, but he'd lied to her for an entire year. She shook her head and looked away from his face, that face that had represented strength and safety to her.

Clearly reading her expression of disbelief, he cursed under his breath and stepped back again. "Go sit. Let Alena feed you. You can tell us where my boy is being held."

She winced at his word choice, but the important thing was getting Zane out of her father's hands. She could sort the rest after. "That's the problem, Steele. They refused to tell me. I think they're moving him around, but I don't know for certain. They send me pictures, so I know he's alive. I have a number I'm supposed to call when I have the information on you and then again when I kill you."

"Where were you planning on going when you left here?" Czar asked.

She turned to face him. She'd almost forgotten the others were still in the room they were so silent. It was eerie being with so many people and not one of them made a whisper of a sound. Her gaze touched on them one by one. They looked grim. Dangerous. Very sober.

"I know them. I know their haunts. I know where they think they're safe. My father won't be able to take having a toddler around. He'll need a woman to take care of him. One of the younger girls. A teen, but old enough that she would have been beaten into submission. Or one of the women who is desperate to be an old lady — desperate enough to go with my father and try to please him." She was revealing way too much about her life, but they already knew. They'd been there. They'd witnessed it.

"That was always the trouble with you," Steele murmured. "You're so damned smart. You observe everything."

She didn't know what was wrong with being intelligent, and she didn't care.

"Keep going," Czar said. "And sit down before you fall down. Driving yourself to the point of collapse isn't going to get that boy back. You have to eat, sleep and be in good shape. We've got a little time because they aren't expecting you to succeed so quickly when they failed in finding us. We need to take that time to plan things out, so we get him back the first time and there's no chance that he can be injured or killed."

She flinched at the thought. She'd been avoiding the idea that her father and brother might kill her son, but it was a very real possibility if they got angry enough.

Steele put his hand on the small of her back and gave her a little push toward the chair where she'd been sitting. She might have protested, but Alena was back, putting a steaming bowl of soup on the table and a small basket of sourdough bread beside it. Lana added a bottle of water.

There was sense in what Czar said, and it gave her the added idea that he was considering taking her along with them when they went after Zane. She was going even if she had to hitchhike after they left; it would be better for her to be there. She knew the way her father thought — and she could track him once she figured out one of the places he had taken her son.

She slipped into the chair, trying not to wince when she settled into the seat. She had to be careful of angles because her ribs were sore, and she knew Steele was watching her with hawk eyes. They all seemed to be watching her.

"Did you go to a doctor?" Steele asked.

She sent him a look. Was he crazy? She was beat all the hell up. A doctor would report it to the cops. She knew that. If her father or Braden caught wind the cops were looking for them, they'd kill her son and bury him where no one would ever find him.

"After you eat, I'm going to have to take a look at you."

"Like hell."

"Watch your mouth."

"Like you do?"

"Breezy, I'm pissed with good reason. No matter what was happening between you and me, I had the right to know you were pregnant with my child — and you know it."

There was truth in what he said, but she didn't want to give that to him. She couldn't make one single concession to him. She'd been so young and so afraid. She'd never been outside the club, and her father certainly hadn't encouraged her making her own decisions. She had the lowest self-esteem possible and a baby on the way.

To avoid answering him, she put a spoonful of soup into her mouth. The flavors were perfect. She'd never had such good soup. She looked at it. Not from a can. "I've never actually tasted anything as good as this in my life." She blurted it out without thinking.

Alena beamed. "I'm so glad you like it. I'm opening a restaurant soon and that's one of my original recipes. Do you think it needs more black pepper?"

Breezy shook her head. "This is as perfect as it can get. Seriously."

Alena shot a glance at Lana. "At last. I was pretty certain this batch had the right everything."

"I'm hungry," Ice said. "Did you make enough for all of us?"

"Got any of that bread to go with it?" Storm, his twin, added.

"There's plenty for everyone," Alena assured.

"We're going to need clothes for the baby," Steele said. "Breezy, you'll have to make a list for us. We're not up on what babies need. We'll need a room ready for him, so include furniture . . ."

"He has clothes and furniture bought and paid for with money I worked for," Breezy said, glaring at Steele.

"I'm well aware of that." Steele took the chair beside her while the others drifted out to get food, presumably from a kitchen somewhere in the enormous building. "Those things aren't going to do us any good. I told you, we can't go near that place. If there's really something you absolutely need, papers, things irreplaceable like photographs, I'll go in at night. They'll be watching your apartment. We don't want to lead them back here . . ."

"By all means, stay as safe as you can," she muttered sarcastically.

"We're bringing our son back here, Breezy." Steele was back in control, no flares of anger. Just absolute control. "That means we don't want a single Sword to know this location or the name of our club."

That made sense too. She detested that Steele made any kind of sense at all. "I'm not raising Zane in club life, Steele. You can get pissed if you want, but I'm not going to do it. If I have to stay close for a while, I'll find a place to live and work near here, and that's a huge concession. We can set up visitation if you think you're going to take an interest in him, but —"

He leaned close. Took the spoon from her hand and set it on the table. "Look at me, Breezy."

It was a command, nothing less, triggering her heart into overdrive. She couldn't help but lift her apprehensive gaze to his.

"Zane is my son. Mine. You aren't going to dictate to me what I can and can't do with him. You aren't going to live somewhere I can't protect the two of you. We're going to talk things out and we're going to do what's right for our boy."

The quiet in his voice alarmed her more than anything. She knew they called him Steele for a variety of reasons. Road names were given for anything from funny incidents to very serious ones. Some of the brothers had called him unbending. Once he made up his mind, no one ever got in his way because he'd just go right through them.

"You're not taking him from me."

"Did I say I was taking him from you? Did I ever indicate that? You're a pair, and as far as I'm concerned, you're both mine."

She pushed away from the table fast, surging to her feet at the same time, knocking the chair over backward. "You're out of your mind if you think that. Completely out of your mind."

He didn't even get up. He reached out, hooked the chair, pulled it upright and pointed back to the seat.

She glared at him, but the smell of the soup was too good, and it had been a long time since her last really nourishing meal. She sat back down and picked up the spoon. "You don't get to dictate to me anymore, Steele. I'm not that girl, the one worshiping you and thinking you walked on water."

"I'm very aware I lost that."

"I don't even know you. You were lying to me. To everyone, remember? So, no, I'm not yours. Zane, I'll concede, is, and you have a right to visit him . . ."

"It won't work that way. You know me, Bree. You *know* me. I might have misled things to the club, but I gave you the real man. I don't back away from a fight, and I win."

She felt herself go pale. Dizzy. So lightheaded for a moment she thought she might pass out. "You're threatening to take him away from me." Her voice was a whisper of fear.

"No, baby" — he leaned close again — "I'm threatening to lock you in a house with our son until you come to your senses. I told you, he isn't going to be raised with one parent."

"And I told you, he isn't going to be raised in a club."

"We'll see. Eat your soup and then I'll show you to your room, so you can get some sleep."

"I slept all day."

"You dozed on and off all day waiting for dark, so you could carry out your hare-brained scheme. Don't remind me. It will just piss me off."

She *was* tired, and she wasn't going to argue with him for argument's sake. He could posture all he wanted; it didn't mean he would get his way. She finished the soup and then stood up, taking the bottle of water with her.

Breezy followed Steele down a long hallway. He pointed out a bathroom as they passed a door and stopped at the room just beyond it. He shoved the door open and stepped back to allow her inside. She knew instantly it was his room because his scent was everywhere. Steele always smelled masculine but very clean, as if he'd just stepped out of the shower. That was unlike most of the Swords members, and she had spent a great deal of time inhaling Steele and taking him deep into her lungs.

"I'm not staying with you," she informed him, putting on her stubborn expression. She couldn't stay there, breathing him in. Surrounded by him. God help her if he decided to stay in the room with her or get in the bed. It didn't matter that he'd thrown her out and made her feel as if she were nothing; he was still Steele, the love of her life, the man she dreamt of. Fixated on. Obsessed over. She didn't want him, or anything to do with him, but her body didn't seem to know that.

"I'm through arguing with you. You're staying here and I'm examining you, so get on the bed before I just tie you to it." When she didn't move, he stepped inside, slammed the door and pointed to the bed. "You know I'll fucking do it, so stop stalling. I've had just about enough for one night. Learning I have a son and the woman who is my old lady didn't even bother to tell me was enough of a shock for one day."

"I'm *not* your old lady. You were very clear on that, Steele. Don't you dare turn this around and act innocent. I wasn't about to go near the club once I left and you were riding with it, remember? As I recall, you had me banned from the Swords. You pretended your loyalties were with the Swords, just like you pretended your loyalties were with me."

"There's an explanation."

"Of course there is, but you know what? I don't want to hear it. I just want my son back. Just get him back. That's all that matters. That's all that should matter to you."

"We're going around and around about things we aren't going to settle right now. Get on the bed, let me take a look at you and then you can take a shower or a bath and sleep. The club has a few things to take off the table, so we can turn our full attention to getting Zane back. You can sleep in here while I'm doing that."

Breezy hesitated. She hadn't been able to take a bath since she'd left the club. Her tiny apartment had a little shower stall, just big enough for her to get into. She doubted most men could have showered without turning sideways and stooping. Certainly, Steele couldn't. She knew the exact width of his shoulders, and there was no way he could get into that little stall.

She wasn't going to argue with him anymore. What was the point? She was going to lose, and every minute she spent arguing was more time in his company. She sank onto the mattress, and of course it was far nicer than any she'd ever slept on in her life. Tearing off her boots, she resisted throwing them at him.

"Do you have things at your place you need me to get for you?"

God. His voice. He could turn her inside out with that voice. "A few things matter to me, but not at the risk of your life. I'd prefer you get Zane for me."

"Make a list and write down the address of your apartment."

She nodded and started to lie down.

"I'll need your jeans off, Bree. I have to look at your thigh, and I have to examine your ribs, so lose the tank as well."

She lowered her lashes, her sex clenching hard. She didn't have the same figure she'd had when she'd left. Her breasts were larger, and her hips fuller. She hadn't had a lot to eat during her pregnancy, so she hadn't gained a lot of weight, but she still had a couple of small stretch marks. She told herself she didn't care. She wasn't trying to impress him.

Refusing to look at him, she peeled off her jeans and tank and then draped them over a chair. It wasn't like she was wearing a really pretty bra and panties. They didn't even match. She bought the cheapest cotton bikinis she could find and the cheapest bras that were functional. Stretching out on the bed, she looked anywhere but at him.

The room was larger than she'd expected and far nicer than the flop rooms for the Swords members to sleep in. He sat on the edge of the bed, and instantly she felt caged in.

"Damn it, Breezy. You're covered in bruises." There was genuine distress in his voice.

She closed her eyes at the brush of his fingers. She'd forgotten how gentle he could be. That whisper of a touch on her bare skin. The moment he did that, every nerve ending sprang to life. She hadn't wanted a man since she'd left him. She hadn't thought of wanting a man. She'd avoided them like the plague, first because she'd been pregnant, then because she'd been a single, harassed mother and then because men were disgusting creatures and she'd wanted no part of them. Lastly, and maybe most importantly, if she was honest, it had been because they weren't Steele.

Those fingers whispered along her ribs, so gently she thought she might cry.

"Hurts here?"

He was bent over her, his hair falling toward her bare belly while his hands slid over her ribs. A healer's hands. A lover's hands. He'd been both before he destroyed her.

"Yes."

"They aren't broken, thank fuck. Your old man do this, or Junk?"

Now his hands were on her thigh, sweeping over the large bruise. Everywhere he touched her, there was heat, and then somehow, miraculously, the terrible ache would subside. He had magic in his hands. "He kicked you in the ribs as well, didn't he?"

"Yes. It was my father. Junk had Zane. He had his hand over Zane's mouth and I thought he was going to kill him." She breathed deeply to keep from sobbing. She would never forget that moment. Lying on the floor helpless, her father kicking her while her brother had his hand over her baby's mouth, a grin on his face.

"I'm going to beat the shit out of both of them before I kill them," he said. "Break every bone in their fucking bodies."

He sounded like Steele. Calm. But she knew he meant it.

"If you think I'm going to object, Steele, I'm not. They took my baby." This time the sob escaped before she could prevent it. She turned on her side, face to the wall, jamming her fist in her mouth. She didn't want him there to witness her breakdown. That was hers alone. He'd thrown her out like trash, and she'd made something of herself. She hung on to that. She'd even finished high school, but she wasn't about to tell him that.

He leaned into her, his mouth against her ear. "We'll get him back, baby. That's what we do. We don't let perverted clubs like the Swords take children. We'll get him back."

He was gone before she'd turned to face him. What had he meant by that? That was what they did? What did that mean? And how had he made her ribs and her bruised body feel so much better just by touching her? Steele. He broke her heart in so many ways.

THREE

"We're going to have to clear the calendar to get Steele's boy back," Czar said, the moment the twenty fully patched members of Torpedo Ink took their places around the large oval table made of oak.

Czar looked over at his vice president. "You get her settled?"

"She's going to give me trouble, but I deserve it. I'll handle it." Steele knew Breezy wasn't going to be won over easily, but as far as he was concerned, there was no other choice. He *had* to win her over for his own self-preservation.

Czar nodded. "First business, where are we with the boy we've been bidding on? Is there anything new popping up?"

Code shook his head. "They shut down the auction, saying some member of the crime unit had bid on him. They sent out a warning and disappeared. I had traced them to Las Vegas, but they may have moved the kid and the operation. I've done everything I can do to be alerted if they pop back up. My friend Cat is also working with me and she's got just as many alerts up as I do. Sooner or later they'll try to sell the kid and we'll be back in business."

Finding the little boy they'd heard was being auctioned on the Internet was a fierce need for all of them, and frustration showed on their faces. Now they had to find Steele's child as well. There was no way they could sacrifice one child for the other. If necessary, they would break into two teams. They'd done so often enough that both teams ran smoothly.

"Ice, Storm, if Code gets anything at all, you may need to head to Las Vegas to poke around. You might uncover something he can't find online," Czar said.

"No problem," Ice agreed without hesitation.

Storm just nodded.

"Anything else pressing before we move on to finding Steele's son?" Czar asked.

Gavriil nodded. "I've been contacted by a former schoolmate. He's living in the Trinity area and he's got about twenty others from our same school riding with him. They have no affiliations with any club, and they want to come in under Torpedo Ink. They all have residences and work in the Trinity area and want to stay there. They're on their way and have requested a meeting with you."

"Another chapter?" Czar said, speculation in his voice. "You know them? All of them? I imagine he sent names to you."

"Our school wasn't quite as brutal as yours, but our instructors did like to torture those of us whose parents Sorbacov particularly hated. I know most of those in their club. I can vouch for a few personally, but not all. I can give you the names of those I know well. They're assassins, Czar, trained just as we were."

Czar tapped his fingers on the table and looked to Steele.

Steele knew what that look meant. "Like us, I doubt they fit anywhere." He looked around the table. "Input?"

"Could be trouble for us," Reaper said. "The Diamondbacks are looking very closely at us. Pierce" — he named the enforcer for the Diamondback Mendocino chapter — "is no pushover. He saw right through us and knows we're lethal as hell. Allowing twenty or twenty-five of us in their territory is one thing. Knowing we've got another twenty or twenty-five a day's ride away is something else, particularly if those men were trained the way we were — and he knows we were assassins for our government. He can't prove it, but he knows it."

Gavriil had attended one of the four schools that had been a training ground for assets for the Russian government, although that really meant assassins for Sorbacov. All of the schools had been brutal in various degrees. The school Steele had attended had been the worst. Gavriil's had been right behind it in cruelty to the children being raised and trained there.

"They're lethal enough," Gavriil said. "If they went after the Diamondbacks, the club would never know what hit them. They'd take them down one by one silently, and they'd have patience to do it over time, just the way we would. They'd be in and out like phantoms and the Diamondbacks would never know who the enemy was."

Czar had six biological brothers and Steele had been around them for a while now. He knew they had attended the other schools, but they were dangerous men, particularly Gavriil. If those asking for acceptance into Torpedo Ink were like Gavriil, they were trained in the art of killing. The Diamondbacks, Pierce in particular, wouldn't like it, but it would be good for Torpedo Ink to have that kind of backup.

"The Diamondbacks are an international

motorcycle club. They're 1-percenters, outlaws, living their lives their own way. We're here because they've given us permission to be here, but we've always treated them with respect and played nice," Maestro said.

Keys nodded. "We tried flying under the Diamondbacks' radar, but more than once now, we've inadvertently showed our fangs to their club, risking retaliation. It would be extremely dangerous to bring more attention to us."

"On the other hand," Savage began.

The others fell silent immediately and paid attention. Savage rarely offered anything to the table. He just listened most of the time.

"These are men like us with nowhere to go. They need what we have to survive. A brotherhood. A family. They need a leader. They need Torpedo Ink."

That was the damn truth, Steele decided. Savage was right. How could any of them possibly fit into regular society? None of them knew the rules. They didn't know how to behave. They'd been taught to kill to survive. They knew a lot of ways to kill, but few ways to integrate into society. They certainly didn't know how to have relationships.

Ruthlessly he turned his mind away from the woman in his bed — at least he tried to. It was hard not to think about her lying there, curled up into a little ball, as if protecting herself. The way she slept had always stolen his heart. He'd wrapped his body around hers to show her she was safe. She'd been so fragile and yet she really wasn't, he was beginning to realize. She'd had his baby alone. She'd found a way to support the child and care for him when she'd left, not even knowing how to make a decision.

In the world of bikers, Breezy had appeared to be a leader of the women and children, one of the reasons he'd thought she was older. She anticipated problems and dealt with them ahead of time. She knew the language of bikers and her father's particular club. Outside that environment, she was in an entirely different world and had no idea how to interpret or fit into it or make decisions accordingly — yet she'd managed. She'd done it for herself and their child.

She'd depended on Steele entirely when she'd been with him. She'd looked at him as if the sun had risen and set with him. Now that adoration wasn't there, and he found he needed it back. She'd been the one. He hadn't said a word to the others. Czar had been sent by Sorbacov to kill Evan Shackler-Gratsos, the international president of the Swords. He had crossed Sorbacov one too many times and the order had gone out.

Evan Shackler-Gratsos had inherited billions from his brother. Those billions included freighters that Shackler-Gratsos had turned into snuff ships. His very wealthy clients paid for sexual partners of any age — from very young children to men and women — used them and killed them after or during sex, and then disposed of the bodies at sea. Of course Czar would want to shut that shit down. He'd risked everything to do so, not just his life but his marriage to the woman he loved. One by one, the other members of Torpedo Ink had followed Czar into the Swords club in order to have his back. Steele couldn't have left him when a war was brewing, and he couldn't have left Breezy there, where the Swords would name her a traitor.

Steele had seen Breezy for the first time, and all hell had broken loose inside him. He'd been trained, like the others, to have complete control over his body, and that had gone right out the window the moment he'd laid eyes on her. He'd watched her, couldn't keep his eyes off her. He'd taken every opportunity to talk to her. She'd been responsible, always looking out for those younger than she was. She cooked for the club. She cleaned up after them and never complained. She was a problem solver when things went wrong and had to be fixed. She never asked for help; she just quietly did what needed to be done.

She was beautiful, and it was impossible to guess her age. She looked young, but her eyes were old. She'd seen too much. Endured too much. He should have known he was looking into the eyes of a child who had been horribly brutalized. He'd certainly seen it enough.

"You with us, Steele?" Czar asked.

Steele nodded. "Savage is right. These men may not have been from our school, but they're brothers. They need Torpedo Ink, in my opinion. I'm certainly willing to listen to any other opinions with an open mind."

That phrase was used a lot. Czar had taught them the importance of hearing everyone out. Each person's input had counted when they were children, no matter how young — and Steele was one of the youngest. All were heard, and Czar had emphasized they should be heard with an open mind. He'd encouraged participation from everyone. Steele had caught on early that by listening to each child, Czar had made them feel important and the group cohesive. They were tight-knit and rarely fought. They often had lively and heated discussions, but they didn't get angry with one another as a rule.

"I'm all for giving them a chance, Czar," Ink said. "But we have family now. We've got Blythe and the children. Gavriil's and Casimir's women. Anya, Reaper's lady. Lana and Alena. We've got more to protect than ever."

"I don't need protection," Lana said with a little sniff. She tossed her head so that her glossy black hair fell around her face, framing its beauty.

"Neither do I," Alena echoed. She was a true platinum blond, her hair rioting down her back in waves. Her eyes were that same startling blue her older brothers, Ice and Storm, had.

Ink ignored the byplay. "Pierce is going to be watching us closely, Czar. You know that. He's very suspicious of us."

"I can handle him," Reaper said. "A quiet accident."

"Not you," Savage said decisively. "You have Anya. I'll do it."

Pierce wasn't going to be easy to kill. Both knew it. All of them knew it.

"Oh, for heaven's sake," Alena snapped. "He doesn't have to be killed. Leave him to me. He advocated for us. It was because of Pierce we didn't go to war."

"He may have advocated for us, Alena," Reaper said, "but don't kid yourself. He was there to kill us if anything went wrong."

"He would have tried," Savage said. "I was on him the entire time and he had no idea."

Alena shrugged. "If it comes to that, I can do it myself."

"We know if our club grows it will make the Diamondbacks nervous, but there was no limit put on how big our club could be. We're charter members, but they expected growth," Czar said. "They knew we had a couple of prospects."

"Maybe not twenty-five new members," Master said with a faint grin.

"Put it to a vote whether or not to meet with them," Czar said. "This has come at a bad time for us, but we may as well get it done if we're going to do it."

"We'd have to send someone to Trinity for a few weeks. And then Savage will need to go back and forth. We have to trust these men if they're part of us," Steele said.

"I could go," Casimir volunteered. "Lissa

likes to travel, and she's all I need for backup." Lissa and Casimir had done what no one else had been able to do. They had freed all those trained under Sorbacov's brutal schools by assassinating Sorbacov and his son. Now they were free to live their own lives and choose what they wanted to do. The problem was, they only knew how to seduce and kill. All of them were struggling to find their way.

Czar nodded. "Let's take a vote on whether or not to bring them here for a trial."

Steele knew the vote would go through. He actually liked the idea of having another chapter, men trained as they'd been trained in the art of assassination and warfare. If it came to war with the Diamondbacks — and that was always a very real possibility — Torpedo Ink was outnumbered. The Diamondbacks would have an endless army, just as the Swords did.

Financially, they'd broken the Swords. The money had been earned from trafficking, and Code had siphoned off every penny from every local chapter as well as international ones. They'd taken out a number of members in a massacre, as well as the president, Evan Shackler-Gratsos. Before they killed him, they'd hit his personal bank account as well as every one of his businesses. Code had made certain the money couldn't be traced to their accounts. Torpedo Ink was wealthy beyond its wildest dreams. They were trying to spend the money wisely, using it to establish themselves in Caspar with legitimate businesses. They tried to do business with locals as much as possible. Czar wanted their club to have a good reputation.

There was no 1-percenter patch on their vests. The local law enforcement didn't believe them, but that was okay. No one could prove anything against them. They wanted to keep a low profile and fit in with their community. That was the plan — and the hope.

Steele glanced down at his watch. For the first time, he realized he wanted out of a meeting, so he could get back to Breezy, even if it was just to watch her sleep. It had been so long. He had made up his mind he would never have a woman of his own again. He'd had her, the right one, the only one, and he'd lost her. The ache in his chest hadn't ceased, not from the moment he'd put her in a car and watched her go.

She'd been crying when she'd left him. Sobbing. That had torn out his fucking heart, but there had been no way he was going to risk her life. He'd known the war was coming and her father would never forgive her for being with him — even though her father had handed her over to him to incur favor. At first, after she was gone, he couldn't stand another woman touching him. Then, no matter how many women blew him, he'd been desperate to feel something — to get relief from the agony of dreams waking him nightly with a raging hard-on that wouldn't seem to go away.

The vote was unanimous to bring the others in, if they were suited for Torpedo Ink. That didn't surprise Steele in the least.

"All right, Gavriil, let them know to come up for a meet," Czar said. "Anything else?"

"There's the mandatory run with the Diamondbacks coming up. We can't forget we have that," Preacher said. "It's a couple of weeks away, so no worries yet, but if we don't find Steele's boy in that time period . . ."

"We have to," Steele said. "He can't be left with Bridges, you all know what he's like. He'll hurt him. He likes hurting anything smaller than him." Bridges was Breezy's father, and he was the type of man to kick a sleeping dog just to hear it yelp. He'd done so numerous times and laughed as the dog turned tail and ran away from him.

"You want to tell us what happened, Steele?" Czar invited.

He'd known the question was coming. These were his brothers — and sisters. They would risk their lives for him. For his son. They were silent. Patient. Just waiting for him to give them any kind of explanation. If he didn't, they'd still help him. He knew that.

"She's my Anya. My Blythe. She always was. It wasn't some bullshit white-knight rescue-her thing. You know my . . . appetites. The women in that club were always up for anything." He stopped and shook his head. "Let's just say I thought having them would be a way to get through rubbing shoulders with those sickening men. They weren't anything I really wanted, but they were bodies and they were willing. Then I saw her. The first time I laid eyes on her I was a prospect and she was the daughter of a fully patched club member. There was no going there."

He couldn't help shoving his hands through his hair, betraying his agitation. "I watched her, though. I couldn't stop myself. I didn't have to tell my body to react. It was there. One fucking look at her. She was it for me. I thought it was just sex. I just wanted her because she looked like an innocent angel among all those she-devils, but . . ." He broke off.

"She was different," Lana agreed.

He shot her a grateful look. That was Lana, always ready to back one of her brothers.

"She was very different. I watched her closely over that first year and the next. Talked to her every chance I got. Her father used her to cement deals with the scum they did business with. She'd come back battered and bruised, and he didn't seem to mind. I minded. I started figuring out ways to kill the bastard, and I should have done it. Eventually, I made it known I wanted her. I made certain her father knew. He wanted in with you, Czar, so he offered her to me."

Czar nodded. "I thought you took her to keep her from having to do any more drug runs or be given to Bridges's friends."

"That too, but it really was for me. I just didn't want Bridges to know how much she mattered to me. It wasn't safe for any of them to know. I had her for a year. Best fucking year of my life." He looked down at the table, the pain in his chest that had been there since that car had driven away, taking her from him, increased in strength. "What

I didn't know was her age."

He dropped that bomb right on them. He had to get it out fast. They hunted pedophiles. They weren't men to tolerate any kind of sexual predator.

"What are you saying?" Code asked.

"She was fourteen years old when her old man gave her to one of his friends. She was fifteen when I was a prospect perving on her. She was barely seventeen when her father gave her to me."

There was a stunned silence. It was Czar who broke it. "That's impossible."

"She was just shy of seventeen by a few days," Steele repeated. "I didn't think to ask her age. Her eyes said thirty, but I should have asked. I should have fucking asked her. I still would have taken her, claimed her for my old lady, but I wouldn't have touched her."

He hoped that was the truth. He doubted it though. A part of him was certain he wouldn't have been that strong, not with her sleeping in his bed, and she would have had to out of necessity, in order to keep her safe from everyone else. He cleared his throat. These were his brothers and sisters. Men and women ready to lay down their lives to help him. "That's not true. No way could I have had her in my bed and not touched her. I lived for that woman."

"Why didn't you tell me?" Czar asked.

Steele knew why. Every man at the table knew why. Without Czar, none of them would be alive — at least none of the original eighteen. He had to make certain Czar lived through the coming war with the Swords.

"You would have sent me away with her," he admitted, making the truth more about Breezy and less about Czar.

Czar sighed and pressed his fingers to his eyes, looking weary. "What tipped you off to her age?"

"There was a younger girl there, she was about fourteen or fifteen. She had a mop of red hair, freckles and bright green eyes. I think they called her Candy. Do you remember her? Bree was worried about her, worried the club would start using her the way they used Breezy. She said it had started for her around the same age. That made me wonder how old she was. I didn't think she was a kid. She never acted like a kid. Not how she talked. Not the way she thought. Not the way she took care of everyone. Not the work she did. Not in or out of bed. I didn't have one inkling, so when she told me how old she was, I nearly fell through the fucking floor."

He would never forget that moment of complete shock. He was guilty of statutory rape. Worse, he was everything he hated most. He was in a relationship with a teenager, and it was a very sexual one. He was demanding of all sorts of things, and she gave him whatever he wanted. He pressed the heel of his hand to his forehead.

He'd felt sick, bile rising. "I couldn't look at her and I knew I had to send her away immediately. I'd planned to, to keep her safe from the Swords when war broke out, but now, I needed to keep her safe from me. I was also extremely angry. Angry at everyone for not knowing. Mostly at myself for not even asking, but her as well, for not telling me. A part of me knew she wasn't to blame, she probably didn't think anything of it since her own father had turned her over to his friends at fourteen, but I couldn't get past the rage."

Steele wanted to hit something. Hard. Smash Bridges's face in. He detested the man. He should have been looking out for his daughter, but instead, he'd used her ruthlessly. "I didn't even ask her when her birthday was. I was so fucking glad to have her, I just didn't take care the way I should have. I was so angry that I was losing her — that the fucking universe had tricked me again, robbed me of the one decent thing I had in this world."

There was a small silence and Steele realized that fury was in his voice. No matter how much he breathed it away, it came back to choke him whenever he thought about the injustice of that. He'd never had one single thing for himself. Never asked for anything. He'd had her and then she was gone — and he'd done that.

"Why didn't she contact you when she realized she was pregnant?" Lana asked. "Breezy doesn't seem the kind of woman to keep that information from a man, even if she was hurt."

Steele didn't want to answer her. Shame didn't sit well on his shoulders. He deserved to feel it. He knew they were blaming Breezy, not him. Like Lana, everyone thought Bree should have contacted him. He couldn't let them think that about her. He'd told them the worst, admitted that he'd slept with a girl, not a woman, and that he would have done so no matter what.

He sighed and ran his fingers through his hair repeatedly. "I told her I didn't want her, that she'd been nothing more than a warm body to use. I made it very clear I didn't love her and that she was absolutely nothing to me. I had her banned from the club so she couldn't even go to another chapter. I told her she was nothing and I never wanted to look at her face again."

"Steele," Alena whispered. "You didn't. She was so young. That must have annihilated her. You had her for a year and you just scraped her off?"

He winced at the pain in Alena's voice. She was putting herself in Bree's shoes and she felt that pain — the twisted agony on Breezy's face when he'd coldly told her to get the hell away from him.

"I gave her money. Lots of it, and I did it in an ugly way, implying I was paying for a year's service. I was as harsh, as brutal, as I could possibly be. I made it clear I was going to be with other women. I didn't want her to stay in the hopes that we'd get back together. I wanted her so far away from there her father and brother — and me — could never find her. If I didn't make it seem as if she meant nothing to me, she wouldn't leave, and I knew I wasn't strong enough not to keep her."

"Fuck, Steele," Reaper said. "You've always been the smart one. What were you thinking?"

"You dug yourself a hell of a hole," Maestro said. "Bree thought you walked on water."

She had. She would have done anything for him. Now she looked at him as if he were the same as her father and brother. He didn't like that. Maybe he deserved it after the disgusting things he'd said to drive her away, but he didn't like it.

There was a long silence. Czar shifted in his seat. It was clear even their president didn't have any advice for him.

"I'm not giving her up," Steele declared. "Not again. The chemistry is still there between us whether she likes it or not — and she doesn't like it. I don't much give a damn. We're getting my boy back and then she's going to stay with me."

"You can't make her stay," Keys said. "Women have a way of making up their own minds, bro."

"Why the hell can't he make her stay?" Ice demanded. "If there's chemistry and he uses what we spent a lifetime learning, seducing her into staying shouldn't be that difficult."

The others nodded. Lana rolled her eyes. "Ice, you're an idiot. You already nearly lost Anya for Reaper. Don't even try to advise Steele."

"No, wait," Player said. "Ice actually has something there. She never could resist you, Steele. You know that. Ice has me thinking about when he was telling Reaper to knock Anya up. You did it once pretty easily with Breezy. A woman might take care of one kid alone, but two?"

"If you keep her in the compound instead of taking her to your house, there's no way she could leave," Preacher added. "Especially now that we've 'lost' her truck."

Lana narrowed her eyes at her brother. "I can't believe you'd even think that, let alone say it. We're not keeping Breezy against her will."

"I am," Steele said. "Until she sees reason, I'm keeping her by whatever means I have to. I had to save her from what was coming. You know I did. Bridges would have killed her or sold her into slavery. He's that sick of a bastard. I had no choice. It was hell and has been every fucking minute she's been gone. I didn't go about it the right way, mostly because I was so pissed finding out I'm a fucking pervert, but I'm not giving her up again. I just need time to get her to change her mind about me."

"Holding her prisoner isn't going to change her mind," Lana said. She glared around the table. "Let's take this to Blythe. See what she thinks."

"She isn't going to understand what's at stake," Steele said.

"What is at stake?" Czar asked.

"My sanity," Steele admitted without hesitation. "My fucking life."

Czar looked around the table. "Your brother just put it on the line. All of it. Breezy's young. She's just shy of twenty-one now, and that makes her an adult. She belongs to Steele. She's got a child. Steele's son, so that woman and that boy are ours. We do whatever it takes to help him keep her."

He waited for each person to agree. Lana sighed heavily but she nodded, the same as every other man and Alena. They would do their best to keep Breezy there with Steele.

"Let's talk about getting Zane back," Czar said. "We need a plan."

"Bree says they're probably moving him every few days, and I agree," Steele said. They were back on firm ground. He'd felt as if the ground had been shifting out from under him ever since he knew he would have to confess to the others that he had been with this woman even when she was underage. He hadn't known, but he blamed himself because he should have known. He should have taken an interest in every aspect of her life — especially something as important as her birthday.

Torpedo Ink hadn't celebrated birthdays.

Most didn't know when they were born, not months or days anyway. Czar had started to keep track of ages when new children were brought to the school, but so many died, and after a while he'd stopped. Time passed slowly in that prison they'd been raised in, and there weren't dates. Or birthdays. There was only survival.

"Does she have any idea where to even start looking?" Maestro asked. He had dark hair streaked with silver, which matched the beard he wore. His eyes were intense, a light gray like liquid mercury or silver, and when he focused on anyone, there was no doubt they were looking at death. Strangely, at odds with his appearance, he was a gentle man, but that had never stopped him from defending his brothers and sisters when necessary.

"If she didn't, she wouldn't have tried to strike out on her own," Player pointed out.

"That's true," Ink said, looking to Steele. "Did you ask her where she was going?"

"I haven't had much opportunity," Steele said. "I think we need to bring her in on our meeting about this, but she needs sleep. She looked exhausted." She had dark circles under her eyes and it was clear, from the way she'd reacted to Alena's soup, that she hadn't eaten in a while either. "Bridges hurt her. You should see her body. Bruises everywhere."

Those around the table exchanged long looks with one another. Steele was a healer, a very gifted surgeon, but he was also a stone-cold killer when he needed — or wanted — to be. No one ever crossed him, unless it was Czar. Not ever. Steele could take a man apart without working up a sweat. Bridges was not going to like what Steele would do to him, and there wasn't a doubt in anyone's mind that Steele was going after Bridges and making the fight personal.

"We don't have even an inkling what state they're in right now?" Keys asked.

"We have to figure Louisiana," Czar said. "Half the chapter was left behind. Habit only brought some of us. Bridges and his son were pissed they didn't get to go. I kept track of what was going on back there, just to be safe, and Bridges became the chapter president, not that he had much of a chapter left to run. We shut down their trafficking ring, closed off every pipeline they had and gave the cops so much evidence on every chapter they're still indicting members across every state."

Code nodded. "There are warrants out on just about every member, especially the

Louisiana chapter."

"Bridges is a vindictive man," Reaper said. "A straight-up coward and bully, but vindictive as hell. He thinks we were the ones to bring down Habit and Evan."

"He might think that, but he can't know we took their money or provided evidence to the cops," Code said. "That's impossible to trace." There was satisfaction in his voice.

"He is vindictive," Steele agreed. He knew him better than any of the others, and he detested the man. "He'll bring that chapter down even further than it has already fallen, and he'll do it for his own gain. At least Habit had loyalty to his brothers and he understood what that is. Bridges only thinks of himself. He knew we had an aversion to those using young girls. I'll bet any amount of money he kept Breezy's age back on purpose."

"You would have taken her anyway," Czar said. He massaged the back of his neck, trying to ease the tension any conversation having to do with the Swords always put there. "You would have had no choice whether you wanted her or not. Any of us would have claimed her the moment we knew her real age."

That was true, but for Steele there hadn't been any choice at all. He would have protected Breezy with his life. Had Torpedo Ink not been on a vital mission, he would have killed Bridges and taken her out of there long before her father offered her to him. As it was, he felt guilt that he'd waited so long. They'd been so careful not to blow it, all of them despising the club they had to ride with but making certain not to show it.

"Code, can you find out who his close friends are? I don't recall anyone in particular other than his son. Look into his money. Make it difficult for him. Wipe out his account. He'll have a secret one, money he stashes away, probably club money he's taken and no one knows about," Steele said.

"Will do," Code said.

"If we take his money, it will make it harder for him to move all the time. Look into his past women as well. He didn't have an old lady. Not even Braden's or Breezy's mothers. No one knows what happened to them, but he would definitely have no problem taking over a woman's home if he knows any of them."

"Grandparents? His mother and father?" Maestro said. "I never heard him talk about them, but if they're alive, he might go to them."

"I'll look into that as well," Code said.

"As soon as I can get information from

Breezy, I'll give you any names she might know," Steele promised. "I've never seen her so scared."

"I like the name Zane. Where did she come up with that one?" Alena asked.

Steele shook his head. "She talked about names once. I wasn't into having kids. I don't know the first thing about them, so I didn't participate in the conversation. She mentioned several names and I just ignored her." It had been right before she left. Right before he'd told her he didn't want her around.

They'd never talked about love. She'd said it to him once, and he hadn't responded. He didn't know how to respond. She'd never repeated the sentiment. He'd been gruff when she brought up having a family. He'd told her he didn't want children and he'd cut off all conversation, including the choosing of names. Zane was Breezy's choice.

"Did she know she was pregnant when she left?" Lana asked.

"It's possible. Even probable," Steele admitted, which made the things he'd said even worse. "I made such an ass out of myself. I should have been more careful in the things I said. I was so busy shoving her away, I didn't think about how she was going to feel. I wanted her gone. Away from me. I'm too damned old for her. Away from her father and brother. Away from the war I knew was coming."

"Stop beating yourself up," Czar said. "You're always the voice of reason. You're the one who says we can't change the past so let it go and figure out a way to undo the damage."

That was easier said than done. Steele believed there was no changing the past and that one just learned from it and moved on, but now that it was his royal screwup, it wasn't so easy. He glanced at Reaper. Their enforcer had managed more than once to put his relationship with Anya in jeopardy. Steele cringed a little trying to remember what advice he might have given.

He just nodded because the others seemed to be waiting for something. "We have to assume Bridges has some woman taking care of Zane. No way is he changing diapers or taking him to the toilet. He wouldn't feed him or get him to bed at night. Neither would Junk."

"How old would he be?" Player asked.

"Around two and a half. Just shy of that," Steele answered, and his heart contracted.

"I'll get looking for the women in his life," Code assured him. "Has Breezy ever mentioned her grandparents on either side to you, Steele? Names? Where they might live?"

Steele wanted to kick himself. He'd never even asked. Had he asked her any personal questions? She certainly hadn't volunteered any information about herself. Damn it, why hadn't he asked? Because he didn't think in terms of extended family. None of them did. There was so much to learn about relationships.

He shook his head. "Sorry, Code, no clue."

Code shrugged as if it didn't matter, but Steele knew not having any information made it all the more difficult for his brother to track down Bridges's parents. Steele had been happy with Breezy, mostly because she was there to do every little thing for him. Give him everything he wanted. He'd never had that. He'd never once in his life, that he could remember, had anyone see to his every need. He'd selfishly been happy with that arrangement.

"Anything else?" He wanted to get back to her. He needed to see her in his bed. Make certain she hadn't found a way to slip out. He'd left Fatei, the prospect he trusted most, just outside his door. Fatei had been in the same school with Gavriil, Czar's brother, and it had been brutal. The man was dangerous, quiet, and he could be counted on. Steele hoped that when the others showed up, those seeking entry into Torpedo Ink, Fatei would opt to stay with the original chapter. He didn't want to lose the man. He knew the others felt as he did.

He heard the clock ticking on the wall and his gut tightened. Somewhere across the country, his son, no more than a toddler, huddled alone without his mother, probably terrified. Most likely he was crying himself to sleep, just like Breezy had most likely cried herself to sleep — if she slept at all. He wanted to leap up, get on his bike and ride, find his boy and bring him home to Breezy. He had no idea where to start.

"We'll find him," Alena assured softly and put her hand over his.

The others nodded. He looked around at them. These were the men and women he could count on. These were the men and women who would stand by him. They'd stand by his woman and their child.

"Thanks," he muttered.

"Before we call it a night," Czar said, "anything on the Demons?"

"I'm not certain what the Demons were looking for on us," Steele said. "It was less of a cementing of relationships between our clubs and more of an information hunt.

They brought their club girls and used them to try to pump us for personal information, at least it seemed that way to me." He looked around the room for the others to confirm.

He couldn't help cringing when he thought about Breezy looking on as he rose up out from under the three women who had partied with him so hard the night before. Her face, that beloved face, had shown hurt and betrayal. There was no excuse, he knew that. He'd tried numbing himself, believing he'd lost her. Believing he didn't deserve her. He didn't. That was the plain damned truth. He didn't deserve Breezy, and he never would. That wouldn't stop him from claiming her or from keeping her because he was that big of a selfish bastard.

Maestro nodded. "Absolutely. The women were asking all sorts of questions, but all personal. They weren't going for club secrets so much as trying to figure out where we all came from and what we did before we ended up here."

Lana nodded. "Before I left, a couple of the men were plying me with compliments and liquor, asking similar questions."

Alena agreed. "They've figured out that there's more to us than a few friends getting together and riding. We rescued Hammer's wife from the Ghosts when they couldn't, and we did it fast. I imagine they're wondering about us." Hammer was president of a Demons chapter that had come to them looking for help.

"I believe we can count on them as allies in a pinch," Player said. He looked around the table. "Did you all get that same impression?"

Czar had taken Blythe home after the barbecue. He looked to Reaper. Reaper and Anya had attended and stayed longer. Because Reaper had a woman of his own, he had more of an opportunity to observe the men and women who had come to party.

"They want to know who they're getting in bed with, Czar," Reaper said. "They want us as their allies, but they don't want to get caught with their pants down."

Steele seconded that. "I have to agree. We're looking for just as much information on them. Code does that for us. They aren't going to find jack on us, no matter how hard they look. Code can feed them bullshit, small random pieces on us he manufactures, if you think it's necessary."

They already had enough enemies, and they were right in the middle of Diamondback territory. That was an uneasy alliance.

Adding another chapter to Torpedo Ink might make that alliance even shakier. Having the Demons at their back was a good thing. Of course that meant doing business with them, but that was the name of the game. And they were very good at the game.

"It's not necessary," Czar said. "We'll meet back here tomorrow and hash out with Breezy where to start looking for Zane."

FOUR

Steele entered his bedroom at the compound quietly. The room smelled different. He'd always kept it clean. He was a doctor, and often, his room was nearly sterile. He used anti-bacterial spray on everything, but mostly it was antiseptic. He wanted his room sterile. It was the one place he never brought a woman — or women. This was where he was most vulnerable, and he wasn't going to allow anyone or anything that might remind him of his childhood and the place he'd shared with the other members of Torpedo Ink as well as those who didn't make it.

The moment he thought of it, the smell of blood and death was there, the moans and cries of the dying. Of the brutalized. Boys and girls. Sometimes they waited in rows of two, lying on the floor curled into bloody balls of what was once human flesh and now was just a mass of blood he was supposed to miraculously cure. It had been cold. So cold, there was no way to warm those bodies, or himself.

He shook his head, his hands curling into two tight fists. He couldn't go there, not now, not when he had a second chance at life — a real life. It was dangerous to go back, at least for him, to even think of those days when he was too young and had no way to save the dying. He could only whisper to them, tell them not to be afraid, and that someday, he would avenge them. That was all he had to give to those little boys and girls with the open, weeping sores and infections that smelled so bad he knew they were rotting from the inside.

Deliberately, he inhaled, taking Breezy's scent deep, knowing his woman could drive out every bad thing, every ugly place, the smells that seemed to follow him wherever he went, and replace it all with her. It didn't matter if it was temporary; she gave him what no one and nothing had ever been able to.

Right now his entire room smelled fresh and feminine. He leaned one hip against the door, looking at his woman lying in the middle of his bed. She'd always done that — curled up like a little cat right in the center of the bed. She had all that thick tawny hair, and it spilled across the pillow, covering most of her face from his sight.

A thin sheet was pulled over her body and she shivered continually. Her knees were drawn up to her chest and her arms were held tight into her. He moved closer to her, leaning down to look at her face. She'd been crying, and his heart turned over. Still, there wasn't a single line there. She looked like an angel with her fair, rose-petal skin and the sweep of those thick tawny lashes. He should have known she was underage when he'd met her. Maybe he hadn't wanted to know, not with his body's reaction to her.

He'd never had that — a real reaction — not that he could remember. His training had been brutal, just like the others'. The beatings. The sex. Learning to kill. He hadn't had it like some of the others. Reaper. Savage. Ice. Storm. Maestro. They'd been nearly wrecked as human beings. He didn't know how they'd survived — but then he didn't know how he had. In truth, there were parts of him that hadn't.

Steele couldn't help himself, he covered Breezy with the blankets and then stepped back. All the way across the room to the door again. Away from her. Just having her that close was dangerous to both of them. He wanted her with every breath he took —

he had from the first time they'd met. His body reacted the moment he inhaled her scent, fresh from the bath. He tended to get his way in all things — especially with her. Breezy had given him that. She might have continued if he hadn't sabotaged the relationship.

He recognized what he'd done. He was intelligent. He felt he didn't deserve her — and he didn't. He'd sent her away as much for his own punishment as to save her. He was that screwed up. Now she was back, and he had to find a way to keep her. He'd tried living without her, and it hadn't gone very well. He would be fighting her as well as fighting himself, because if he didn't find a way to keep her, this time there would be no survival for him.

He looked slowly around his room. He was a doctor. A surgeon. He'd had more specialized training than most doctors. Over and over, he'd violated his oath — his need — to heal others. He'd murdered his enemies, keeping his promise to the dead. He'd assassinated for his country. He'd been following orders — but it was still murder. He went after child predators, but he'd made the same mistake he killed others for. He hadn't known her age, but then he hadn't bothered to find out. He was guilty as hell

— even if the law didn't condemn him, it didn't make him less so in his own eyes.

Breezy moved. Those long lashes fluttered. "Steele?"

The ache in her voice was an arrow piercing his heart. "I'm here, Bree." He stayed right where he was, planted against the door, afraid to move. He'd walked into a room filled with enemies, never flinching, and would do it over and over, but this woman held the power to ruin him.

"I want him back. I want my baby back."

The little sob was his undoing. She was weeping. It was heartbreaking and so unlike Breezy. She didn't cry. He'd noticed that before he'd ever been with her. He'd seen her father backhand her, sending her flying. She'd picked herself up without even putting her hand to her face. She'd simply done the task Bridges had wanted, without a comment or sound. He'd wanted to kill her father, and that had been the first time he'd ever had to be physically restrained by Savage and Czar. It wasn't the last. *He'd* been the one to make her cry the last time, telling her he didn't want her, that she was nothing to him. Could he hate himself any more? Yes. The answer was yes, because if he was any kind of a good man, he'd get their child back, give him to her and get her out of the country.

There were Swords overseas, and they'd look for her as well — that was what he told himself. He knew he was just a selfish son of a bitch and he was keeping her because no way in hell, after seeing her like this, could he let go of her twice.

"We'll get him back." He poured confidence into his voice because he believed it. He moved to the edge of the bed, every step slow and deliberate, his boots making a whisper of sound on the floor. He didn't want her to reject him. He needed her in that moment. Zane was his child as well. He might not have known about him, but that connection was already there — through Breezy. Now, someone had his son, his worst nightmare coming true.

She sat up, moving until her back was against the wall, pulled her knees up and held her legs tightly to her chest. There were tear tracks on her face. He sank down on the edge of the bed close to her and reached out to brush wet strands of hair from her face.

"It's what we do, Bree. We're good at it."

She blinked at him, her long lashes fanning her cheeks. "I don't understand."

"We hunt pedophiles and we get the children back. Your father may not be a pedophile, but he kidnapped a child. We've been hunting since we were little kids, so for all of our lives. We'll find Zane and we'll bring him home."

She wiped at her face. "I still don't understand."

"The man who was the international president of the Swords ran the largest human trafficking ring in the world. He had what we referred to as 'snuff' ships. He took women, men and children onto the ships with his very wealthy and sick clients and gave those chosen to them. They used them, got their kinks satisfied and killed them. The bodies went overboard."

He'd told her all of it before but in an offhand way, as if he was making excuses for himself — and he had been. This time he wanted her to know what Torpedo Ink was capable of because he would never stop until he had their son back, and neither would any of his brothers and sisters.

"Czar joined the Swords and worked his way up to enforcer. He joined that particular chapter because it had been the chapter of the international president. Czar knew if the man came back, it would be to that chapter."

Breezy lifted her head and looked at him. Met his eyes. It was the first time since he'd last seen her that she really looked at him without anger or hurt. She studied his face for a long time and then frowned. He'd fallen hard for that little frown. He'd traced it with his fingertips more than once just to memorize it.

"You're MC," she said with conviction. There was distaste in her voice.

He was. He was Torpedo Ink, and he lived and died for those colors and his brothers. He nodded slowly, sensing he was on very shaky ground. "Yes. Torpedo Ink is my club. I'm VP. We've always been Torpedo Ink and we always will."

"You can't hide the MC in a man." The distaste had deepened to revulsion.

He couldn't blame her for disliking clubs. She'd been born into the Swords club, and they hadn't treated any of their women with respect. They saw them as assets to be used. Even the old ladies. "Not all clubs are alike, Breezy."

"It doesn't matter as long as you get Zane back. I swear to you, Steele, he's your son. I wouldn't lie about that."

"I know that. I wasn't the one asking." He hadn't been. It hadn't occurred to him that Breezy would lie to him about the child. Apparently it had occurred to the others, and they'd made certain the boy was his by using Absinthe, their own lie detector. "It wouldn't have mattered though, Bree. We would have gone after him no matter what."

She rubbed her chin on top of her knees. There was a scant four inches between his fingers and her ankle. He was acutely aware of that short distance. He could touch her, she was that close. Feel her skin. Feel what had always belonged to him.

"As soon as we get him back, I'll be gone. You won't have to worry that I'll ask you for anything. I'm working now, and I've been able to support us. I have most of the money you gave me, and I've been saving a little bit here and there in order to pay it back. To get started, I needed some of it, but I was careful. I'll have all of it."

He heard the pride in her voice, but it didn't matter. Anger swept through him. "I gave you that money to give you a good start, Bree. That was me taking care of you."

She drew back. He felt that withdrawal, although she had nowhere to go. Their conversation was so careful, so stilted, when they'd always laughed together and talked so easily about everything. Or had they? He tried to think back to the nights they lay in bed together chatting. They'd been comfortable, but he'd done most of the talking, not Breezy. If she spoke, it was to tell him about her day, about some of the children she supervised. Sometimes it was her worries for the girls. They hadn't felt distant from each other, not like this.

She laughed easily, that was one of the things he remembered most. Her laughter. The sound of it. The way she turned everything bad into something good. It didn't matter how he was feeling, and often it wasn't good. He had nightmares and woke up dripping in sweat. He'd sit on the edge of the bed and she'd wrap her arms around him, and the next thing he knew he wasn't thinking, only feeling. She could drive away every one of his demons so easily.

"It's important to me to pay you back, Steele," she said. "I never want to feel like that again, the way I did when you set me straight. It was hard to hear, but I know I had to learn to stand on my own two feet."

He shook his head. "I was full of shit, baby. I wanted you safe and I said whatever I could to drive you away."

She sent him a false smile when there had never been anything false about Breezy. "I appreciate you saying that, Steele, but you had plenty of time to look for me. If that's what you do, find people, you could have found me. You didn't. And that's okay," she added hastily. "I'm fine now. I needed to learn about myself and my own strength. I knew Zane was coming and I figured it out."

"Baby . . ."

She winced. Visibly. "Please, don't call me that. We're not . . ." She trailed off, waving her fingers in the air as if that said everything. "It's best if we keep this as impersonal as possible. Once we find Zane, I'll leave, but if you want to stay in touch with him, of course that's all right."

His temper kicked in. He'd thought he'd mastered that long ago, but his woman had forgotten who she belonged to. If nothing else, she should have remembered who *he* belonged to. It was written on her skin, right where he'd had Ink tatt it.

"Impersonal?" He nearly roared the word at her. He leapt up and paced across the room to keep from hitting the wall just beside her head. "There's nothing *impersonal* about us. You may have forgotten what it was like when I was moving inside you, but I sure as hell haven't. I'll call you anything I damn well please, and yes, we are . . ." He waved his fingers in the air just as she had done. "You aren't leaving when we find Zane."

She regarded him as if he'd grown two heads. He realized she'd never really seen him lose his temper. In all the time he'd been with her, he hadn't raised his voice. They weren't that kind of couple. He'd always led, and she'd always followed. Breezy didn't do things to upset him. Clearly, that had changed.

"You can't tell me what I can and can't do anymore, Steele," she said quietly. "You threw me away and made it *very* clear what you thought of me —"

"That's bullshit, and you know it. You had to leave. I told you that you had to leave, and you wouldn't. You refused. I knew war was coming. It was too damned dangerous for you to stick around. I had to get you out of there."

"You could have come with me."

"I had to back Czar up."

She shook her head. "Czar had everyone else to back him up, Steele. I had no one. You chose to stay with your club, and you threw me out, knowing I didn't have a clue how to take care of myself."

He wished she would yell back or cry. She did neither. More, there was truth in what she said. It hadn't occurred to him to leave the others. They were whole together. Safe. Had he tried to point out that logic she would simply counter that she hadn't been safe or whole without him. Now she was. Now she was complete without him.

"There are eighteen of us, Bree." He made an effort to drop his voice down to the level of hers. Quiet. Calm. "We were outnumbered and didn't expect to walk away from that battle."

Her eyes were on his face, moving over it, focusing completely on him in the way he remembered. He'd always loved that look, yet at the same time he had always found it disconcerting. He'd often turned away from her, afraid she'd see into him. Afraid she'd see what a fuckup he was. How damaged. Still, he had liked that she nearly always gave him her complete attention.

"You went against how many Swords with eighteen men?"

Steele wanted to curse, and he did — in his own language so she wouldn't know what he was saying. Yeah, there were eighteen members of Torpedo Ink, but they hadn't fought that fight alone. There had been others working with them, including Jackson Deveau, the deputy sheriff. If he told her that, came clean and was honest, it would negate everything he'd said.

He took a breath. It was important to tell her the truth no matter the cost. He wanted a relationship. A partnership. He had to treat Breezy with the respect he gave his club, even if the price was that he looked bad to her. "It wasn't just Torpedo Ink. There were others, men and women Evan Shackler and the Swords had done things to. We were still very much outnumbered, but there were others with us." She would never know just how hard it was to tell her the truth.

Those green eyes hadn't moved from his face. He felt a little bit like she was seeing inside, into those dark, ugly places he didn't want her to know about. The tip of her tongue darted out to moisten her lower lip, reminding him of all the times that tongue had moved over his body, taking him straight to paradise.

"You chose the club, Steele," she said quietly. "Don't lie to yourself or me. That isn't going to do us any good."

There was something about the new version of Breezy that appealed to him even more than before. In that moment, he realized his woman had lived the same life he had. Not, obviously, with sexual predators when she was a child, but as a teenager. She'd still been beaten while she'd been young. She'd learned survival skills, just as he had. She knew when to go silent. She knew when to keep her head down. She knew how to make a drug deal and keep from getting killed.

She had done all that, but she'd never learned social skills or how to survive in the outside world — in a completely different environment. But Breezy had adapted because she was a survivor, and she'd done it on her own, needing to provide for a baby. She was quiet still, not belligerent, not accusing, just stating the facts. And they were facts — as she saw them. He had chosen the club, but he hadn't *not* chosen her.

"That's true from one point of view, Bree," he conceded. "But I wanted you. I had no business keeping you when I knew all hell was going to break loose. I had to protect you."

Her gaze never left his face, as if she could see straight through to his twisted way of thinking. "Then why didn't we have a plan to meet up later?"

That was a fair question. He didn't want to answer that one either. The rules of their club were very simple. Respect. No lies. Have one another's backs at all times. If he wanted Breezy in his life, those rules had to extend to her, no matter how painful the telling was.

"We have a code we follow. It's what we live by. It's how we survived. Being with you broke that code. You were underage. I had no idea. None. Not one clue, Bree. You have to understand, that's a sacred rule. By being with you, I fucked up worse than you could possibly imagine. It was wrong."

She was silent for a long time. A flush slid up her face and her chin rose a fraction of an inch. "I see. Well, you don't have to worry. I understand completely. No one wants a reminder around that they're a complete fuckup because they were in a relationship with someone. Or a semi-relationship, whatever you want to call what we had. Well, we know what to call it — your worst fuckup."

"Damn it, Bree, you're twisting everything I say into what you want to hear." Steele raked both hands through his hair in an effort to keep his hands off of her. She had always been amenable, eager to please him, to do whatever he asked. The worst was, he could see why she would think that way. He'd certainly led her to believe he didn't want her or value the time they had together.

A faint smile touched her mouth — that mouth he fantasized over. "If you think that, Steele, you don't know me at all. The last thing I want to hear from you is that you think being with me was the ultimate fuckup." She rubbed the top of her knees with her chin. "This doesn't matter anyway.

The only thing that matters is getting Zane back. If you think you can do that, and the rest of your club backs you up, then we're good."

"It matters, Bree, because you're going to stay here with the baby and we're going to parent him together. In order to do that, we have to straighten things out between us."

Her eyes flashed at him, that vivid green crackling, like a flame that might consume him. His cock jerked hard and something inside him that had been held tight and closed since he was a child broke open. Shattered. Left him vulnerable and exposed.

Steele clenched his fists at his sides, breathing hard as he tried to work off the panic and adrenaline. Self-preservation had kicked in, and he stayed as far from her as possible. He'd always known she had the potential of crawling inside him — she had found a way to steal his heart. But this was so much more.

Now he was aware of the difference in her in a big way. Before, he'd taken care of her. Looked out for her. Made certain she was safe. He'd been the dominant in their relationship. It hadn't been a true partnership because she had no way of knowing any kind of life outside the Swords community, and she'd stayed quiet and followed his lead. She'd been so young, and yet he'd expected her to be grown-up. By staying quiet and observing, she'd done what was expected of her, but she hadn't participated as a partner — because she couldn't.

He'd never been in a relationship before. He didn't even know what one was until he'd met Czar's Blythe. Breezy had a valiant spirit. He had seen so many children succumb to death because they just couldn't — or wouldn't — fight back. Breezy would have survived the horrors of the school Torpedo Ink had endured. So many others didn't have what she had. He recognized it because he'd seen so many die. He'd held them in his arms. He'd cried so many tears he was certain he didn't have any left.

He leaned against the door, dragging in deep breaths, realizing that his woman would take more than he'd ever thought he had it in him to give. When he could finally look at her again, the anger was gone from her face and in its place were concern and speculation. She saw things in him he didn't even allow his brothers to see. He'd had to be so careful, always guarding every emotion, never letting on, even to the other children, staying very low-key and calm for his brothers and sisters, never sharing the turmoil and chaos that could rise unexpectedly. She seemed to see that in him, no matter how much he tried to hide it.

He turned away from her, knowing by her expression it was already too late. He needed to lash out, to save himself. He opened his mouth.

She got there first. "Zane is a beautiful little boy," she said, unexpectedly, as if giving him a gift.

He reached behind him for the door. For the knob. He could take all kinds of punishment. Fists. Whips. You name it, he'd managed. But she undid him in ways he hadn't expected and had no idea how to handle. He realized she believed she was giving him a gift, and she'd done it to soothe him, the way she'd done with all the women she'd taken care of after they'd been beaten or used cruelly. The way she'd done with the children when they were frightened. It was ingrained in her. Deep. A part of her character in the same way it was ingrained in him.

"He's very much like you already. His personality, I mean. He's already thinking he needs to look after his mommy. He tries to feed me with his spoon and he always shares with me. Once I tripped and fell down. Of course I protected him, but he was so upset and kept trying to make the 'boo-boo' better." She smiled at the memory.

He couldn't respond. His chest hurt. His gut twisted. His woman. That was so like her, to try to turn things around for him. She did that for everyone. It sucked that her man was the one needing her instead of the other way around.

"I've got pictures of him on my phone. It's in the pocket of my jeans if you'd like to see him. He's absolutely beautiful, Steele."

It was a gift she was giving him. He took the opportunity to turn away from her and find her jeans on the chair. She'd always done that, placed everything so carefully. Once she realized it was important to him to keep his room and things clean — not just clean, nearly sterile — she'd done so. He'd bet any amount of money she kept wherever she was living the same way.

Her phone wasn't the most up-to-date one, but it had a decent camera on it. He turned it over. The case was one of the ones that was shatterproof, so she protected it. He stole a glance at her. The tension in the room had gone up slowly again. She didn't like her phone in his hands and that annoyed him.

"What's your passcode?"

She held out her hand. "I'll do it and get his pictures for you."

He kept the phone. "You got another man in here or something? You been cheating on me?" The moment he said it he knew he'd screwed up again. He was totally sabotaging himself. Was he that afraid she'd discover what he was inside? He shook his head. "God, baby, pretend I didn't say that. I don't know what the fuck is wrong with me. I know who the screwup is, and it isn't you." He rubbed the bridge of his nose and then pressed his fingers to the corners of his eyes. "I need another chance here, Bree. Would you mind giving me your passcode?"

"Not at all, if you don't mind giving me yours."

It was a challenge, and she should have known better. He didn't have anything to lose. He didn't keep women in his phone — with the exception of her. He had quite a few Breezy pictures. He'd kept every single one he'd ever taken of her, including ones, if she saw them, she wouldn't be happy he'd taken, but he spent a lot of time alone with those particular photographs. Without hesitation, he handed her his phone and gave her his code.

She frowned, that adorable little frown he'd fallen for years earlier, but she reciprocated, giving him her code. "It's Zane's birthday," she added. "My boss gifted me with the phone and I'm on her plan, so my name doesn't show up anywhere."

He understood why Code had never had her name pop up anywhere. She was smart, and she wasn't using her own name — something he'd taught her. "Your boss put her name on your apartment?"

"Yes, I was terrified Bridges would find me. He thought I left you, didn't he?"

"No. I told him straight up I sent your ass away because I was done with you. Told him I wanted you gone, didn't want to see your face anymore. I made it clear I wanted you banned from every Swords clubhouse. He wasn't happy, but I was spoiling for a fight and he let it go."

He saw the relief on her face that he'd protected her enough to tell the truth — he had sent her away. It would have been so easy for him to tell her father she'd run off, and Bridges would have sent an army of Swords after her. As it was, he couldn't do that; Steele had made certain by saying he didn't want to see her around.

She indicated her phone and he forced himself to look down. His heart stuttered. The boy looked about two. He had wild tawny hair and, just like Bree'd said, his eyes. He looked beautiful. Perfect. Innocent. Everything a child should be. He looked healthy and happy. She'd done that without him. Breezy had given birth to his son and she'd kept him healthy and happy.

He wanted to hold his son. Get on his bike and go after him right at that moment. Yell at Code to hurry up and find Bridges so he could beat out of the man where his child was. The need was so strong in him that he turned toward the door, dropping his hand on the knob. He stood there, head down, breathing in long, deep, calming breaths.

"You have to be going out of your mind, Bree," he said.

"I have been, but I tried to stay calm and think it through. Not at first," she admitted. "At first I did a lot of screaming and crying. When I got that out of my system, I thought things through very carefully. I knew I had to get to you, warn you, provide you with evidence that you had a son and hope you'd go after them if I wasn't able to get him back."

He turned back to her, looking down at the screen, picture after picture breaking his heart and yet, at the same time, giving him hope. His son was a miracle. Never, not once, even when he was with Breezy, did he think he could actually have a child.

"Steele."

Her voice. It was a warning. He tried to keep the grin from his face as he slowly raised his gaze to hers. He let one eyebrow go up. She'd lost this battle and she knew it.

"All of these photographs are of me."

"You're my woman."

She narrowed her eyes at him. "Don't keep saying that to me, not when you crawled out from under a pile of naked women, Steele. That ship has sailed."

"And circled right back." He indicated his phone. "No one else is there. You can search it all you want. Only you."

She suddenly went still, and he knew what she'd found. He moved closer. Her lashes fluttered. Lifted. "When did you take these? Who took them? Oh my God, Steele. These are so wrong. In every way. I can't believe you took these. And kept them."

He reached out and snagged his phone, sure she would delete the pictures. They'd saved him more than one night. "Needed them. Once I knew I was sending you away, I had to have them. Only thing that ever gets me off."

"He says, after crawling out from under three women," she repeated. Breezy snapped her fingers. "Give that back to me."

"Not happenin'. I know exactly what you'll do. You're not deleting my photographs. I'm programming me into your phone and taking some of these pictures of Zane."

"Steele, those pictures are . . ."

"Beautiful. Fuck, Bree, you're so beautiful in them I can barely breathe lookin' at them."

She rolled her eyes and snapped her fingers at him again. "Hand it over or delete them yourself."

"Babe. These pictures are going up in my den."

"They are not."

"Then in our bedroom."

"Who took them, because it wasn't you, and I didn't give my consent. That's so wrong."

She had a point, maybe. He needed those pictures, the proof on her face that she was into him. Completely. She was beautiful when he was inside her. Her face, the way she looked at him. But he had taken them without her consent. He didn't take them because he was into porn, he took them because of her face. Yes, they were having sex, but he needed to see that look. There was no way to describe it, but love for him was there, completely focused, wholly on display.

"I'll let you know next time."

"There isn't going to be a next time, Steele. Get rid of those pictures."

"It isn't happening, so drop the subject." He needed to make that very clear. He didn't want her to ever sneak his phone and get rid of the ones he needed so desperately.

"You are the most exasperating man, and we're not done talking about this."

"I'm done talking about it. We need to talk about things that matter to you. To us. We have to fix us before we get our son back."

"There isn't any fixing us."

There was that resolve in her voice he liked to hear, just not on this particular subject. He studied her face. How had he not seen how young she was? He'd always thought she looked like an innocent angel, and she still did. So many of the patch chasers had looked hard and used up. It had been her eyes. He'd stared into them enough to know she was old inside. He found himself swearing again in his own language.

"We'll get him back," she assured softly, just as he'd assured her. "I know them so well, Steele, they can't hide from me forever."

He should have let it go, but her voice was

magic to him. His woman. So beautiful and so damned young. "Why the hell did you have to be a child? Do you have any idea how I felt when I found out? The bottom dropped out of my world."

She nodded. "Actually, your reaction when I told you my age is something I'll remember for the rest of my life. You weren't very nice. In fact, you were a complete bastard. I realized, when you shoved the money into my hands and told me it should cover the year, that you weren't at all the man I thought you were."

"I never once called you a whore, Bree," he said. "I never thought it and I never called you that. I was shocked and angry and a part of me wondered if Bridges deliberately put you up to it in order to blackmail me."

"I doubt if Bridges remembers how old I am. It wasn't like he wanted a child around, Steele. In any case, you know, you're kicking yourself for something that isn't even real." She watched as he put his number into her phone. "In Louisiana, I was of legal age when I was with you. My father gave me to you. That was his consent. I was above the legal age."

"You were underage." He knew he sounded terse about it, but he couldn't go there. Not again. Not in his mind.

"Not in Louisiana. In any case, I was far older. You know the difference. The things I had to do made me older than my birth age, as I imagine happened with all of you. I suppose it would be much like a soldier who goes off, fights for his country and then comes home and can't walk into a bar. I didn't think about my age because in my life, age didn't matter. I could be of use to Bridges by him giving me away. You saved me from all of that. You treated me with respect. For the first time in my life, I knew there was something called happiness. I may not have had it long, but I know I want to find that again, and I'm not about to settle for less."

"Breezy —"

She cut him off. "Just listen for a minute, Steele. At first, I was so scared and hurt that I couldn't think about anything but how much it hurt and how scared I was. But I was lucky, and I met a woman, Delia, and she took me under her wing. She owned a diner and gave me a job. She helped me get a place to live and my GED. Once I could breathe, I had a lot of time to think, especially at night because I had never been alone before. I realized that year with you was a gift to me. A revelation. Whether or not it was to you didn't matter, because it was to me. I was nothing like my father or brother. I could love someone wholly. Give myself to that relationship. You gave me Zane and he became my world. I'm good with that. I really am."

She could break him so easily. Hell, how did one reply to that? He was as broken, as damaged as they came. He didn't look it on the outside. He had brothers who appeared far more screwed up than he did, but he was so far gone he had no business even considering a relationship. What the hell did he know about one? He'd gotten along with Breezy because she'd given him every little thing he'd wanted. The sex had been off the charts.

He should know, he'd been trained practically from the time he could remember, and the training had been brutal, but there wasn't much he didn't know how to control during sex with the exception of a natural erection. Those had been stamped out of him until Breezy. The sex hadn't been about luring a victim and controlling them. With her, sex had been all about pleasure, something he hadn't been able to achieve again without her. Not at all. No matter what he tried. He never felt like he was swept away, consumed by another realm. That was all

Breezy. That belonged to her.

"I'm glad you're so good with that one year we had, Bree, because we're going to have many more together. The three of us: you, Zane and me."

She was already shaking her head and he ignored her protest. "We have a chance to make this right."

"Steele, I've done a lot of reading, mostly because I know my childhood was shit. I wanted to make certain I was in a good place to raise Zane, so I read everything I could about traumatic childhoods and bad relationships. Not," she added hastily when he glared at her, "that I think ours was bad. I told you, I was happy. But I wasn't your partner. I was happy, but it wasn't a healthy relationship. You have to admit that. You gave me the slightest wish and I knocked myself out fulfilling it."

It was the truth. He couldn't deny it. His breath caught in his lungs. No matter which way he came at her, there was always a refute. He forced himself to give her the respect he gave to his brothers. He listened, hearing her out when he wanted to form his protests. He knew she made sense. Breezy always made sense. When it came to the two of them, he didn't. He didn't care whether or not they made sense together. He needed her to survive. It was that simple, but he would listen.

"We set those patterns and they're there whether we like it or not. I'm not that same person, Steele. I wouldn't be happy with you dictating to me and you would never be happy with the new me. You need a 'yes' woman, one who would be happy living with you, doing whatever you asked. I don't want to raise my son in the club life. I don't want to be second to the club. I know what that's like and I'm not going back there again. Those parties with all the drug deals and men doing whatever they wanted to the women. I can't go there again. Never again. I'm different. I like who I am now."

"We don't do drug deals and we don't hurt women. New patterns can be established, Bree," he said. "We've been apart going on three years. That's time enough to break those patterns. We'll take time and get to know each other. You're a pleaser, baby, whether you want to admit it to yourself or not. I'll be more careful of making certain I'm not too demanding and that I see to the things you want and need to make you happy. I was without you those three years and believe me, I know what I lost."

She sighed. "You know you're going to

stay with your club. That's a deal breaker."

"It doesn't have to be. You have to stick around anyway for protection. You can get to know the others and maybe you won't feel the same."

He could see on her face that she was very closed off to that possibility, and his heart sank.

"Steele, honey, I don't need saving. I'm fine now. Really. You can get on your Harley and ride off to save another damsel in distress, because I'm good."

He found himself staring at her for a long time. Shocked that she didn't know. That she couldn't see. Then he was laughing. He didn't know if he was slightly hysterical, but his laughter wasn't humorous in the least.

"Baby, you're reading the situation completely wrong. I know you don't need saving. *I* do. I need you to save me."

Five

"Welcome home, Breezy," Maestro said as she emerged from the bathroom. Fortunately, she had dressed in the surprisingly nice room.

"Hey, Maestro," she replied. The hall was empty. It was at least ten o'clock. She'd slept in. The others should have been lounging around — at least the Swords always had. Ten was early for them to move. She'd been so lucky that Steele hadn't tried to sleep in the same bed with her. From the moment she'd laid eyes on him, she'd thought of sex. Her body was so wound up she hurt. That was what Steele did to her, even in the worst of circumstances.

"Where's Steele?" She wanted to get started on finding Zane.

"Waiting outside for you. He showed me a picture of the boy. He's beautiful. Can't wait to meet him."

Breezy couldn't help the smile because

any mention of Zane made her smile, but the anxiety for his safety was nearly overwhelming, to the point that she just wanted to run out, jump in her truck and tear down the road, as if she could find him that way — with action.

"You'll love him, Maestro. He's so into music. When he cried, if I turned the radio on, it would soothe him to sleep. That and me rocking him."

"I can teach the little guy to play the guitar. Or the piano. Have one in my brand-new house. First thing I put in there. They delivered it the other day. We get our boy back, I'll take you there and play for you."

That stopped her in her tracks. It didn't make sense. These men didn't own property. They were in the wind the moment the whim took hold. "You have a house? Like an actual home?"

"Sure, we do. All of us. Czar wants the roots down deep. Seemed kind of dumb until Reaper got with Anya. Then it made sense."

"Reaper has a woman?"

"Old lady, and he's damn serious about her. Czar has Blythe, and now Steele's got you back . . ."

"I'm not back. I'm just . . . here." It had bothered her for the rest of the night, the last thing Steele had said to her. The voice he'd said it in. He was the one who needed saving. She'd always thought of him as invincible, but his tone resonated with honesty. He'd believed what he was telling her. "Wait. Blythe? I thought Alena was Czar's old lady." She was more confused than ever.

Maestro shook his head as they entered the large common room on their way outside. "No. Alena provided cover, so it didn't seem strange that he didn't sleep with any of the club girls. Blythe is his wife."

Breezy frowned. "Czar rode with the Swords for five years. Do you want me to believe he didn't sleep with anyone else in all that time?"

"Why do women think they're the only ones who can be faithful?"

She saw Steele sitting on his big Harley, surrounded by several of the Torpedo Ink members, all ready to ride. Her heart pounded instantly, and she stopped walking so abruptly Maestro nearly plowed into her. His hands caught her shoulders as he came to a halt behind her.

"Because most men are like him." She indicated Steele with her chin. "You know, that man who needs three women all over him to satisfy him." She murmured her reply, her gaze fixed on the man she'd fallen so hard for she hadn't been able to get through a single day without thinking of him. Or dreaming about him. Nothing had changed after seeing him. Maybe that longing had gotten even stronger.

He was beautiful sitting there on his bike. He belonged, his rugged good looks and his colors worn so easily, as if they were part of his skin. She knew they were. She'd seen the tattoo of the tree on his back often enough. Before, it had only been a cool tatt, and his body was covered in them. Now she knew it was his life. The club would always be his life. His first loyalty was there. The lifestyle of parties, women, alcohol.

"Men can be faithful, Breezy," Maestro said softly. "Steele —"

"Don't," she interrupted softly. "There's no need to explain. He's free to do whatever he wants to do. I'm not in his life anymore. Whatever he says now, knowing he has a son, he told me in no uncertain terms what I was to him for that year. It wasn't his old lady. He's free. I'm free. We just need to focus on getting Zane back."

She would decide what to do after her boy was back in her arms. In the meantime, she knew how to act in a club. She knew she didn't have a say. She just had to keep the conversation away from controversial subjects, and she had to guard her heart at all times.

She hadn't been on the back of a motorcycle in three years. Not since Steele had sent her away. He'd long since destroyed her vest, the one she'd worn so proudly declaring she was his old lady — she'd watched him do it. It had been her protection, but more, she'd been honored to wear it. She'd felt as if, for the first time in her life, someone really cared about her and she was safe. She belonged. She was Steele's. Now she was just Breezy, Zane's mother, standing on her own two feet. No one was taking that away from her — not even the man she loved.

"Why aren't we just having the meeting here?" she asked, nervous to get on the bike with Steele. It was too intimate. They had been one on his bike, man, woman and machine flying down the open road.

"Steele said you were uncomfortable in the clubhouse and he asked if we'd all go to Czar and Blythe's home to make you feel more relaxed."

That was *so* Steele. He had always paid attention to the little things. He didn't think he gave her much back in the relationship, but he noticed if she didn't like something.

She didn't have to tell him. If she did mention something — which was rare — he knew she *really* didn't like it and from that moment, she'd never been put in a position to either have to do it or be around it. That was Steele.

She'd learned to be careful before pointing out something in a window she thought was pretty. The next thing she knew, it was hers. Steele was always strange in that he seemed offhand with her in front of others, although very protective. When they were alone, he'd been very different. Now she knew why. She had to continually remind herself of how he'd thrown her out, like a piece of garbage, treating her the way the Swords members treated the club girls — and their old ladies — like trash.

She took a deep breath, feeling the pressure of Maestro's hand slipping from her shoulder to the small of her back, all but pushing her toward Steele and his bike. As they approached, Steele turned his head toward them and her breath caught in her throat.

He looked the epitome of a dark knight. The outlaw. The man who could ride straight through hell and probably had. Everything feminine in her rose up like a tidal wave. She turned her face away, not meeting those dark, midnight eyes. She couldn't look at him. She didn't dare, not after what he'd said to her the night before.

She'd thought far too long about his parting shot — she needed to save him. She couldn't. If it hadn't been for Zane, knowing she was pregnant with Steele's child, she might not have made it. She might have humiliated herself and run back to the life she'd known and detested because she'd been so scared. Her victories were small, but they were hard won. She was a mother and she had to put her son before anyone else — Steele included. Certainly before her own ridiculous fantasies. Already, those fantasies had come back full force. She wanted Steele to find a way to make it all right. To find a way for her to take him back. She wanted to be in his arms and have him moving in her body. She wanted him to love her.

"I would much prefer to ride in a car or truck. I can drive, Maestro, if you would return my keys, please." She'd managed calm when deep inside she was a mass of nerves. She couldn't get on that bike behind Steele just as she'd done every day for over a year, her arms around him, her body pressed tightly against his while his bike roared under them.

"Babe, are you kidding me?" Maestro said, one dark eyebrow shooting up. "You can't think that truck is safe."

"I've been driving it for over a year."

"It's a mess. Mechanic has it in the shop torn apart."

That was so like a club. The men didn't consult, they just did whatever they wanted. She glared at him. "I bought that pickup myself. It belongs to me. No one has the right to touch it without my permission."

"You have to talk to your old man about that," Maestro said with a small shrug.

Steele frowned, was off his bike and stalking toward them. "What's the holdup? Get a move on, woman. We're going to be late."

When Steele moved toward her, Keys shadowed him. He looked like a menacing jungle cat, muscles rippling beneath a tight tee, his cut declaring him Torpedo Ink. He didn't have a sergeant at arms on his vest. He had nothing to declare he was an enforcer, but like Maestro, he clearly guarded the vice president of Torpedo Ink. That made her wonder about Steele and what he did for his club to have two men on him at all times the way Savage and Reaper were clearly on Czar, the president.

Breezy lifted her chin at Steele in pure defiance. "If someone is going in an actual vehicle, versus a motorcycle, I'll ride with them. I don't ride on bikes anymore. Ever."

There was a stunned silence at her announcement. The other members, already on their Harleys, turned toward her, shock showing on their faces.

Steele burst out laughing. "Very funny, sweetheart. That's good." He held out his hand. "Come on. You love the bike."

She did. She had. She'd loved riding with him. She saw the exact moment he realized she wasn't joking, that she meant it. She also saw the brief flash of understanding in his eyes. He knew why she didn't want to get on his bike with him. Steele had always been quick. Intelligent. He could figure things out faster than anyone she knew. He put pieces of a puzzle together with only fragments of information, and he was always right.

Her heart clenched hard in her chest. She knew immediately there was no getting around this. She would have to get on his bike with him. If she made a stand, she would lose, and she'd lose in front of most of his club.

Steele moved in toward her, taking up her personal space. His arm slid around her waist and he pulled her into him. She'd forgotten how strong he was. He was careful of her though, cognizant of her injuries in the way only Steele could be.

He bent his head to hers, his breath warm against her ear, moving tendrils of hair as he breathed against her skin. He smelled of leather and man. So Steele. "Bree, get on the bike. We're going to figure out how to get our son back. I made certain you didn't have to sit in the clubhouse to do it."

He was already walking her over to his Harley. He reached into a compartment and pulled out a jacket. She stepped back, her breath coming in a ragged protest that hurt her lungs. He shook it out. It didn't say *Swords.* It didn't say *Property of.* It simply was a denim jacket. Still, it was his. Steele's. The moment she put it on she'd do nothing but breathe him in.

He stood there unmoving, holding out the jacket to her. Breezy lowered her lashes and took it, telling herself she was doing this to get her son back. She just had to get them all moving to find him. Once they did, she knew Steele. Once he'd made up his mind to go after Zane, nothing would stop him until he had his son. Then she'd have to figure out how to get Zane away from him and disappear again.

Swallowing her protest, blood thundering in her ears, she stepped close as Steele slipped the sleeve over her left arm, wrapped her up and then she found herself sliding her right arm into the other sleeve. That put her squarely in front of him. His hands dropped to the metal buttons.

Breezy wanted to protest, but no sound would escape. She should have remembered the way he did this. He always held her coat or sweater for her, and when she was in it, he was the one who buttoned it. Before, what seemed a million years ago, his actions had thrilled her. Now she could barely breathe.

He couldn't touch her like this. He couldn't bring back those memories. She knew she was weak when it came to Steele. He was in every dream. Every waking thought. Zane had his eyes and his smile. He was already showing bits of his personality. Steele said he needed her. Breezy knew herself very well, and she needed to be needed. It was that simple. She wanted to make a difference in someone's life. She thought she had to Steele.

"Don't, baby," Steele whispered, cupping her chin in his palm. He brought her head up, so she was forced to look into his eyes. "Don't think about anything but the two of us getting our son back. That's our first priority. We can do that. We're a good team.

We always were, and I know you remember that. Let's get him back and sort out the rest later."

She could drown in his eyes. That deep, deep, dark blue. So blue one could get lost there. She nodded mutely because Zane was the only thing that mattered. She'd die if she had to in order to get him to safety. She'd do anything to get him back.

Steele bent slightly to brush a kiss over the top of her head. She had thick hair. Very thick. It didn't matter. She felt that kiss, that soft touch, all the way down to her toes. She told herself she had no business feeling anything but stark terror. For the first time in three years, since the last time she'd been in Steele's presence, she remembered what it was like to feel feminine. Like a woman. It was the last thing she wanted or needed.

He caught her hand, led her to his bike and swung his leg over in the casual way he had, the one that she'd always thought was so cool. "Use the helmet, Bree."

It was her helmet. He'd bought it for her. She hesitated, wondering how many other women had used it. She hated feeling jealous, even just a momentary flash. She didn't want to be that woman. She should be a decent ex; after all, they shared a son.

"Haven't had another woman on my bike,

sweetheart. It's never going to happen. That's your place. Put the helmet on and let's go. The sooner we hash out how to find him, the faster we get him back."

His voice caught at her. She wished she could see his face as she pulled the helmet over her head and tucked in her hair. He caught her hand, put it on his shoulder and waited. She slid in behind him, closing her eyes when her bottom settled on the seat. It felt natural. Right. Like she belonged.

Steele's body was warm. Too warm. They were surrounded by cool air — fog coming off the ocean — but it didn't matter. The moment she settled behind him, heat was there, warming her as nothing else could. She didn't know where to put her hands. She'd always wrapped her arms around him and gotten as close as possible. Now, she was afraid to do that. Afraid it would be too much, and she'd never recover.

Steele reached for her hands and brought them around him. "Hold on, babe. Tight. I've lost my son, I'm not chancing losing you. We're going to get him back."

That was firm. She laid her cheek against his back, allowing her body to settle against his. That was a mistake. Her body knew his. It knew his bike. The moment he started down the road, the others riding around them, the sound of the pipes, the wind tearing at her body, his heat, the feel of his finger stroking the back of her hand, was all too much. Her body melted into his of its own accord.

Breezy had forgotten what it was like riding in the wind. Riding in a pack. Feeling freedom. She had ridden with Steele when he was pretending to be a member of the Swords, but each time they'd gone out, these very men had surrounded him. They'd been wearing Swords colors, but they had been there to protect Steele. She knew that now. Even then.

She made herself look at the world, the ocean going by, whitecaps high, waves splashing against cliffs. Trees and sometimes homes. The fog touched them, a dense mist that rose like a darker cloud from the great expanse of water much farther out and traveled like a reaching hand with fingers outstretched. A little shiver went through her and she pressed closer to Steele. Immediately his hand dropped down to cover hers.

Everything she did communicated her emotions to him. It had always seemed to matter to him just how she was feeling, and that had been one of the reasons she'd thought she meant so much to him. She'd noticed that he was very observant. He caught details, even small ones, others seemed to miss. The thing was, she had to keep reminding herself, it wasn't just her he was like that with. She wasn't anyone special. Her son was. He wanted her son. She had to keep her guard up and tell herself a million times a day, if necessary, that she wasn't anyone special to him and she couldn't save him at the expense of herself. She had Zane. He was the most important person in her life.

She'd forgotten how much she loved to be flying down a road, a highway, anywhere, on the back of Steele's bike. He seemed to own the road. He drove with complete confidence, inspiring immediate trust in him. Her body moved with his, as though it was born to be there. Each movement was perfect together, as if the three of them shared the same skin and were one entity, not three separate ones. Man. Woman. The Harley.

She pressed herself deeper against Steele, biting back a little sob. Her emotions were all over the place. She couldn't allow herself to think too much about Zane. If she did, she'd lose all control. She was terrified that her father would beat him the way he had her. She could only hope that whatever woman he'd forced to care for her baby would do her best to protect him.

Breezy tried to shut it off, that flow of terror that left her unable to breathe properly or think. She wanted to scream. Just open her mouth and scream out her hatred of the Swords, of the clubs, of the men and women who allowed such ugliness to be perpetuated against children.

Before she realized it, they were off the main highway and going through ornate gates to what appeared to be a very well-manicured farm. Through a flood of tears she desperately tried to control, she caught glimpses of a house in the distance off to her left, but they continued on the winding road in the direction Steele had set.

Eventually he slowed the bike, and she found herself looking at a very large two-story house with a wraparound porch and a large parking area. There were six bicycles parked neatly under a roof that enclosed the space between a garage and the house.

Her heart clenched hard. There were children here. There were children's bikes among the adult bicycles. One of the roll-up doors on the garage was open and she could see three small dirt bikes parked inside, along with a sporty little car and a larger RAV4.

Steele shut down the bike and she took a deep breath, struggling to get herself under control. It was one thing to sob like a child going down the highway in the fog, it was another to face him and his brethren doing it.

She put her hand on his shoulder and forced her legs to hold her up after the experience of riding. Turning away from him, she removed the helmet.

"Bree. Look at me."

She shook her head. "I can't do this right now. I can't lose it in front of everyone. Give me that, Steele. I need you to give that to me." Her voice trembled because she was trembling. Her baby. She wrapped her arms around her middle, feeling sick. He was alone. Scared out of his mind. Did he think she'd abandoned him? "He's so little. He's never known anyone but me. I've never even raised my voice around him. Not once. He has to be so scared. He saw them hit me. He saw them, Steele. What if they —"

He dragged her into his arms and pressed her face tightly against his chest. She could hear his heartbeat, so steady, so strong. She couldn't help herself, just for that moment she needed his strength or she wasn't going to get through what had to be done. Most of the time, she'd learned to push the terror to the back of her mind, so she could function, but at times like this, it pushed through the gates and took her over. She wrapped her arms around his waist and sobbed.

She hated that the others were silent witnesses of her breakdown. Steele kept her wrapped up tight in his arms but walked her away from the house, down a little path that meandered through an overgrown garden. Through blurry vision, she could see the neat little pavers that made up the trail through vines climbing up and over archways and a mixture of grasses warring for room in a variety of colors of green, blue and even pink.

"I'm sorry." She hiccuped. Tried to pull herself together. His arms were strong. His body warm. It was impossible not to cling even when she'd promised herself she wouldn't — not ever again.

He stopped in the middle of a round circle, surrounded by neatly carved wooden benches and covered with a small roof so one could sit, even in the rain. Roses of several varieties were planted around the little sitting area. Climbing roses, tree roses and bush roses, all different colors, some exotic. The place was ringed and shielded by very large grasses, tall ones, that made the area extremely private.

"Bree, you have every right to fall apart. I feel like falling apart."

"But you don't. You hold it together." She detested that she couldn't stop weeping and he was so stoic.

"Only because I've had a lot more practice shutting off emotion when I need to. You're supposed to be emotional. You give that love to him openly. You make him feel it. I know you, sweetheart. You always were good at that. Every child in the Swords club felt it from you, and they needed it. I know Zane felt it every minute of his existence. He'll feel it again because, baby, I swear to you, nothing will stop me from getting him back for us."

She believed him. She had to believe him or she was going to lose her mind. She let herself cry it out because no matter how hard she tried to stop, she couldn't close the door on terror. She had to take back control one minute at a time until she managed to find a way to breathe again.

Very slowly she became aware she was clutching his jacket in her fists. His colors. She had the leather bunched tightly. Immediately she let go and tried to step back. "I'm such a mess, Steele, but I can do this. I just get so scared sometimes, afraid for him. Bridges isn't a good man. Unfortunately, Junk follows in his footsteps. My hope is, Bridges hates being around children so much he'll have someone else watching Zane."

She stepped back, and he let her, his arms falling to his sides. She turned away before he could see her red, swollen face. She wasn't a pretty crier. She'd read about women who wept in front of men and just looked all the more beautiful. That wasn't her. She pushed at her hair, hoping she didn't have helmet hair. It shouldn't matter how she looked, not when her son was missing, but this was Steele. *Her* Steele. He'd crawled out from under three women, and she could describe each of them. They didn't look anything like her with her red face, swollen eyes, messy hair and stretch marks.

"I'm counting on you. I know you're tenacious. I know once you make up your mind, you won't stop. I'll help. I won't keep falling apart." It had happened every hour the first day. Then she'd managed to let it happen only at night. She hadn't thought she'd have a complete breakdown in front of him.

"Stop apologizing, Bree. I would think it was strange if you didn't have a meltdown once in a while. Just take some deep breaths and we'll go join the others and come up with a plan to get our son back. You'll love Blythe, Czar's old lady. She's an amazing woman."

She needed him to keep talking so she could get herself under control; hopefully the cool air would help with the results of her loud, noisy sobbing. "Tell me about her." She walked to the very edge of the circle and pretended to examine a particularly large rose.

"We were hitting the Swords' traveling prostitution houses. They would set up with the girls they kidnapped. Some were 'trained' right there, gangbanged and beat. We divided into two teams. Czar took one out and I took another. We'd hit as many of the chapter's houses as possible and shut them down. Czar's team hit a group that had several young girls being trained. One had fought back hard because her little sister was there. He had a feeling about them. Not all kids have homes. Blythe looked them up later and found them in foster homes. There were the two girls and a younger sister who hadn't been there. Czar and Blythe adopted them."

She swung around, forgetting all about her tear-stained, swollen face. "The Swords 'trained' kidnapped young girls?"

"For human trafficking," he said. "I told

you, they had the biggest ring going that anyone knows of, worldwide."

"No. You said the international president did. You said he had freighters for his clients." She could barely breathe all over again. "The Swords run drugs and guns. They force their women to sleep with other clubs to make alliances. A lot of the women are prostitutes for the club and they do it willingly, but no one ever said a word about kidnapping children."

"You knew some of the women were sold to other clubs. Your father threatened to sell you," Steele pointed out.

It wasn't the same thing. How could she make that distinction to him? "To other chapters. I was born into the club. We're considered club property. That isn't the same thing as kidnapping a child outside the club and selling their body to the highest bidder." She was outraged. Sick. Was her father involved? He was scum — she knew that. She knew he considered women to be far less than him, but would he really kidnap an innocent child and force her into sexual slavery?

"Baby." Steele's voice was very gentle. "Just because you were born into the life doesn't give anyone the right to use you or sell you. When you wear my colors proclaiming you're mine, it means I take care of you. That you're protected, not only by me but by every one of my brothers and sisters. It means I'm responsible for you and willing to take on that responsibility. It means you're loved and that everything I do, I do with you in mind."

She turned away again, not wanting him to see her face. He was too good at reading her expression. She couldn't respond to that. It was too dangerous. That was for fairy tales, not real life. She knew better than to dream. To trust him. To trust any club.

"These girls . . ."

"Darby, Zoe and Emily. Darby is the oldest and she's been through hell. Zoe is still fragile and probably always will be. She was so traumatized she barely talks, although I think she feels safe with all of us now and she's happy. She doesn't like leaving the farm, but she goes to visit Blythe's sisters, who have their own homes on the farm. They aren't sisters by blood, but she regards them that way and the children think of them as aunts."

"I don't know what to say, Steele. How are they going to feel with me being the daughter of a member of the Swords? Maybe this isn't a good idea."

She needed a little time to process the facts he was giving her. She could tell he wasn't lying to her and it fit, now that she had time to put together some of the behavior she'd noticed that hadn't made sense years earlier. Small things. Snippets of conversations hastily shut down when she was close. Her father suddenly furious and then smug.

"You were victimized just the way they were, Bree," Steele said. "Blythe hadn't even accepted Czar back into her life all the way when we brought home Kenny. We'd made a run to stop a pedophile we'd heard about and found him chained in the basement with nowhere to go when we freed him. We brought him home to Blythe. She took him in immediately."

She was beginning to think Blythe wasn't real. She couldn't equate a woman like the one he talked about with her measure of Czar — or any club man for that matter. And for Czar to take those children in . . . Breezy shook her head, rejecting the idea that the man could do anything decent.

Steele ignored the small shake of her head, although he had to have seen it. He saw everything. "We've got a line on another little boy. He's being auctioned on the Internet. We were bidding on him, trying to find the nest. Code traced him to Las Vegas but then the operation was shut down. As far as we can tell, there's no family looking for him. If we can't find his family, Blythe and Czar will take him in. She's got good counselors for the children and the patience of a saint. I've never heard that woman ever raise her voice to those kids."

Now that she thought about it, Steele had only raised his voice to her last night — for the first time. He'd always been gentle with the children from any of the Swords families. He hadn't said much, but he'd been unfailingly patient with them. She could imagine he'd be that way with their son.

That brought her up short. Their son. It was the first time she'd ever thought of Zane that way. He'd always been her son. It was the two of them. Zane and Breezy. She would whisper that to him all the time. That she would always keep him safe. A fresh flood of tears welled up, burning behind her eyes, and she turned away from Steele before he could see.

"How old is he?" She whispered it, unable to find her voice. That could be Zane. Terrified. Alone. He could be sold off by his own grandfather. Bridges would do it too. She hadn't wanted to think of him as capable of kidnapping children and selling them to the highest bidder, but she knew Steele was telling the truth. Now Bridges had their son and she had to worry, not just about him hitting her boy but about him selling Zane to some horrible pervert.

She staggered over to the bench and put her head down, dizziness welling up along with the tears. She *had* to pull herself together. She wasn't going to be of any use to Zane this way, and Steele would never agree to her going along to find him if she didn't stop.

"He's six, at least that's what he was advertised as being." Steele's voice was grim.

She glanced up at him, unable to help herself at his tone. His face was a mask of anger. Every line was carved deep and shouted retribution. He really despised those who had that little boy and she could read his intentions to take the child back. That was *her* Steele. The one that made her heart flutter.

"That could be Zane," she whispered. "Steele, that could be Zane."

"It won't be, Bree." Resolve was there. Absolute resolve. "Even if something happened to me, every one of my brothers and sisters would keep after him, never stopping. It isn't just me. I know you don't like clubs, and you have every reason, but we're not all the same."

She took a deep breath and forced her head up. "Maybe. Clearly there are degrees of depravity. The Swords are disgusting, but I walked in after one of your parties, Steele. I saw the place and I saw all of you. You were buried under three women, and most of the rest of your brothers were draped over others. No one had a stitch on. I remember the parties, even after we were together."

He frowned. "What was wrong with the parties after we were together, Bree? I took care of you. I made certain no one came near you. When it got insane, I took you to our room, away from everyone else."

She shrugged. "It doesn't matter anymore. I don't want to talk about it."

"Babe. We have to talk about the things you object to."

"No, we don't. We just need to get Zane back. After that we can talk all you want, but right now, it has to be about Zane."

His eyes went even darker. He walked right up to her and held out his hand to help her up. She hated touching him. He made her weak. He made her want things she couldn't have. She had to wrap herself in the hurt he'd caused. Real pain. Three years of it, going over every word, repeating it endlessly, looping the ugly things he'd said to her over and over until they were etched into her very bones. She had to cling to that agony in order to survive this.

His fingers closed around hers and he tugged. His hold on her was at odds with the way he pulled her to her feet. His hold was gentle, but he yanked her up aggressively. Her stomach bottomed out as her body fell against his. His other hand was there, cupping her chin, tilting her face up, and then he took her mouth.

The moment his lips touched hers there was fire. Hot. Burning. Wild. Out of control. She tried to cling to the hurt and pain he'd caused, but the storm of flames burned right through those memories, consuming them until there was no way to think. Only feel.

Steele was rough. He was aggressive. Dominant. Totally taking control of her and wielding a fire that burned so hot there was no resisting. Her brain refused to function as every nerve ending in her body sprang to life after a very long hiatus. Blood thundered in her ears and pounded through her clit. Her sex clenched hard and her nipples felt like they would shatter if they continued to rub over his chest.

His body felt so hard, like coming up

against a wall of pure steel. His arms were strong, his hold on her just exactly the way she needed — the way she wanted. She liked that he took control. She'd always needed that from him. Now her body just melted into his, her tongue following his lead, dueling with his, a dark tango that had her clutching at his hair and sliding one hand under his jacket to try to feel his skin.

They had to breathe, and it was Steele who breathed for both of them, kissing her over and over, refusing to let her come up for air. Refusing to allow her to think of anything but what her body needed — and she needed him. She would have done anything for him right then. Given him whatever he wanted as long as he put out the fire building like a volcano inside of her. Need coiled tighter and tighter, winding until the pressure was unbearable and she needed release. All from his kisses.

He lifted his head just an inch and proceeded to kiss his way over her chin to her throat. One hand was there at her nape, controlling her so easily. Her mouth chased after his, but then she felt the sharp sting of his teeth. That echoed through her body, sizzling like a lightning strike, straight to her sex.

She remembered how he did that. Those

nips with his teeth, the bite at her shoulder, her neck. The sting on her breasts that was like a lash of pure heat, an arrow of desire that pierced her skin and drove straight to her pounding clit. Blood thundered. Her breasts ached. She hadn't felt truly alive in all the time without him. Not once. She hadn't known her body was even capable of feeling pleasure, not like this.

His hands slid under her jacket and found her shirt. Those hands of his. Big. Strong. Stroking fingers knowing exactly how to arouse her. She heard herself moan and then, before she could come to her senses, his mouth was back on hers, devouring her. So hot. So perfect. So completely dominant, taking her over, taking her body over, demanding nothing less than a complete surrender from her. God help her, she gave it to him just like she always had.

Every touch of his hands, every stroke of his fingers, his mouth moving over hers, his tongue demanding things she didn't know how to give but impossibly did, all of it was pure Steele. He was addicting. His taste. His mouth. The way he kissed. The way he touched her. He didn't seduce her gently. Had he tried, it would never have worked. For some reason, Breezy responded to his strength, his aggression. To that pure control he always exuded.

He was the one to step back, lifting his head, those dark eyes watching her, compelling. She could see the mixture of lust and something else she didn't want to believe. She couldn't believe. She'd never allow herself to believe again.

She pressed two trembling fingers to her swollen lips. There was a sting there where he'd nipped her bottom lip, and she licked at it, her heart pounding. "What was that for?"

"I can't resist you. I never could, not even when I should have." His gaze never left her face.

He was expecting her to get hysterical or run. Something. She just stood there, trying desperately to draw air into her lungs. Trying to wait for her body to return to her. He'd taken possession of it, just the way he always did, and she didn't dare move until she was whole again. The problem was, she hadn't been complete in three long years. She wasn't now. She never would be again. Not without him.

She touched her tongue to her bottom lip one more time, forcing herself to remember those three naked women surrounding Steele when she'd first come to the clubhouse. She could imagine what they'd done to him, to his body, the body that she thought had belonged to her.

"Don't do it again." She turned away from him, determined to be Breezy Simmons, on her own, mother of Zane. Independent. She was that woman now, and she liked who she was. She wasn't about to let a man like Steele drag her back under.

He paced along beside her. "We're going to revisit what you didn't like about the parties, baby, but not now. Later. When we have Zane back."

Of course he would have the last word, but she didn't dare refute him. All she cared about was getting her baby back, so let him talk. Let him say anything he wanted.

Six

Blythe was tall, blond and beautiful, with brown eyes and a ready smile. She looked elegant, as if she'd just stepped off the cover of a magazine. She didn't look as if she belonged in the world of motorcycle clubs, and yet she fit perfectly. Breezy didn't know exactly how to act around her. The others, all members including Lana and Alena, treated her with the utmost respect. It was clear she was very loved.

Czar, the president of Torpedo Ink, was a different man around his family. He couldn't get near Blythe without hooking his arm around her waist. He kissed her often and his gaze followed her everywhere she went. When he wasn't looking at his wife, he had his arm around one of his adopted daughters.

Darby, Zoe and Emily looked very Irish, especially the youngest, with her red hair and freckles. It was easy to see the three girls were close, and Darby watched over her sisters very attentively. Kenny was seventeen and filling out, although he still appeared a little coltish.

It was interesting, and revealing, to see the interaction between the children and the Torpedo Ink members. Breezy could see the affection between them. When one of the kids talked to a member, he or she immediately got their entire focus.

The house was large, with high ceilings and extremely spacious rooms, and the space was needed. The club members were all inside, even Reaper and Savage, although they were close to the doors. There was a woman with Reaper, his old lady, Anya. It was a revelation to see the enforcer of Torpedo Ink with his woman. As far as she knew, he'd never touched a woman in the Swords, although several patch chasers had tried to snare him. Emily, the youngest of Czar and Blythe's children, hung off of Reaper's arm while his other was around his woman. That shocked Breezy as well. Reaper didn't touch anyone, and no one ever touched him.

None of it seemed real to her, the transformation the club made the moment they were at Czar's property — it was too surreal. Clearly, they all felt at home there. The men immediately pitched in, getting leaves in the tables to make them much longer. She was even more shocked when they set the tables for breakfast in the huge dining room while others helped Blythe, Darby, Lana and Alena in the kitchen making eggs, bacon, potatoes and toast.

Steele walked in with Breezy, going in through the door to the kitchen. Immediately, there was silence, the conversations stopping as heads turned toward them. Breezy couldn't help herself, she slowed, dragging her feet reluctantly. She'd always felt that initial inferiority complex she could never quite get rid of when she entered a new, unfamiliar place. She was a whore, a mule, lower than low, passed around, and it had to show on her. It had to be etched into her forehead. At school, the few times she'd managed to convince her father to let her go, girls had whispered behind her back. She detested new environments because she still had those moments when she lacked confidence.

Steele stepped close to her, took her hand and pulled her beneath the protection of his broad shoulder. "Blythe. Thanks for letting us meet here. I've wanted you to meet my woman. Bree, this is Czar's old lady, Blythe. Their daughter Darby. Anya, Reaper's woman. You know everyone else. This is Breezy. We all call her Bree." He transferred his hold, circling her shoulders with one arm.

He was a big man and she wasn't that tall next to him, not like Blythe. Not at all like Blythe. She couldn't be elegant if she tried. Ordinarily, she would have corrected the impression Steele was giving to Czar's wife, but right then, she couldn't even open her mouth. She hadn't looked in a mirror and she'd been on a terrible crying jag and then she'd let Steele kiss her. A terrible thought occurred, and she glanced down quickly to make certain her clothes weren't all over the place.

"Bree, it's wonderful to meet you. I'm so sorry for the circumstances. I know the boys will bring your son home. You must be out of your mind with worry."

The sympathy in Blythe's voice was genuine and nearly got her crying again. She didn't understand, when she'd managed to stay in a semblance of control, why she was breaking down so much all of a sudden. Well, she knew, she just didn't want to admit that a part of her was already allowing Steele to take over so that she was free to collapse with grief.

"Thank you for lending us your home,"

Breezy said, blinking back the threat of tears. She tapped her lip with the pad of her finger, hoping the tiny bite mark didn't show. She detested her voice. It was too shaky, but she did manage to stop herself from moving even closer to Steele. If she was any closer, she'd be crawling into his pocket.

What had happened to her hard-won independence? She felt as if she were reverting right back to that scared girl who had walked, pregnant and alone, into the diner, hoping for a job and guidance. She'd gotten both. She didn't want to be this girl. She wanted to be *that* one.

"I'm so happy to meet you, Breezy," Anya said. "We could use more female voices around here to even things out. I know they'll bring your son home to you."

Breezy managed a smile. "Thanks, Anya. It's nice to meet you as well." Anya seemed to genuinely welcome her, and that helped to restore a little of her confidence in spite of her tear-stained face.

"It's so exciting to meet you," Darby said. "I'm really sorry about Zane as well, but I know Uncle Steele will bring him home to us."

Uncle Steele? Darby had been one of the children rescued from the human trafficking ring. The Swords had been the ones to kidnap her and her sister Zoe. There was no ill will there, only genuine sympathy. Darby was far too young to be able to fake anything. Breezy was adept at reading people. She had to be. If she'd misread any member of the club, they'd have beaten her. Right now, she could see that Darby was honestly concerned for her son.

"Come help," Alena invited, moving over to make room for Breezy. "I'm making French toast. You can help Anya peel the potatoes for hash browns if you'd like, unless you want to go into the dining room with all the men. They're annoying, but . . ."

"Annoying?" Maestro tossed a wadded dish towel at Alena. She caught it right out of the air and flung it back at him.

"Children," Blythe said drolly. The others erupted into laughter. Blythe shook her head with a little grin that told Breezy she wasn't in the least upset and was used to the type of teasing the club members did to one another. "Get out from under our feet, Maestro, or you'll be cooking the eggs."

Alena rolled her eyes. "I asked him to cook once. *Once.* He sucks at it. The house smelled burnt for a week. Every smoke detector went off and the neighbors called the fire department."

"She's lying her ass off, Darby," Maestro said and kissed the top of the teenager's head. "Don't believe a fuckin' — a thing she says." He hastily tried to correct himself at Blythe's glare.

Darby giggled. "You're in *so* much trouble." She winked at Breezy. "Both Zoe and Emily have swear jars. Emily had hers first, and I think she has enough in it to pay for college already thanks to the club and the way they talk, so Zoe's decided she wants in on the money making. I can't say that I blame her."

Maestro groaned. "I'm going broke as it is just paying Emily." He looked around. "Neither one is in here, so it doesn't count."

Darby laughed. Her laughter sounded relaxed and genuine. Breezy couldn't remember feeling relaxed when she'd been growing up and working in the kitchen or cleaning the clubhouse. She'd tried, for the sake of the other children, and she'd made jokes and laughed a lot for them, but she hadn't felt safe enough to relax. It spoke volumes that Darby, who had gone through hell, did.

Breezy took a step toward Alena, her heart pounding. Once she joined the other women at the islands, Steele would disappear, go in with the other men, and she would be alone.

It was shocking how scared she felt.

He stopped her by circling her waist and pulling her back against him. "You don't have to help them."

He whispered it in her ear, but she knew she did. She would look like a coward otherwise, and she couldn't afford for Alena and Lana, who had known her before, who knew her past, to look down on her any more than they already did.

"I'm good," she lied. She straightened her shoulders and gave him a small, false smile before stepping toward the aisle where Alena and Anya were working and a large mound of potatoes was waiting to be peeled.

Steele pulled out a chair from the smaller table by the window, toed it around and straddled it. "How's school going, Darby?"

Breezy knew he'd stayed because he'd read her reluctance. He'd been like that. Always watching her. Always looking out for her. The way he focused on her had been what had made her fall so hard for him. He didn't make a big deal, he just seemed to do it so naturally that no one questioned his continuing presence in the kitchen.

"Good. Airiana has a way of making physics easy, and that was the one subject I was having trouble with. Zoe's even getting some of the easier stuff just by listening.

I'm pretty proud of her."

Breezy could hear the pride in her voice. She picked up a knife and began to peel potatoes. They were already cooked partially so it was easy enough, and the work allowed her to keep her head down and concentrate on the task rather than look at those in the room.

"Uncle Steele!" Zoe came in and flung her arms around Steele's neck. "You snuck in when I wasn't looking."

"I did," he said. "Brought my woman to meet you."

So much for not looking up. Breezy glanced over at Steele, her heart lurching in her chest at the way his arm, so muscular, surrounded the little girl.

The child looked at her with solemn eyes. "I'm sorry about your little boy," she said immediately. "Uncle Steele will get him for you. Czar came for us when bad men took us, right, Darby?" She looked to her sister.

The room had gone electric. Alena leaned toward Breezy. "She never talks about what happened," she whispered in her ear.

"Thank you," Breezy said immediately to Zoe. "I know he'll bring him back to me. It's just that Zane is so little and I'm very scared right now for him. I keep thinking he's all alone and probably wondering where I am." She couldn't help the little catch in her voice.

Steele half rose from his chair but stopped when Zoe came across the room and put her thin arm around Breezy.

The little girl looked up at her face. "I was scared, but I had Darby. When Czar came to get me, I was really afraid, because he looked so scary, but they took us out of there, didn't they, Darby?" She looked to her sister for confirmation and then turned back to Breezy. "They'll get your little boy and bring him home. You'll see, and he'll be happy here." She spoke with absolute conviction. With confidence.

Darby held herself very stiffly. Beside her, Alena went still. Breezy looked to Blythe for an explanation of why everyone had gotten so emotional and was clearly trying to hold it in. For a moment there was a faint trembling to Blythe's lips and then she nodded at Darby.

"They did, Zoe," Darby verified. "Czar, Reaper, Savage, the others, they came for us, and all of them will help Steele get little Zane back for us."

"I can babysit him when you need me to," Zoe declared. "I know all about nightmares and if he has them, I can make them go away." She believed so completely in Torpedo Ink, it clearly hadn't occurred to her that the club might not find Zane.

Breezy didn't realize she was crying until a tear splashed down on the pile of peeled potatoes, drawing her attention.

Zoe immediately tightened her arm. "Don't cry. They brought us Kenny. They're looking for another brother who is in trouble. They'll find him." She looked up at Steele. "Won't you, Uncle Steele?"

Steele was there, putting his arms around Breezy from behind and pulling her body in tight to his. "Absolutely, Zoe," he assured. "He's my little boy and his mama is right, he's very scared right now and feels alone. That's why she's upset. She knows we'll get him back, she just doesn't like him all alone."

A shudder went through Breezy's body and he turned her into his chest, so she could bury her face there. Hide. She didn't even care that the others saw. She did care that Zoe was witnessing the breakdown though. She recognized, from the way the others were acting and from what Steele had briefly told her, that Zoe still struggled, and she needed to keep her faith in the club. She needed to know she was safe.

Steele's arms enclosed Breezy, as he moved closer to Zoe. "You're good to babysit, Zoe?"

She nodded and reached up to take a bit of bacon that was near the end of the aisle in front of Blythe. No one stopped her. No one smacked her hand. Through her blurred vision, with her ear over Steele's heart, Breezy could see the child lick her fingers. She didn't get in trouble for that either, although Blythe handed her a napkin and another full piece of bacon.

"I am, Uncle Steele," she said. Then she looked up at her sister. "Almost. I have to do the CPR class. We all do, right, Darby?"

"That's right, Zoe," Darby said.

"You gotta pay for that class?" Maestro asked.

Breezy had forgotten he was there, and she turned in Steele's arms to look at him. He was looking down at the little girl with open affection on his face.

"Of course we have to pay, Uncle Maestro," Zoe said.

He heaved an exaggerated sigh. "Fine." He fished out two dollar bills. "I said *ass* and *fuckin'* just now. Here's the money."

Zoe giggled as she took the money. "You just said the bad words again."

He scowled at her and looked as menacing as possible while pulling two more dollar bills out of his wallet. "This is highway robbery, Zoe."

Breezy knew immediately he'd said the offending words on purpose in order to give the child more money for her bank. Not a single club member of the Swords would have given a child money, especially for swearing. She probably would have been slapped for getting the bacon before the men.

Zoe's giggle turned to full-blown laughter. Maestro swept her up and whirled her around. When he set her down, his hand enveloped the child's as they danced around the kitchen and through the door. It was so different from anything she'd ever seen in the Swords club that she was almost jealous of Zoe's relationship with the members. She'd grown up around the Swords and not a single one had ever treated her with compassion, let alone affection.

"That's beautiful," she whispered and looked up at Steele.

His eyes met hers and her stomach did a slow somersault. His smile was brief, but genuine. "You good now, sweetheart? Even Zoe knows we're going to get our boy back." He lifted one hand and wiped gently at the trail of tears down her face. "As soon as we all finish eating and the kids go off to school, we'll come up with a plan. They're homeschooled. They go just down the road to one of their aunts' homes."

She swallowed down every fear and forced herself to nod. She had faith in Steele. She did, otherwise she never would have informed him they had a son. She had to keep believing. It didn't matter that she wasn't his old lady anymore. Or that he preferred to have several women, not one. She wasn't buying into him needing saving. He looked . . . invincible. She doubted anyone could take him down. She just had to believe he would go get Zane and get him to safety.

The pad of his finger stroked her chin. "Bridges has no imagination, Breezy, you know that. He's not going to have some intricate scheme we can't unravel. It will be something convenient for him. He won't think it's convenient, but he's all about his own comfort."

It was a good observation. Her father *was* all about his own comfort. Everything had to be done his way because he refused to be inconvenienced. She took a breath and nodded again, trying not to lean into him. Steele was just so solid. A wall of pure strength. Her legs felt rubbery and she couldn't stop shaking, as if she were very cold. Her teeth wanted to chatter.

"I don't know what's wrong with me. I held it together until I got here." She needed him to understand she was capable of being strong. She had been strong the entire time she was alone.

Steele lifted his gaze across the aisle to Blythe, as if she might have all the answers. Breezy followed his example. Blythe smiled at her.

"I'd be a little in shock too if someone stole one of my children. I think you're handling it very well. It's natural to fall apart when you have someone strong standing by, ready to pick up the pieces. Before, there was only you to handle everything, so you did. Now you have all of us to help, and especially Steele, a man you know won't stop until Zane's back with you both. Of course your body is going to react to that."

Breezy took a step away from Steele and back to the aisle. She picked up the knife to finish peeling the potatoes. Steele stepped up behind her, trapping her between the aisle and his hard body. His arms wrapped around her middle, just under her breasts, and he dropped his chin on top of her head.

"What are you doing?" She tilted her head to look up at him.

"Seeking solace."

She blinked. That was such a Steele thing

to say. It meant everything and nothing. "Well, you can't have it, go away. I'm working here."

"You have to give me solace. That's your job as a woman, Bree."

Alena, Anya and Blythe both laughed. Alena rolled her eyes. "Don't listen to him, Bree. He's playing the sympathy card on you, which means he's up to no good."

Blythe nodded. "Be on the lookout for treachery of some sort."

"Blythe. Not you too," Steele said. "That's betrayal, plain and simple. I'll be having a word with Czar about this."

Breezy noticed that even with the easy teasing all around her, Steele's hold on her didn't loosen at all. She turned back to peeling potatoes, a small smile on her face. She couldn't help it, Steele made her want to laugh. He had a way of making her feel as if she were part of everyone else, and very important to him. She didn't want to let her mind go there. It was too easy to reach for that fantasy, even when he'd torn out her heart.

"I feel that not sticking up for you is fair payment for the fact that, knowing I have four children, you're in heavy negotiations to bring back a fifth."

"That was all Alena and Lana," Steele denied.

"We voted," Alena explained hastily. "It was put to a vote. Only Czar didn't get a vote, the rest of us all agreed we'd spend every penny we had to get him and bring him to you."

"How many more children do you think I'll be able to handle?" Blythe asked, her voice infused with a mixture of laughter, genuine puzzlement and a touch of exasperation.

Alena and Steele looked at each other. They looked at Darby. Then Lana. All of them shrugged at the same time. It was Steele who answered.

"Any number, Blythe. However many need you."

They all nodded. Blythe met Breezy's eyes and she looked a little lost, as if to say, *See how they are?*

Breezy sent her a faint smile. "That could be a lot. Of course Steele's good with children. He could take on a few."

She expected him to laugh and when he didn't, she turned her head to catch the thoughtful expression on his face.

He nodded solemnly. "Bree's right, Blythe. It shouldn't be all you. Bree's good with kids. She spent her life taking care of them, and they all loved her. She has a big heart, and if you share your counselors with us, we could do it. We could help out by taking a few."

"Wait. Wait." She couldn't turn around and face him because his arms were solid bands holding her prisoner as surely as if he'd chained her to one spot. There was no getting away from him, even with a major struggle. "What are you saying? Why am I included?"

"You're my old lady, silly," Steele said, as if he hadn't crawled out from under three naked women. He was matter-of-fact. "If I'm taking on a child who has been abused in any way, that means you are as well. It's the two of us."

"That's *wonderful,*" Darby said. "I knew you were going to be awesome, Bree, the moment I heard Steele had someone. It would be so great if there were two homes providing for children who had nowhere to go and needed us desperately."

"Honey," Breezy started cautiously. She was only a few years older than Darby. Did the teen really think she was capable of taking on a child with such an abused background? It was nice that Darby had said "us," meaning Torpedo Ink and all of them, but ultimately, she would be the one responsible for any child they took on.

"Not this child," Steele qualified. "It's too soon. Zane has to get to know me. And I can see by Blythe's face that she isn't about to give this new boy up."

Blythe burst out laughing, but then it slowly faded, and she was looking at them all with a sober face. "No, I won't give him up. Czar showed me the video of him in that horrible little room. I really can't get him out of my mind. Darby feels the same way, don't you?"

Darby nodded. "We have to find him and bring him home with us."

"We will," Lana said. "These things take time and you just have to wait for the right tiny bit of information. That's what we're doing for both Zane and this little boy."

"It feels like it takes forever," Darby complained. "I guess I just want them safe."

Breezy sent her a faint, knowing smile. "I understand exactly what that feels like." Steele wasn't going anywhere, and she wasn't going to make a fuss in Blythe's kitchen, so she leaned her head back against his chest while she worked. She should have protested his "old lady" reference, but what difference did it make how much she protested? It wasn't helping get her son home.

"We all do, honey," Alena said.

Anya stuck her head into the kitchen. She'd gone out to make certain everything was ready for the meal. "Tables are set and ready. The boys want to know what else you need done. Well, with the exception of Kenny. He says he's on strike and no matter what you say, he won't help."

Darby snickered when Blythe looked to her for an explanation. "He's mad because I told him he had to set the table and he thinks that's a girl's job. Women's work. You know what a chauvinist he is."

"All the boys set the table," Blythe pointed out.

"Doesn't matter, Blythe," Darby said. "He just wants out of work."

Anya laughed. "I want out of work. I'll go tell him to follow Reaper around and make certain he doesn't get into any trouble. The man was born for trouble." Her soft laughter faded as she walked away.

Breezy liked them. She liked the way they interacted with one another. The way they all pitched in to help. She didn't want to like anything about them. They belonged to Steele, and even if the club was everything he'd said they were — and she counted on that to be fact — she wouldn't take the man back. She just couldn't. There was no living through another heartbreak.

She kept her head down and finished taking the peel off the last of the potatoes while talk swirled around her. She was conscious of every breath Steele took. Of the masculine way he smelled. Of his colors worn so perfectly on his body. It fit him to be MC. He was hot enough and masculine enough to need three women, not one . . .

"Stop it, Bree, or I'm going to put my mouth on yours, and then I'm not responsible for what happens." His teeth tugged at her earlobe as his voice whispered in her ear.

She turned her head, smiled up at him, circling his neck with one arm to bring his head down so she could reach his ear. "You never are responsible for what happens when it comes to women, are you?" She kept her voice sweet, trying her best not to allow him to see how much that had hurt.

She went to turn her head, keeping her lashes lowered so he couldn't read her expression, but his hand was there, under her chin, preventing movement. His mouth came down on hers and then he was just possessing her. Taking her over. Leaving her with nothing of herself because she'd burned up in the fire he generated.

The sounds of men's voices and laughter faded away. The noises of the kitchen receded. There was only Steele and the heat of his mouth, the commanding way he kissed, demanding her surrender in the way it always had. If he had put her on the counter and ripped her clothes off right there, she would have let him. Nothing mattered but him. It was Steele. Her man. It didn't seem to matter how many roadblocks she threw up — and rightfully so. It didn't matter how many times she told herself she had to protect her heart from him. She gave herself to him.

His mouth was a flame, pouring down her throat, spreading through her body, rushing through her veins like a wildfire. Every cell, every nerve ending, came to life, out of control, so that need pulsed through her and roared in her mind. She kissed him because she was helpless to do anything else. She kissed him because she loved him, and she could only pray he didn't taste that love on her tongue or in the flames rushing back through him.

He lifted his head first, his eyes so dark her heart pounded wildly. She'd seen that look before he'd all but thrown her up against a wall and taken her hard. She tried to step back, shaking her head, desperate to save herself. One hand covered her mouth as she pressed herself against the aisle.

"You can't do that. Not ever again. Kissing is off-limits, Steele." Her voice was a thread of sound. She was oblivious to anything and everyone but him. He filled up her vision until she could see only him. It had always been that way. "I mean it. We're done. Over."

"Damn it, Bree, we're not. Why do you keep saying that? I explained why I sent you away. You know I'm not lying about it. That should be enough."

"Should it? God help me, but I might have been weak enough to take you back if you hadn't crawled out from under those women. *Three,* Steele. Not one. *Three.* Even for you, you have to admit, that was excessive. No way am I getting involved with a man who needs that."

Somewhere far off, she heard Blythe gasp. She might have turned her head, embarrassed that she'd said something so private aloud, in front of others, but then she remembered there had been nothing private about Steele in the common room of the club. She tried to step away from him, but he caught her firmly against him, locking her there.

"Are we finally going to talk about that, then?"

"No. Not ever. There's no need, because I

don't care what you do. I'm not your woman, your old lady or anything else to you. Have at it, Steele. Why stop at three women? Why not take on more. You can handle it." Now her voice was belligerent, and maybe hurt; that was there too, but she didn't care. "Stop touching me. Stop telling people we're together. I'm not with you and I'm not going to be."

The worst was, she was certain he could handle any number of women. He had more stamina than she had imagined possible, and she'd certainly seen the men in the Swords' club with women. They didn't last anywhere near as long as Steele, nor were they able to go multiple times as he could. She hated that it was the truth, that he probably could handle several women.

"I hate to tell you, baby, but you *are* with me and you're going to be for the rest of your fuckin' life, so get used to the idea. The only way we're going to work out our issues is by talking. So, yeah, we're going to talk about this."

"Don't you *dare* use that tone of voice on me." The one that made her freeze. The one that shook her right to her deepest core and shredded every bit of hard-won self-confidence she had. She couldn't bear for him to be angry with her. Worse, she was programmed to freeze if anyone raised their voice to her. "I didn't do anything wrong. That was you. Oh. Wait. You don't consider that wrong." Sarcasm dripped from her voice.

"Maybe it isn't wrong, Bree, but it isn't something a man with a commitment would do, especially a man like me. You were gone. Three years, woman, and I didn't think you were ever coming back. Three fucking years, Breezy, and you had my son. You could have written . . ."

"Really? Written to where? I had no idea where you were. When you threw me out, you wore Swords colors and you made it clear you wanted nothing to do with me and you had no intentions of having a family. I wasn't coming back. I didn't come back to you. So, have at it. Next party, drown yourself in as many women as you like, and I'll do the same with men. We can celebrate the fact that you're an asshole."

There was a long silence. Her heart pounded when she dared to look at his face. She'd never seen him look like that before and his expression shook her.

"If you never hear another word I say, Bree, you hear this." Steele framed her face with both hands and stared straight into her eyes. "Another man touches you and I'll kill him. He won't die easy, baby, but he'll die." His voice was pitched very low. Each word was annunciated clearly so there was no way to misunderstand what he said. "You think long and hard about that before you ever let another man put his hands on you."

There was no way one sliver of doubt could creep in. He meant what he said. A frisson of fear crept down her spine because he wasn't finished. He kept staring into her eyes, and it was more than intense. He was taking her somewhere terrifying. For the first time, she could see the killer in him.

"I know more ways to take a man apart than you can imagine. I kill easily, sweetheart, and not many can say that. Call me a psychopath, call me whatever the hell you want, but don't you ever be stupid enough to allow another man to touch you if you don't want that man dead. Are we clear?"

She couldn't take a breath. There was no air. He had always had the ability to scare her. He was a big man and clearly dangerous. He was also MC. But not like this. He was different, and that difference wasn't exciting or thrilling — it was just plain scary.

"Have I made myself clear, Breezy?" His voice had dropped another octave, dropped lower so he was nearly whispering, but that felt more compelling, more menacing, than if he had yelled at her. "Because if I haven't, we need to go over the rules again. Do you understand the rules?"

She nodded mutely. His thumbs slid over her cheeks, barely there, but she felt his touch winding through her body slowly, leaving behind a flutter of wings, a need that just wouldn't leave her no matter how hard she tried to get over him. Even now, seeing this other side of him, the one that scared her to death, she still responded to his touch.

"We're going to talk through every issue we have. You have to be willing to at least talk about things, Breezy. You can't just shut the door on us. Whatever we had between us is stronger than ever. Now we have Zane."

Zane was the reason she didn't want to take any chances, but she couldn't say that to him. She was too afraid of him getting angry with her again. He'd never done that before — as in never. She didn't know how to respond to him when he was like this, so she remained that frozen little mouse she hated, the one that went still when she was threatened.

Steele sighed and stepped back, giving her space, allowing her to breathe. Her mind was still shut down, and she didn't move, but at least he couldn't feel the tremors wracking her body.

"Would you take the platters of eggs and bacon into the dining room, please, Steele?" Blythe asked.

Her voice startled Breezy. She'd forgotten anyone else was in the kitchen with them. Steele, still looking at her, nodded. Blythe put the platters into his hands and waited until he was out of the room. The women gave a collective sigh.

"I had no idea Steele could get so intense," Blythe said. "Are you all right, honey?"

Breezy shook her head. "I don't know him at all. And he doesn't know me, not the way I am, or at least the way I can be when he isn't around. I'm not going back to him." She lifted her chin and met Blythe's eyes. "I'm not."

"It's clear," Alena said, "that you're in love with him. Why don't you want him back?"

"I've had my fill of club life and coming in second. Being treated like trash. I'm not going back to that life or raising my son in it."

"Steele would never treat you like trash," Lana objected. "Nor would he put you second to the club."

"Really? He did. I was so terrified when he told me to leave and told him so. It didn't matter to him. He stayed with the club, with Czar, and told me he didn't want anything to do with me. That I was nothing to him. As for club life, I walked in after one of the famous club parties. It looked and smelled the same to me. He doesn't need me. He's got any number of willing women."

Breezy knew she sounded bitter, but she couldn't help it. "While he was partying, I was having a child alone and learning how to survive outside a club. I did it, and for the first time, I felt pride. Self-esteem. I'm not going back to that scared little mouse standing frozen in front of him, too terrified to say what I think."

"Honey," Lana said, her voice gentle. "You've heard me tell my brothers to go to hell. Do you think they hit me? That they would *dare* hit me? I'd slit their fucking throats if they tried it, not that they ever would. They aren't like that."

"Steele just threatened to kill a man, and he meant it, Lana," Breezy reminded.

"He threatened to kill the man, Bree," Lana pointed out. "Not you. He would never lay a hand on you. Not like that, no matter how upset he was with you."

"Bree." Darby glanced at her mother and then her gaze jumped back to Breezy's face.

"I know you don't know me very well, but Czar and Blythe always encourage us to say what we think. I'll admit I've never seen Uncle Steele like that, but I did see the way he touched you. So gentle. He wasn't going to hurt you. When we first came here with Czar and Blythe, we were scared, and every time one of the men moved too fast or sounded scary, we jumped — or froze. The men who took us tried to train us like that, and they only had us for a few days. They had you for years."

Breezy's heart nearly stopped beating. She had never considered herself a victim. She was born into the club life. She was a daughter of a high-ranking member. She was a useful club asset. She was a lot of things, but not a victim. What Darby said to her made sense. She'd been trained to be a mouse. To stand still and never voice her opinion. To stay as quiet as possible, to soothe tempers, to anticipate needs, whatever they might be.

To some extent she was still that girl and always would be. She had trained herself to notice details, to observe, so that had translated over to her waitress work in serving her customers. She knew what Zane needed almost before he did. She'd always been good at anticipating Steele's needs or wants. She hadn't considered that training; she'd thought it was her nature. Now, having heard Darby and giving it consideration, she knew it was both.

"He'd never hurt you," Blythe said with complete confidence. "You're Torpedo Ink whether or not you claim them. You belong. They will surround you with protection. They'll surround your son with protection. You love Steele. There's not a doubt in my mind that you love that man. Just give it a chance."

"I don't share." She didn't care how they all tried to explain things away. No one could explain Steele and the other women.

"Men are idiots," Alena muttered and slipped off her stool. She picked up the platter of potatoes and went into the dining room.

Blythe handed Breezy two pitchers of fresh-squeezed orange juice and picked up the other two. "My sister grows oranges in a greenhouse, so we're very lucky. Player and Transporter did the honors this morning."

"They squeezed all the oranges to get the juice?" Breezy was shocked.

"We do have a little machine," Blythe clarified. "Although if you ask, I'm certain they'll act like they did it by hand."

She went out with Lana following behind,

carrying the platter of French toast. Breezy stood there for a moment staring at the archway between the kitchen and dining room. She felt like that mouse all over again.

Darby reached out and touched her arm. "They're all here to figure out how to get Zane back. Think about that. Just keep it in your head that they're here to help. I told myself that thousands of times and it sank in. Now, for the first time, I think it's sinking in for Zoe."

Breezy nodded her head, took a deep breath and followed Darby into the dining room.

Seven

Breezy forced her body to work when it wanted to do its frozen-in-place thing. The only chair open at the table was next to Steele. The men were heaping food onto their plates and pretending to stab at the bacon and pancakes on Zoe's plate. Kenny sat beside Darby. He'd clearly put food on Darby's plate, afraid the others would eat everything before she even arrived. The plate beside Steele's also had food on it, evidence that he was looking out for Breezy in spite of their argument.

She placed the pitchers of juice apart on the lower end of the table because Blythe had put her two pitchers on the upper end. The table went from one end to the other of the dining room and had clearly been custom-made. It was beautiful. She couldn't help admiring the woodwork.

Steele held her chair for her as she slipped into it. She didn't look at him but at the amount of food on her plate. There was no way she could eat it all, not with her stomach churning the way it was. She couldn't stop the fine tremors running through her body, over and over. Steele noticed because he always noticed everything about those around him and her in particular.

He leaned into her. "This is good, baby. Just eat, and when the kids go to school, we'll hash this out. We'll ride out tomorrow morning before dawn, starting for Louisiana. Code will continue to feed us information so by the time we get there, we'll know where we're going. This morning is mainly for him to get as much information as possible." He picked up her fork and held it out to her.

She took it because she didn't want to make a scene. The others were talking and laughing together, like one big family, but she knew they were all very aware of her. She didn't want to give them any reason for turning the spotlight on her. Besides, she wanted to observe them together. The atmosphere was very different from that of any function with the Swords.

"Do you want some of Blythe's weird pink salt?" Maestro asked and held out a salt shaker. The salt really was pink.

She took it, looking at it suspiciously.

"What is this really?"

Steele nudged her with his shoulder. "Blythe lies and tells us it's salt, but I don't think it is. Kenny usually has a contraband salt shaker if you want to try to get it from him, but if you're caught, Blythe gives you her stern look. It's pretty cute, but only Czar gets away with saying that to her because she thinks that scowl makes her look badass." He didn't bother to lower his voice, although he pretended to.

Blythe was quite a distance down the table from them, but she glared at Steele. "I heard that. I don't look cute when I'm giving you my meanest look."

Czar hooked his arm around her neck, brought her in close and took her mouth. Breezy nearly dropped her fork. The kiss wasn't a little peck. It was intimate and hot, and she considered fanning herself. She should have looked away, but she couldn't. When Czar let her up, Blythe was pinker than the salt.

"I love that look," Czar said. "Gives me a hard-on, baby. Every single time. And yeah, it's cute as hell when you get all badass on us."

Blythe shook her head, but she was smiling. "It's salt, Bree. It's just natural, not processed, and so much better for you. It has all the minerals in it as well. And Kenny, if you have processed salt anywhere on your person or hidden in your clothing . . ." She broke off. "I saw that handoff to Ice." She snapped her fingers and held out her hand. "I'll put that with the other two hundred salt shakers I've confiscated from the three of you."

"I wasn't in on that," Storm protested, trying to look innocent.

In spite of everything, Breezy found herself laughing with the others. They seemed more like one huge family, the way they interacted. She didn't know that much about real families — hers had been more than dysfunctional — but each of the club members was so in tune with the others, it was almost as if they knew exactly what the others would say and do before they did it.

Steele was a part of that. He'd always been a part of that, even when he rode with the Swords. These people had ridden with him. His brothers and sisters. Breezy looked around the table as the teasing continued. This was Steele's family. He belonged. She could understand why he'd chosen them over her. She didn't know how to be like them. She didn't fit in because she had no idea how to act.

Darby leaned close. "They're all crazy."

There was affection in her voice. "When I first came here with my sisters, believe me, I was afraid, leery and felt totally out of place. They make a place for you. It's as if once you're accepted into their circle, they just somehow absorb you and you're a part of them. It's really cool, Bree. It took me a while before I could make myself give them a chance, but I was really glad when I did."

Did she look that uncomfortable? Probably. It was more that she didn't understand what was happening, and that always paralyzed her. She had a tendency to try to make herself small and invisible until she figured out protocol. These people baffled her. A good deal of the problem was that she had known them all first as Swords. They'd blended in with the club seamlessly, although they all looked, even then, as if they could eat their prey. They were like chameleons, blending in wherever they went.

How did she know what was real? She'd thought Steele's feelings for her were real during the time they were together. Although he'd never once told her he loved her, she'd felt it when he touched her. Maybe she just had never known kindness and she'd mistaken that for love. It was also possible he'd felt some affection for her, and she'd mistaken that as well.

She forked the eggs into her mouth. This food was as different from the Swords fare as the table filled with obvious friendship and brotherhood was. Everything about Torpedo Ink was different. She just didn't know if she could trust them to return Zane to her if — when — they got him back.

Steele's hand slid up her back to the nape of her neck. She froze at his touch. There was no way to stop the flutters in her sex, or the weird sensation of a somersault in her stomach. She accepted that her body would always react to his touch no matter how much she tried to keep it from happening. She turned her head slowly toward him, bracing herself to meet his eyes.

"Everything's going to be all right, Bree."

"I want to go with you when you go after him." She was going, no matter what they all said. They would have to lock her up to keep that from happening. She wasn't going to say so though; she was going to stay quiet. If they left without her, she would find her own way to Louisiana, because she was going to be there to hold her son in her arms and comfort him.

He nodded slowly. "I've been giving that a lot of thought. We could communicate by phone, but having you with us to direct us to the next possible place would be the smarter thing to do. I need you safe though, Bree, so you have to give me your word you'll follow orders. I'm not going to be telling you what to do just to be bossy. These situations can get dicey fast and can deteriorate in moments. We're adept at reading what's happening."

That made sense as well. She let her breath out, nodding. "I have no problem with that." She'd always let him take the lead because she'd trusted him. Now she wasn't sure how she felt about him — what she trusted and what she didn't. She was elated that she didn't have to argue, beg or try to deceive him. She wasn't good at deception. Not like he was.

"Good. Eat, baby. You're going to need your strength."

A shiver of awareness snaked through her body. His admonishment could have been about keeping her strong for travel, but his eyes and tone said something else altogether. Steele was a very sexual being. He was demanding, and often, they'd had sex several times a day. More than once, he'd just caught her, slammed her against a wall and drove her out of her mind. It hadn't mattered where they were; she'd lost her ability to think around him.

He'd never had a problem being naked in

front of others or having sex with others around. She didn't either. The moment he touched her, it didn't matter where they were, his entire focus seemed wholly on her, and she loved that. Once at a party, he took her right on the bar, and when someone else tried to touch her, he'd gone insane, beating the shit out of him. It had been a thing of beauty to watch him, his body like a machine.

Sometimes when they had sex, it was wild and crazy; other times, so intimate she wanted to cry. Always, no matter where they were, no matter if others were around — frankly, Steele had always seemed more comfortable and relaxed if some of his friends were close by — whatever the situation, they burned together hot and perfect.

Club life to Breezy, especially the parties, meant drug deals and the members forcing the women to make the deals with their bodies. She'd hated that. Dreaded every party. Until she'd been with Steele. Surrounded by Steele's friends, she'd felt safe and protected, especially when Steele had her naked and mindless, crying out with orgasm after orgasm. The way he was had been thrilling and made her feel as if he couldn't get enough of her. Now she felt it was just his incredibly strong sex drive and had nothing whatsoever to do with her.

His breath came out in a hiss of displeasure. "Stop it, Bree. Stop thinking. Just give it a rest until we can clear things up. Right now, finish your food. The kids are leaving, and we'll get this operation under way. After, we'll talk about us."

She didn't want to talk about them. There was no "us." As far as she was concerned, there never had been. That fantasy had been in her mind. She accepted it like she accepted everything else that had happened to her. Steele had been too good to be true. She kept her head down and finished the eggs, although now, nothing tasted good to her. Everything was like cardboard.

Darby got up and began carrying plates and platters from the table. Several members of Torpedo Ink helped. Transporter and Mechanic along with Keys gathered up more dishes. She could hear water running as if they were rinsing them. Lana stood up and gathered more.

"Here, babe, take mine too," Ink said.

Lana glared at him. "I didn't know your legs were broken."

"Muscle strain. At least that's what Steele said," Ink informed her.

Instantly the glare disappeared, and her expression changed. "Are you hurt? No one told me you were hurt. I was teasing."

"So was I," Ink said.

A roar of laughter went up around the table. Lana shook her head, a small smile playing at the corners of her mouth. "I don't know why I fall for your crap every single time." She placed the pile of dishes she had gathered directly in front of him. "For that, you can rinse."

Ink got to his feet, picked up the dishes and sauntered out, more laughter following him. Lana gathered up the condiments and followed. Several of the others finished stripping the table and washing it down until the wood gleamed.

Darby caught up a book bag and took Emily's hand. She waited by the kitchen door as Czar crouched down in front of Zoe. "You have a good day at Airiana's."

She nodded solemnly.

"What do we always do, Zoe?" he asked.

Breezy's heart clenched hard. Clearly, this was a ritual. His hands were gentle and loving on her, rubbing her arms and then her hair.

"We always give our best, treat others with respect and we keep our business private. What we see, what we say and what we do stays here."

"Very good. What else?" Czar smoothed

back Zoe's hair with gentle fingers.

"Anything I don't like, I tell you, Blythe or one of my uncles or aunts, but our business in this home is private. My uncles' business is private."

Czar's smile held pride and affection. "Exactly. We don't share with the outside world, but we don't keep secrets from one another. Anything upsets you, darlin', day or night, you call us immediately. And if someone tells you it's a secret, there are no secrets from us. Even if someone tries to scare you by saying they can hurt us, you tell us."

Zoe hugged him tightly and then turned to her sister. "Darby too, right? I can tell Darby."

Czar nodded as Darby took Zoe's hand.

"Hey, what about me?" Kenny said. "You can tell me anything, Zoe. I'll look out for you." He ruffled her hair. "The club's been giving me lessons in . . ." He broke off abruptly and looked up at Czar.

Blythe moved closer. "Lessons in what, Kenny? I can't imagine what all your uncles might choose to teach you." She looked at her husband, not at her son.

Czar gave her a lazy grin, wrapped his arm around her and pulled her in tight to him. "Woman, you have a dirty mind. Not sex.

Basic self-defense. We're working with Darby and Zoe as well."

Blythe rolled her eyes.

"Don't pretend you weren't thinking we were giving him instructions on sex, woman. I can read you like a book."

Another roar of laughter went up, and Blythe shrugged. "I wouldn't put it past you."

"Where else is he going to learn how to give his partner pleasure? He needs to hear it from us, not read about it on the Internet or learn it from watching porn."

"Is this an appropriate subject in front of the children?" Blythe demanded, but she was laughing and let Czar kiss her until she was breathless.

"Sex is a part of life, baby. It's a part of intimacy with their chosen partner. I don't want them to ever feel shame."

Breezy didn't think any of the Torpedo Ink members had inhibitions when it came to sex, but then she'd been around the parties and somehow, she didn't think Blythe had. Breezy had no inhibitions either, none at all, not when she was with Steele. Watching Czar with Blythe, she doubted if Blythe had many, but she was far more reserved than Bree would ever be.

She watched both kiss the kids good-bye

and usher them out of the house. Instantly, the atmosphere changed. Code leapt up and got his laptop, opening it. The others positioned themselves around the table again. She found her heart pounding as they all settled, with Czar at the head of the table.

"Bree." Code addressed her first. "I need to know names and everything else you can tell me about your grandparents. I've found Bridges's birth certificate, but only his mother was listed, not his father. Can you give me any information on them now? I haven't found any information on his mother since about forty years ago. Did you ever meet either of them?"

Breezy took a deep breath. This was important, although it had been drilled into her never to talk about her father's parents. "According to my father, my grandmother Carlotta detested children. She had my father alone because my grandfather, Boone, was in jail by the time she had him. He was in for armed robbery. Carlotta and Boone were never married. From what I understand, Carlotta beat the crap out of Bridges, and any lover she took was encouraged to do the same. She hated him for messing up her life, and then loved him because he belonged to her. The moment Boone was out, she handed Bridges over to him. Boone was in the Swords club, so Bridges grew up in the club."

"Last names," Code demanded without looking up.

"Carlotta's is the same as Bridges. Simmons. Boone is from a very wealthy family, at least that's what I was told by Junk. He said Boone terrorizes his family when he's out of jail and they do anything he says. It's Abernathy."

Code's eyebrows shot up as if he recognized the name, and maybe he did. Breezy had heard enough about the old man that she didn't want to ever meet him or his family. "Boone was pretty nasty, from what Bridges said, and I only saw him once or twice."

"Do you know where they live?"

Breezy was horrified. She could feel the color draining out of her face, and her heart beat wildly. She tasted fear — no, terror — in her mouth.

"Do you really think my father would take Zane to either of them? He detests his mother and father with every breath he takes." The sound of her voice was thin and wavering.

Immediately, Steele shifted closer to her, as if he could protect her from the idea of Bridges's father or mother having anything to do with her son. She pressed her hand to her chest and leaned against Steele's hard strength. She needed him. She didn't care that he'd hurt her. Or thrown her out. Or crawled out from under naked women. She needed strength, and he had it in abundance. She was so dizzy she could barely find air. The room spun and tilted crazily.

"Breathe, baby. We're going to find him. I promise you that. Code is covering all the bases, that's all. If we can rule them out, we'll have two less places to check."

The absolute confidence in Steele's voice penetrated the terror. She forced air into her lungs, but she didn't pull away from him. Did it matter if she was embarrassed later? The only thing that truly mattered was getting Zane back.

"Carlotta is with a man, Jacob Daltry, who owns a plantation house just outside of New Orleans." She gave Code the parish. "Boone is much more difficult. His family owns a ton of properties. When he's not in prison, he chooses one and just moves in, regardless of who is in it, from what I understand. That's what makes him hard to find when the cops are after him."

"What about Bridges? Are there places he likes to go when he wants downtime? Or when the cops are after him? A fishing or hunting camp? Tell me about him," Code persisted. "The more I know of him, the more we can narrow down any of the Abernathy properties that he might choose to go to. If his father does that, maybe he thinks he can do what his father has always done — use the family holdings to hide."

The questions forced Breezy to think about her father. She realized she never did that. She tried to put him out of her mind as much as possible. She had when she was a child as well. She'd been a frozen little mouse, afraid if she even thought about him, she would come to his attention and he'd hurt her. For a long time, the emotional damage was far worse than the physical. At least Bridges tolerated Junk, but she didn't seem to be worth anything at all to him — and that had hurt for the longest time.

"When he's not on his Harley, he drives a Jeep. He only will drive a Jeep. Once, he needed to rent a car and he nearly beat up the attendant because they'd rented the Jeep they had to someone else."

"That's good, that's the kind of thing I need. I can find Boone's family properties easily, but Bridges's habits are what is going to trip him up," Code encouraged.

"He drinks Jack Daniel's and smokes Marlboros. He prefers to get his gas at a mini-mart, where he can load up on snack foods, like Twinkies. He likes diners but not a restaurant if you understand what I'm saying."

"People have habits, Bree," Code said. "He has them. Patterns. Keep talking about him."

"He uses women all the time. I can't tell you how many women he moved in with and then pawned me off on when I was little, so they were forced to take care of me. He said he could avoid mortgages by letting the women pay."

"Did he stay friendly with them after he left?" That question was from Transporter.

Breezy shrugged. "He beat the hell out of them, terrorized them so they wouldn't dare leave him or report him, and then he would leave, but often, he'd go back time and again just to scare them. I don't think you could call them his friends."

"I need a list. Every name you remember. Every town. Every address. If he had no problem dumping you on them, he might not have a problem dumping Zane on them," Code said.

Breezy closed her eyes and pressed her head into Steele's chest. She hoped Zane was with one of Bridges's past ladies and not at one of the Abernathy properties. At least he'd be safe. The women hadn't always liked taking care of her, but they'd done it, and some of them had been nice.

"Medications?" Code prompted after she had rattled off the last of the women's names she could remember.

Her head was still pounding from all the wild crying earlier, and thinking about her father wasn't helping. She thought about trying to be strong and sitting up away from Steele, but it seemed like too much trouble, especially when he was rubbing her arm soothingly. She could feel his chest moving with every breath he took. When he exhaled, it was warm air against her neck and it felt familiar to her. Familiar. Intimate. A connection between them when she desperately needed someone.

"He takes heart medication and always gets it at a Winn-Dixie. He doesn't like the other pharmacies. It's the same with actual groceries. He refuses to go to any of the bigger supermarkets."

Reaper stirred. "Sergeant at arms for the chapter? Anyone know? If Czar took off, I'd be on him immediately. If we know who it is, we can track him as well."

"That's a good point, Reaper," Czar said. "You don't let me shave without one of you checking the shaving cream."

There was laughter, but it didn't ease the terrible weight pressing down on her. They spent the next couple of hours questioning her about every detail of her father's life, going as far back as she could remember. In the end, she felt worn out and drained, but somewhat hopeful. If they were that thorough, then maybe they wouldn't be looking for the proverbial needle in a haystack.

"We'll take the majority with us," Steele said. "Everyone volunteered to go, and Bree and I thank you for that. Czar, I think it best if we leave your team with you and I'll take mine with me. We're used to working together, and Reaper and Savage will —"

"I'm riding with you," Savage said and got up. He pushed his chair back to the table, nodded at Blythe, leaned down to brush a kiss on the top of Anya's head and prowled out.

Savage prowled. He never just walked, Breezy decided. There was something very scary about him. His declaration was met with silence.

"Should I be worried about him?" Breezy asked. "I don't need a powder keg."

They all looked at her. Focused entirely. She felt familiar fingers of fear creep down her spine.

"You should worry about your man, not

one of us," Reaper said. "No one goes up against Steele when he's pissed. No one. Not me. Not Savage. You're sitting next to the powder keg." He got up, held out his hand to Anya and they followed Savage out.

Steele stood next, his fingers an iron band around her upper arm, so that she rose as well. "We're riding out at three this morning. Dress warm. We're traveling fast. You'll need weapons but prepare for a search. We'll be riding through Diamondback territory and into Swords territory so no colors."

Breezy had never heard the authority in his voice like that. He'd certainly told her what to do on occasion, but she realized that power came naturally to him. He wore it easily on his shoulders, so much so that she should have caught it, but they all deferred to Czar. They'd played up his role as the badass when they'd ridden for the Swords. He'd been the one the Swords club members feared, and that had prevented them from really seeing the others. What did Reaper mean about Steele when he said he was the one to watch, not Savage? She was very confused by the changes in all of the Torpedo Ink members.

Steele pulled her under his shoulder, his arm locking her front to his side, and took her with him right out the door, not even giving her a chance to say good-bye to Blythe or Anya.

Breezy knew she should pull away from Steele and stand on her own two feet. He wasn't the kind of man one could give a few inches to, he'd take the mile every time, but she was trying to puzzle out how she had missed the way he carried himself with such complete confidence.

"Are you really a doctor?"

He glanced down at her but didn't slow down on the way to his Harley. Behind them, Maestro and Keys kept pace. She didn't hear a sound, not even the whisper of their motorcycle boots. The only way she knew they were there was the glimpse of them she caught when she looked back.

"Yes. A surgeon actually, but I had advanced training in several fields. I don't practice here for anyone other than the club. Code makes certain I have up-to-date licenses, so if I had to perform surgery on one of them, it would be legal. We're putting together a little clinic with the latest equipment, so Blythe can bring the kids."

She didn't know what to say to that. It was one more reason why she didn't belong with Steele. He was intelligent. Really gifted. Off the charts. That, she'd always known. One couldn't be with him for even a brief time without realizing just how intelligent he really was. She had common sense, but she wasn't book smart. She'd never had that chance. Bridges had pulled her out of nearly every school she'd ever attended. She'd been lucky to have Delia help her figure out how to do the adult classes to get her GED.

Steele slipped onto his bike, backed it out and waited for her to tuck her hair into the helmet and climb on behind him. She surrounded him with her arms, locking her hands at his waist. The moment she did, she felt the same rush that had happened earlier, adrenaline moving through her veins like a drug. Motorcycle. Steele. Freedom. In her life, on the back of Steele's motorcycle was the only time she'd ever experienced the feeling of freedom. She'd loved it. She tried not to love it now, but when the pipes roared and the machine vibrated, coming to life, and they were in the wind, the exhilaration was instantaneous.

She pressed her body tightly against his and let the wind take away everything the way it had always done. They were leaving in the early morning hours to go find Zane. She couldn't do a thing about it until then. They had a plan. She wasn't alone, and she had a much better chance at getting her son back than she'd had before. There was something about Torpedo Ink that inspired confidence, and for the first time since Zane was taken, she really believed she would get him back. Because of them. Torpedo Ink.

The moment Steele, Breezy and the bike moved together, she felt whole. She knew, because she'd had multiple talks with Delia, that needing someone wasn't healthy. Wanting them in one's life was okay, but she said Breezy needed to stand on her own two feet. She'd done that until her father had kidnapped Zane, but she'd never felt whole. It was as if a huge piece of her was missing. Riding with Steele completed her.

Maybe it was because she was as screwed up as he was. She was a victim of abuse and knew no other life. Steele was the same way. He was complete by being in Torpedo Ink, and she was certain he would always need them. It was just possible she would always need Steele.

He didn't turn back down the road leading to the compound but took them up to the highway. She didn't ask. She didn't even care. She wanted to ride. They had a lot of hours to kill before they started out, and she just wanted to ride for a while to stop feeling so afraid for her son and to breathe again.

She knew Steele had already mapped out the shortest route from Caspar to New Orleans. He planned to go right through New Mexico and stop by her apartment to pick up the items on her list — mainly the earlier pictures of Zane. She had told him, during the meeting, that she could live without the photographs if they all believed someone was watching her apartment, but Steele had insisted he couldn't live without them.

The members of Torpedo Ink had exchanged looks, ones she couldn't read. At the time it had felt significant; now she just didn't care. She would when they were in New Mexico, but going down the highway, she let the roar of the pipes and the wind carry away every problem.

She blanked her mind against the images of Zane with Bridges or Junk. She had to believe he was in the hands of a woman who cared enough to try to protect a toddler. She refused to think about the pain and humiliation of Steele throwing her out or discovering him with other women. She simply allowed herself to enjoy every second on the motorcycle.

He took them to the little village overlooking the ocean. Sea Haven extended from the highway to the headlands, spreading out with numerous cute little shops and historical homes. Old water towers rose into the air, making the town feel quaint and authentic.

He parked the bike in front of the local market. Maestro and Keys parked right beside them and took a careful look around. She saw their gazes sweep the buildings and rooftops, the cars and street. Steele took her hand once she removed the helmet, and she didn't fight that either. She wasn't going to allow anything to ruin the joy she got from riding.

If she wasn't lying to herself, she had always been proud walking with him like that. Close. Hand in hand. Steele liked to touch her. When he'd been with her, he'd almost always been touching her. She'd liked that. It had made her feel cared for. Now, she knew, that was just part of who he was. It had nothing to do with her. She hoped he'd always be that way with Zane and that it would give her son that same feeling of being cherished as it had her. She wanted that for their child, especially if Steele insisted on being in his life permanently.

"Inez," Steele greeted as they entered the grocery store.

The older woman behind the counter

broke into a smile. "Steele, Maestro, Keys, good to see you."

Her gaze went to Breezy and then dropped to their linked hands. Immediately, for reasons she was uncertain of, Breezy tried to let go of Steele. It was impossible with his fingers wrapped around hers. He had a large hand, and it completely enveloped hers.

"Inez, I'd like you to meet my woman. This is Bree Simmons. Baby, this is Inez Nelson and Frank Warner." He indicated the man seated behind the counter with the older woman.

Inez beamed before Breezy could put in a quick disclaimer to the fact that she was *not* Steele's woman. Truthfully, she didn't have that kind of courage. One kept club business, especially personal club business, in the club. That had been drilled into her from the time she was a toddler, just as it was being drilled into Zoe, Emily and Darby.

"Nice to meet you, Bree," Inez said.

"Have you thought any more about our proposition?" Steele asked.

Inez nodded. "It's a good one. We took it to our silent partner and he agreed it was a very good plan, but he can't be a part of it. Still, even without him, Frank and I are very interested. When would be a good time for us to drop by and talk things over with you and Czar?"

Breezy let the conversation flow around her while she watched others in the store. Clearly the sight of three very rough-looking Torpedo Ink members wearing their colors didn't strike fear into anyone's heart. More, several greeted them. She noticed the women looking more than once.

Her heart clenched, and she looked down to the floor, an old habit she couldn't quite break. The moment she did, Steele transferred his hold from her hand to around her waist, his arm a bar, locking her to him. It was a claiming hold. She remembered how he'd done that when they were together. He'd always made her feel so safe and secure. He'd made her feel *his.*

"We've got a few things going on right now, but Czar will be in touch in a few days," Steele reassured Inez. He flashed a small smile and urged Breezy down one of the aisles, snagging a basket as he passed it. Maestro and Keys trailed behind them.

Breezy had no idea what was going on so she remained silent as Steele filled up his basket and the two baskets the other members of Torpedo Ink had with all sorts of food. She recognized that most were her favorites. She tried very hard not to be thrilled that Steele remembered what she liked. He would. Steele didn't forget things.

She just couldn't let herself buy into anything Steele was saying to her. She had before, and she'd gotten her heart broken. This time, she had to look out for Zane. There was no risking herself twice and coming out of it healthy and whole. She forced herself to remember the women Steele had partied with. She closed her eyes and conjured them up. Not one looked anything like her. He couldn't even say they were a substitute for her.

"Stop."

The whispered command came straight into her ear. She felt his breath exploding in a warm, exasperated puff.

"Seriously, baby, let it go. Just for now."

"You can't know what I'm thinking." She tried scowling at him, but she couldn't meet his eyes because he was right. He was always right.

"Your face is an open book, sweetheart," Steele said and caught up a small bag of baked pretzels, her favorite kind. "You're thinking about walking into the clubhouse and seeing me with those other women. I asked you to hold off thinking about them until I had the chance to explain."

"I don't want your explanation. I'm grateful I saw you with them." She tilted her chin at him. "Every time I think I might be buying into what you're selling, I think about them and remember none of it was real and you're very, very good at conning people — especially women."

He nodded. "I am. There's no question about that, but I wasn't conning you, and I'm not now."

"Because I'm so different from every other woman." Sarcasm dripped from her voice. "I might have swallowed all this, Steele, if you'd come looking for me, but I have your son and you want him. You think I need to be part of that package, but you're wrong. I don't have to be. There are so many couples making it work when they aren't together. We'll do just fine apart."

"We're not going to be apart, Breezy. We're going to talk this out."

He made it a decree. There was nowhere to go with that, so she changed the subject. "What kind of deal are you making with that very nice woman?" There was a bite to her voice she couldn't quite keep out of it, because Inez seemed extremely friendly and not at all a woman involved in anything illegal.

"She owns this store and we were hoping

to get a smaller version up and running in Caspar. We have the funds and she has the name. If we can get her to work the store for us even for just a few days a week for a few months, just to get it going, we can make a success of it. We need her to bring the locals in. She knows her value too." He flashed a smile Inez's way.

"Are you going to be laundering money through the store? Or selling drugs out of it?"

"No, baby. All businesses in Caspar are legit. We're putting down roots here. This is our community. You don't fuck with local royalty, and Inez is just that. Everyone loves her. Besides, her silent partner is Jackson Deveau, and he's a sheriff."

She mulled that over as they paid and got back on the bikes. Could it be the truth? Was Torpedo Ink that different from the Swords? She hadn't been around any club other than the Swords and those they did business with. The local people here seemed to accept Torpedo Ink — but then there hadn't been locals at the party taking place at the clubhouse. The Demons had been gone, but she'd seen their colors. She knew patches and what they meant. They weren't angels any more than Torpedo Ink was.

Steele took them back down the highway

to Caspar, but he didn't turn toward the Torpedo Ink clubhouse. Instead, he chose a winding road leading to the cliffs above the ocean. From there, he chose a lane that seemed to be more of a long drive than a public street. He slowed the bike even more once he turned away from the ocean and back toward a slight hill all overgrown with tall shrubbery. The road narrowed more, the vines climbing high on trees lining the road, so thick they formed an impenetrable wall on either side, preventing anyone from seeing the landscape, other than the occasional glimpse of light.

They went through a long archway created by the tree branches. She found herself looking upward at the flowering limbs. It was really quite extraordinary. Breathtaking even. How had Steele found such a place? It was an avenue of pure beauty.

Then he slowed even more and came to a halt. Breezy sat up straight and looked around her. A house sat straight ahead, tucked into the hillside, rising up like a great palace. It was something out of a fairy tale. Unreal. There weren't houses like that in real life. The structure stretched out in length, with rounded turrets and wide long windows facing the sea. It rose up maybe three stories, but she couldn't be sure because one of those stories was tucked into the hillside.

Steele took her hand and helped her off the bike. She kept her eyes on the house while she removed the helmet, afraid such a beautiful home couldn't be real.

"Who lives here?" She didn't want anyone to call the cops on them and she really, really wanted to look around.

"It's ours."

Her heart clenched hard in her chest. She scowled at him. "First, Steele, there is no us, so nothing is *ours.* Second, this place has to be worth millions. *Millions.* I don't have a huge concept of real estate and what it's worth, but this place is enormous. The grounds alone are worth a fortune, and it overlooks the sea."

He nodded slowly. "Seven million and some change. We got it for a steal."

She felt a little faint. "Steele." She whispered his name. Shocked. It didn't occur to her, not even for a moment, that he was kidding her. He wasn't. She could see that on his face and hear it in his voice. He meant every word.

"And yes, we are together. There is an us. You. Me. Zane. This is our home. I bought it because we're putting down roots here. I like the view."

"That's it? You like the view? Where did you get that kind of money?"

A slow grin transformed his face from dangerous to gorgeous. He looked mischievous, as only Steele could look. "The Swords."

Eight

Steele never did anything without a plan. That was why he was vice president of Torpedo Ink. Like Czar, he saw an entire picture, the problems and every possibility along with solutions that worked. His brain worked at an extremely fast speed and remembered details, right down to the smallest particular. Nothing got past him — until Breezy.

His body had responded to her immediately and, worse, his heart. He'd never had that happen. Not once in all his years. Torpedo Ink was a closed society. They were whole when they were together and none of them — with the exception of Czar — had ever considered that anyone else might be brought into their very fucked-up family. He'd been thrown. Completely.

He'd known if Czar or the others were aware of how he really felt about Breezy, they would have insisted he take her and leave. He couldn't do that. He knew that none of them worked away from the others. They functioned because they were together. Whole. They had tremendous gaps in their social education, but they could function and survive. Alone, they would fall apart. He couldn't take the chance that things would go haywire with the person that mattered to him. He also couldn't leave his family when they needed him. Every gun counted — every single one — when they were up against an international club like the Swords.

He knew Breezy better than she knew herself. He knew her insecurities. He knew her character. He knew every unselfish thing about her. He especially knew what to appeal to in order to keep her with him. This plan was more important to him than anything in his life had ever been because, like those dark days of his childhood, it was about survival.

Steele had found that once he had a glimpse of what life could be like when it was good, he couldn't go back to dark, ugly days and nights. He had existed before Breezy. He'd thought he was free, so it was better than when he'd been a captive forced to do his master's bidding, but it hadn't been good. He hadn't been alive. Breezy had changed all that. Once she was gone, he was back to — nothing. To empty. To an existence he didn't want anymore.

Her fingers on his skin, her mouth on him, his body moving in hers, she'd taken away every trace of those earlier days, the nightmare existence he'd lived. The more he'd taken her, the less he'd felt that yawning abyss threatening to swallow him whole. Now he had her back, and he wasn't about to lose the most important war of his life.

He had a campaign already planned out. Each step. He couldn't afford a misstep. It was Breezy. He didn't know anything about love, not in the accepted sense of the word, but anything he did know — or feel — all belonged to her. He had a *serious* battle plan. He was going to use everything he knew about her, everything he'd ever been taught and everything she felt for him, to get his woman back. Nothing was going to be too big or too small in his campaign, but he wasn't losing her a second time.

Now that he knew Zane existed, he would move heaven and earth to get the boy back, and he'd learn to be a good father. He was eager to be a father. He couldn't imagine what that would be like, but already, just knowing Zane was out there, he felt connected. Bonded to him without ever having laid eyes on him. Just as he had a point-by-point plan to win his lady back, he had an equally well-thought-out plan to get his son back. And he would. There was no question in his mind. No room for failure in either endeavor.

Maestro and Keys carried the groceries up the walkway to the house. A fountain was on, and the sprays of water erupting into the air looked like diamonds as they landed in the circle surrounded by a wide swath of white flowers set among dark green leaves. Stonework and wide white stairs led up to a landscape of plants, trees and small expanses of lawn.

Breezy let him take her hand and tug her up to the front door, which Maestro had left open for them. The floors were white oak and travertine. They gleamed as if they'd just been put in. Light fixtures and chandeliers were brand-new throughout the house. All the chandeliers were blown glass. Lissa, Casimir's wife, was a very famous glassblower who had earned quite a reputation, first in Europe and then in the United States. Of course she had made a fellow Torpedo Ink member first priority. He particularly loved the chandeliers.

"The way the house is set, we have the best view of the ocean from this side on all three levels. There are five complete bedroom suites. There's a home office, which I need, but if you want one, we can allot one of the rooms for you. Each of the suites has views and balconies. There's open social spaces."

"Social spaces?" Breezy echoed faintly, looking at him like he'd grown horns. "Steele . . ."

"I know, at first glance, it looks like too much house. When we were choosing homes, Czar made it plain to choose something we'd be comfortable in. This has a temperature-controlled wine and cigar room."

She frowned up at him and then blinked, those long lashes fanning her cheeks. "Do you even drink wine? Do you smoke cigars?"

He grinned down at her. "No. But that doesn't matter. It's just fuckin' cool. There's an indoor home spa, Bree, with heated floors, a steam room and a quick-fill tub. That doesn't include the outdoor one. There's a home gym you might like too. The best is the master suite. I can't wait for you to see that."

He took her farther into the house. She was staring all around her, looking at the ceilings with recessed lighting and wide-open spaces. The floor-to-ceiling windows were really movable pocket electronic doors that brought the outside inside. When they were open, one had access to an extremely large patio with an infinity-edge pool and spa, a fireplace, a built-in barbecue, a covered dining area and the lawn.

She stood at the glass staring out, looking as if she might faint. "Steele, this isn't real. No one has a home like this. Maybe a movie star or someone like that, but you're in a club."

"*We're* in a club, Bree, and this is really ours."

"I work in a diner. I couldn't afford the electricity on a place like this, let alone help with a mortgage payment. Does being a doctor really make you that kind of bank?"

"Baby, we own it outright."

"The Swords didn't have this kind of money." She shook her head and stepped away from him, nearly pressing her nose to the glass, staring at the backyard with wonder.

"They had the biggest human trafficking ring in the world, Breezy. They had money. Their president was a fucking billionaire. We took his money too."

She was silent. He watched her closely. She looked pale, but her shoulders were straight. She used to hunch a little. He had continually told her to stand up straight when they were together, especially around her father and brother. Now she did that all on her own. She was absorbing everything he said to her — with the exception of the "we" he kept throwing in. He did that on purpose, knowing the more she heard it, the more accepting she would eventually be.

"That's a good thing, then. I hope you broke their backs."

"We did. And Code keeps his eye on them. Anytime they try to reestablish those pipelines, or they kidnap fresh girls, we take that shit apart as well. We sub some of the work out if they're in states too far for us to ride to."

She turned toward him. "Sub it to who? Steele, I really am not understanding any of this. Who exactly are all of you? Where did you come from?"

At last. He'd been waiting for genuine interest. She wanted to know. That was step number two. Getting her was step one. That had been the trickiest because he knew she would be royally pissed at him and she'd equate him taking her prisoner with a club. He knew few clubs would have done such a thing, but it was ingrained in Torpedo Ink members to get what they needed at any cost to others. Blythe was trying to help them find a way to appear to assimilate into society, but all of them knew they would be forever living on the fringes.

Phase one was complete. Phase two was in progress. He had to seduce her first, get her in his bed, make certain she was mellow and on board and then he'd talk to her about the difficult subjects, things he wished he didn't have to explain but knew were necessary to address if they were going forward in a relationship — and they were. It was a good battle plan, but there were quite a few things that could go wrong.

"You good?" Maestro asked. "The security system is up and running, groceries are put away and you've got the place mostly to yourselves. We've taken a couple of the suites. There's a kitchenette and the home theater we're using, so give us a shout if you need us."

Breezy's face showed her panic at the idea of being alone with him. Steele immediately stepped between her and the other two men. "We're good," he assured.

Maestro saluted him, and the two men sauntered off, leaving him alone with Bree at last. He took her hand and led her away from the panels of floor-to-ceiling glass so he could show her the rest of the house. He took her up the winding staircase. It was wide, the stairs curving around to the second floor.

Unlike most of the other members of Torpedo Ink who had purchased homes in Caspar, Steele had furnished his. Why, he had no idea, because he didn't actually stay there. He had bought this particular home because he loved the outside, the views and the master bedroom, but more importantly, he knew when he found Breezy, she would love it.

The suite was enormous, and he needed the space. Lots of it. He had spent so much of his time in confinement that he couldn't take closed-in places. He liked to be able to see what was coming at him long before it reached him. The house was mainly white, ivory or a light gray, making it aesthetically pleasing to him.

The bedroom had a gas fireplace with a long row of flames. The television was recessed into the darker stone above the thick white stone surrounding the built-in fireplace. The throw rug was white with gray accents. He especially loved the view from the huge window and glass door leading to the balcony. The room also had a frameless, stand-alone shower and tub and his and her closets that someone could live in. The frameless shower was a large rectangle made of glass. The sprawling views were tremendous in almost every direction.

He indicated the shower. "I fuckin' love that."

For the first time, a ghost of a smile touched her mouth. He watched her eyes dance for just a moment.

"You would. You have a thing about wearing clothes."

"That's true." He caught her hand and dragged her to the large window that took up nearly one wall. "Look at this view. Nothing like it, unless you're outside in the backyard."

She pressed herself up against the glass, staring, just as he knew she would. The view was spectacular. "Oh my God," she whispered in awe.

Steele removed his colors and put them on the table beside the bed. While she was staring out, looking at the wide expanse of ocean, the waves crashing and rolling, he sank down onto the bed and removed his motorcycle boots and socks.

"I can't believe you own this, Steele."

He came up behind her, sliding one hand under her jacket and shirt so that his palm covered bare skin. He was a master at seduction. Every Torpedo Ink member was. It was what they'd been raised from birth to do. Seduce. Kill. They had complete control of their bodies. They also controlled the body of their chosen victim — or partner.

Breezy was his woman, and he knew everything that aroused her. He'd made it an art to seduce her. To please her. To bring her every bit of pleasure possible under their circumstances. Now he had her without the Swords surrounding them, which gave him endless possibilities. He hadn't forgotten one detail. Not one. He'd introduced her to so many pleasures and intended to introduce her to many more.

He kept his hand there, the pad of one finger stroking her bare skin. She was soft. He closed his eyes and savored the way her skin felt. She didn't move. She didn't make a sound. He had known she wouldn't. Breezy might not want to be his, but she was. She belonged to him and she always would, just as he knew there would be no other for him.

He knew as much as he was deliberately seducing her, she was doing the same for him, although innocently. She wasn't in the least trying, and his body was already hers and always would be. He pushed the hair aside from the back of her neck and leaned in to inhale her scent and then blow warm air on her nape. He felt the little tremor that went through her body. It was subtle, but he was acutely tuned to every nuance.

He pressed his lips against her nape. Just touched her there. "Isn't the view incredible? I did worry about lighting. If, for instance, we wanted to sleep in, the morning light would wake us up early. On the other hand, I'd hate to cover the view, so I had electronic blackout drapes installed. What do you think?" He kissed her again, more for himself this time.

"Steele."

There was apprehension in her voice. Caution. She wanted to escape, but both of them knew there was no way that was going to happen.

"Breezy." He let the genuine ache into his voice. The absolute need. He knew, above anything else, that would be seductive, even irresistible to her.

She shook her head, but she didn't move, not even when he reached around her and unbuttoned the jacket. His jacket. He had been careful to pack one that didn't have his colors on it. The club was a problem, and that was way down the line of things to address. He slid the jacket down her arms, not moving back even an inch so he had to carefully work the denim from between them.

She shivered. Shook her head a second time. "This isn't a good idea."

"It's the *only* good idea I've had in a very long time." He pressed another kiss to her neck this time, and then her shoulder. That was always one of her very erogenous spots, and nothing had changed. Her breath hitched.

He felt her hesitate again and then she started to push away from the glass, away from him, and he knew she was thinking of those three women he'd partied with. Dick move. Stupid. And it hadn't done a damn thing for him except nearly lose his woman all over again. He also knew she had known the moment they entered the house that he would have her. She knew what would happen, and she'd entered anyway. He knew that was her consent. Intellectually, she didn't want him, and he couldn't blame her, but her body needed his nearly as much as he needed her. Still, he didn't want to give her the time to talk herself out of it, and she was thinking about doing just that.

He knew Breezy. He knew what got her going fast, and it wasn't a gentle seduction. That was foreplay, but it wasn't what would tip the scales in his favor. He caught the hem of her shirt and ripped it over her head, tossing it aside. At the same time, he took control of the nape of her neck and pushed her against the glass aggressively.

Her breath exploded out of her lungs in a gasp of pure need. He stripped away her bra and had his palms filled with her generous breasts. For a moment he heard the roar of his blood in his ears, felt the chaos in his head. That fever of need only Breezy could bring him. He woke up night after night needing her. A frenzy of desire. A fever. His head pounded as if someone had taken a sledgehammer to it. A million ugly images poured in, images only Breezy could drive out.

He took a breath and let himself just feel the soft weight of her breasts while his mouth took her neck, trailing burning kisses, using the edge of his teeth and his seductive tongue from her neck to her ear and back to her shoulder. Then his fingers were at her nipples. He'd fallen in love with her nipples. He liked that she was sensitive in a way he could play, not so sensitive that she didn't like the things he did.

"Kick off your shoes." He didn't ask. He made it a command.

Breezy responded to his demands, and the more he poured authority into his voice, the more she wanted him. It was the first thing he'd noticed about her and the one that turned him on the most. She was perfect for him. Made for him. He needed that from her, and she'd always given it to him. She did now. She toed her shoes off obediently.

"Open your jeans." His voice had turned gravelly. A growl more than human. His cock felt as if it might explode. The first time wasn't going to be slow. It had been too long for him. Far too long.

Steele knew her body, and the moment she complied, dropping her hands to the waistband and opening her jeans, he spun her around and yanked on the offending denim, almost desperate to get to her. He wasn't a desperate man. He was a deliberate one. His seductions were always thoughtful, methodical, all about his intended prey. He didn't know if he could keep this time all about Breezy. Fortunately, she responded to his aggression.

He felt aggressive. He felt dominant. He wanted her a million times in a million ways. He never wanted her out of his sight again. She thought it was a great concession that he said she could go with them to get their son. He would never have left her behind. When he stripped her jeans from her, he took her panties as well, leaving her completely naked.

She took his breath away. For a moment, all he could do was look at her. "You're so fucking beautiful, Bree." Before she could respond, he swept his arm around her, locking her close and bent his head to her breast. He wasn't gentle. She didn't like gentle. She liked — him. His method of seduction. She thought he fucked her. He had fucked hundreds, maybe more, in his earlier years. He knew this wasn't that. With Breezy, it had never been that, no matter how rough with her he got — and he needed rough.

His mouth was hot and wet, and her breasts were soft, made for him. He used his teeth and tongue, tugging and rolling her nipple. Suckling hard and then abruptly changing it up, so that she never knew which sensation she was going to get from his mouth or hands. He could spend hours working her body. Hours. He had before, keeping her on edge, right on that very brink, never letting her tip over until he allowed it. He loved that shit. Loved that she gave him that. He knew the sound of her voice. Those mewls. Those pleas. The little sobbing gasp of his name. He knew when she was ready and that she'd go big. So big. The orgasms would rush over her, taking them both, drowning them, rolling them in so much pleasure he couldn't see straight.

His woman. Breezy. There was no one else in the world like her. No one else for him. No one else could make him as hard as a fucking rock. They couldn't make him fight for control. That was all her. He kissed his way down her stomach. So soft. She'd nestled his child there and he hadn't been there for that. He hadn't kissed her the way he was doing now, showing her he loved every inch of her, pregnant or not.

He dropped to his knees, yanking her legs apart, and then he had the taste of her in his mouth and she was keening that soft little sound that drove him out of his mind. Breezy. She gave him solace. She gave him everything. Things he didn't think possible. He gave her everything he was and more. When he was with her, he was a man, not a monster.

He drove her up fast, using his teeth and tongue. His fingers. He was greedy for her, that aphrodisiac only she could provide. For him, her taste had been addicting from the first moment he'd put his mouth on her.

Her hands went to his shoulders, gripping hard, fingers digging into his flesh right through his shirt. She threw back her head as her body came apart, rippling around his fingers. She'd had a baby, yet she felt tight to him, and there was always that thrill of wondering if he was going to fit, to stretch her beyond her means to take him.

He was up, spinning her around, pressing her to the glass while he undid his jeans with one hand and took his heavy cock in his hand, positioning, pressing home. She was home. She would always be home.

"Use a condom."

"I'm clean." He didn't want anything between them. He never had.

"You don't know that, Steele. Use a condom or we don't go there." Even as she dictated to him, she was pressing back against him, her breath coming in ragged little explosive gasps.

"Baby, I'm telling you I know for a fact that I'm clean. I had to be inside those bitches to get unclean, and that didn't happen. Let me. I need you right now, Bree. I swear to you on my fucking colors that I'm clean."

He was lodged there, her heat and fire surrounding the crown of his cock. Squeezing him tightly. Pulling at him. Her body as greedy for his as his was for hers. He waited, and it nearly killed him. Thunder roared in his ears. He felt a jackhammer pounding relentlessly at his brain, the one that was sometimes there when she was close, and he needed her desperately.

"Please be telling the truth," she whispered and nodded.

He slammed home, not taking chances she might change her mind, plowing through those tight folds that drove him out of his mind. Instantly he was gripped in a silken, fiery fist. Her sheath felt like paradise, so perfect there was no way his memories or his imagination could have prepared him for the feeling of ecstasy.

He gripped her hips and pulled her back into him as he surged into her again and again, losing himself in her body. Losing his demons, driving them away for the priceless time he had. He'd lost her, so he knew what it was like without her. He knew he needed her far more than she would ever need him, and he was okay with that. He didn't have a lot to give her. He didn't know the first fucking thing about relationships, only that he'd screwed theirs up.

Her breath was coming in little sing-song sobs and he slid his hand up her back to her nape and then around, so his palm cupped her throat. "Not yet, baby. Hold on for me."

"I can't."

"A little longer. Hold on for me." He knew she would. She always had, although the fire was so much hotter. Her body was tighter than ever, gripping and squeezing until he thought he might go insane. He felt her heart beat against his palm. It was there in the fiery silk of her sheath, beating around his cock. That fire. That beat. That breath. His again. His chance at having it all when in his life, there was no such thing as living.

"I'm going to give you fucking everything, Bree," he whispered, meaning it. The world. Whatever he could to make her happy. He'd get their son back, and he'd find a way to keep from screwing things up again with her.

"Just get there."

He loved that little demand in her voice. His woman. Bossing him. She always did that at the end, when she was desperate for release and he was holding her on the edge. He moved in her, his cock so hard, so in need, surrounded by her. That perfect moment, balancing on the edge. He thrust hard again and again, feeling the exquisite tightening of his balls, the fire moving like hot magma through his body. He threw his head back.

"Now, baby. Let go now."

She obeyed immediately, her body clamping down hard on his, gripping his cock, constricting the blood flow for a moment, her body that tight. Then he was exploding, rocketing into her, the release flinging him to a place where nothing could touch him. Nothing. Not his demons. Not the whispering voices of the dead. Not the ones he'd failed. There was only Breezy and this — paradise and the reprieve that only she gave him.

Her soft little cries tugged at his heart. Gave him satisfaction. He loved when Breezy came, when her body was right there with his, and he knew no one knew her the way he did. No one knew what she liked or needed the way he did.

He held her up, his cock pulsing in her, feeling every ripple. Every powerful aftershock. This was the moment he had to be the most careful of. He could lose her right here. She would try to distance herself from what they had together. He couldn't blame her, there was too much unsaid between them. There were things he didn't want her to know. Even now, through her hurt, she looked at him as if he were someone amazing and special. If she really knew him, she wouldn't. He wanted to keep that look, but there could be no half measures this time. If he demanded her commitment, then he had to do the same.

He wrapped his arms around her, holding her steady when he could feel her shaking, as he withdrew. He hated leaving the haven of her body. For a moment, he rested his head against her back and then pressed kisses down her spine.

"Thank you, baby, for believing me. I know that was difficult for you. I needed you more than I needed to take my next breath." He had no problem telling her the truth of that. There were things he didn't want to share, but she needed to know — to be reassured after the vile things he'd said to her — that she was his world.

He kept his arm around her waist as she straightened slowly. Very gently he guided her across the room to the wide, deep bathtub. He turned on the ridiculous golden taps before he settled her on the bench beside the tub. She wasn't looking at him, and her breathing hadn't settled. She was definitely gearing herself up to run or at least try to distance herself.

"Steele."

There it was. The warning in her voice. He let her have her say because, God knew, he deserved whatever she wanted to throw at him.

"Just because we . . ."

She waved her hand at him to include his

cock, which was still at half-mast. It had been too fucking long, and his release had been a volcano, but there was so much more. Three long years of more.

"We're not going to get back together. I'm not going to lie to you and say the attraction isn't there because obviously it is. But we can't go back. I'm not the same person, the one that you wanted."

He was silent, listening to the water pour into the tub. Listening to his heart beat. This was too important to jump in with protests and risk saying the wrong thing. Every word had to be what Breezy needed. He had to choose wisely. He was walking through a minefield, but he excelled at that. He excelled at strategy.

He sat on the edge of the tub, letting her look at his body. The scars she was so familiar with that he'd never explained. The tattoos covering most of them. Her name wound through the lock and key he'd had Ink put on him after she was gone. He saw her eyes widen when she realized it was there and he had to have had it done some time after she left. He wanted her to think about that and the pictures of her he had on his phone.

"I have a lot of explaining to do, Bree," he said.

She shook her head quickly, one hand going defensively to her throat. His palm had been there, feeling every beat of her heart.

"Don't, Steele. You don't need to explain anything to me."

He kept his face an expressionless mask, but triumph burst through him. She was terrified to listen to him because she knew he could persuade her. She wanted him every bit as much as he wanted her, and it wasn't all sexual the way she wanted to make him believe.

"I know. You've never asked for that, but you deserve to know. I couldn't tell you before, when I wanted to. When we were together, and you were all mine. Essentially, I was undercover. I couldn't even tell you my real name." He ignored the fact that she all but fell off the bench shaking her head to prevent him from giving that to her. "It's Lyov Russak. Clearly, I'm Russian. I wanted to drag you to the nearest courthouse and put a ring on your finger, but I couldn't break cover or tell you I was Torpedo Ink and we were bringing down a human trafficking ring."

Deliberately he reminded her of what Evan Shackler-Gratsos had been doing with his perverted ways of making money rather than tell her the end game had been his assassination. He wanted her to think about those women and children they'd saved. The little boys, so like his brothers and sisters. So like him.

She made a small sound and pressed her fingers to her lips. That was a habit she'd acquired to remind herself to stay silent when she was afraid. She held herself very still now, becoming the little mouse she thought no one could see. He always saw her. He held out his hand to her, detesting that she relied on being frozen and small like prey. She was his and under his protection, and he had started teaching her how to defend herself. He wanted her confident. He wanted her to be able to stand up to anyone — including him.

She put her hand in his and stood. There was satisfaction in seeing her gleaming thighs, his seed coating them. He loved that. Loved that he was on her skin.

"There are hair ties in the drawer there. Your favorite kind. Those scrunchy things as well. I put them there after I furnished the house, hoping you'd be here someday to use them." He indicated the acrylic drawers stacked to one side, with their towels and everything he knew she liked in her bath. Breezy loved baths. He had introduced her to bath salts and fizzing bath bombs.

She loved citrus scents, and he'd stocked up on the ones he knew she'd like. He bought her small things because she loved the little things more than extravagant gestures like multimillion-dollar homes. He'd supplied the bathroom with everything he knew she would feel was a luxury and more. Things he wanted to introduce to her.

He watched her put her hair in a high ponytail and then a messy knot on top of her head. Immediately, Steele helped her settle into the large tub. He stepped in behind her, forcing her body forward so she was sitting between his legs. He pulled her in tight to him. He liked her close. She'd always liked being close, but now she tried to hold herself away from him, and he wasn't having that.

He tightened his arm until it was a bar locking under the soft weight of her breasts, and he tugged until her body was right up against his. Until his cock was pressed tightly against the tattoo he'd designed for her. His ink on her. That statement proclaiming to any other man who dared touch her that she belonged to him.

"I want to talk about the party and the aftermath you walked in on."

She stiffened, but he refused to release her. Instead, he put his head on her shoulder. She made a single sound, but it pierced his heart like an arrow. Straight through. Fuck. He'd hurt her so much. So, so much.

"Breezy, baby, I know this is difficult for you. I know that, but I swear to you on everything that matters to me, I'm going to tell you the truth and answer any questions, so we have a chance. That's what I'm asking, one chance. For our son. For me. Especially for me."

She remained silent and still, holding herself as if one wrong word would make her shatter.

"You saw the pictures on my phone. I didn't just manufacture those out of thin air. You saw my ink, right over my heart. The lock and key with your name in the barbed wire and roses. Only you, Breezy. That's what it says. That's what it means. I belong to Breezy Simmons. I want to belong to Breezy Russak. The things in this house, I bought them for you before you ever showed up. Give me this chance, baby."

There was a long silence. He heard his heart beating. Hard. Aching. Fear gripped him, turning his stomach to knots.

"You tore me apart, Steele," she admitted in a small voice. "Completely and utterly apart. I didn't think I could survive, and I didn't even know if I wanted to. Until Zane.

Until I knew I had that little part of you. I don't think I can go through that again."

His heart stuttered. She hadn't known she was pregnant when she left. She might have had a woman's intuition, but she didn't know for certain. If she had, she might have told him, and he would have found a better way to keep her safe.

"Hear me out. That's all I'm asking."

"I don't know if I can believe you."

He knew that wasn't it. She was afraid she *would* believe him.

"I'm a damn good liar, baby. And I can con anyone. But this is us. You and me. You're my world and I want you back. I'm giving you everything if that's what you want, and trust me, Bree, it's damned hard to tell you some of the things that need to be said."

"There's the club. I don't want that life. I don't want it for me or for Zane."

"You saw Czar's family. You saw the way they were together. We aren't the Swords. We'll never be that club or treat our women and children the way they do." Before she could protest, he bit her shoulder gently and then tugged at her earlobe. Keeping his voice a husky whisper, he continued. "In any case, we're getting ahead of ourselves. Let's start with the party."

Before anything, he had to get those three women he'd partied with out of the way and hope she believed him. If he couldn't put that to rest, nothing he said after would matter because she'd always come back to that one moment. He cursed himself for hurting her.

She didn't reply, but she stopped straining away from him. He felt the little goose bumps on her skin and tasted her excited heartbeat on his tongue when he used his teeth and lips on her. She was very susceptible to his particular brand of sex. He kissed his way up her neck and then pressed another one to her nape, his other hand coming up under her left breast to hold that soft weight in his palm.

"My parents, in Russia, ran afoul of a man by the name of Sorbacov. He was very powerful and had the backing of the man he wanted in the presidency. All those opposed were made to disappear, including my parents. I was very young, a toddler at the time."

She stirred just a little, enough to tell him she was about to stop him. He forestalled her protest by rubbing his thumb over her nipple. She liked breast and nipple play, and he wasn't averse to cheating. There was satisfaction in feeling the shiver that ran through her body in spite of the heat of the water.

"I know this doesn't sound like it has anything to do with that party, but it has everything to do with it — and with me — the way I am. I want you to know the real me — Steele, and why I'm Steele. Why I choose Torpedo Ink and my brothers and sisters. Why I choose you. It's important, Breezy, so I'm asking that you'll hear me out. Really listen to me without trying to think up shit to keep us apart. Just listen. Can you do that for me, baby?"

She let out a sigh and pressed her head against his chest. "You have no idea what you're asking of me."

"I do, but it's important. Think about raising Zane with two parents. You'd have help. No matter what, Bree, you'll be fine financially, I'll see to that, but give us this shot."

Their son was clearly her first priority. Steele remembered when *he* had been her priority. Her every thought had been for him. She was made that way. Some women weren't and that was fine, but she had a way of making him the center of her existence. He should have done the same. Now they had Zane, and Steele had no doubt that she had a big enough heart to make them both her world. She just had to let him back in.

"Just start talking. But don't break my heart again, Steele. I'm feeling a little fragile right about now, terrified for my — our — son, and I don't think I can take much more."

He cupped her face and turned it toward him, so she was looking at him over her shoulder. He needed to see her. To look into her emerald eyes. His heart stuttered again. Those eyes of hers, two large gems that held his heart. He could fall into them forever. He remembered all the times he'd laid her out on his bed and moved in her slowly, staring into those eyes. They were large and vividly green, surrounded by the thickest lashes he'd ever seen, lashes that matched the color of her hair.

"I'm not going to hurt you, Bree. I'd shoot myself in the heart before I'd do that again." He'd sent her away and his life was shit. He'd had one year with her. One perfect year — or as perfect as it could be when he was riding with a perverted, fucked-up club like the Swords. That told him all he needed to know. If she made his life something to look forward to when he was with the scum of the earth, then being with her was far better than being on his own. He just needed to figure it all out. He was intelligent. He was Torpedo Ink's strategist.

He leaned forward and took her mouth. The moment he did, the sparks were there, arcing between them. The fire poured from her mouth to his. Or maybe it was the other way around. All he knew was that his cock was once more as hard as a rock and she was kissing him back. Really kissing him. Participating. Her tongue chased his and danced and stroked, flame on flame. Velvet on velvet.

He kissed her over and over. Her nipple pebbled in his palm and he couldn't resist stroking and then tugging. She gasped into his mouth, her body stirring beneath the hot water restlessly. He dropped his hand to slide it down her tummy and curl two fingers into her. That tempting sheath was hotter than her mouth.

Again, it was Steele who pulled back, forcing himself away from that path he took with her. He could — and would — win her back with sex if that was his only resolution, but she deserved explanations, and he wanted more than a one-sided relationship. If she didn't truly know him, and know why he was so fucked up, the chances of him screwing things up were far more than if he just came clean.

NINE

"The water's cooling, Bree," Steele pointed out. "Let's get out of here and go down to the spa. It's hot, and I want you to see the ocean from that view."

"You do know this house would be impossible to clean. Even if we did do this, Steele, we couldn't live here. It's beautiful but intimidating. I don't know the first thing about taking care of a mansion."

"You don't have to take care of it, baby." He stood up, pulling her with him. He loved the way the drops of water shimmered on her skin. "We'll have help come in. Cleaners. We have plenty of social space to have everyone over, and when we throw a party, it will be mostly outdoors where we have the fireplace and barbecue. I'm pretty damned good with a barbecue."

She just shook her head and took the large towel he handed to her, drying off without a hint of being self-conscious. He'd done that — made her comfortable in her own skin when she was with him. They stepped out of the large, room-size bath, and she looked around for her clothes.

"Leave it. You're not going to need clothes in the spa. There are extra towels in an outside linen closet. We can grab them if we need them and I can turn on the fireplace out there for additional warmth if you just want to sit outside while we talk."

She glanced around the bedroom and then nodded. "The fireplace."

He knew she chose that because she thought she'd be safer. She wasn't, not from him. Not when his cock was still raging and she was right there, all soft skin and gorgeous body. He liked breasts, and she had them. He particularly loved the shape of her ass and the way she looked walking away from him. She had curves, more since she'd had the baby. He shut down that thought because he didn't dare think too much about Zane in the hands of the Swords club, not and keep his sanity. He had to concentrate on winning his lady back and making sure Zane had a home and two parents to come back to.

It was still early afternoon and the sun was shining brightly. The fog had burned off. He knew the wind would come in off the ocean, because it often did, but the chairs in front of the outside fireplace were comfortable and the house curved around on either side, providing a good shelter. The patio was enormous, and the area in front of the fireplace was spacious.

He'd thought about barbecues with his brothers and sisters, not parties with other clubs. He didn't want wild at his house, he was too fucked up for that. Breezy, like him, preferred clean. Neat. She would oversee the house and make certain it was the way he favored because she wanted it the same way.

She started to wrap the towel around her body, but he couldn't stand not seeing her. It had been too long for him. He took the towel out of her hand and draped it over his arm before holding out his other hand to her. She kept herself shaved, other than a little landing strip, again, his preference. He liked that she still did that, three years later when he hadn't been around.

The stairs were wide enough to allow them to walk side by side, hand in hand, their bodies close. His thigh brushed hers. Their shoulders. Her breasts jolted with each step she took. He wanted to put his hand on her ass, but knew it was too soon. He wanted to mark her breasts with his mouth, put a claiming bite on her shoulder or neck, but he resisted every urge and just walked with her to the huge glass wall that took up the entire back of the house and slid or folded open depending on the room.

Breezy stood watching him, her eyes wide. "Who knew people had houses like this?"

"The moment I saw it, I knew this was the one. I bought it, furnished it with you in mind and then couldn't even sleep here."

"You always had trouble sleeping," she commented, preceding him onto the patio when he stepped back to let her through.

"Still do. Always will. Too many fucking bodies. All those voices calling out to me." He shook his head. "You're all that takes them away, and only for a short while." He rubbed his temples. "Some nights I think I'll go insane."

She frowned at him, that adorable little frown he always wanted to kiss off her face. "Bodies? What are you talking about, Steele?"

He used the remote to get the fire going. The chimney ran up the side of the house, between two turrets, wide and made of rock. It was nearly as beautiful as the house and fit right into the landscape. He gestured toward one of the chairs positioned close so she could feel the heat if she needed it.

She curled up, pulling her knees in and tucking her feet under her. It was such a Breezy thing to do. She was always curled up in some way. Making herself smaller. Just in case. She had no idea how she looked to him, sitting there in her soft, glowing skin. Her breasts were high and firm and very round. Temptation itself. He could just see the peeking of her sex between her legs, enticing him further.

His woman. Hotter than hell. He sank onto the chair beside her, his hand dropping casually to his hard cock. Circling it with his fist. It was more automatic when he was around her than anything else. He didn't even think about it. Instead, he pumped slowly while he thought about how best to explain it all to her. She didn't break the silence but watched him, eyes on his face and then dropping lower.

Steele took a deep breath. When he figured out what he needed to tell her, his hand dropped from his cock to his thigh and began kneading his muscle there. Fingers digging in. Fist curling and thumping on the heavy muscle, his cock forgotten. Everything forgotten but the past that continually haunted him.

"I'm no longer Lyov and I haven't been since I was a little toddler, terrified out of my mind. I'm Steele. I had to become Steele to survive. My parents were murdered, and I was taken to what the outside world thought was a school to shape me into an asset for my country."

He couldn't hit his thigh hard enough to keep the pain physical and in the present. The past was rising like a specter. "There were four such schools. I was taken to the one Sorbacov called his own. No one was allowed to inspect it or see us for any reason. Sorbacov was a pedophile, as were his friends. The instructors at the school were vicious, disturbed criminals who enjoyed torturing and raping children. I was one of those children."

There. He'd said it aloud. To her. He kept his voice expressionless. Disconnected. He let the pain of his fist hitting his thigh push the reality to the back of his mind. He needed the distraction to recount those early days to her, and she had to hear it. She had to know. It was his only shot at keeping her.

He heard her soft gasp and knew he had her. Breezy had more compassion, more empathy in her little finger than anyone he knew. He had to keep talking before he couldn't make himself continue.

"In the end, there were two hundred and

eighty-seven children brought to that school. A prison really. Only eighteen survived." He stumbled over that. There should have been nineteen. He closed his eyes against that knowledge. His fault. His responsibility. That was on his shoulders. Only eighteen, not nineteen. They'd been so close to freedom.

"Steele."

Her whisper was like a breath of fresh air. Breezy. Blowing away the memories. The knowledge of his failures — failures that had cost others their lives. When she said his name, every person and place, every horrific situation, every failure, was gone, leaving only his woman with her green eyes and perfect mouth and beautiful skin.

He forced himself to continue without looking at her. If he looked at her face, she would see his guilt. Those green eyes saw too much. "The children were all ages, and our keepers had carte blanche to do whatever they wanted. The more they hurt us, the more they became depraved, and the tortures got worse. I couldn't save the others no matter how hard I tried."

Now there was no distraction. Not her breasts. Not her sex. Not her green eyes or his pounding fist. There were only those faces staring up at him with pleas and cries and suffering. "I was the only one we had to help, to doctor them, and in the beginning, I was a child being brutalized myself." He had a gift, healing hands, except he'd been too young and had no idea how to use it.

He scrubbed his hand down his face, trying to wipe away the filth and dirt, the blood, sometimes black mixing with feces, vomit and filth on the unkept floors. "The conditions were intolerable. We were crammed into a basement with no bathroom. No way to clean. Very little food. It was freezing all the time. The wounds on bodies went septic very fast. There were rats and cockroaches everywhere. The smell . . ." He shook his head, trying to clear it. He couldn't go back there. He couldn't let his mind take him there.

"We didn't have clothes, and that became the norm for us. It was Czar that gave us all a sense of hope and kept our humanity in spite of what was happening to us. The daily rapes. The tortures. There were so many children so traumatized they were catatonic. The wounds were open, and we didn't have antibiotics or any way to treat them. Eventually the sexual training. Training to kill."

Breezy pressed a cold bottle of water into his hand. She'd found the little refrigerator behind the outside bar and had gotten him something cold to drink. He wished it was alcohol, although he'd found over the years even that did nothing to help. Only Breezy. Only his woman. Looking up at her, the wind tugging at her hair and her eyes overbright, wearing her empathy and compassion on her face, he knew what love was.

Steele pressed the bottle of water to his forehead. He was hot. "It was always cold there. No blankets. Always naked. We had very little water to share. Czar rationed it just like he did the food. Everyone was always hungry and thirsty. The smell of rotting flesh permeated the room. Those gaping, horrible wounds. Children rotting from the inside out. Sometimes, Bree, there were rows of them, lined up for me, begging me to help them. I was eight or nine when they all began to look to me to save them."

"Why you?"

He shook his head. "I was born with an ability. I can heal, or at least get the process started, and that's without any formal training as a doctor. I wish —" He broke off. He wished he wasn't a healer, that he hadn't known or felt the tremendous drive to try.

"Honey, you don't have to tell me this."

"I do. You have to understand me and why I'm so damn fucked up. You know I am, so don't pretend. I don't." He always turned the spotlight on himself. He had to. He had a monster crouching inside, waiting to emerge, looking for a chance to escape. He was careful, and that meant assessing his mental state at all times. "There were no adults looking after us, they were the ones hurting us. We had to make up our own rules. Our own code. We had to look after one another, watch one another's backs."

He took a long drink of the cold water, letting it slide down his throat, feeling the cool relief of it. Savoring it. He appreciated every time he drank water. He never took it for granted. Never. He never took having a clean environment for granted.

"We were trained to control our bodies, to give pleasure to others no matter what was happening to us. They would whip us, laying open our flesh while we were forced to continue performing. Some had it far worse than others, but all of us had to train to become experts at anything sexual."

He raised his gaze to hers. He had to. He had to see if she understood, even a little, what had been done to all those children. Children he couldn't save, no matter how hard he'd tried with the little tools he had. As always, his woman didn't disappoint. There was compassion softening her expression. Her eyes were liquid and her long lashes damp. For a moment his throat closed. It was no wonder that he loved her.

"Anything sexual, Breezy. Any type of sex. We were beaten severely if we didn't succeed in arousing our partner while controlling our bodies. Every type of rape you can imagine was done to us. I couldn't keep up with all of them. I would come back, just as bloody and just as beaten, hurting so bad I could barely take a step, and there would be two rows of broken kids lying in filth and blood, bugs crawling over them, waiting for me. Looking at me as if I could save them. As if I could come up with a miracle and stop what was happening to them."

He pressed his fingers to his eyes as if that would stop the flood of memories he had unleashed. Rage, he knew, wasn't hot and loud. It was ice-cold and gathered into a powerful weapon, one trained in anatomy. One trained in every kind of sexual behavior. One trained as an assassin. He was a very effective weapon.

"The point I'm trying to make with all of this is I have complete control of my body unless it's you. I don't have normal erections, not like every other man in the world. My body doesn't react to women or men because I was taught never to allow my body to react. I had to be in control at all times. We all did."

He studied her face without appearing to do so. It was a lot to take in and he knew that. People shut down when they heard horrific stories. Their minds couldn't accept that others were that deviant, or cruel, especially to children. They didn't want to hear or comprehend that boys and girls were raped, tortured and killed for the pleasure of adults.

Breezy had taken it all in. He could tell she knew he'd whitewashed it. There was no way he was going to describe the particulars to her, not if he could help it. He needed her to understand him. Why he was in control when they had sex. Why he touched her all the time. Why she had to be in his sight. Why he would be the same, maybe worse, with his children. Why his house had to be so clean and pristine. Why he struggled to give her space when he needed everything his own way just to stay sane.

"I'm so sorry, Steele. It's no wonder that you're so close with the others. Sharing something so horrendous will either drive you apart or weave a bond so close, you can't be without one another."

"That was how we survived. Czar came

up with a plan. So many died from infection. So many bled out. Others were killed for pleasure. We had to fight back. All of us had to do our part so we could make it out of there." But he'd failed, and one of them, one they all loved, hadn't survived just when they were about to taste freedom.

He took another slow drink of water, appreciating how it cooled the strain on his throat. "The point I'm making is about sex, Bree. After you left —"

She held up her hand. "As petty as this sounds, given what you're telling me, I don't want you to ever rewrite our history or get the idea in your head that I left you. I didn't. I never would have. You forced me to go when I would have walked through hell with you and would have been happy to do it as long as I had you."

The truth was an arrow piercing his heart because she was right. Worse, he'd known that when he sent her away. He'd been cruel and ugly about it to get her to go because nothing else would have made her leave him. That was on him, that hurt she carried. He'd flayed her right to her soul, and Breezy was a gentle, sensitive woman, filled with compassion and a quiet strength that called to him.

"I'm very aware I sent you away, Bree."

He pressed the bottle to his forehead, wishing the vise that was squeezing his skull would let up. Just for a few minutes. Just so he could try to explain the party to her. His needs. His desperation. "I needed to know you were safe. You were all I had, and the Swords would have destroyed you. I had to make you go."

She nodded. "I'm beginning to see that."

His heart leapt and then clenched hard in his chest. He rubbed over the spot. "After you were gone, I had no interest in women. I wanted nothing whatsoever to do with another woman. I spent a lot of time with the bottle, trying to find a way to sleep at night. It was too much of a bother to force my body to try to cooperate."

Breezy got up and went to the bar. He watched her walk, wondering why a woman would ever want to wear clothes, and why her man would want her to. When she moved, he knew the meaning of poetry. The female form was beautiful, no matter what. Her body, to him, was stunning. Gorgeous. It was no wonder, knowing her the way he did, that he reacted physically to her. She was as beautiful inside as she was outside.

She bent to get another water out of the refrigerator for herself. When she bent, the firm globes of her ass with his ink dripping over the curves, declaring her forever his, sent his cock into a frenzy. Blood rushed, pooled. Low. Wicked. Sinful. The ache turned to pain. For a man like him, one who couldn't have a normal erection, the sudden steel running through his cock was a miracle.

She didn't return to the chair but instead stayed a distance from him, leaning on the bar. The sun shone on her breasts. He wanted to spend hours on her breasts and devouring her spicy honey, drawing moans and cries from her. She was so responsive, genuinely so, and he loved that about her. Breezy was always unexpected — a mixture of submission and demands.

"Once we were here, away from the Swords, and we began to interact with other clubs, going to their parties and inviting them to ours, I decided to try to find a better way to sleep than drowning myself in alcohol. I didn't want to be in any other body but yours. I knew that. I also knew if I wanted a release, I had to work at getting one. Or have the woman work at it."

Her eyes were on his cock, mesmerized by his fist circling the rigid shaft, once more sliding slowly up and down, fingers tight. Her tongue touched her upper lip, and his cock jerked hard. Little pearly droplets made an appearance on the broad crown.

"One woman never got me off. Not ever, no matter how long I was in her mouth. Then two didn't. No matter how much I commanded my body to obey, how much I needed the release, I couldn't get there. I'd had your body, your mouth, your ass. No one else was going to do it for me. I haven't been inside another woman. Not one time since you've been gone. There's only been you."

He watched her expression carefully. She didn't have a poker face. He was telling the absolute truth. It was possible the copious amounts of alcohol he'd drunk had contributed to his inability to get hard, but it hadn't mattered. He hadn't wanted to be inside another woman.

"I got off looking at those pictures of you. So fucking sexy." He pulled out his phone and texted Maestro. Needing his help. Needing to know his woman was his again.

"How did you get those pictures? You were inside me and you didn't have a camera."

"I asked Storm to take them. He likes that shit. Gets off on it. Apparently, I do too, as long as it's you. Come here, baby." Just the idea excited him. "Don't you get a little hot thinking about getting pictures of us fucking? Just a little?" He folded the bath towels and dropped them in front of his chair.

She sent him an enigmatic smile and a small shrug. “I don’t know. Maybe. It’s hot knowing you jerked off to them.”

“Are you damp? Touch yourself and let me see.”

Breezy dropped her hand between her legs and curled her fingers into her body. He nearly groaned aloud watching as her hips did a slow undulation, and then she raised the two fingers into the air to show him the liquid coating them before licking them clean.

“I want your mouth on me and I want pictures of that. The photographs are just for me, or us. I love looking at you. That look you get on your face when I’m sending you over the edge. It’s hotter than hell and so beautiful.”

She moved toward him slowly. The sun added a glow to her skin and put highlights in her hair, which was still in that messy knot on top of her head. Every step she took had her breasts moving suggestively. Her hands followed the indentation at her waist and moved over the curve of her hip.

“You okay with the boys taking a few pictures? I brought the camera, just in case. They’ll be somewhere out of the way.” He held his breath. He could tell her he knew why he needed those pictures, what had started him down that path, but he didn't know what he'd do if she said no. He'd taken a huge risk asking her permission. She had to trust him implicitly to give her consent for such intimate pictures.

"I know you have a problem with the parties. You never seemed to mind when we had sex and the others were in and out. Surrounding us. Protecting us. I don't want you to be uncomfortable, Breezy."

"I'm not uncomfortable with that," she admitted. "I never notice when you're in me."

"The pictures, babe. I want the pictures of you."

She shrugged. "If it's important to you, then I don't mind."

She put her hands on his shoulders and leaned into him, arching her back, pushing her tits right into his face, so that he latched on to her right breast and caught at her left with his hand. He had turned the chair just slightly, just enough to present a profile, so a zoom lens would be able to record everything for him. She threw her head back, closing her eyes the way he loved, looking as if she was in ecstasy.

He would never have trusted her in the hands of anyone else. He wasn't exactly like

Ice, who enjoyed a bit of exhibitionism, or Storm, who preferred to be a voyeur. They'd been taught that from the time they were little. Encouraged in it. His training had taken a different turn. He hadn't realized until he was with Breezy that it had stuck with him in the way Ice's and Storm's trainings had stuck with them.

He needed to look at her face in the throes of ecstasy. He needed to see her in every position he demanded, giving him that. Giving him whatever he asked her for. It was all about proving she was his. He knew that. He also knew it was completely fucked up. Still, right now, he gave into his needs. He hoped in fulfilling his own, he was meeting hers. He hadn't taken the time to find out before; now he needed to know. She had to get off on it, not just want to please him.

Her hands went to his neck and she held him to her. He was rough because that was his way, but one hand slid between her legs to feel her response when he pulled his head back to look up at her. "You like the idea of pictures for us, baby? My cock in your mouth? Inside you? Taking you in every way I can? You like the idea of that?" He kept his eyes on hers, refusing to allow her to look away. "We can look at them together anytime we want."

A fresh flood of liquid heat coated his fingers. She nodded slowly. "Mostly, I like the idea that I don't know someone's taking the photographs so any time it could be happening."

He leaned into her breast, caught her nipple with his teeth and tugged, watching her face the entire time. The gasp. Her breath exploding as another rush of cream found his fingers. "Get on your knees, Breezy. I've waited three long years to feel your mouth on me again."

She slid her hands down his chest and leaned in to kiss him. That fire was there. Instant. Hot. She gave him everything without hesitation. Then she lifted her head. "Those photographs are ours alone."

It was both a statement and a question. Hell yeah, the pictures were just for them. He nodded. "I'll make sure no one else ever sees them." His heart hurt, it pounded so hard with exultation he could barely breathe.

Breezy slowly sank to her knees between his thighs. His fist was already surrounding his cock. He felt like titanium. So hard. It was perfection. Her lashes fluttered and then a sea of green was looking up at him. Waiting. Hungry. He wanted that look on her face recorded for him for all time. A shudder went through his body. Hot blood rushed through his veins. An electric pulse slid down his spine. He held them both there, stretching the moment out, drinking in her look.

"You want this, baby? You want my cock?"

"You know I do."

"It's been a long time, Bree. I'll try to be gentle, but with you, control goes right out the window. I start out feeding you and giving you what you want and then it's all about me."

"I get off when it's all about you," she reminded.

That was the fucking truth. With Breezy, it had always been all about Steele, because he was a selfish bastard and he took everything she gave him and more. The worst of it was, he would always need her to be all about him. That was never going to go away for him. He needed her adoration as much as he needed air to breathe. He didn't deserve it, but he'd try. For her, he'd try.

"You tell me when you want or need something, baby. I might not notice . . ."

She threw her head back, exposing the clean line of her throat. "You'll always notice, honey. You see everything."

He did, but now he vowed to double his efforts to watch closely. To make certain she never had to do one fucking thing she didn't want to do. He knew her favorite color, not because she'd told him but because he'd observed. He knew what kind of towels she liked, and the house was stocked with them. He'd gotten everything with Breezy in mind. And she wasn't going to do the cleaning. Not ever again. Not in their house and not in the clubhouse.

He noticed everything about her, that was the truth. She didn't like loud noises, the kind that startled her. She liked to be aware of anything coming at her. He'd chosen the house because he knew he was going to find her. He had Code on it already, but once his club was settled, he had planned on getting on his bike and tracking her down. The house, with its wide-open spaces, high ceilings and state-of-the-art security system, was just for her.

Every stick of furniture had been chosen with her in mind. The dishes and cutlery. He knew what she liked almost better than she did. His woman didn't know how to be pampered — not the way she deserved — and that was about to change. Looking down into her upturned face, his heart nearly exploded.

He'd always faced reality and the many flaws he had, but he'd learned even more about himself in the time she was gone. He had always thought himself strong, a rock the others could lean on, but without Breezy, he was crumbling inside. Breezy. So young and so mature. So willing to give others whatever it was they needed. Who protected her? She'd been out there on her own without any protection, and that was on him. On his shoulders. He should have found a different way.

He'd panicked once he'd learned her age — and once he'd known he was really in love with her. He didn't know the first thing about a relationship, and other than Savage and Reaper, he figured he was the most fucked-up human being in the world. He'd said terrible things — things he could never take back.

He wanted to kiss her, but kissing would break the spell he'd woven for her. That mesmerizing sexual web he'd caught her in.

"Stop holding out on me," she whispered, the smile fading. "I've waited as many years as you for this. It makes me hot, but I'm going to have a heart attack if you don't let me have what I want."

"Try asking nice." That was another thing he got off on. He liked to hear her say over and over to him that she wanted him. Or needed him. He liked her to ask him. Beg him. Plead with him. Breezy, being Breezy, only took so much and then she made her own demands.

"I *need* your cock in my mouth, Steele." She wasn't being a parrot. She wasn't snowing him. She meant it. She loved sucking him off, blowing him big. She enjoyed it and she had made an art of it. "Please, honey."

"What do you like most?"

"The way you taste. The way your cock stretches my lips and fills my mouth. The heat of it too. The way your face looks when I swallow you down. I love that look on your face."

Just the matter-of-fact way she stated what she liked made his blood rush hotter. He loved the look on her. Greed. Hunger. Adoration. His fist continued the slide, but it wasn't so slow now. He could get off just talking about her blowing him. It was a far cry from the desperation he'd tried with other women.

"I don't know. I might just jack off and coat your breasts. I like the way I drip down your body. You could lie out in the sun and see if it helps you tan, although I love all this smooth, white skin." He ran one finger from her collarbone over the swell of her breast to the nipple. He flicked that tight little bud experimentally.

"Steele."

There it was, that note that told him in a minute the balance of power would shift from him to her, although, truthfully, she always had it. She just didn't know.

He caught the back of her head in his palm. "Open your mouth."

She did instantly, and he gave her the crown. Her mouth was hot and wet. She closed her lips tightly around him and used her tongue to stroke and caress. She found every spot he liked as if she had his cock memorized, and knowing Breezy, she probably did. She sucked hard, taking him deeper, and he fed her, one thick inch at a time.

He had to force himself to go slow. There was no way to hold the memory of just how good her mouth felt surrounding him. Just how strong her suction was, or the way her tongue danced and stroked. It was paradise. He let her get used to his girth and length again, let her set the pace, take her time, even when he thought the top of his head might come off when her mouth took him deeper.

Hot. Wet. Tight. She took him deeper and deeper, and then he couldn't stand it. He caught that messy knot, yanking back as he surged to his feet. Her head tilted far back, giving his cock the opportunity it was now demanding. Her gaze jumped to his, widening a little with shock at his unexpected move.

He wanted that look recorded as well. That total surrender to him. She made his pleasure hers. He moved his hips, thrusting deeper, feeling the momentary resistance and then she was taking him down. Strangling him. Her eyes watered but she didn't pull away. It took effort to pull back and give her air. Three long years he'd been away from her. Away from paradise.

She had practiced for him. No one could just naturally take a cock like she did, but she'd put time into learning how to please him. She was good at controlling the muscles in her throat and her gag reflex. Her tongue was a weapon of pure pleasure.

Even more, just the visual was stimulating to him. Breezy on her knees looking up at him with her neck exposed so he could see his cock disappearing into her mouth and her throat expanding as she took him deep. It was an extremely erotic visual and made him that much harder, if it were possible.

She was so tight around that sweet spot, constricting there, just under his crown, the sensation intense, her muscles massaging, and her mouth working him hard. He held himself there as long as possible, his eyes on hers, on the sight of her holding out for him as long as she could. Nearly choking on him, but still holding. Unable to breathe yet, for him, holding.

The flat of her tongue together with the heat of her mouth nearly destroyed him. Then there was the way she suckled, as if she were desperate for what he could give her. He knew there was no way to prolong the ecstasy, not when it was that good, but he tried. She didn't use her hands to try to control his movements or how deep he went. She let him have complete control.

His hips found a fierce rhythm. His cock went deep. Her eyes were pure liquid, like a deep emerald sea. His balls drew up. Tight. Boiling. He dragged her head back farther and plunged. Air left his lungs in a rush. His blood felt on fire. He looked up at the window above the patio, the one overlooking the conversation area, and sent up a silent prayer that the camera was picking up every detail.

"Swallow me, all of me," he demanded, his voice guttural. He could barely see straight.

Then he was gone, the explosion hot and violent, pouring into her. His fist tightened in her hair, keeping her head back. His eyes were mere slits, watching her, needing this from her. She was Breezy, so she did what he asked, although he could see it wasn't easy because he had a lifetime stored up for her. He liked that it wasn't easy, and she still took him. That made him a selfish dick, and he accepted that about himself.

He pulled out but not away, keeping possession of her hair, his spent cock against her lips. The release had been explosive, liberating. It had been too long since he'd come like that. Her tongue slid up his cock, a gentle velvet rasp, and he shuddered again with pure pleasure. The way she did that, easing him down, easing him back into the real world, always left him shaken.

It took a few minutes to recover his breath, but he managed to snag his bottle of water and hand it to her. She'd always needed to drink water after a particularly aggressive and physically demanding session. She sank back onto her heels and poured the cool water down her throat.

He waited until she put the bottle down. "We're not finished."

Her gaze jumped to his. He reached down and lifted her into his arms. It was easy. He was extremely strong, and she wasn't that big, although she thought she was. He took her to the bar and laid her out, her ass right on the end so he could put her legs over his shoulders. He kept one hand on her belly so there was no moving and, without preamble, attacked her clit.

She cried out, trying to squirm. He held her in place and took everything he wanted. Each time she got close, he backed off, listening to her soft little cries and pleas. She was there fast. Blowing him always made her needy. Always made her close. She'd told him repeatedly she loved it as much as he did. He didn't see how that could be true, but she was always hot and damp and desperate to get off.

He slid his hand from her belly to her left breast. He liked playing with her because she was so responsive. He knew when to be gentle and when to be rough. She liked aggression, but when she was coming up on her cycle, he gentled things down. She didn't like sex during her time of the month because she said it hurt. It was the only time she'd asked him to back off, and he had, although as a doctor, he'd wanted to find a way to ease her cramps.

He tugged and rolled while he raked her clit with his teeth and then used his tongue to fuck her. Her breath was coming in ragged little pants when he suddenly switched tactics and jerked her thighs wide apart and flattened his tongue. He added his fingers into the mix, wishing he had thought to bring an ice bucket and heated stones. He liked to change things up with her, so she never knew which sensation she was getting.

Breezy went out of her way to give him pleasure of any kind he asked for, and he had no problem returning the favor. He loved every single moan and cry he extracted from her. More, he loved the way her body responded to everything he did. She was made for him, always ready for him.

Breezy had never told him no when he'd asked to try something new, and he'd given her every opportunity. Some of the things he'd asked for, she'd been a little intimidated by, but she'd trusted him enough to allow him to lead her gently into it. He'd always been careful when introducing her to something new. He loved that she'd always been willing.

Steele had taken her often, more than once a day, and it had never mattered to him where they were. He'd never taken her in front of the Swords, but he had in front of his brothers more often than not. They'd rarely paid attention, and if they had, it hadn't been to leer at her. They felt safer losing control with the others around. No one could hurt them because someone was always on guard. It was the way they were, and none of them really questioned it. Breezy hadn't. When his mouth was on her, she didn't care about anything else.

He glanced up at the window. He needed these shots. He hoped, over time, as Breezy was with him, he would be able to forgo having tangible memories of the way she gave herself to him. The way she loved him. That look he needed so much.

"Steele." Her voice hitched. It was a plea, not a demand.

He couldn't help the smirk. "I want to see that desperation, baby. Look at me. Turn your head this way." He needed the camera to catch that look for him. To record it. He pressed his fingers around her opening and leaned down to sip at the nectar. "Tell me what you want."

"I need to come."

He stroked her with his tongue and then raked her with his teeth. Suckled and then pulled back to rub his face on her inner thighs. "I don't think I believe you." He blew warm air on her and then started all over again.

Only when she was writhing, hips bucking, and he heard that soft little panicked note in her voice did he send her crashing over the edge. Breezy wasn't absolutely quiet when she came, but the sounds she made were always low and musical. He loved hearing them. Sometimes he wondered if he initiated sex so much just to hear those sounds.

She lay stretched out on the bar, her body rippling with pleasure, fighting to get her breath back. One hand went to his hair, fingers sliding in, and everything in him went still. It was the first time she'd really touched him of her own accord. The way she used to. She could communicate love with just one caress of her fingers. This touch was natural to her and had nothing to do with sex and everything to do with love.

She could convey her emotions so easily, so much so that to him, she was an open book. The way her fingers moved through his hair meant everything to him. He wanted time to stand still so that moment would last forever. His chest hurt. Ached. The pressure was unbelievable, but it didn't matter. He didn't move. Not as long as those fingers stroked little caresses in his hair.

TEN

The pool was heated. On the Northern California coast it had to be if they were going to use it much, and Steele knew Breezy liked to swim. He'd discovered that little nugget of information on a warm day when she'd looked longingly at the river and told him one of her longtime wishes before she died was to own a pool where she could swim every day. The pool had been a requirement when he'd looked for a home.

He spent most of his time stretched out on a lounge chair, watching her swim laps. The way her body sliced through the water, as if she were a little fish, fascinated him. But everything about Breezy always had. Why she gave him everything he asked, he didn't know, other than it was in her nature. Giving her everything was something he intended to do, and watching her sudden smile at him when she rose up out of the water, the happiness on her face, made him realize giving to Breezy was going to be his greatest joy.

He wanted to talk about their son, but he knew she was holding herself together by a thread. She didn't even mention his name if she could help it. As much as it cost him waiting to know every detail about the boy, he had to curb his impatience and give her this time, this small reprieve before they hit the road and tore through Louisiana looking for Zane. The way she'd cried, her heart clearly broken, had reached into him and slipped the lock he kept on the door where the monster resided.

He closed his eyes against the sun. His captors, the guards, the trainers, so brutal, had won in the end. He'd been sensitive, a healer. Now he was a killer. A monster. He had the ability to shut down all feeling and become something else. Something no human being could possibly be. To get his son back, he would become what he detested. The thing he knew his captors had tried to shape him into and he had resisted for so long. Until . . . Until he had gone insane and the monster had emerged for his survival.

He thought about that while he listened to the sound of the water playing over Breezy's skin. Survival instincts were strong in him or, like the other children who had succumbed to the torture, he would be dead. If he had died, he would never have met Breezy. He wouldn't have a son. He wouldn't be lying in the sun, hearing his woman as she emerged from the pool and tried to sneak up on him. He wouldn't feel so alive and so happy.

Cold water hit his warm skin and then she was in his lap, laughing, her wet body stretched out over his. He brought his arms up as she buried her face against his throat. Holding her. "Settle." He growled the order when she went to pull away. He didn't care that she was wet; he wanted her in his arms.

She relaxed against him. "You bought this house for me, didn't you?"

He was silent a moment, his breath caught in his lungs. Clouds overhead rode the slight breeze. They looked like white fluff flung into the blue haphazardly. "Yes."

"You really were going to come for me, weren't you?"

His gut clenched. So many knots. She was working it all out. At last. He was afraid to hope. He didn't want her to ever think he had meant one word he'd said to her the night he'd sent her away. He didn't want her to think he was taking her back into his life because they had a son and he wanted the boy with him.

"Yes. Code's been looking for a direction on you for the last year. One little footprint was all we needed. You listened when I told you how to go off the grid, didn't you?"

"Yes. After you sent me away, I knew you'd told me all those things for a reason. In your way, you were still protecting me. That's what you're all about, Steele, protection of everyone around you. Just know, I really can stand on my own two feet."

"I'm very aware of that, Breezy." He wanted her to depend on him. At the same time, he was proud of her. He relied on that strength she had.

"Why didn't you tell me straight-out that you had plans to come for me?"

She tried to draw back so she could look at his face, but he held her easily in place, refusing to let her move.

"You wouldn't have believed me."

She nodded. "No, I wouldn't have. Still, there's more."

"Didn't need you knowing you're my world." He made the confession gruffly, feeling like a fool. Feeling so fucking vulnerable she might as well have driven a stake through his heart.

Breezy pressed cool lips to his throat. There was a long silence and he didn't know what that meant. Finally, her hand slid up his arm to cup the side of his face. "You've always been my world, since the moment I first saw you. I knew it was you. I don't mind you knowing that."

"That's because you're courageous, Bree. You don't mind if I have the upper hand in all things. Why is that? Why doesn't it bother you that I need to be the one in control?"

Her slender shoulders shrugged, the movement sliding over his skin like a caress. "Control is an illusion, Steele. I learned that a long time ago. It doesn't matter who appears to have it. We really only can control ourselves. We have choices. You were my choice. Just listening to the sound of your voice always made me happy. I knew you were a good man, even though you rode with the Swords. I have control over me and my wants and needs. You're both to me. It doesn't matter what happens in the future, or if we're together, I know that isn't going to change."

He didn't like that. "We're going to be together." He made that a statement. He didn't like the feeling of vulnerability being with her gave him. He hadn't allowed himself to be vulnerable to anyone other than his brothers and sisters in Torpedo Ink. That was the reason he hadn't told her. He didn't want her to know how vulnerable he was.

"You're insisting we stay together, Steele. You're demanding I tell you how I feel and trust you implicitly. I did that once and, in the end, it didn't work out for us."

She pushed back hard, and he reluctantly let her up. She sat on the edge of the lounge looking down at him, staring right into his eyes. "You have to commit to us. Just like you're part of Torpedo Ink, I have to be part of you. You have to be all in. You have to be able to tell me the hard things and not worry that I'm going to do something to hurt you."

She could tear his heart out, and there was that monster, crouching inside of him, waiting to slip out. What if the pain she caused was so bad the monster got loose? He closed his eyes and started to turn his head away, afraid she would see.

"No, Steele. Look at me. This is our chance, right here. I saw the pictures on the phone. I see this house. Everything in it. I choose to believe that you weren't inside those women, that your cock always has belonged to me. I'm willing to give us another chance, but you have to give me your full commitment this time."

"Do you have any idea how fucked up I

am, Breezy? How difficult your life is going to be with me? I can give you the world. I can show you in a million ways what you mean to me. I can do that. But you have to live with a control freak. I don't want you out of my sight. Do you know how many cameras there are in this house? I have an app on my phone so I can look to see where you are and what you're doing at any time. I'll smother you. I'll make you crazy. You have no idea how crazy I can get."

"I lived with you for a year. You kept me with you every moment and I knew it was for my protection."

"That was nothing. *Nothing.*" He spat the word at her because he knew, the more she became aware of the real man she was choosing, the more she'd want to run. Her thumb was moving along his jaw, a soothing gesture because that was Breezy's way. She soothed him no matter what was happening.

"What do you think I'm going to be like with Zane?" he demanded. "With our children?"

"I think you'll protect them, because that's what you do."

"Damn it, woman. You persist in seeing what you want to see. I want you to be realistic."

"Then tell me, Steele. Let me decide what I can or can't live with. Then you won't have to worry, and you can jump in with both feet or let me leave."

He shook his head. "That's the problem right there, baby. You don't know me. You don't know that I'm not capable of letting you walk away. I'm willing to put my life on the line so you can live happily with our son if that's what it takes, but I know as long as you're somewhere in this world, I'm going to be with you. That's fucking stalker mentality and if another man did that to you or another woman, I'd kill him."

Breezy should have been horrified, but instead she smiled serenely, that same old Breezy smile that made him think she was older and wiser than most. "Honey, you're so far off the mark about yourself you don't even know. If I didn't love you, if I truly wanted out, you wouldn't want anything to do with me. You can protest all you want, but just as you watched and studied me, I did you. I spent nearly two years watching you. Talk about being a stalker."

"Bree . . ." He tried to protest but she shook her head, that smile never faltering — as if she knew absolutely what she was talking about.

"Steele, you might spend time trying to

get me to fall back in love, but in the end, if I didn't love you, you wouldn't want me. We didn't have fights . . ."

"Because every single thing went my way. You never opposed me."

She smiled at him. Sweet. Breezy. Setting his heart on fire. Sometimes looking at her hurt. Really hurt. How had he ever sent her away from him?

"That isn't true, honey. Think back. Whenever I wanted something, you moved heaven and earth to get it for me. When I didn't like something, it wasn't done. I didn't have to fight with you because you gave me anything I wanted. I'm not a pushover, Steele. I loved belonging to you. I'll admit I don't know the first thing about relationships, and maybe ours wouldn't have suited every woman, but it suited us. I was happy, and I thought you were as well." She tilted her chin at him. "What are you so afraid of? What are you holding back?"

She was too damned intelligent. She had always asked the hard questions. She did know him more than he thought she did, to be able to guess he was hiding something big from her. Hell. "I don't want you to give me everything and then take it away from me when the going gets tough. And it will." That was all true.

"I don't give up, Steele." She rubbed her hand down her leg. "It's surprisingly hot out here this afternoon."

"I don't want you to get burned, baby. Let's head into the house. You can shower while I cook something for us."

"I can do the cooking." She stood up and wrapped the towel around her waist, leaving her breasts bare. There were faint marks there, little strawberries from the scrape of his teeth. Like a brand. His. He found satisfaction in that.

She had always enjoyed making meals for him when she'd had the chance. He'd set up the kitchen with her in mind, but it was important that she didn't think he expected her to do all the cooking.

"After your shower, come join me in the kitchen." He stood up as well and wrapped his towel around him, letting it ride low on his hips. He needed to cover up the fact that just looking at her brought him to attention. He wanted to make love to her. Slowly. Gently. Take his time in the bed, not take her like the wild animal he could be.

Breezy laughed softly. "I'll never find it. I'll get lost in this place."

He grinned at her. "Code came with me to look at it and he got lost, either that or he found the racquetball room and just got stuck there."

"There's a racquetball room?"

He nodded.

"Do you play racquetball? Any of you?"

"Nope. But it's there."

"What in the world were you thinking, buying this house?" she asked.

He slung his arm around her neck and pulled her beneath his shoulder. He was taller than Breezy by quite a bit and his arm circled her shoulders and draped down so that he could caress the curve of her breast with the pads of his fingers. Each stroke sent a little electrical charge through his bloodstream.

"I was thinking my woman deserves the best and I was going to find her and bribe her to come back to me with this place."

She looked up at him, her green eyes moving over his face. Searching. It was the truth, and he let her see that it was. He knew he'd told her repeatedly, but she would need reassurance often after the things he'd said to make her leave. He stopped abruptly just at the glass door and took her mouth.

Kissing Breezy was a singular experience and one he would never get enough of. He was addicted to her taste and the fire in her mouth. The way she gave him everything that was her instantly, the moment his lips settled over hers. He made his demands with his tongue and then waited to feel the delicate stroke of hers, such a contrast to his aggression and insistence. He loved that. He loved everything about it.

Steele couldn't believe his woman was there — in the home he'd bought and furnished for her. He knew it would overwhelm her at first. He'd intended to overwhelm her. She wasn't getting a bargain. She might protest as much as she wanted, but he knew. He knew the way he was, and he knew what was locked up inside of him. Chances were, when they made their run to find their son, she'd see, because once that monster was loose, there was no putting him away until he was satisfied.

He walked her up the stairs and waited to see if she chose the frameless shower or the one in the enormous double bathroom that was part of the master suite. She went with the smaller free-frame. He loved that. He loved that she would choose the one he was certain she'd like. He left her to it and headed down the stairs.

Maestro and Keys were already in the kitchen. Maestro indicated the camera with his chin. "Got your shots for you, bro. She really is beautiful."

"Always liked that girl," Keys added.

"Sweet. She was always fuckin' sweet to everyone. Never saw her pass up one of the kids without stopping to talk to them."

Steele nodded. "Yeah, she's amazing. She can forgive anything. That's a good thing because I'm going to fuck up royally most of the time."

No one argued with him. He took out the chicken he'd bought. Breezy liked chicken, and he was good at grilling. He'd learned when he rode with the Swords.

Keys washed potatoes. "You good?"

Steele shook his head, looking down at the chicken that was already cut up. His stomach rolled as images pushed into his brain. Children he knew. Children with the skin flayed off of them looking up at him, expecting a miracle he couldn't deliver. It was all too close after opening that door.

Breezy thought the worst had been the beatings. It hadn't been the beatings, and the ones he'd endured, the ones the others had, hadn't been done with slaps or fists. Punches and kicks had been frequent, and there had also been chains and whips and cattle prods. There'd been all kinds of torture devices. Beatings hadn't been the worst.

He looked up, his eyes meeting Maestro's and then Keys's. "Breezy thinks if Bridges kicks or slaps Zane that's the worst that can happen to him. She's so worried. I held her last night while she cried herself to sleep, just wanting him safe. That's all she wants, our little boy safe. She has no idea what the worst can be. I know the Swords sell children to predators. Bridges will know the kind of bank he could get for a boy that age."

"Steele," Maestro began. He glanced at Keys. What was there to say? One of their own, one of their family, was in the exact position they had all been in as children. Someone had taken him from a safe environment and might give him to vile predators for money. Steele had every right to worry. Bridges had sent his daughter out to seal deals when she was no more than a child. He wouldn't care about his grandson, especially when the boy was Steele's son.

"We'll get him back," Keys said. "He's ours."

Steele didn't voice his worry, that even if they did get him back, he'd be like those children lying on that filthy floor, staring up at him with despair. Bloody. In pain. Infections raging. He'd fought rats off of them. Laid on them to keep them from freezing to death. Stayed up all night to keep the bugs and rodents off of their dying bodies. So many.

"Fuck!" He yelled it, wanting to throw the cut-up meat. Those children had been nothing but meat to the predators, and he'd been a child himself, unable to save them. Unable to help them in any way.

"Steele," Maestro said softly, trying to call him back to the present. "It's over."

Steele shook his head. He knew better. Maestro knew better. "It's never going to be over, and you know who's going to pay the price? That woman up there. She's going to pay it just like Anya pays it for Reaper. Just like any woman you find that does it for you will. We're so far gone and there's no coming back from it."

"We can learn . . ." Keys began.

"What? Social norms? We feel safer fucking our women when we're together because we've got eyes watching out for danger. Our childhood was spent on survival, on killing to survive. We don't know how to be without one another and we sure as hell don't conform to other people's ideas of bullshit rules. We're assassins. It doesn't matter how far we put down roots here, our first inclination when someone crosses us is to eliminate them."

Maestro shrugged. "We're getting by,

Steele. Reaper found Anya. Breezy's back."

"Bree has this misguided belief that I'm a nice man and will be a good partner to her. She had a year with me; how she doesn't remember what I was like, I'll never know. She also thinks that if she wants out, I'll let her out."

Keys snorted. "She ought to know better than that. She was raised in the life."

Steele looked down at the chicken again and the churning in his stomach grew worse. His past was too close. All those children. Dead. Over two hundred and fifty deaths. On him. It hadn't mattered how many of the bastards they'd killed. Even when they'd just been kids, Sorbacov had replaced their guards with even crueler wardens — or he had until he'd begun to run out of criminals.

"I can't do this." He shoved the offending chicken away from him. "Not yet. Give me a few minutes and I'll be back."

He had to get himself under control. He didn't lose control. That was too dangerous. He'd done so on occasion and the results had been . . . monstrous. He stepped away from the work aisle and started toward the glass door that led to the extensive patio.

He caught her scent and turned, his breath hitching in his lungs. A knot rose in his throat. Breezy stood in the doorway, her gaze on Maestro and Keys, a soft flush rushing over her, making her skin glow. She had discovered the clothes he'd put in the drawers just in case he found her. Things he liked. Things he wanted her to wear in their home.

The little shorts were nothing but black stretch lace, showing all that beautiful skin, highlighting her little tawny landing strip. The matching bra barely stretched across her full breasts. Both nipples pushed through the lace. He could see his marks on her.

Keys saluted her. "Hey, Breezy. You shouldn't stay out so long in the sun. I know it's cooler here, but you could burn."

All three men had been raised with no clothes. Their brethren as well as Alena and Lana had never been given clothes unless they were being sent out on an assignment. They'd been forced to have sex in front of one another until it was commonplace. Breezy was Steele's. She was part of their family. They didn't look at her as a woman simply because they'd been conditioned not to. Their bodies were totally under their command and didn't react at the sight of a beautiful, naked woman.

"I'd forgotten you two were in the house,"

she said hesitantly, taking a step back.

Steele went to her and circled her waist with his arm. "I'm having a little trouble fixing the chicken, Bree. My stomach isn't settling."

Instantly her expression changed to one of concern. "Do you want to lie down? I can fix us dinner."

He shook his head. "I'll take a shower and be right back down. Maestro and Keys wanted to take a dip in the pool but were going to help with dinner."

"I don't mind. You all go ahead and do whatever," she said.

Steele jerked his chin toward the door and his brothers got the message, heading out to the pool. Both wore loose-fitting jeans slung low on their hips and they had them off before they got to the pool.

"You really don't mind starting dinner? I can be down in a few minutes."

She shook her head. "I'd better go change though."

He frowned. "Why? You look beautiful. I can come back and watch you moving around the kitchen just the way I imagined. Does it make you uncomfortable to have them see your body? Because if it does . . ."

She glanced through the glass to the pool and the two men swimming and splashing each other. Steam was rising from the surface of the water as the outside temperature dropped.

Her adorable little frown was on her face. "No. Not really. If you think I'm safe."

His heart stuttered. He framed her face with both hands. "Don't you feel safe with Maestro and Keys? Have they done something to make you feel uncomfortable?"

"No. Not at all."

"They aren't going to notice, Breezy. Stay in that outfit for me." He wasn't asking. She might as well know how he was, demanding his way. At the same time, if she was feeling in the least like she wasn't safe, he had to find a way to rectify that. "Your choice, baby." He softened his voice, so she knew he meant it. "But you're perfectly safe."

She shrugged. "Then I'm comfortable."

He leaned down and took her left breast into his mouth, his tongue flicking her nipple as he suckled right through the lace. Instant heat exploded through his groin and hot blood rushed through his veins. He dragged her closer, pulling strongly, wanting his mark on her. His other hand slid down her belly to find that stretchy lace and the openings in the fabric that gave him access to her. Her sheath was already damp and hot as hell. Beckoning him.

"I'm hungry all over again for the taste of you." He growled it. Lapped at his fingers, watching her the entire time. Her eyes had gone dark with desire. She was always responsive to him. Always.

"You're hungry for dinner," she countered, but she didn't move when his mouth found her other breast and his fingers returned to bury themselves in her channel. She immediately cradled his head to her as if she loved standing in the middle of the kitchen with her man working her body.

He licked at his fingers again. "I'll be right back. Whatever you don't have done, I'll do, and then I'll be playing some more."

She laughed softly. "Is that a threat? You made it sound like one. I like the way you play."

He couldn't resist spinning her around and rubbing her ass. The black lace stretched over her pale skin, framing it beautifully. He crouched for a moment, thrust his fingers into her and bit her left cheek. Not hard. Just enough to sting. The flood of liquid heat rewarded him. He stood up slowly. "Fuck, woman. You're going to shatter my cock into a million pieces if I keep this up. I'm so damn hard I feel like I'm going to break in half."

Her hand found him under the towel, her

fist closing around his girth. "I love the way you feel, Steele." Her thumb slid over the crown, smearing drops over the broad head. "Maybe we'd better do something about that before you head upstairs."

Steele didn't need a second invitation. He yanked her panties down. She took away the darkness that always threatened to consume him, and right then, it was far too close. He caught at her and easily lifted her into his arms. "Put your legs around me. Lock your ankles."

She obeyed and threaded her fingers together at the nape of his neck. Her legs being spread so wide apart opened her sex to him, and his cock pushed against her, seeking entrance. Very slowly he lowered her over him, sheathing that thick, steely spike one inch at a time. He felt the reluctant give of her tight muscles as he relentlessly pushed home. Her body swallowed his, took him in, gave him that perfection.

He let it take him. That feeling of euphoria. She was strangling him she was so tight. He pressed her back against the counter and began to move, slowly at first, watching her face, watching her breasts jolt with every savage thrust. He buried himself deep, wishing he could live there. Every time he withdrew and surged forward again, his body sang and his blood grew hotter. Flames licked at him. Burned.

Every sound she made was pure music. He loved the way she moaned. A soft little cry accompanied each thrust. His hips picked up the pace because it was a necessity. He couldn't continue slow. He needed hard. Fast. He leaned forward, sinking deep, catching her nipple between his teeth and tugging. The liquid heat turned fiery hot, surrounding him. He switched sides and flicked with his tongue and then used his teeth, this time scraping over the curve of the sensitive mound before finding her nipple and biting down.

She cried out and once more flooded him with liquid fire. He took her hard. Over and over. Behind him the door opened, and his brothers sauntered past, both barefoot and naked, heading over to the folded towels they'd placed on the table. Her fingers tightened in warning at the nape of his neck. He moved harder in her. Deeper. Wanting her to know that he would take her where he wanted, when he wanted. He'd done it often before. His brothers guarded him when he was at his most vulnerable, and fucking her made him as vulnerable as hell.

She moved with him. He loved looking at the way her breasts jolted in that stretchy fabric. The visual of her laid out over the counter, her legs wrapped around him and his marks coming up under the lace, added to his pleasure, just as the sight of her had when he'd watched her blow him.

The messy knot on top of her head began to unravel with each hard thrust. He loved that too, but it was the expression on her face when she looked at him, her eyes, so dark with a mixture of love and lust. So his. He hoped that Maestro or Keys had thought to pick up the camera and capture that look for him, but he couldn't take his eyes off her to check.

"You close, baby?" She was, he knew it. He could feel her body tightening around his. He could hear the soft little pleas begin to change notes.

"Yes." She barely managed the assent.

"Take me with you," he commanded.

Her body clamped down on his. Hard. Vicious. A milking squeeze of tight muscles that caught at him and worked his cock until his head spun. Her low, keening cry had him emptying himself like a volcano into her. The splash of his hot seed triggered another strong wave through her body.

He lay over her, feeling the strong ripples of her body. His face was buried in her neck and he took the opportunity, in spite of fighting for breath, to suck on that soft, pale skin. Gently. She needed gentle care now. He'd been rough, and the counter was a very hard surface.

"You okay, Bree?"

"Yes, it was spectacular as always with you. I can't think when you're inside me like that."

He couldn't think either, which was a damn good thing. The churning in his stomach was gone, and suddenly his world was right again. All because of Breezy and her amazing body. All because of her response to him. She gave him what he needed.

He pulled out of her slowly. Reluctantly. Very gently he set her feet on the floor and held her with one arm around her waist. He reached around her to turn on the warm tap water and soak a small towel. "Put your legs apart for me."

She widened her stance and he washed her gently and then his cock. He looked around to find that Maestro and Keys had headed up to their rooms to take showers. The camera was on the counter, but in a different spot than where it had been. His brothers were looking out for him.

Breezy's gaze followed his. "They took

pictures of us, didn't they?"

"It looks like it. I hope so. You looked beautiful. Your face when I'm inside you is so beautiful, baby."

Her hand cupped his jaw, her thumb sliding over it. "Why do you need photographs?"

He sighed and caught her hand, pressing a kiss to her palm. "That year without you, I think I would have gone insane if I hadn't had those pictures."

"Our intimacy should be just for us, shouldn't it?"

That shocked him. "It is just for us. Why would you think it would be for anyone else? I'm not like Ice or Savage, baby. I don't need an audience. I just don't give a fuck if they walk in while I'm in you. That just reinforces you're mine and they'd better protect you. I need the look on your face as a reminder sometimes. If it bothers you . . ."

She shook her head. "I don't know if it should, but it doesn't. When you're moving in me, I don't honestly care who walks in. I barely notice."

Love for her welled up so strong, so intense, the pressure in his chest made him feel as if he might be having a heart attack. He pressed his hand over his heart and then bent his head to capture her mouth with his. She moved into him and circled his neck with her arms, her body tight against his.

"Hungry, woman," Maestro said. "If you're not cooking dinner, vacate the kitchen with your man and let me give it a try."

Keys snorted his derision. "Don't do it, Bree. He can't cook worth a damn. Give him any instrument to play and he can do it, but a stove? It's too complicated."

Maestro snapped a towel at him. "Shut the fuck up. I'm hungry."

Breezy laughed and dropped her arms from around Steele's neck. "Get out of here and I'll call you when dinner's ready." She went to the sink and washed her hands.

Steele came up behind her and pressed his body against hers, his hands cupping the firm globes of her ass. "I can help you, baby."

"You'll just distract me. Go away. I'll get this done and call you."

He kissed the back of her neck. "I've asked Lana and Alena to get a jacket made for you. One with my patch declaring you're my property." He kept his body pressed tightly against hers knowing he was pushing her hard.

Breezy went completely rigid and he felt

her rejection of his club. His jacket. His declaration. She gave a slight shake of her head, but he didn't move, didn't let her slide away even when she pushed at the sink to try to make an inch or two between them. This was one of those defining moments when she had to understand what he'd been telling her earlier. Some things were going to go his way and he wouldn't budge on them.

The club was as necessary to him as breathing. He lived and died by those colors and what they stood for. His colors defined him. His brothers and sisters completed him, filling in all the gaping holes that were there in him. They weren't eighteen individuals; they couldn't survive without one another. There was no way to explain that to Breezy, she had to understand by observing it firsthand. They were one unit.

"No."

"Yes." He said it firmly. "My club made me the man you fell in love with. That's who I am. You're afraid of club life, and I don't blame you after seeing the Swords, but our club isn't like that and I wouldn't be in it if it was."

She gave a little shake of her head, staring straight ahead at the sink. "I can't do that. I swore I would never go back to that life, and I don't want to raise Zane that way."

"What are you afraid of?" He kept his voice low, inviting her to share her worst fears with him. If she didn't tell him, he wouldn't know. Clearly, the fact that his brothers went in and out of the room while he had sex with her wasn't part of her fears. He wanted her to tell him so he could fix the problem.

"No. I'm not part of the club."

"This isn't up for debate, and you know it isn't. I'm Torpedo Ink. The colors are inked onto my skin. Every one of my brothers will protect you, Breezy, not use you. They'll protect Zane. You're mine. I told you that we'll be doing things my way and I expect you to follow my lead. You knew that going into it. You knew that when you gave me your body. When you gave me your heart. The club is me, Bree. If you reject the club, you're rejecting me."

She stayed rigid, her head down, breathing hard. She gave a little shake of her head again. "I don't see why we can't be together without me being a part of that life. I can get a job and we can —"

"You know better." He kept his voice low. Gentle. Absolutely in control. Of him. Of her. Of what their life was going to be. "You will wear my jacket. Do you understand me?

You knew who I was, and you still gave yourself to me. I told you there would be no backing out. Fix dinner. I'll go shower. We're not going to argue about this. When you're ready, I expect you to tell me what the problem is."

Her breath hitched and for a moment his heart pounded, afraid she would cry. That couldn't happen. He couldn't give her this. There was no way to resolve it for her if she wouldn't talk to him. She had to accept who and what he was. He was Torpedo Ink. Every inch of him. She was his choice. The woman he loved, and this was too big a battle to lose, especially when they had to be completely on the same page when they hunted for their son. The things they might find . . .

"What if I can't do it?"

He put his arms around her, surrounding her with his strength. "You trusted me before when I rode for the worst club there is. You trusted me to keep you safe. You didn't want to leave me, even when you had the opportunity, Bree. I had to lie to push you away, to keep you safe. You're trusting me with your body. You're trusting me with our son. Trust me to take care of you in the club. To know that those in the club would lay down their lives for you and Zane. You won't just have me protecting the two of you; you'll have all of them. Every single one of them was trained the same way I was, to be an assassin. The people who took Zane don't stand a chance against us. You'll be safe, and so will our children."

He felt a shudder go through her and he turned her around to face him, his hands gentle. He was shocked at her expression. She was as white as a sheet. Her eyes were wide with shock and she couldn't seem to catch her breath.

He caught her by the back of her neck and pushed her head down. "Breathe, baby. Take in air." He had seen that look before too many times. His woman not only didn't want anything to do with a club, just the idea caused her to flash back to her childhood. He should have known. His heart sank. More than anything, he wanted this. He needed it. But Breezy couldn't give him something that put that look on her face. Not now. Maybe not ever.

"I'm right here, Breezy. I won't let anything happen to you." He crouched down beside her and breathed with her, looking into her eyes. "I've got you, baby. I'll always have you. You don't want to wear my name on you yet, we'll shelve it until you can see absolutely that Torpedo Ink is different.

That we're different."

This was no longer about him. About his need to have her accept him. He was Torpedo Ink, and if she rejected the club, she really was rejecting him. He was expecting too much of her. It had always been Breezy giving him everything. He just expected to get his way.

"Forget I said anything, Bree. Just breathe this away. We'll talk about things at a later date."

She straightened slowly, her lashes reluctantly lifting until he was looking into all that green. "I'm so scared," she whispered. "I was scared every single minute I was growing up."

"You don't have to be afraid anymore. We'll get Zane back and then we'll talk about it."

She moistened her lower lip with her tongue. "I'll try, Steele."

He shook his head. "Not like this. Not when you're terrified. I pushed it too soon."

"Swear to me." She turned her head to look at him. "Swear to me Torpedo Ink isn't anything like the Swords."

"You have my word, baby, but we're going to shelve this for now. I don't want you worrying about it."

She wrung her hands together, but she

was breathing easier. "I'll say yes, Steele . . ."

"No, baby, you won't. We're going to wait until you're able to talk to me. I know you don't like disappointing me, but I want us to wait."

"You're certain?"

There was a hopeful note in her voice. He rubbed the pad of his thumb gently over her chin. "Absolutely. And you work up the courage to talk to me about what you're most terrified of. Not now. After we have Zane. I'm good with this, understand?"

She nodded.

He brushed his lips back and forth over hers and then kissed her gently. "Give me ten minutes to shower and then I'll be right back to help you."

She nodded again, and he stepped back to give her room to slide away. He was uneasy. They were riding to get their child back. He was willing for the monster to come out to get his son back to her. He was willing to die in order for her to have Zane. His club members would do the same.

Those riding with him were willing to risk their lives. He hoped she would see that, but in doing so, she would also see what they all were. It was one thing to talk of killing other human beings in the abstract, or because she was afraid for her child, but to actually witness it was something else.

Bridges was her father. Junk her half brother. They weren't good to her, but they were all the family she had. He hadn't been blowing off steam when he'd said he was going to take them apart before he killed them. Bridges had punched and kicked Breezy. Junk had held his hand over Zane's mouth and nose, laughing while he did so. They'd taken the toddler from her. They were dead. Steele was willing to do whatever it took to make that happen. His club was willing right alongside him. Breezy was about to see the worst in him, and it had nothing whatsoever to do with being a controlling bastard. He loved her enough to curb that. Killing those who threatened her and his child was another matter altogether.

ELEVEN

Breezy was exhausted. They'd been riding for hours. She was warm enough. Steele had seen to that. He even had gloves for her. They weren't riding with their colors and she was grateful. She wasn't a club girl and she didn't want to be associated with a club again. She didn't want to feel the way the Swords had always made her feel — worthless.

She was a little shocked at how many of the other members of Torpedo Ink had elected to go with them. Thirteen of the eighteen surrounded them. Even Savage. For some reason that surprised her. Savage had always, along with Reaper, stayed near Czar to protect him. The little she'd seen of him had made her believe nothing had changed. Reaper remained behind to watch over Czar and his family, but Savage rode with them. They'd brought a truck with them and Transporter was driving it. A car seat was in the backseat and just looking at it made her feel as if they were really going to get Zane back.

The Swords wouldn't have considered getting a child back from a kidnapper an emergency. Most wouldn't have bothered to go, and if they knew there was a risk, most likely none would have gone. It wasn't because they didn't have a brotherhood; it was simply that a child was as worthless to them as she had always been.

Breezy pressed her face against Steele's back, trying not to think about her breakdown in the kitchen. Panic attacks happened, but not very often. She'd been a little shocked that Steele had been so gentle with her. That had continued for the rest of the evening and night.

They'd made a few stops to stretch their legs and eat the food Alena had prepared for them. Lana rode with them, but Alena was home, helping to watch over Blythe and Anya and the children with the skeleton crew left behind. They'd left right at three A.M. and were now in New Mexico approaching Santa Fe. It was one in the morning and they'd been riding hard nearly twenty-four hours.

The club members were machines. No one looked or acted tired. It was as if once they'd started on their chosen mission, they were different individuals. They looked as dangerous as they felt. When they stopped at a rest stop, no one came near them. Steele stayed close to her, walking her to the women's room and waiting until she came out. He had a hand on her at all times. Holding her hand. Slinging an arm around her shoulders as they walked. Placing his palm in the middle of her back. When they ate, his thigh was tight against hers. She found it comforting — and she needed comfort.

She had done her best to keep Zane out of her mind because if she didn't, she might go crazy. Now, as they got closer to the apartment where Bridges and Junk had found her, she began shaking. Immediately, Steele dropped his gloved hand to cover hers. She tried to keep her teeth from chattering as the motorcycles slowed and turned up a street three blocks above her apartment building.

The night before, Steele, Maestro and Keys had eaten dinner, proclaiming her ability in the kitchen rivaled Alena's, which she knew it didn't. She could make decent meals, but she didn't have the knowledge Alena did. It was nice that they'd acknowledged she'd cooked for them. When she'd been with the Swords, she often cooked meals for quite a few of the men and no one, not once, had said thanks to her.

Steele had taken her to bed and he'd been so sweet and gentle, worshiping every inch of her body, making her feel loved. That was what he was so good at. He made her feel loved. His entire focus was on her no matter what they were doing, and when he moved in her, staring into her eyes, his fingers threaded through hers, it was almost magical. He stole her heart every time.

She knew, more than any other reason, it was the way Steele touched her, the way his hands moved over her and the look on his face when he stared down into her eyes, that kept her tied to him. He couldn't hide that. She didn't have to wonder if he cared. When he was with her, she knew. It was always there in the things he did. Even when he ordered her around, she knew he was looking out for her, and that control made her feel safe when she'd never felt that way.

She hadn't wanted to think too much about his declaration that she would wear his colors. Somehow, she'd let the way she felt about Steele, the explosive chemistry between them, make her forget about the fact that he was a member of a motorcycle club and she would have to accept that. She lay beside him afterward while he looked at the pictures in the camera, showing her the occasional one.

In each photograph he shared, her face showed every bit of her love for him. The intensity. It was caught on camera. She could see it etched into her skin. The feeling, so stark and raw, was in her eyes. She found it interesting that most of the photographs focused mainly on her face, not on what they were doing. It was those pictures, the ones he didn't delete, that gave her the best insight into him. He needed to know she wanted to be with him. He needed to know someone loved him. He didn't believe himself worthy of love, so he had a difficult time believing she really wanted to be with him.

That was a shock, and she'd laid next to him watching the expressions on his face as he held the camera up and looked at the viewer. Steele always appeared to have absolute confidence. He was the man people turned to in a crisis, and he came through. He was calm and never faltered. Looking at him, feeling his abnormal strength, knowing how skilled he was, it had never occurred to her that he might not believe himself worthy of love. That only made her want to show him how she felt about him all the more.

He'd nudged her and held up the viewer to show her other pictures taken. She couldn't help but see how sexy it was when she was kneeling in front of him, his cock in her mouth, or when he had her laid out on the bar and his mouth was between her legs. Her face had shown pure ecstasy, because Steele gave her that.

He had her with sex. There was no question. They had explosive chemistry. She couldn't resist him. She'd never been able to. She liked the way he took control. It was hot, and she reaped all the benefits. He could take her in the middle of Grand Central Station and she wouldn't be able to say no. She'd forget everyone was around her because once he touched her, there was nothing else for her in the world.

On the other hand, she loved him with all her heart. *Loved* him. Her heart ached when she was close to him. She'd heard every word he said to her about his horrific childhood and she knew there was far more to it than he'd given her, and she could barely stand hearing that much. She wanted to be that woman for him, the one he needed. He told her she was, and she felt, deep down, that it was true.

She didn't mind when he needed to know where she was. When he had to touch her when they were together. She didn't mind that he wanted his way most of the time because she knew he would give her whatever she wanted when she protested. He always had. It was just that things didn't matter to her as much as they seemed to matter to him. She didn't mind that he had to have ridiculous photographs to remind himself that she loved him. None of that mattered to her.

Breezy didn't even care about the men drifting in and out of the room when he made love to her — because every single time Steele touched her, no matter if he was rough or not, it felt like love. He didn't look anywhere but at her. His focus was so complete that she knew he didn't see the men moving around them. He felt safe because they were there. Safe to give her his complete attention. None of that mattered. But being in a club did.

The apartment she'd rented wasn't in the best part of town, but it was affordable. In the year she'd been with Steele, he had insisted she learn self-defense and he'd worked with her daily. He'd talked to her about keeping in shape just because sometimes it came down to winning by outlasting your opponent. She'd taken everything to heart, but it still came down to money, and she hadn't wanted to use Steele's because it had made her feel like a whore. She'd taken what she needed to get started but had told herself she was saving the rest for emergencies.

She knew Steele's body language and he wasn't happy when he saw the neighborhood she lived in, and it made her ashamed. She should have swallowed her pride and used the money to provide Zane with a better home. Three blocks over was the warehouse district. The seedy buildings were in long rows, some occupied, some not. The riders pulled to the curb just a short distance from the buildings and Savage and Keys rode forward toward them.

Breezy turned her head to put her mouth beside Steele's ear. "What are they doing?"

There was a moment of silence. He turned his head toward her, and her stomach dropped. Concentrated fury met her gaze. His eyes blazed at her. "Best not to talk to me until I calm down, Bree."

She had known if he saw the neighborhood he'd be upset. She squared her shoulders and opened her mouth to protest. He hadn't been there. He didn't know the first thing about her life without him. She couldn't make the kind of money it would take to live in a better neighborhood, and sooner or later his money would have run out and she would have had to move. By being careful, she'd been able to live just on the fringe, save money, so she could move them when Zane needed to go to school.

He shook his head. "I have no problem pulling your ass off the bike and across my knee. Right here. Right now. I'm so fuckin' pissed I can't think straight and believe me, woman, when I tell you that doesn't happen to me. The thought of you sitting on all that money, exposing yourself and our baby to this, for the sake of your pride, I want to fucking beat your ass until you can't sit down for a month. So don't talk to me right now." He turned his face away from her.

She took a deep breath, anger rising at his accusation. Unfortunately, she knew he was right. He'd given her thousands of dollars. She could have found a better place, especially once she had Zane, but it hadn't made sense to waste what she had when she would need it when he went to school. She knew that wasn't the only reason. She'd been hurt, and she'd nursed that hurt. She kept it to the forefront so she wouldn't go looking for him. For Steele. The love of her life.

She wasn't the kind of woman to hold a grudge, and she couldn't sustain anger. Part of that, she knew, was because of her childhood and how helpless she had been. It had never mattered if she'd been angry. She hadn't dared voice it, or any other protest. She had learned to find other ways to make her life better. Anger hadn't been an emotion that was useful to her survival, so she'd discarded it early on.

She hadn't noticed that Steele was angry very often — as in never when they'd been together. She'd had more of a temper than he had in those days. She rubbed her hand on her thigh, wanting to apologize to him, but she didn't know how to tell him that saving that money had been a form of self-preservation. She'd needed to have pride to survive. Once Zane was born, she'd held on to it for emergencies. With the whole sum intact, she'd known if she ever saw Steele again, she could hand it all to him. So many reasons. None were good enough to risk their child's life in this neighborhood.

Breezy was almost so distracted by her guilt that she didn't see the man coming out of the shadows to approach Savage and Keys, who had stopped two buildings along the row. He handed something to Keys and took a small flat package in exchange. Keys gave him a small salute and waited until the man had gone to his own bike and disappeared up the street.

Steele had never turned off his motorcycle and he reached back and caught her hands, jerking them around him before moving forward with the rest of the group to the rows of buildings. They followed Keys and Savage, who drove past the first two rows straight to the middle building in the last row. Behind it was a stream, snaking its way through a deep carved gully and over jagged rocks and boulders.

The moment he shut down the bike, she slipped off, her legs weak and rubbery. She tried to pace away, needing a little space, knowing Steele was that upset with her, but he caught her wrist and pulled her back to him.

"Don't walk off."

"I was just going to stretch my legs a little bit." Her gaze was on Keys as he unlocked the rolling door and lifted it. They pushed their bikes inside and he closed the door as Savage flipped on a light switch.

The first thing she saw were colors proclaiming the space belonged to a club. A skull grinned eerily through a field of black roses and gun shells. Her heart dropped. Involuntarily, she took a step back, right into Steele. Both arms came up to cage her in. He rested a chin on her shoulder.

"I'm sorry I got upset, Bree. I just don't like the idea of you with a baby in this hellhole. I saw needles on the sidewalk and something in me just went south. It's called guilt and it's on me, not you. I drove you away."

She leaned back against him, hearing the regret in his voice. "To protect me, Steele, because that's what you do. And you were right. I didn't want to hear or admit it, but it was pride that kept me from spending money on a decent place. I wanted to keep hurting so I wouldn't go looking for you like one of those pathetic women who won't take no for an answer."

"You notice that when you came looking, baby, I pounced."

She turned her head and smiled at him. Even here, in this old warehouse with its smell of drugs and burnt something, he could make her feel wanted. She wrinkled her nose and inhaled again. Alarm skittered through her. "What is this place? It smells like burnt flesh." She couldn't help the suspicion. She'd been around the Swords since she was a child. She'd heard rumors about places like this.

"Yeah, Bree, you got it right. This is a place a club would take an enemy to extract information or to make a statement. I need information. They set a couple of Swords members to watch your apartment. I'm going to bring them here and ask them a few questions. We'll know where Zane is if they know. If not, we'll know who might be with him. Or if they've already sold him."

Alarm nearly choked her. "Sold him? What do you mean, *sold him*?" She spun around and clutched at his jacket, her nails nearly meeting her palm right through the material. "You think they sold him?"

He framed her face with his hands. "Take a breath, baby. I don't want to miss a possibility. Lana will go with you and a couple of guards into the apartment and get the things you want. You're not ever going back there after this, so this is your last opportunity. We've got the truck, so get what you want now."

"I'm not leaving. I might have a few questions of my own."

His expression turned hard. "You can't stay, Breezy, and don't give me any grief. I've got to do this and I want you safe."

"Well that's too damn bad. You aren't Zane's only parent. And I know Bridges better than you do. I know the right questions to ask."

"Bree, when we're on these kinds of runs, we have to know everyone works together.

You can't oppose me over every little thing."

She didn't feel as if this was a small thing. "If you're getting information, Steele, I should be there."

He shook his head, his eyes merciless steel pits. "No way, baby. I'm going to take them apart to get every bit of intelligence that I can from them. It won't be pretty, and it won't be humane, and I don't personally give a fuck. You will. You think you won't, but you will. You can't disconnect, and I've been doing that shit since I was seven. You'll ask me to stop, you'll beg me to stop, and I won't. You'll never look at me the same way again."

Her stomach lurched, not because he was implying he could take a human being apart but because she saw that he could. He would. He intended to do just that. Steele, no matter what, had always seemed to be a dangerous man, but not a cold-blooded killer. He'd tried to tell her, but she couldn't conceive of him being that.

"You said you were trained as an assassin. Was this part of your training?" Her voice came out shaky. A whisper. She didn't want to sound like that because she needed to hear anything the Swords guards could tell her, but this side of Steele scared her.

She didn't think he would ever hurt her, it

wasn't that. She could see that he was capable of compartmentalizing, shoving all emotion away and acting without any feelings. Disassociation. Her heart pounded as she looked around the large room. There were tools everywhere, and she could see that several chairs were bolted to the floor.

"Yes, it was part of my training. This isn't for you, Bree. I don't ever want you to be part of something like this, even if it's necessary that I do it. There's not a need for you to be here."

"I don't want to be," she said. "But what if something he says triggers a memory and I can ask him a question that will lead to Zane."

She pressed harder on her stomach. Was she really going to be part of this? What was wrong with her? Steele wouldn't back down or stop because she couldn't take it — and she knew herself — she would be screaming for him to stop the moment blood started flowing or a Swords guard started screaming.

"You'll know them, Breezy." He kissed the side of her neck. "You will have grown up around them."

"They probably raped me," she pointed out, trying to steel herself.

She felt his body go taut. His arms tightened around her, and his fingers, locked together at her waist, dug in. It probably hadn't been the best time to remind him of her childhood.

"It's not going to happen. You're leaving with Lana and two of the brothers."

She closed her eyes, wishing she wasn't such a coward. It wasn't right to leave Steele to do the dirty work. Zane was *their* son. She had a responsibility as well. She had told Steele she would do anything to get him back. He was willing, but . . .

"I hate myself right now, Steele."

"You're not the one asking questions, sweetheart. That would be me."

Could he sound any farther from her? He thought she was condemning him and blaming herself for not being able to stop him. She shook her head and turned, sliding her arms around his neck. "I hate myself because I'm not capable of being you, Steele. I'm forcing you to do all the dirty work to get Zane back for us. That's not right. It leaves you with the nightmares and gives me freedom to pretend I wasn't part of any decisions."

"You're not going to have to pretend, Bree." His voice was implacable. Cold. "You don't have a say in this. I wouldn't listen to you arguing with me about my decision. I'm going to take them both apart, and I'll know every single thing they know about Zane's disappearance. No one, not even you, the one person who might have influence over me, will be able to stop this. They took him from you. They have him somewhere. He's alone. He's terrified. I know what that's like. They shouldn't have taken my boy."

"I'm so sorry I couldn't stop them." She whispered the apology, tears burning behind her eyelids. This was bringing it all back to him, it had to be. The murder of his parents. The things they'd done to him. What things? He had said torture. Rape. Repeatedly. She hadn't asked questions; she didn't know how long it had gone on. He'd barely scraped the surface and she hadn't asked him questions because she could see it was making him sick. She'd done what she'd always done when Steele was upset: she'd turned his attention to her body.

Breezy pushed her forehead into his chest, desperate for air. "What if Bridges did sell him?" The idea made her want to vomit. "What if they're doing to him the things that happened to you, Steele? Our baby. Why didn't I have a gun? I should have bought a gun. I should have used that money to find a safer place, one they couldn't get into." She was babbling, and she couldn't stop. The pressure in her chest was enormous, so much so that she thought her heart was shattering.

"Stop it."

Steele's low command startled her. His hand went under her chin and he jerked her head up, forcing her gaze to meet his. There was that arctic cold there and little else.

"This won't help. You have to stop, Bree. You can't go there. We have one job, and that's to find him and take him back. I'll kill anyone in my way. I'll take apart anyone who can give me information and won't when I ask politely for it. We will get him back. When we do, I'm going to beat the shit out of Bridges and Junk and then I'm going to kill them. I intend to make them both feel every pain you ever felt in your life, and if they hurt Zane, it will go twice as bad for them. There isn't anything you or anyone else can say to sway me from that path. Ask any of my brothers, nothing stops me. No one stops me. I got the name Steele because I'm unbending. Zane is coming home. You hang on to that."

She concentrated on his strength. Steele was unbending. That's what he'd told her, and she could see that trait in him. She might not like it all the time, but right now, in this moment, she needed that from him.

The Swords would make the mistake of taunting him, just as they would have had she been asking the questions. They would try to scare her with tales of what was happening to Zane, and she would fall apart. Steele wouldn't. She could see that.

"You're going to go with Lana —"

"I don't need anyone but Lana with me," she said softly. "Keep everyone else with you. Lana can keep us safe. She's like you. I've seen it in her."

Lana was beautiful, but more than once, Breezy had been uneasy in her presence. The woman gave off a deadly, dangerous vibe if you were around her for very long. During her time riding with the Swords, Lana was never far from Ice's side. They rode together, and Ice made it known that no one touched Lana. Ordinarily, that wouldn't have been good enough. The other members would have harassed her, touched her as she walked by, groping and stroking, making lewd comments, maybe even pulling at her clothing. No one did. That said it all about Lana.

"I'm sending two brothers. I won't lose you, Bree." He framed her face in his hands. "I'm a killer, Breezy. That's who you have in your bed. I have more blood on these hands than you can possibly conceive of, and I touch you with them. I'm not losing you over this. Just know that. The bullshit you told me about how I would let you go if you wanted to leave is just that — bullshit."

She knew better but it didn't matter because she loved him. She loved him as the healer, the doctor who protected everyone and looked out for them. She loved this man, the one with the strength to do whatever was necessary to get their son home safely. No policemen could find him before they killed him or sold him. She knew that.

"When I was fourteen years old, my father gave me to one of his friends. I'd never been with anyone, and Bridges owed them a favor. I was what he wanted, and he gave me to him and walked away. He hurt me, Steele. He hurt me beyond anything I thought was possible. My father laughed when he tossed me on the floor in front of him, broken and bloody. He got up and got beer. They sat around the living room drinking while I lay in front of them."

"Damn it," he whispered.

"I tried to go to the cops. It was the biggest mistake of my life. My punishment was Bridges letting that man and his two friends do what they wanted with me short of killing me. I couldn't get up for a couple of weeks and I was lucky I lived through the punishment. I know the police aren't going to be able to help us. I know you have to do this to get our son back."

His eyes never left hers as she told him what her father had let happen to her. Those dark blue eyes went so dark they appeared black, gleaming at her like a vicious cat's, growing colder and more predatory with every word she said. His hands never wavered though, framing her face gently, his thumb stroking caresses over her skin.

"I'm telling you this so you'll understand that I know what you're doing is necessary and I'm ashamed that I can't do it for us, that I'm leaving that to you. I'll never blame you for something that you did to get our son back. Not ever."

"You will give me the names of those men."

Her heart clenched hard. Her man. He believed in vengeance. "Steele." She said his name softly to deter him. "This is about Zane, our innocent sweet little boy."

"This is about disgusting pedophiles who would hurt a fourteen-year-old girl or take a two-year-old boy from his mother by force."

She'd never thought of her father's friends as pedophiles, mostly because at fourteen, she was already so old in her mind she didn't think of herself as a child. "Just get us our son back and we'll call it good."

"Give me their fuckin' names, Breezy. I'm not asking again."

She knew what his brothers were talking about now. She was coming up against the unbending man. He wouldn't give her this, and she had to yield. She wasn't protecting them, she just didn't want Steele to put himself in harm's way to extract whatever vengeance he felt was necessary on her behalf.

"Donk, Favor and Riddle."

"Donk is Bridges's sergeant at arms. Code's been looking into him. He's disappeared as well, so the general consensus is that he is with Bridges." He dropped his hands from her face, but his arm locked her in place, a bar across her back.

"That doesn't surprise me. You know Donk. He's a brute and he likes hurting people."

"You mean women. He likes hurting women and kids. He kicks them around. He does the same with the prospects because they can't fight back. He's a pussy, Bree. He wouldn't have lasted ten minutes in one of our schools."

Breezy bit her lip to keep from arguing that point. Donk was a huge man. Yeah, he had a beer gut, but he was strong, and he liked to punch anyone who looked at him wrong. Quite a few members of the chapter were afraid of him.

"If Donk is with Bridges, then Favor and Riddle know where they are, and there isn't a doubt in my mind they'll visit them at some point. Favor, Riddle and Donk hang together all the time. What one does, they all do."

"That's good, Bree. I'll put Code on it." He bent his head and brushed a kiss over the top of her head. "Take off now." His gaze went beyond her. "Lana, I'm trusting you with what means the most to me."

"I won't leave her side, you know that, Steele." Lana very gently caught Breezy's upper arm and tugged her away from Steele. "Who's the bait?"

"Master's going in. Preacher will watch his back. You hang back with Bree until they tell you they've cleared the entire area. The others will be close if something goes wrong."

Lana shrugged. "I can handle a couple of Swords idiots with my eyes closed."

"I'm not worried about the ones we know are there. I'm worried about the ones we aren't aware of. Don't be cocky."

"Steele, you know I'm always cocky. Got

my brothers, don't have a worry." She blew him a kiss and started to step away, tugging on Bree's arm.

Steele reached out and caught the front of Breezy's jacket, jerking her back to him so hard she nearly stumbled into him. She looked up, blinking, and he took her mouth. He didn't start gentle. He was rough. Demanding. Hot as hell. He ended gently, pulling her close to him, his mouth moving over hers, his tongue stroking love into her mouth until she wanted to cry because, even now, she felt that. Even now when he had to become the killer, she felt his love surrounding her.

She'd told him once that she loved him, and he'd shut down. She watched his expression go from happiness to pure ice, to the mask. He had turned away from her, and she'd never repeated the sentiment — and she had no intention of making that mistake again. He was never going to tell her, never going to say it aloud, but it didn't matter because she *felt* love in his every touch or kiss.

She kissed him back, trying to convey the fact that she was with him every step of the way. She might not be able to do the things necessary to get their son back, so she was doubly grateful that he could. He lifted his head and a shiver went down her spine. He had that look again, the cold, deadly one. She cupped the side of his jaw for a brief moment and then turned to go out with Lana.

"Thank you," Lana whispered under her breath as she shortened her steps to walk beside Breezy. "He needed you to understand. He would say it didn't matter, but you're the one person whose opinion of him does matter."

"I'm ashamed I can't do it myself and that he has to be alone."

"He's not alone, Bree." Lana handed her the helmet. "He's got all of us. We're like him. We can do whatever needs to be done. We've only got you, Anya and Blythe who can't. We're happy we have you. We need you. All three of you. We're hoping you pull us a little more into the light."

Breezy had never thought of it that way. "Is that what you think I do for Steele?"

Lana swung onto the bike. It was Ink's. No Sword would ever trust his bike to a woman, not even his old lady, and Lana was not Ink's woman. Lana had her own bike, but because they knew they would have times when they needed extra hands, she had opted to leave hers at home. It was obvious that Lana and Alena were an integral part of Torpedo Ink.

"I know you do that for him. He was desolate without you. Steele's a strong man and we all rely on him. It wasn't the same after you were gone."

Breezy wrapped her arms around Lana and they were moving fast down the road, straight toward the block where her apartment was. Her heart began to pound. She had learned some self-defense from Steele, but clearly it hadn't done any good when her father and brother broke in. She needed to be more of an asset in situations like this one.

Her breath left in a rush. What was she thinking? More like this? She couldn't consider living the club life again. What kind of responsible mother would that make her? She was in this situation because she'd been part of a club. It was Torpedo Ink, another club, helping to get Zane back. Torpedo Ink had contacted yet another club in New Mexico, to aid them with a place where prisoners were taken to interrogate them.

Before they turned onto Breezy's block, Lana turned onto the street that ran parallel. She drove right into a driveway and then turned around and went back out onto the street. Between the houses, they could see Breezy's building.

Bree watched as Master sauntered up the broken, uneven walkway to the door of her apartment. The door had chipped paint, and all around the other apartments on the lower story, ones like hers that had a semblance of a front yard, litter and needles and sometimes dirty condoms were thrown around. Drug deals were common right out in front on the sidewalk. She wanted to groan and hide her face, she was so ashamed.

Master opened the door with the key she'd given him, looked carefully around and disappeared inside.

"What if they're watching and someone goes in the back way?" Breezy asked, anxiety beating at her. She didn't want anything to happen to Master. She should have told Steele the records and photographs weren't worth anyone's life. Oh. Wait. She had. He hadn't listened. That had evidently been one of those times when he made the rules.

There was silence. It stretched out for minutes, each second ticking away so slowly she felt the pull on her nerves, but like Lana, she remained still. Lana had slipped off the bike and helped her off, indicating to her to remove the helmet. She kept her eyes glued to the apartment, looking between the buildings to see. A man emerged between two structures to cross the street, angling toward Bree's apartment, his hands in his pockets. He glanced up and down the lane.

Lana had parked the bike in the shadows, and Breezy knew not to move or they'd draw the sentry's eye in spite of the fact that they were a distance away and one street over. The newcomer was wearing Swords colors. She held her breath. He turned and looked to his left, letting out a low whistle.

The streetlights had long ago been smashed and no one had bothered to replace them, but it didn't matter. She recognized him. The Swords had given him the name Bruiser, not because he liked to fight but because he bruised easily and was very clumsy. His closest friend was Dart, a man who was very skilled with a dart and often used them in fights. She would bet her last dollar that Dart was there right now, circling around behind the house to go in from the back.

Lana didn't move, nor did she say a word, so Bree kept silent as well. Lana appeared completely unconcerned by the fact that Bruiser was entering the front door and at the same moment, most likely, Dart was going through the back, trapping Master between them.

A few minutes later Lana touched her ear where she wore a tiny radio and then smirked. "Master took them both out easily. He's called for the truck."

Seconds later, an old beat-up truck with a deep bed pulled up in front of the apartments. It fit right in with the dilapidated building and the mostly broken-down cars lining the dirty street. Breezy knew the engine in that truck was in top condition and ran like a dream. Transporter slid out from behind the steering wheel and sauntered up to the walkway as if he owned the entire building. A few minutes later, he came out with Master, Dart between them. Dart looked more drunk than hurt. They deposited him in the back of the truck and they weren't gentle about it. Bruiser was next. Breezy winced when the man hit the bed of the truck hard enough that it made noise.

Transporter didn't seem to mind. He jumped up into the bed, bent over and worked for a few minutes, presumably to secure the two men. He began tossing things on top of them. Old, torn boxes and other rubbish that had been in the back of the truck. He leapt out when he was satisfied and saluted Lana and then got into the cab. They waited for a minute.

"Preacher's given the all clear," Lana said aloud. She glanced at Breezy. "He's lying up on the roof across the street with a rifle. He would have killed the Swords to get the boys out. They were safe, Bree."

Breezy let out her breath. "I don't think I have nerves of steel the way all of you do," she admitted. "And you can all go for hours, days. I'm exhausted and need to sleep; I know I can't because time is important. I wish I was more like all of you."

"No, you don't," Lana said. "Never wish for that, Bree. You're perfect the way you are. We don't need more of us. We're . . . flawed. Every single one of us. There's no living on our own. We don't know the first thing about how to live with society's bullshit rules. Blythe works with us all the time, but we forget them. There are too many rules and they seem so unnecessary."

The two of them walked toward the apartment building. "Like what?"

"Clothes. People make such a big deal about clothes. What others wear or don't wear. Are they designer? Supposedly your clothes say things about you. It's all bullshit. I don't even feel good in clothes, they hurt my skin. And you have to know if a beach is swimsuit optional. You have to know if it's topless or not topless. What's the big deal?"

"Steele said you wanted to open a clothing store."

"If we have to wear clothes, I'd like to choose what I'm going to wear. People are so hung up on what their neighbor is wearing or not wearing, they aren't paying any attention to their own lives."

Breezy laughed. "That makes sense."

"And Blythe says people are really hung up about sex. Are they? Are you? She says they have so many inhibitions that sometimes they can't even enjoy it." Lana opened the door to the apartment.

It was one of those moments, after seeing Steele's house, that Breezy worried that Lana would judge her for living in a really bad place. She always kept it neat, but right now, her things were smashed and broken. It was obvious to her that the two Swords members had been using her apartment to stay in while they waited for her, or someone else, to return.

"I'm not, no, but that's because I understand Steele and his need to have all of you protecting us. He feels vulnerable, doesn't he?"

Lana nodded. "It's better if we're close. No one can hurt us, or the one we're with. It's just so much safer and we can relax."

She shrugged. "I guess others don't feel vulnerable. Blythe says that to most people, having sex is very intimate, an expression of love between two people, and adding others around takes away from that, which I don't understand at all."

Breezy shot her a smile. She wasn't the person to ask. She didn't know about a good relationship any more than Lana or Steele did. She'd grown up in the Swords, and apparently they weren't even like other clubs. "I don't know much about that, having only had it with Steele, but I do remember feeling safer when his friends were close. It's always intimate with Steele." She was surprised that it was true. She did feel safer with members of Torpedo Ink close.

She stood in the middle of the living room, hands on her hips. "They really made a mess, didn't they?"

Lana toed a broken chair with the end of her boot. "This was deliberate, honey. They were sending you a message if you came back here."

"I got the message when they took Zane."

"Let's get your things and get out of here," Lana said. "You can rest at the motel."

Breezy agreed. She wanted out of there as fast as possible. "The photographs are in my bedroom in the top drawer along with his birth certificate," she said and led the way.

Twelve

Bruiser was a screamer. He was the one Steele was certain was going to break first. Dart's eyes were all over the place, but he was fairly stoic. That wouldn't last. Steele was far too good at his job. He had begun to study anatomy and the human body when his trainers had first discovered that he was exceptional when it came to healing. It hadn't bought him any favors. Not one.

His training as a killer had begun when he was four years old. He had been given to both male and female pedophiles at the same age. He was beaten and brutalized. He was raped and tortured. At seven his sexual training began, mostly to please women. Then men. Then they discovered he retained all information and was good at healing. He'd been given to his first doctor, a close friend of Sorbacov, who shared him. The man happened to have a problem he couldn't solve, and Steele had solved it for him. At seven.

After that, the doctor was a regular who wanted to talk as much as he wanted to fuck up a child. He was the first to educate him as a doctor. By ten he had outgrown the doctor and needed someone with more knowledge. At his friend's request, Sorbacov shared him with another doctor.

Through it all, Steele continued to learn how to kill. He mastered weapons and hand-to-hand combat. He was good with poisons because he retained any information given to him. He knew what common household cleaners would cause the most pain when he poured them down throats or splashed them on skin. They were in a warehouse used essentially as a torture house for interrogation, and that meant, with all the tools and car shit around, he had easy access to even worse chemicals.

He knew where, on the human body, he could inflict the most pain and still keep someone alive. He had no problem visiting that on either of the two men. Bruiser had made the mistake of taunting him, just as he knew the idiot would. They were so predictable. Screams didn't bother him. He barely paid attention to the sound, just enough to hear a breaking point. If it wasn't there, and no questions were answered, he took it up a notch. If they were at a breaking point, he took it down.

"This isn't going to stop for you. I can keep it up all night, all day and all week. I don't give a shit. If I get tired, which I doubt, one of the brothers will take over while I lie right there and take a nap." He indicated the long table where a carburetor had been laid out. "Paid two weeks on the place."

His tone never changed. It wouldn't. His pulse wouldn't change either. He'd buried his emotions deep. These men were part of the club that had taken his two-year-old son. He'd kill them all, one by one, until he got his boy back. That would start next if they couldn't get to Bridges.

Torpedo Ink was good at what they did. They'd acted as assassins for their country and Sorbacov for well over twenty years. Most had been sent out as teenagers. Most had started killing, striking back at the men and women who'd abused them, when they'd not even been ten. They knew killing and they were comfortable with it. Far too comfortable, and all of them knew it. This was their element. What they knew best.

He'd been at them for going on three hours now. He sent a deliberate grin to Maestro. "I hope the Guns and Skull club used really good soundproofing. It's going to get a lot louder in here as the day goes on."

Bruiser squeaked and shook his head so hard it looked as if he might break his neck. Steele let the smile slip as he turned back to the two men hanging from the chains. Both were naked. There was water right beneath them, their bare feet in it, but it did nothing to blot out the smell of urine.

"Would you like to tell me again what you planned to do with my son? Or my woman? I'm really interested in knowing. Since you don't want to tell me Zane's location, entertain me with your plans for them both. I've forgotten what you said. What was that, Bruiser? Dart? You remember?"

Steele picked up the cattle prod. "Not as effective as the battery Mechanic is hooking up for me. I'm getting tired of this little thing."

Bruiser screamed and screamed, the sounds of agony filling the wide warehouse the Guns and Skull club had made into a garage just in case law enforcement questioned them. Few did, and Steele hoped they kept it that way. He hadn't even gotten started. A cattle prod was nothing in his arsenal of tools.

"Let's start again."

He was patient. He'd learned patience in a hard school. While he'd been with any of the four doctors/surgeons he'd trained under, he had tried developing ways to combat infection. He had stolen antibiotics and done everything in his power to save the children in that prison of a school he'd lived in.

Their lessons weren't about etiquette like the other schools. They didn't learn manners and what kinds of rules society cared about. They learned languages, so they could be sent out to kill. They learned sex, so they could be sent out to kill. He'd learned to become a doctor, so he could be sent out to kill. Everything they did was for that one purpose — their only purpose. No one expected that any of them would survive, let alone go free.

Sorbacov knew they were killing their instructors, the pedophiles who were there to commit whatever atrocity they chose without fear of retaliation. He knew what the children were doing, but he didn't know how. He set up cameras throughout the school, so that every room was covered. He'd done so with the intent to blackmail any participant that might later oppose his chosen candidate. Films of them as children being raped still circulated among child predators, but Sorbacov had never caught any of them on film killing their wardens.

That was all Czar. His brains. His plans. He had slowly recruited those children he believed wouldn't betray the others — and they hadn't. All of them had been interrogated at one time or another, and those sessions had been pure torture. None of them had broken.

"I don't know where the kid is. Bridges took him. He's in the wind," Bruiser sobbed. "You have to believe me. I'm telling the truth."

Steele shook his head slowly. "The thing is, Bruiser, I don't have to believe you. You told me that you were going to personally take my son and sell him to a guy you know who loves little kids. You told me you would then go after Breezy and do all sorts of things to her — some, by the way, I'm not certain you could actually do. So, no, I don't believe you when you tell me you don't know where Zane is. We're just going to have to keep going."

"No. No. Really, I didn't have anything to do with it," Bruiser sobbed. "You can't blame us. We weren't going to help him."

"Didn't you just tell me you were going to shove your dick down my woman's throat until she choked on it? Didn't you say that to me?"

Bruiser opened his mouth and the cattle prod was pushed inside. Dart's body shook as he watched his friend's face contort. As he watched the body nearly seize with shock as Bruiser took the prod to the back of his throat.

"Steele, for God's sake, he doesn't know shit. He was talking crap, that's all. Bridges was higher than a kite when he came back to the clubhouse with Breezy's kid in tow. He acted like he won the lottery. Ever since Habit's been gone, we've had to lick his boots. He told Lizard to get Candy and bring her to the clubhouse. While he waited he told us that he had you by the balls and he was forcing Breezy to kill you and Czar both. He kept laughing and doing lines of coke. That boy made a sound, and Bridges lambasted him across the face. Even Junk didn't go near Bridges, he was so fucked up."

Steele could hear the ring of truth in Dart's voice. It didn't shock him that Dart told the truth about Bridges. He couldn't imagine how anyone would want to back a man who put himself before his brothers. Habit had run a trafficking ring, but he'd put his brothers first. Bridges had no idea how to do that. He was too far gone on booze and drugs. Had Czar gone that route, any one of the Torpedo Ink members would have put him down. They would have forced him to dry out first to see if it worked, but if it didn't he would be dead.

"Not our fault," Bruiser sobbed when he could find his voice. "We didn't have nothing to do with it."

"You were sitting on a stakeout waiting for my woman to come back to her apartment, or for one of us to show up. You planned on killing Master, didn't you? You had your gun out." Steele kept his tone mild.

Maestro handed him a bottle of water, and Steele opened it and drank. Both prisoners stared at the water, unable to take their eyes from the bottle with the condensation on it. Bruiser's tongue lolled, and Dart's touched his dry, cracked lips.

Dart heaved a sigh. "We were following orders. We had no choice."

"Bruiser here told me all about how he planned on raping her. The details were very well-thought-out. Seemed to me he was fixating on her and what he could do to her," Steele said as he applied the cattle prod to the man's most precious part. He was casual about it, as if he wasn't in the least bit even thinking about it.

Bruiser's screams hit a note Steele had never heard before. He circled around behind the shrieking man. "Seems to me, Bruiser, you thought you were going to put your filthy dick in my woman. I don't take kindly to that shit, do I, Maestro?"

"No, Steele, you don't," Maestro replied.

"You said you were going to put your dick up her ass, didn't you, Bruiser?"

Bruiser began screaming before the cattle prod even touched him, let alone was applied to any area he'd been threatening on Breezy.

A couple of the other Torpedo Ink members snickered. "Breezy's been off-limits since Steele laid eyes on her," Keys said. "Isn't that right, Ink? You notice any man touched her even before she was with him, that man got the holy hell beat out of him, cuz I noticed that shit. But I got a healthy dose of self-preservation that's clearly missing in these two."

"Everyone knew, even then, you didn't touch Breezy," Mechanic agreed.

"Guess they must have missed that memo," Maestro said. "You get that now, Bruiser? Maybe a little late for you, but hopefully you get it now."

Bruiser was sobbing and nodding his head up and down.

"I been thinking on this for a little while now," Keys said. "Wondering about how a man that protective of his woman might feel about someone taking his boy. His son. If it was me, I'd walk through hell to get that man. Follow him right down into flames so I could fuck him up. That about right, Steele?"

"The minute Lizard walked in with Candy, Bridges grabbed her by the hair, shoved the kid into her arms and went out, barking orders at everyone," Dart said. "He didn't tell any of us where he was going, but once he had Candy in the truck with Junk, he came back and told Bruiser and I to come here and if Breezy came back, to teach her a lesson. A *hard* lesson."

"Where was Donk? He's never far from Bridges." Steele's voice was mild. Deceptively so. The thought of Dart and Bruiser teaching his woman a lesson of any kind made the monster in him show his teeth.

"He was still in the clubhouse. He'd been drinking with Bridges and snorting cocaine. The two talked in whispers and then Bridges left. Lizard jumped up and ran to his truck, probably worried Bridges would kill Candy he was so far gone. Donk was still there. I think he was waiting for Riddle and Favor."

Just the names of the three men who had

raped Breezy when she was fourteen made the monster emerge even more. He felt cold inside. Cold outside. Just plain ice. There were no compassionate feelings in him at all, as if his personality had split and this one had come forward to allow him to do everything necessary to survive. He remembered his monster. He had needed him, the block of ice that couldn't be stopped.

"Did Donk follow Bridges?"

"We left. I gathered my shit and got out of there. Donk was getting crazy with the cocaine and I don't like being around when he's like that. Bruiser and I headed out."

"Have you heard from Bridges?"

Dart hesitated just that fraction of a second too long and retaliation was swift and brutal. Steele wasn't playing around. He was on the move now, Code gathering intel his way and Steele taking it forcibly. One of these two men would put him on the right road to finding Zane.

When Dart stopped screaming, Steele looked at him impassively. "My son, Dart. He's out there somewhere scared and alone without his mother. He's with a man who beat the shit out of his daughter daily and gave her to three of his friends to be raped when she was only fourteen years old. I don't know about you, but that's not a man

I want my son with. Not even for a minute or two, let alone this long. So, if I were you, I'd just tell me whatever I want to know and get it over, cuz this isn't going to stop."

Dart coughed and spat blood and then shook his head. "I got no call to love Bridges. If I knew something worthwhile, I'd tell you. He called me a time or two looking to see if Breezy showed up. When I told him no, he cussed me out and hung up."

Steele glanced at Mechanic, who quickly picked up the two cell phones and walked away where he had a quieter space to get into them.

"Need your passcode," Steele said to Dart.

Dart gave it immediately.

Steele called the code out to Mechanic and waited for the man to nod his acknowledgment that it was correct.

Steele touched Bruiser with the cattle prod without triggering it. Bruiser's entire body shuddered. "Need yours as well."

Bruiser broke into another sob. "I'm sorry. I'm really sorry."

"I don't give a fuck, just give me your code."

Bruiser turned his head to look at Dart, his eyes wild. "I'm sorry, man, I had to do it."

"Do what?" Dart asked. Involuntarily he moved his body to try to ease the strain of the chains he hung in, but it only hurt more, and he couldn't stop the groan that slipped out.

"The fucking code, Bruiser. You don't give it to me now, I'm going to slit your belly open and watch your coward's intestines slither all over the floor." Again, Steele's voice was low and mild, completely at odds with his words, but that only made it worse.

Bruiser called the passcode out loudly and then burst into loud sobs. Steele ignored him and wandered back toward Mechanic, who was moving quickly through Bruiser's phone. He scowled down at the text messages he was reading, and then handed it to Steele.

Steele took the phone and walked back to stand in front of the two men. "This is very interesting, Bruiser. Seems you had a very special arrangement with Bridges. You two were buddies, who knew?" He nudged Dart. "You know that, Dart? You know that Bruiser here, your best friend, had a close relationship with Bridges?"

Dart frowned but he didn't say anything, instead waited to see where Steele was going with it.

"Bruiser here says to Bridges he's willing

to do whatever it takes as long as Bridges gives him Breezy. You really wanted my woman, didn't you, Bruiser? Seems Breezy pissed you off by choosing me instead of you. Bridges promised her to you, way back then?"

"He did." Bruiser nodded over and over. "I did everything he asked, and he still gave her to you. He said when you were tired of her, I could have her."

Dart glared at him. "What the fuck were you doing for him?"

Bruiser shook his head, sobbing, trying to squirm out of the chains.

"He was skimming drugs and money from the club, giving what he took to Bridges," Steele said. "He stupidly admits it right here in his texts, throwing it in Bridges's face as a threat. Bridges comes back saying he had nothing to do with skimming, and the club would cut off Bruiser's balls if they found out."

"No fucking way," Dart said, but the shock on his face confirmed that he knew Steele wasn't making it up.

Using the cattle prod, Steele pushed at the two spheres hanging between Bruiser's legs. "Not very big, but still there. You really are a dumb ass, aren't you? But that's not the interesting part. Bruiser, what did you tell Bridges you'd do to get my woman?"

Bruiser swung his body in a complete rejection of admission.

Steele shook his head. "This is the most fucked-up club I've ever come across." He showed the phone to Dart. "I'm reading this shit. I couldn't make it up if I tried. Bridges tells Bruiser if he wants Breezy, he has to kill you, Dart, because you're becoming a pain in the ass with your continual opposition to Bridges's lifestyle and presidency. Apparently, if you question your president or call for another election, that makes you treasonous and it's okay to put out a hit on you."

Steele pulled the phone out from under Dart's nose and switched his attention to Bruiser. "You agree with that? You think because Dart questioned Bridges's sanity, that he deserved killing?"

Bruiser let out another deep sob and then shook his head wildly.

"Now that's just a glaring lie, Bruiser, and you know it. It says right here in your reply to Bridges that Dart has been talking shit about him for months. You've given him the names of every man in the chapter wanting to take Bridges down. That was nice of you. You really are his little bitch. That makes me think you know more than you're telling me, Bruiser, about where Bridges is right this minute."

"I don't. I'm not." Bruiser made the denial looking wild-eyed at the phone.

Steele shook his head as he thumbed through the texts. "Says he'll do you no problem, Dart, just reiterates that Breezy is his after. Bridges goes on to say she might need a few hard lessons, and look here, Bruiser, you were more than happy to oblige." Steele looked up from the phone. "You plan to beat the shit out of my woman? Is that what this means?"

"You're saying that Bruiser really agreed to kill me?" Dart demanded. He couldn't believe it, not even after Steele had shown him the texts.

"Kill you. Beat the shit out of Breezy. And there's more. So much more, isn't there, Bruiser? No wonder he sent you here. You've been his private little bitch for years. Stealing from the club. Spying on your friend. Spying on your brothers. Doing whatever he wanted. But I especially love this. You'll personally, and that's *personally,* but with one *L,* slit that fucker's son's throat right in front of her if Bridges will give you that privilege."

Steele looked up at Bruiser. "I assume the 'fucker' you're referring to is me. You're going to kill your best friend, presumably when his back is turned. Beat the shit out of Breezy and rape her in every way possible. Slit my son's throat in front of her, and all this is to get favors with Bridges. Nice, man, really nice. You really are a piece of shit, aren't you?"

"Get me out of these chains," Dart said. "I'll kill him myself."

"Sorry, can't give that to you, Dart." Steele stepped closer to Bruiser. "He's going to die slow. But first, you piece of shit, you'd better tell me where Bridges is."

"I don't know. I don't know!" Bruiser screamed.

Steele glanced at Savage and nodded slightly. He admired Dart in some ways. The man rode with the wrong club. He should have chosen better. He rode for his colors and backed his brothers, but whatever his personal code was, it included trafficking women and children, and that wasn't okay with Torpedo Ink. Dart didn't know a thing about Bridges, but Bruiser did. Savage stepped up behind Dart and cut his throat, the blade slicing deep. It was fast and quiet, Dart never even suspecting that Savage was behind him.

Bruiser screamed, a high-pitched wail. He fought the chains with almost superhuman strength and then subsided abruptly, his bladder letting go for the third time. Steele just watched him impassively until he quieted to a soft sobbing.

"We just carried out your intentions for you, Bruiser. It was merciful. You've been his best friend for what? Twenty years? Since you were kids? That's the way he always told it to everyone. Since you were in grade school."

Bruiser continued to weep, shaking his head as he did, looking down at the floor and the blood mixing with the water under Dart's body.

"Where is he?" Steele asked quietly. It was going to be a very long day. He knew Bruiser wasn't going to give up the information easily. Somehow, in his twisted brain, he still thought he was going to get out of this with his plans intact.

Steele was rarely wrong. He'd thought Bruiser would break first, but Dart had sacrificed in order to try to save his friend from suffering. The brotherhood at work.

Breezy was very cognizant of the fact that they were traveling on mainly motorcycles and she didn't want to fill the truck with unnecessary sentimental stuff. It wasn't that she had lots of beautiful things. She didn't have beautiful things. She had *necessary* things, but she had managed to acquire them, piece by piece, from hard work. She looked around the bedroom. There wasn't much there in the way of furniture, but she hadn't needed much. The room was small. She could walk across it in several long strides. The carpet was old and threadbare with several stains in it.

She was comparing this tiny apartment on a bad side of town to Steele's multimillion-dollar house, which was all white and pristine. She didn't know the first thing about caring for a house like that. It was absurd to think she could live there. She sank down on the edge of the bed and buried her face in her hands.

"Honey, talk to me. We're going to get Zane back. Everyone's looking, and Czar's called in favors from other clubs we've helped. We're owed a lot of favors. We'll find him."

Breezy shook her head and looked up at Lana. "I'm just so confused right now. I swore I'd never live in a club, and I sure as hell wasn't going to raise my son in one, but here I am, letting a club risk everything to get my son back."

"We're not risking everything," Lana objected. "We have certain advantages."

"Steele's risking everything. His soul. I don't know. He's doing things a doctor, a man as sensitive as he is, shouldn't ever do."

"He's done them all his life. He's had to, for his own survival, and for ours."

"Maybe, and then there's that house. Have you seen that house?"

Lana flashed her a smile and sank down onto the bed beside her. "It's a gorgeous house."

"It's too much. I don't know what he was thinking, buying that house."

"He was thinking he was getting the best he could for his woman. He might not tell you how he feels about you, but he definitely has no problems showing you."

"You know about that? That he won't say he loves me?" Breezy met Lana's eyes, wanting to find something there, but she didn't know what she was looking for.

Lana nodded. "He told me what an ass he'd been to you. The moment you were out of his sight, he wanted to run after you. He forced you to leave because he was afraid you'd get hurt or killed in the war between our clubs. He knew we were going to take down the international president and that the Swords would always be looking for us."

"And my age," Breezy said. "He was upset

when he learned my age."

Lana nodded. "None of us guessed you were that young. You were always so calm when chaos reigned in the clubhouse. No matter how big a party was, you had the food and the drinks ready. The other women looked to you for their orders. You took care of problems and looked after the kids. You never seemed to get upset. There was no giggling or teenage behavior. Never."

"I grew up knowing if I made a mistake, no matter how small, I would get beaten. It was expected of me to take care of all things in the clubhouse or at home no matter whether Bridges told me about it or not. If I drew attention to myself in any way, he would beat me or hand me over to his friends. I was lucky in that no one could just put their hands on me. Bridges had to approve, and he was stingy. Growing up that way, I had to think like an adult."

"Let Steele spoil you, Breezy. You gave him everything when you were with him. You met his every need, and that's nearly impossible for anyone to do for anyone, but you managed. Let him have the chance to give back. He wants to give you a huge house and let you do anything you want with it, let him. Just remember he needs . . . clean."

Breezy nodded. "I'm very aware. Fortunately, again growing up the way I did, I prefer clean as well. Maybe not like him, but it's easy enough, at least it was until he decided we needed a mansion the size of Texas."

Lana burst out laughing. "I'm sure he'll hire cleaners to come in."

"They'll need to live there permanently and work twenty-four-seven." Breezy rubbed her hand over her face. "He's told me a little about his childhood. About the things that happened to you. I'm trying to understand what it was like for him to have his need for such a completely ascetic home. The walls are white. The floors and ceiling, the stairway. It's beautiful, but every speck of dirt shows, and there's Zane. He has to be allowed to be a little boy, and honestly, Steele's obsessed with cleanliness."

Lana sighed. "You can't imagine what the conditions in the basement of that school were like. It was really a prison they'd made into a school. We were shoved into the basement. The floor was filthy, covered in dirt and feces. There were rats down there and cockroaches. When we were returned from one of their sessions, we were bloody and raw, usually from several different areas on our bodies, front and back, so whichever way we lay, we were lying in filth and germs were multiplying. Often they used knives to cut us or whips, so open wounds. It was the worst nightmare possible for a boy like Steele. He felt responsibility, even when he was just very little. Something in him *needed* to help all of us."

Breezy's stomach churned and she pressed a hand to it. She couldn't imagine Steele as a little boy in those conditions, let alone surrounded by wounded or dying children.

"Sometimes they left dead bodies down there with us for a few days to teach us a lesson. I was never certain what the lesson was, but it added to Steele's distress and sense of guilt. He's so protective now, I can't imagine how that trait will manifest itself with you and Zane. He'll go crazy trying to keep you safe. The fact that one of our worst enemies has his son has to be killing him right now."

Breezy sighed. She knew it was killing her, and the fact that Steele was forced to do horrible things to get information for them was making it worse. She hadn't been able to protect either one of them.

"If Absinthe can get truth out of people, why didn't you use him?"

"Absinthe's gift is extremely hard on him. None of us know how it works. Simple things, like pushing a suggestion into someone's mind, are easy enough; forcing truth when someone is resisting can damage him. There's levels of resistance, and what we need now is too important — you can bet there will be major resistance. Absinthe wanted to come, but both Czar and Steele refused him."

Breezy pressed her fingers to her temples. There was no saving Steele from his task. "Lana, I love Steele with everything in me, but there's things I don't know if I can handle. He's pushing me hard and I have this inclination to give him whatever he wants, but I don't know if I can give in about the club. I'm sorry if that hurts, because I like you. I like all of you, well, the ones I know fairly well, but that doesn't mean I trust the club life."

"It was unfortunate that you arrived when we were entertaining the Demons. That chapter has been trying to thank us for helping the wife of their president out of a bad situation. They brought women because they knew most of Torpedo Ink was single. I know Steele looked bad coming out from under those women but —"

"He explained that to me. I choose to accept his explanation." Breezy hesitated and then took the plunge. "He had photographs of me on his phone. Dozens of them."

Lana frowned at her. "That's a good thing, right? He kept them because you matter."

"Some of them were of us in very intimate positions. I had no idea we were being photographed. He never told me. He likes to have photos. I think he even needs it."

"Does it matter to you?"

Breezy rubbed the pad of her finger over her lips. Back and forth. Thinking it through. "It doesn't bother me to have the photographs or that someone he trusts is taking them. It bothers me that he needs them. I think he uses them to reaffirm that I care about him. That he's my man, the only one I want. He shouldn't need photographic proof, Lana."

Lana shrugged. "We're all fucked up in some way. You are too, or you wouldn't be able to handle him. You know that's true. Steele might not look as scary as Reaper or Savage, but no one, not one single person in our club, would ever be stupid enough to cross him. But you, Breezy, you stand up to him. You smile sweetly, and you somehow get him to see reason."

"Steele's pretty reasonable."

Lana nodded her assent. "That's true, in a fight, or argument, he'd never lose his cool. But with you, in terms of your safety and Zane's, I wouldn't bet on it."

Breezy took a deep breath and let it out, fighting a yawn. "I'm very tired and as soon as Steele is finished, he's going to want to ride, isn't he?"

"He'll want you to get rest and eat," Lana said and stood up. "What do you really need from here? Or want? We'll bag it and go."

Breezy stood too and looked around her. She didn't need — or want — anything but her child back. She emptied the papers and photographs into a plastic bag and added the two small albums she'd already made up. "This is it. I have his birth certificate and Social as well as all his early photographs. I think Steele will like those."

"Any favorite blankets or toys Zane might want?" Lana asked.

"Why didn't I think of that?" Breezy asked and hurried to the crib. She caught up the blue blanket with the rows of sailboats on it and added a stuffed dog that looked a little worse for wear. "He loves animals."

"Great. Steele might lose his mind if there's animal hair anywhere."

Lana started out of the bedroom and Breezy saw her suddenly duck as something whistled through the air. Whatever it was hit the doorjamb, putting a very large dent in the soft wood. A baseball bat clattered to the floor and rolled. Stepping up to the door, she saw someone wearing a Swords jacket facing Lana with a gun in his fist. Even from the back, she knew it was a man named Scalp. She had nightmares about him. He liked to say he could take anyone's scalp off faster than others could shoot, and she believed him. He and her father went way back. Lana was smirking and didn't look in the least intimidated.

Breezy wasn't just scared; she was terrified. She knew how cruel Scalp was. She did the only thing she could think to do. She flung Zane's little blue blanket over Scalp's head, counting on Lana to do the rest. Lana didn't disappoint. She was on the man in seconds, taking him down, knocking him out and calmly talking into her phone. "Need you to pick up trash for us, Preacher, and bring him to Steele. Will leave the bag just inside the door for quick collection."

She grinned at Breezy. "Didn't see that coming. Master and Transporter took the prisoners to Steele, and they stayed because they thought we were safe in your apartment. I was supposed to call them when we were done. Preacher was outside, on the roof across the street, not that anyone, including me, was worried, but this is going to make Steele *really* lose his mind. He'll probably put all eighteen of us on looking out for you."

Breezy was still shaken. She admired the fact that Lana didn't seem in the least bit upset, where she couldn't even look at the man lying on the floor. Gingerly, she caught the edge of the blanket and yanked.

"Is that Zane's favorite blanket, or yours?" Lana teased. "If it's yours, let's get him a new one. I'm not certain Steele's going to want that touching his son after it's touched him." She kicked the man with the end of her motorcycle boot. Lana wore particularly sharp-toed boots.

"It's mine," Breezy said. "I paid more than I really should have. It was new." That made her ashamed. Zane hadn't had a lot of new things in his life.

Lana looked at her sharply. "Let's take it anyway. That's what washing machines are for." She caught up the blanket and bags of papers and pressed them into Breezy's hands. "Grab the stuffed animal. I'll get the trash ready. I swear, when we were with the Swords, if I heard him bragging one more time about practicing scalping on his bed-mate bitches, I was going to do a little scalping of my own."

"It wasn't bragging." Breezy pitched her voice low, afraid the man would overhear her. "I heard my father telling Junk about it. He was laughing. He helped Scalp get rid of more than one body. He said Habit complained that if Scalp kept killing the women, they would go broke because they couldn't sell them without a scalp."

"That's disgusting. I'll make certain Preacher lets Steele know. He likes that kind of information."

"Has anyone texted you? Are they making any progress at all?"

"You can't hurry these things, Bree. It takes time to get reliable information. First, Steele has to scare the hell out of them without really hurting them. He has to get a feel for when they tell the truth and when they don't. Also, there's the whole bravado thing. The macho I-can-hold-out bullshit. We were tortured over and over. We learned to hold out and make it look as if we were caving. We had a lot of experience in that sort of thing. It makes it far easier to see when someone else is bullshitting."

Breezy sank down into the one decent chair she had. "I thought my life was ugly, but there's always worse, isn't there?"

"We made it through," Lana said practically. She caught Scalp by his jacket and dragged him across the floor to the front door. He was showing signs of coming around and she kicked him hard again, driving the toe of her boot into the side of his head.

Breezy watched her, the casual way Lana did it and then turned her back on him and sauntered across the room, her hips swaying, looking like a million dollars. She looked the epitome of confidence in herself. As a warrior. As a woman. As a biker. She was definitely an equal in Torpedo Ink.

"Do you have a full vote in your club the way Steele does?"

Lana's gaze jumped to hers. She nodded. "Both Alena and I do. We're charter members along with the others. Two of Czar's brothers have joined and are fully patched members, and we have a few prospects. The club coming to us, the ones wanting to be patched over, are out of one of the other schools. They reached out to Czar's brothers, who live in the area, and then, after they're vetted, if we agree, we'll have a chapter up where they live."

"What about Blythe or Anya?"

She shook her head. "First, Blythe would be appalled if Czar wanted her to sit in on a meeting. She would refuse." The amusement faded from her voice and she threw herself on the broken love seat and leaned toward Breezy. "Blythe is the best. The absolute best. She will discuss anything with us, talk to us about whatever rule we don't understand, and she's never condescending. I don't know how Czar got so lucky, but she's the best old lady ever born. We all benefit from her. If you need someone ever to help you, Blythe is your girl."

"And Anya?"

Lana's face softened. "We all love Anya. She works as a bartender, and she's really good at it. She never forgets anything. Reaper's got mad love for that woman and none of us blame him. We're hoping she gets pregnant soon, so psycho man will settle a little. He's all over her all the time, but so happy. None of us ever thought he'd be happy. We really didn't. We thought we'd lose him, but she arrived out of nowhere and we've got him back one hundred percent."

"Like Savage?"

The smile faded. She shook her head. "Unfortunately, no. Savage is really different and none of us, Savage included, think there's a happy ending in store for him. He'll hang on though. He'd never leave us unless he thought we could handle the Diamondbacks without him."

Breezy didn't like that, but she knew, just being around Savage, that he was different even from the others.

"Are you happy, Lana?"

Lana shrugged. "The things I want, I can never have, but I'm free and I've got my family. I love Steele, and he's got you and Zane. Reaper's got Anya. I know both men are safe. Those are the things that make me happy."

Breezy wanted to say she wasn't sure yet. She wanted to be, but there was that one huge milestone she was still trying to hurdle. The club. Lana and Alena were treated as full members. She didn't know a single club where women were treated equally as members. Not one. Torpedo Ink was definitely different, and she had to make certain, before making a decision, that she was fair about it. That meant she needed more information.

Preacher threw open the door, glaring at his sister. "What the fuck, Lana?"

She grinned at him. "It wasn't like I went looking for him. You remember Scalp? He liked to practice scalping the women he took to bed, the ones they would have sold if he hadn't insisted on practicing his favorite sport."

"And he's still got his scalp? Didn't you

have a knife on you?"

Lana shrugged. "Breezy was here and I try to act civilized around her, so she'll let me play with Zane."

"Don't let her kid you, Bree. She wants to swim in your pool."

"I have a pool." Lana smirked at her brother.

"True, but you like Steele and Bree's pool better."

"That's true too, it's awesome," Lana admitted.

"Steele owns the house," Breezy corrected.

"Actually, both of you do," Preacher said. He heaved Scalp over his shoulder and walked out, leaving her with her mouth open.

Thirteen

Steele entered the motel room silently. It was well after midnight and he was exhausted but needed to see his woman. She had every curtain pulled and the fan running on high. He could barely make her out lying in the middle of the bed directly under the rotating paddles that fanned the hot air, making the room temperature bearable.

The garage hadn't been. The smell of blood had permeated everything, so that he was breathing it in, so that it soaked into his pores. It didn't matter; he got what he needed, and that meant he could take the terror from his woman's eyes.

He'd been holding it together by a thread, trying not to think that his boy could be sold to some fucking pedophile and that what was done to him and his brothers and sisters would be done to his child. The horror of that was almost more than he could bear. He would do anything to get Zane back. Anything. He'd trade his life for his child. He'd torture and kill if that was what it took.

He had been angry that Scalp had slipped through, hidden inside the apartment's attic. That was a fuckup that could have cost them. Even Dart and Bruiser hadn't known he was up there. Living. His assignment had been to kill Dart if Bruiser didn't and then kill Bruiser. Bridges's plan wasn't to sell his daughter. He was tired of no one taking care of him. He wanted to kill Zane in front of her, or sell him so she would suffer every day, but Scalp was to bring her to Bridges.

Scalp should have shot Lana immediately, acquired Breezy and gotten out of there, but he'd been greedy the moment he saw Lana. That wasn't unusual. Lana had an allure, an appeal that quite a few men found hard to resist. The Swords member thought he could use her, keep her prisoner awhile, and then when he was tired of her, scalp her in his signature way. Scalp had died hard.

Steele moved close to the bed. There was a small lamp on an end table and he put it on the lowest setting so that he could see Breezy. He needed the innocence of her. The brightness of her. He looked down at the smooth expanse of her back. Her hair was braided and twisted up onto her head, presumably to keep her cooler.

He loved the line of her buttocks. The first time he'd ever seen her walking away in a pair of tight jeans, his stomach had dropped, his gut had tightened into knots and his cock had gone to full attention without his order. He'd been so shocked, he almost went after her right at that moment, but then sanity had taken over.

He'd been taught to be cautious, and he'd taken his time watching her. He didn't think it was possible to really be around Breezy and not fall for her. Not feel that overwhelming emotion that tore him up inside and shredded his heart. He glanced over to the chair where his woman had placed her clothes. They were folded neatly. Perfectly. Her boots were right there against the wall, and he picked them up, frowning. There was a hole in one of them.

Fuck. A hole. He had bought her new clothes and put them in the closet at the new house. He had bought sexy lingerie, because he'd been thinking about himself. He hadn't thought to buy her shoes. Boots. Walking shoes. She needed all kinds of shoes. She hadn't said a word to him. They were waiting to ride until the next morning when he could get her some decent boots.

He sent out a mass text knowing she wouldn't like it, but he didn't give a damn.

They had information. They had phones, and Code was so good at mimicking anyone if calls had to be made. Once Code could see a few lines of text, he could replicate style easily. Those phones gave them access to personal information as well as any nicknames they called one another or anything that they might have between them no one else knew about.

He sat on the edge of the bed and pulled off his boots, noting he'd done a good cleaning job. He'd power-sprayed the tread as well as the boot to remove any damning trace of blood. Then he'd made certain to dip the soles in the oxygen bleach the Guns and Skull club had handy. It was a trick they all knew. Regular bleach left behind DNA.

He lined his boots up beside Breezy's and removed his shirt. It was a new shirt, one he'd packed along with jeans to ensure he could burn his clothes. They all burned their clothes. No one took chances. They made certain those ashes were properly disposed of, just like the burned ashes of the bodies they'd cremated in the underground basement oven the Guns and Skull club had for just this kind of problem. Unlike others, Torpedo Ink cleared the ashes and got rid of them as well. They didn't believe in leaving any trace behind.

The phones were broken and disposed of in various trash cans over a three-mile radius. The sim cards were dropped in acid and what remained was also disposed of in different trash cans. They were thorough. They had searched for hidden cameras in the building as well as around it and found nothing.

Steele stood up and peeled off his jeans. He'd taken a shower, knowing he would come to Breezy and wanting to do it as clean as possible, not to mention, one couldn't be riding around in clothes soaked in blood. He'd been slick with blood. Blood didn't bother him. Nothing he did this day or night had bothered him, not when he needed to find his son. Going to Breezy with blood on his hands did.

He sank back down on the bed and ran his hand up her leg. She did something to his insides, twisted and melted them until he sometimes felt he couldn't think straight. She turned her head at the touch of his hand, her lashes fluttering. Then he was looking into her green eyes and his heart turned over.

"How come, with your past, you're not seriously fucked-up, woman?" He stroked his palm up her leg, from behind her knee to where the seam of her buttock met her thigh. One finger ran back and forth along that crease.

"I am, silly, or I wouldn't be even contemplating having a relationship with you, let alone lying naked in this bed waiting for you to come back."

It was a good answer and probably true. He knew she had major issues when it came to just talking about clubs and their life together in one. She had panic attacks. He leaned down and ran his tongue along that seam between her thigh and her ass just to feel her shiver. Sitting back up, he began to trace the tattoo that ran along the small of her back and dripped down over her buttocks, following the curve of both firm globes.

"When Ink was tatting this, putting my name on you, I thought my world was right. That it always would be because you were mine." He gave her that because she gave him so much more. He ran the pad of his finger over his name. "I like you belonging to me, Bree. More importantly, I like belonging to you."

She smiled, and his heart jerked in his chest, matching the way his cock jerked against his stomach.

"Are you going to let me have Ink tattoo *Property of Breezy* on your ass?"

He contemplated that. "Got your name here, right over my heart, sweetheart, but if that's what it takes for you to give me your word you aren't going to run the moment I put our boy in your arms, I'll give you my word I'll have that ink on my ass."

Those long lashes fluttered. Her lips pressed together but he couldn't tell if she was trying to suppress a smile or keeping something from him. He needed to know where he stood with her and if what he'd done this night had pushed her further from him.

"I need an answer, babe."

"I like my name over your heart, not on your ass."

That told him nothing but the fact that she had a sense of humor. He felt like he was chasing an elusive shadow. He wanted to cage her in. Glue her to him.

"I didn't like that you weren't safe tonight."

She pushed up, so he could see the soft weight of her left breast. Then she turned and sat up in the middle of the bed, facing him. "I was safe. Lana handled it so fast, you wouldn't believe it. There was nothing to worry about."

He couldn't help himself. He stroked her breasts, his hands feeling the soft cream that was her skin. So beautiful. A shiver went through her. She was that responsive. His thumbs and fingers strummed her nipples and the soft curves, indulging himself because he could.

"She said you helped."

"She had it under control."

"Said you threw Zane's favorite blanket over his head. I think we'll frame that blanket and put it up on the wall under glass once our boy is finished with it."

She smiled at him, and his heart stuttered like it did sometimes when her face lit up. Lana had told him that she had bought that blanket new with money she'd earned, and it meant something to her. He wanted to make sure she knew he valued it as much as she did. Her smile was worth anything, certainly framing a blanket and putting it on the wall.

"That might be a little silly, Steele, but I like the idea."

He leaned in to her and licked her right nipple. Her arms immediately cradled his head to her. The moment she did, he drew her breast into the heat of his mouth. Her fingers tunneled into his hair. The way she massaged slowly, rhythmically, made his entire body relax. His arms slipped around her waist and he drew her deeper, working her nipple with his tongue and teeth. When he finally lifted his head after worshiping her body for some time, her eyes held that dark green that nearly glowed at him. Her breath came in the ragged little pants he loved.

He traced the marks on her generous breasts gently with the pads of his fingers. "I love how this looks on your skin." He stretched his legs out, his back to the headboard. "Put your mouth on me, Bree. I can't think once your lips are wrapped around me, and I don't want to think right now." He couldn't think about his child in danger, not for one more minute. She had to take that away, the way she took away his personal demons.

Breezy didn't hesitate. She rolled over, kissed her way down his chest straight to his groin. His cock jerked in anticipation and he closed his eyes and buried his fingers in her thick mass of hair. She had a way of giving him comfort when nothing else could. The wailing of the dead. The accusations of their eyes because he couldn't save them. She drove those dead children away from him and brought him peace.

She did it in so many different ways. She

used her body. Her laughter. Her kindness. He felt her caring in her touch, every stroke of her tongue, the way she focused on his cock and gave him pleasure without asking for anything back.

He gathered her braid in his fist and pulled her head back, her mouth off of him. Her gaze jumped to his. "Come up here, baby. I need to ask you something."

"I'm a little busy."

She had an adorable pout. He pulled her hair gently but persistently. "I'm the one sacrificing. I need you up here."

Her hand went to her head to ease the ache, but he didn't relent, and she moved, crawling up his body, sexier than hell, her eyes on his, breasts swaying, body sensual as she crept over him.

"I think I'm the one sacrificing. I was enjoying myself. I find your cock a treat I look forward to." She used her snippiest voice.

He believed her. He had often woken to her lips around his cock in that year he'd had her. It was a fucking great way to wake up. He reached out and tugged on one leg until she straddled him. He pushed two fingers into her. She was slick and hot, ready for him, proving she was telling the truth — she did enjoy sucking his cock.

He fisted his heavy erection and caught her hip with one hand. "Lower yourself on me."

Both of her hands went to his shoulders to steady herself and then her body was swallowing his and he wanted to shout out his pleasure. She could consume him so easily, take his brain right out of the game. She was so tight he had to clench his teeth. Her muscles didn't want to give way and they gripped and dragged at him, surrounding his cock with a fiery silken fist. Air rushed from his lungs.

She faced him, and he refused to allow her to look away from him, holding her gaze captive. It was the most sensual thing ever to stare into her eyes and see the way the green darkened with lust. Most of all, he wanted to see the love in her eyes. She hadn't told him she loved him, not since that idiotic moment when he'd panicked and shut her down three years earlier.

He didn't know the first thing about love or a relationship. All he knew was the moment she'd told him, his heart had felt as if a giant fist had squeezed it, overwhelming emotions choking him. He'd been terrified because he'd lost so many others that he loved, and none of those had been Breezy.

It was difficult to believe she could love

him. How was that even possible? He had to stare at those photographs for hours. Looking at her face. Analyzing every frame, every nuance. It was the only way he could believe that she really was capable of loving a man as fucked up as he was.

He waited until she was fully seated on him, until he was so deep inside her, he felt they were one, sharing skin. Sharing bodies. He couldn't resist the temptation of her breasts, full, round and soft, jutting toward him. Very gently, he cupped her right breast in his palm and once again began stroking with his fingers.

"Baby, look at me and keep looking." He waited for her to obey him. Breezy's gaze had been moving over him, down to where they were joined and now back up to his eyes. "Do you love me?" He didn't beat around the bush. "You once told me you loved me, and I panicked because I didn't think it was possible."

She deserved the truth. He was only giving her part of the truth. He wrestled with that. With his need to be wholly honest with her. He'd lost her once through his own stupidity and he wasn't going to do it again. Instantly she frowned at him, and his cock swelled just a little because he loved that little frown.

"Why wouldn't you think it was possible?"

She squirmed, trying to move, and his hand at her hip blocked her. She stopped instantly at his silent command.

"I'm pretty fucked up, baby. I can get crazy when I don't know where you are. You know that. You've seen me."

A little shiver went through her body. "If I thought you were trying to control me, it would be an issue, but you just want to know I'm safe."

"It's controlling, don't kid yourself. I *have* to know you're safe or I lose my mind. So, yeah, I want to be in control and tell you to check in when you're going somewhere."

She arched her back, thrusting her breasts out, trying not to move her hips but clearly needing to. "You're torturing me." Those tight muscles squeezed down hard on him.

His fingers tugged at her nipple and then slid down her belly to where their bodies joined. He found her clit and began working it slowly. Small circles. A flick. More circles. All the while he kept his gaze on hers.

"Do you love me?"

She opened her mouth, hesitated and looked at him warily, sensing a trap. "It's been three years, Steele."

"Three years you never let another man

near you, Bree." He kept working her clit, holding her in place while his cock jerked and swelled, pressing tight against her sensitive tissue.

"I'm different. You're different. We need time to get to know each other."

"I'm the same. Older. Hopefully wiser. I learned a lot about myself and you while you were gone, but I'm the same. You're stalling."

"Because *I'm* different."

"That doesn't mean shit, baby. Your being different doesn't mean you can't love me. Tell me one way or the other. Stop holding on to hurt and give me the truth."

He began to rock his hips gently. Her breath rushed out. Her eyes went slightly dazed. He leaned forward and took her left breast into his mouth, pressing her nipple tight to the roof of his mouth and stroking with his tongue. She gasped. He used his teeth, raking, then biting down to tug, watching her face the entire time. She moaned, and around his cock came a flood of heated liquid. He licked at her nipple and then sat straight, holding her in place. Waiting.

He'd studied every photograph Maestro had taken before they'd left. Every single one. Over and over. He had them on his phone and he looked at them often. There was no mistaking the look of love on her face when he was taking her. It was there now. He didn't reach for his phone to take a picture, but he wanted to. If he couldn't get her to admit it this time, he would need another photograph to hold on to until she did.

Breezy let out an exasperated sigh. "I do love you, Steele. I can't help it."

His smile was slow in coming, but it was full, originating from somewhere inside. He rewarded her courage by lifting her and letting her slide over his cock. She wanted fast. He kept her slow. The burn was tremendous. The pleasure fierce. Almost brutal. They both needed it so much, but he wasn't ready for that.

He guided her, letting her ride his cock slowly, so that her tight muscles grasped and milked greedily, surrounding him, strangling, all the while growing hotter each time she seated herself all the way and then rose up again. After a few minutes, when she was gasping and trying to wrest control from him, he stopped moving and forced her to stay still. He was immensely strong, and she was no match for him.

"You loved me every minute you were away from me," he prompted.

She nodded, frowning, trying to see where he was going with it. He could feel her heartbeat pounding right into his cock. Every pulse of her blood. It was sexy and hot and made him feel closer than ever to her.

"Say it."

"I didn't want to, Steele, but I loved you every minute, every second, I was away from you. I cried myself to sleep nearly every night, and I dreamt about you."

"And you love me even more now that you're with me."

He lifted her and thrust hard, so that fire streaked through both of them. Her breath caught, and she threw her head back, her lashes lowering.

"Yes," she whispered.

"You want to stay with me." He made that a statement.

She went still. Her gaze searched his face and then she framed it with her hands. "More than you could possibly know, Steele. I want to spend my life with you. I love you and I know no one else is ever going to do for me, but I'm not the same girl. I have a son and I have to figure out what's best for him."

"*I'm* best for him. Can you honestly think I wouldn't take care of him? Protect him?"

"You have to love him, Steele."

"I'm capable of feeling for my children, Bree," he said gently. "More than anything, I want a family with you. You've got one foot out the door, and I need that commitment from you. I need to know you're mine."

Breezy stared at him for a long time, her gaze moving over his face, clearly searching for something there, some sign she needed from him. Suddenly, she leaned into him, the action tightening her sheath around his cock even more, sending fiery spears through his groin and flames licking over his body. She settled her lips on his, kissing him, her tongue stroking and caressing until he took over and kissed her back. He rolled them abruptly, taking her to her back, pinning her under him.

"I want to be with you more than anything. I want a family with you. I can't pretend I'm still not leery of the club. I know you won't leave it for me . . ."

"Baby, don't put it like that. You know I can't. I'm not whole. They keep me from going off the deep end. Not like you do, but I have to be with them. I *am* Torpedo Ink. If you love me, you love the club. It's really that simple."

Blanketing her body, he began to move in

her. Gently. He rested his weight on his forearms, and now he framed her face with his large hands. Staring into her eyes, so she could see his love as clearly as he did hers, he kept the slow building of that inferno between them.

"Give yourself to me, Breezy. Let me have you. I swear you won't regret it. I'll take care of you in the club."

Her eyes went wet, and his heart plunged. She wasn't going to give him what he needed, and she always had. No matter what, when his mind had been chaotic, and his demons had risen to consume him, she had taken it all away, ready to sacrifice herself for him. For a moment he could barely breathe. Barely think. He'd lost her. He'd lost the intense way she loved him. His body went still, and he found himself having to fight for air.

"I've been trying to find out things about the club, so I could better make a decision for Zane. Right now, for me, I would give up everything to be with you. I would accept life in the club and trust you to take care of me. My hesitation isn't about loving you or trusting you with me. It isn't even the club for me anymore. It's about whether or not I think the life is best for Zane."

He forced himself to hear her. To listen

the way every club member listened to the others when they had something to say. Would he want less from his son's mother? She was struggling to find answers because she wanted the best for their son. He had to love her more for that, even though it was unsettling for her not to give him the commitment he needed from her.

He began to move again, showing her with his body how he felt about her. The intensity of the way he loved her. The overwhelming pride and respect he had for her. Threading his fingers through hers, he stretched her arms above her head and kept surging into her. Withdrawing, holding there for a moment, balancing needs with aches and then thrusting hard and holding again.

"You have to decide whether you trust me with our son. To give him everything he needs. To provide for him and keep the two of you safe. You know I'm capable of those things, Breezy. You're just afraid, baby, and I get that. You have to get me. You have to know I'm fully committed to you. You have to trust me when I say my club will protect the two of you and care for you the way they do Czar's family."

He was a good strategist, and he knew that was a huge selling point. She'd been shocked and very intrigued by the way the club members treated Czar's family. More important than the way the club members treated them was the way the children responded to them. They couldn't fake that. She'd also had her son ripped from her. Having an entire club guarding him had to appeal to her.

He moved faster in her, taking her breath. Taking his. His fingers tightened around hers. He buried his face in her throat. "I'm aware, more than any other, that I don't deserve you, but no one will try as hard to make things good for you and our children. Give me a chance."

He hadn't been able to look at her when he told her, because it made him feel so vulnerable and so exposed. He almost wished his brothers were there, surrounding him, just in case he couldn't take it if she rejected him.

"Honey."

His heart turned over and he lifted his head to look at her. Her eyes were soft. That look was on her face. The one that told him above everything else that he still had a chance with her because she did love him.

"I'm going to say yes, *but,*" she added.

It was too late. He wasn't going to let her take it back. Whatever she needed to say, he would hear, but she wasn't taking it back.

He couldn't help the smile and he leaned down to nip at her chin. His hips found a faster rhythm. He let go of her hands and lifted her hips, holding her so he could move harder and deeper into her.

Her breath rushed out of her lungs and he wanted to grin at her. Instead, he made it his one mission in life to bring her the most pleasure he possibly could. The *but* didn't matter. He could handle that. She committed to him and that meant she trusted him with their son in the same way she trusted him with her. No one had ever given him a greater gift.

Her hips matched his fierce rhythm. Each time he thrust deep, her breasts jolted and swayed invitingly. His gaze was glued to her face. That expression. Her lips parted. Her eyes on him. Features expressing her love, her heightened sensuality. That mixture in the green that told him she wanted and needed him just as much as he wanted and needed her.

He took them both to the edge over and over, waiting for that one note that told him she couldn't wait another moment. Only after getting that satisfaction did Steele let his body swell against that fiery sheath, tilting her body so he was hitting her sweet little spot. She rocketed over, clamping down hard on his cock. He felt every tiny movement, every powerful wave. It was brutal. Glorious. Perfection.

She cried out low, just his name. Chanted it. He loved that too. It only added to the aftermath, her body rippling around his. The hot splash of his seed coating her walls triggering more. He loved those moments. Loved after that when he collapsed over her and held her down. She could barely breathe with his weight, but she lay under him, breathing shallowly, never protesting as he covered her, his cock still buried deep. She always had given him that. He loved that she still did.

When he finally rolled over, he took her with him, so that she sprawled over top of him, her head on his chest, his cock still in her. "I know you need to hear me tell you how I feel about you, Bree. I know that's the way relationships go, saying the words out loud. I needed it from you because I'm . . . Hell, baby, I don't know what I am, but I should have told you way back, when you first said it to me. I feel it deeper than I feel anything else. So deep it's fucking terrifying. I'm never going to be good at saying the words. They get stuck in my throat. It's like if I say it out loud, something bad is going to happen. I feel as if I'm cursing us. Everyone they knew we cared about died. I want to give you that, and I swear I'll try, but . . ."

She dug her chin into his chest, those green eyes giving him compassion because his woman was all about that shit. She was everything he wasn't. "Ink it on your skin, honey. You won't have to say it aloud. Just point it out to me and I'll know what you're saying. I don't want something beautiful between us to ever make you uncomfortable or bring up nightmares. You look at photographs, and I'll look at your ink."

She was brilliant. He could do that. Hell, he could have Ink put that shit all over him. It was the fucking truth and always would be. "I like that solution." He pressed a kiss to her forehead and lay back again, fingers buried in her hair. "But just looking at those photographs isn't going to cut it, woman. I'm more fucked up than that."

Her laughter felt warm on his chest. "You are? What else do I have to do?"

"I want you to tell me as well."

"That's not difficult, as long as you're not worried I'll curse us."

"Pretty sure demons can't hear you, babe. You're too good. They're ready to pounce on me." Because he was a fucking asshole and always would be. Demons liked monsters.

Her fingers drifted to just below his belly and began to write letters there. “I have no problem telling you, honey.”

“I’m not done. That’s the most important, but there’s more. I’ll ink it on my skin, but you say it and then you show me.”

Her eyebrow shot up, and once again her gaze jumped to his. “Show you?” she echoed.

“Need more photographs.”

She rolled her eyes. “You already have so many we’re going to have to get you a new phone. I don’t know where you’re going to put them all.”

“I do.” She hadn’t objected, but then he wasn’t kidding. He’d need more. His very large insecurity problem wasn’t just going to go away because she’d committed to him. It would help, but it wasn’t going to disappear.

“Fine. You’ll have your silly photographs.”

“Coming and going, either one of us, you kiss me.”

“I already do that.”

“Yeah, but it should be a requirement.”

“On both sides, then.”

He let the silence stretch out, and she bit him. He laughed and gripped her bottom.

He loved her. Plain and simple. She taught him how to play. How to have fun.

"Fine," he conceded as if reluctant. He would never pass up a chance to kiss Breezy. Never. Her mouth was pure fire. "Waking me up in the mornings —"

"Don't even go there or you'll find you won't be getting any wake-up calls from me."

"Fortunately for me, I happen to know you love my cock, so I'll look forward to you demonstrating that."

"I won't deny that." She laid her head on his chest, ear to his heart.

He tunneled his fingers in her hair. "Tell me, baby. Let's hear your *but.* What are you most worried about? I'll try to put you at ease." He had known all along he would have to circle back around to her worry, but he wanted to have a few minutes of fun with her so she would stay relaxed and mellow.

Breezy didn't start unnecessary arguments. He had always appreciated that in her. She didn't sweat the small stuff. She didn't care if he had a beer with his brothers, she wasn't that kind of woman. Before, when she was his, she popped the tops of the bottles and got cold ones for them. He had no reason to think she'd be any different now.

She tensed in spite of everything they'd just shared. He felt the change in her immediately. Panic set in. Her breath exploded out, hot against his chest. "I won't ever whore for the club. I won't make drug deals. I won't help run guns. None of it. Not one thing."

It was so unexpected, and he actually yanked her head up by her hair. "What the fuck, Breezy? How can you even say that after what we just did? After what I just admitted to you?" The idea of another man touching his woman brought the monster in him far too close.

Her tongue touched her lip nervously. Her eyes went liquid. Steele forced air through his lungs to quiet the fierce need to shake her. She was very, very upset. He had to think beyond his feelings and what it cost him to make the admissions he had and really examine her fears. They were legitimate, just not with his club. Breezy had her own insecurities, and they were as legitimate as his. She came from a similar background and she'd been just as traumatized. She'd been forced by her father to do every one of the things she feared most.

He slowly loosened his fingers from her hair. "Bree, that's part of trusting me to take care of you in the club." He had to reassure her, so she would never worry about it again. "First, we don't use our women for any reason. We don't take money for any woman to sleep with anyone. If she's fucking someone at a party, she's there of her own free will and doing what feels good. She doesn't have to do anything she doesn't want to do. We don't run drugs, so there's no need to expect a woman to carry drugs for us. Our old ladies are sacred to us as well as to the entire club. They are always as protected as our families are."

There were tears in her eyes and he brushed his lips over her lids, tasting the drops. His heart contracted. "Baby." He whispered it against her lashes. "You should have told me right away that was a fear." He pulled back to look at her.

"I didn't because I felt like, after observing your club, the idea was absurd, but I get so scared. I can't help it. I panic at the thought of actually being in a club."

"Sweetheart, you should have told me. When a man finds the right woman, he isn't going to whore her out or make her run drugs for him. He doesn't beat her. He doesn't cheat on her. He doesn't let other men do any of those things. When he has children, he protects those children. He doesn't beat them or make them run drugs.

He certainly doesn't whore out his daughters or his sons. You grew up in a fucked-up club, baby. You're Torpedo Ink now. We take care of our old ladies and our families. I've got to tell you, Bree, most clubs do."

Steele massaged her scalp, knowing he might have yanked her hair too hard. She hadn't protested and that pissed him off too. She should have. She was too used to the violence she'd been raised in.

"I get rough with you when we're having sex, Bree, because I think you like it. If you ever don't, you tell me immediately. It will stop. What I did just then wasn't deliberate, I was startled, but I still should have been careful. I'm strong, and you could get hurt if I get careless like that. You don't put up with shit from me."

"I knew you didn't do it on purpose. I wouldn't put up with it, Steele. I told you, I'm not that girl anymore, and I'm not going back."

He liked the determination in her voice and he believed her. She might love him, and she was more than willing to give him everything he asked for, but she wasn't willing to be his doormat or take abuse.

"Anything else we need to put to rest before you're a little easier about Torpedo Ink?"

"Do you run guns?"

"No." He wanted to give her whatever she needed to lay her fears to rest, but they were skating close to club business.

"What do you do to bring in money?"

"Ink has a tattoo shop. Alena will have the restaurant. Mechanic and Transporter have the garage. I'm a doctor. We're putting in shops all over Caspar." He willed her to accept that. "You know we took money from the Swords and their billionaire president."

She took a breath and dug her chin back into his chest, her eyes meeting his. "What does the club do to earn money?"

There it was. He either was honest, with those eyes of hers staring into his, or he lied, and she'd know it. "You sure you want to know, baby? Because we're in a gray area here."

"I have to know if I can live with it."

He had to take a chance. Either way was a risk. "We hunt pedophiles. We hunt for children that need to be taken from them. We hunt for trafficking rings. In order to do those things, we stay in good with other clubs. We sometimes take jobs escorting people through a territory. Or we eliminate threats to others. We're careful, but we do what we were trained to do."

He didn't take his gaze from hers. She

stared at him for a very long time. He heard the clock ticking. He wanted to put his arms around her and hold her as tightly as he could, but he made himself stay relaxed, as if this moment wasn't every bit as important as every other moment since he'd asked her to tell him she loved him.

"You were trained as assassins."

He nodded. "Yes, we were."

"Is that what you do best?"

Was it? He frowned at her. "Maybe. I don't know. We're damn good. I'm as good at killing as I am at saving lives, probably better, but I don't know if that's what we do best. I'd have to say it's hunting pedophiles. We started perfecting our technique at a very young age. We were like a wolf pack, spreading out, each of us doing his or her job in order to find them, corner them and kill them without getting caught."

She pressed a kiss over his heart and looked back up at him. Waiting.

"They set traps for us, but we always stuck to the plans. Always. No one deviated, because that meant death. We're good at it, baby, maybe the best in the world."

"Okay, then."

"Okay?"

"Just don't get caught in traps or deviate from the plans. I want my man alive."

Relief swept through him. It was so strong that he felt weak. "Need sleep, baby. Just stay there and close your eyes." He glanced at the clock. "I told the others we'd leave after ten. We're buying you new boots, and don't give me shit. You need them." He tipped her face up, took her mouth and kissed her thoroughly.

She laid her head on his chest and he let himself drift off, knowing Maestro and Keys had just switched shifts so the other could sleep. Breezy was well guarded.

FOURTEEN

They arrived in Slidell, Louisiana, at five in the morning. They'd made good time, but stopping had been necessary and that had slowed them down. Steele was getting edgy over the delays. Now it was growing light and all of them were tired. He needed them at their sharpest. They had rented a house neighboring their target overlooking the lake, and they slept, taking turns keeping eyes on the house where Bridges was most likely holding Zane.

The information Steele had gotten from Bruiser and then Scalp had been enough to bring them here. This was where Bridges's old man had a family home. It was right on the lake, a large estate, and the last three of Bridges's texts had come from this area. Code had the exact address and had informed them that Boone was most likely in residence because every other family member was gone. It stood to reason that if

Bridges was in the area, he would be at that family estate.

The Abernathy estate was composed of several acres overlooking the lake. The house was enormous, reputed to be twelve thousand square feet, with six bedrooms and as many full bathrooms and a couple of half baths.

Code had gotten the plans to the house and sent them. It had a marble foyer and grand staircase, a sunroom and a private library with a separate entrance, which was good for them. They had the locations of each bedroom and bath, formal dining room and massive kitchen. Code even found which security company was used and had managed to get a hold of the actual layout for it. That was Code. If it was digital anywhere, it was his.

The back of the house was mostly glass to take advantage of the lake. The backyard of the Abernathy estate was an oasis — a beautiful area specifically for entertaining and enjoying the weather and the lake. There was an inviting pool that lazily wound around a spa and fountain where water spilled over rocks, falling from fountain to spa to pool.

The cabana and bar were located to the left on the expansive lawn that led down to the boathouse. The estate had a manicured landscape that rolled right into the large pier that ran out over the water. Two boats were suspended beneath a covered canopy just beside the pier.

The nearest neighbor was a good distance away, too far to ever question any noises coming from the mansion or guest cabins. Torpedo Ink had gotten a lucky break. The neighbor used his home as a vacation property, renting it out when he wasn't using it, and Code had managed to get them in for a week's use. The house came with all the amenities, including a boat. Of course, they'd paid extra for that, but money didn't matter to them and finding Zane did.

Preacher lay up on the roof studying the estate, looking for signs of life. There were two trucks parked at the back of the house and one near the cabin. He'd been up there for hours — since before dawn. Humidity was a bitch and the mosquitoes could be a problem, but he didn't move, nor did he take his eyes off the house. Transporter was on the other side with glasses, watching the cabin. Mechanic was watching the road.

They'd sent the license plate numbers of each vehicle to Code. He hadn't yet responded but Steele had a gut feeling they had come to the right place. Wealthy families weren't immune from having sons like Boone, mean men who robbed others and felt they were entitled to take what they wanted rather than work for it. Boone seemed to have passed that trait on to Bridges, who'd clearly passed it on to Junk.

That made Steele think about what he wanted to give his son. Certainly, the ability to protect himself. He was going to continue Breezy's self-defense training as well as ask the others to help him with that. All of the women and children should be taught. They needed a shooting range. He'd have to talk to Czar and have it put on the list of businesses they would open. An indoor shooting range would be good as well as one outdoors. Somewhere to teach self-defense classes as well. His mind went over the possibilities, allowing him to keep from losing his sanity as they waited.

It was difficult, looking at the serenity of that house in the early morning hours, to think that his son might be held prisoner there. For one terrible moment he remembered a little boy, no more than four, thrown down the basement stairs where he tumbled soundlessly, rolling until he hit Steele's legs. Steele was in chains and couldn't cushion him. Couldn't reach for him. There was no way to help him. The boy had died three hours later, staring at him. Never once did he make a sound until that last rattle of his breath.

Breezy came up beside him as he stared out the window, looking at the quiet estate next door. Her hand slid up his back as she moved into him and then she was in front of him, frowning. Her fingers slid over his face from his eye to his jaw, and just that small touch seemed to quiet the demons in him.

"Honey." She wrapped her arms around his waist in an effort to comfort him.

He felt like a fucking pussy to have her see tears tracking down his face. What the hell was wrong with him? "I'm good," he said, his voice gruff. He was. He had to be. He wasn't going to be worth anything to his son — or to her — if he didn't stop letting the present situation trigger memories of his past. He couldn't think about his son in the hands of madmen, not when he needed to be sane and rational.

Breezy didn't respond to his bullshit, but then she often didn't. She seemed to know when to soothe him just by staying quiet. He wrapped his arms around her and dropped his chin to the top of her head, inhaling her scent. He was supposed to be the one comforting her, but right at that moment, he knew it was the other way around.

Breezy had a quiet strength that he counted on. He'd taken the lead when they'd been together for that one perfect year. He was always going to take the lead. He'd been doing it since he was a child and had been ripped from his parents and brought to the hellhole Sorbacov called a school. He was good at thinking through problems and coming up with solutions.

Breezy was good at life. She read people, but not in the same way he did. He had been taught to assess people with the idea of getting close to them, so he could seduce and kill them. He looked for weaknesses and he used them against people. Breezy read people with the compassion in her. She did it and quietly set about helping them, giving them whatever it was they needed. She'd done that for him the entire year they'd been together.

His woman had focused on him and given him everything he could possibly want or need. She'd anticipated and provided. She'd done so quietly and without thought of him giving back. He hoped he hadn't taken her for granted, but knew he had. That was one of the biggest lessons he'd learned in her absence. He'd had three years to figure out everything that he'd done wrong.

Steele had no trouble turning the spotlight on himself and analyzing his strengths and weaknesses. He did it all the time. He had no understanding of people who pretended their failings away. How could you fix what was wrong if you didn't admit to it first? He had made up his mind that he would find her and when he did, he would offer her the world. He wanted her to always have more reasons to stay with him than to go.

Breezy wasn't the type of woman who would stay for money or advantage. She would stay for love. He knew that. He respected that. And he was going to make certain she felt it in the way she made him feel when they were together. It was just when they were away from each other that he found his demons rising to tell him there was no way she could love what a monster he was.

"I'm going to have to get quite a few tatts when we get home, baby," he murmured softly.

She tilted her head to look up at him. "One will do."

"When I'm feeling like this, one isn't going to do. Besides" — he sent her a wicked grin — "I need them, so you can see them from every angle when you're busy."

She rolled her eyes. "You're getting out of hand, Steele. Once we get Zane and get back home, I'm going to have to take you in hand."

He pretended to think about it, then shook his head. "I don't mind a hand job, babe, but I prefer your mouth. I'm not saying I'd turn it down, but . . ."

She punched his arm. "Everything is about sex to you."

"Isn't it with you?"

She laughed softly. "Only when I'm around you. I think it's contagious then." She turned in his arms, facing the window. "It's really beautiful here, isn't it?"

"Yes. Does it feel like home to you? You were born in New Orleans."

She shook her head. "The only good times I associate with this place are from the year I was with you. Everything else was just learning to keep my head down and see what was going on around me so I could figure out what Bridges was going to want before he did. I wanted to go to school."

There was longing in her voice that Steele was certain she hadn't intended to show him. "Were you ever in school?"

"He'd put me in and then yank me out, even when I was really young. He liked being waited on, and if I wasn't around to get him his beer, he'd fly into a rage. I was fortunate in that I learned to read early on so I could do the schooling at home. There was a teacher who would come in to work with me once a week. He was afraid of Bridges, and that was never a good thing. Eventually Bridges couldn't help but taunt him, and the teacher stopped coming."

"How old were you?"

"Probably seven or eight. I don't know how Bridges managed to get a teacher to come to our home or the club and for the state to allow it."

"You come from a very wealthy family with a lot of pull." He indicated the mansion situated a few acres from them. Fortunately, the two houses were located on the same rise, so even though it was a good distance away, they could see it. "My guess is, when your father wants something, he makes his demands, just the way Boone does. The family is old-school, traditional, and has old money. They don't want a scandal. Boone joined a motorcycle club. Not just any club, but an outlaw club. Bridges followed suit. The family probably gives them whatever they want to stay away."

She nodded. "He never brought me here or told me much about my grandparents or great-grandparents. What I did know, I pieced together. His mother is worse than his father. At least he acted like she was; he scared me every time he talked about her."

"That place screams money. Code said it's valued at over four million. Here, in this area, that's a lot of bank for an estate." He nuzzled the top of her head, his fingers linked tightly just under her breasts. "Would you want to come back here to live, instead of living in California? It's cold there at times."

She shook her head. "I loved the coast. It seemed wild and I remember thinking I wished I could stay."

"It was very cold in Russia, where we were. The heat here was stifling for all of us. The coast in Caspar is much more moderate, and we've been able to adapt. Thank you for giving me a chance, Bree. I know it won't be easy, but I'll do my best to make things good for you."

"I know you will. I want to be with you, Steele."

They both watched as Savage came into sight, moving around the bikes to the beat-up truck Transporter had chosen to bring with them. Savage pulled open the back door and reached inside to take a hold of Zane's car seat and tug at it, making certain it was snug and properly bolted down.

Breezy looked up at Steele. "They are different, aren't they? The club? He's making sure that the seat is safe for Zane."

"We're different, Bree, but we aren't saints. That truck is a rocket. If we need a fast getaway with Zane, we want that seat not to move."

She smiled at him over her shoulder, and his cock stirred. It wasn't his cock that got to him with its reaction to her. It was his heart. He had a strange fluttery sensation, a curious melting. She did things physically to him that were impossible from a purely scientific standpoint.

"What's he like? I was always afraid of both Reaper and Savage. Reaper joined within a month or two after Czar and Savage showed up with him. In all the time they rode with the Swords, I never said one word to them, not even when I was yours. I was more afraid of them then I was any Swords member, even Donk."

"You have good instincts, better than most of the Swords. They're phantoms when it comes to killing, in and out and no one ever knows they were there. For big men, they walk softly and they can get into places you'd never suspect. Savage is edgy, difficult to predict. He's nearly impossible to defeat when he's fighting with his fists or his feet. I've never actually seen him defeated. We don't let him kill anyone when he's in a ring, but it's always close. I'll admit, it's brutally cool, but equally as scary to watch."

"You admire him."

"Yeah, I do." He did. Savage was implacable when he set on a course. No one got away from him. He'd been one of the top assassins Sorbacov had had. The most elite among the elite.

"And you worry about him."

He glanced down at her again. She was right. He did. They all did. Sorbacov and his "instructors" had twisted all of them, but Savage, with his good looks, had been a favorite, and they'd really twisted him. He was the most damaged of all of them, and there was no cure for the years and years of the kind of sexual torture and abuse their instructors had used to shape the boy into the kind of man they'd wanted. Each of them had been shaped by those years, and no amount of counseling was going to overcome their needs. What seemed natural and right to them was considered deviant in society — or so they were learning.

"Yeah, baby," he conceded softly. "I do worry about him. The things they did to him and made him do were cruel beyond anything they did to others. They wanted him to be like they were, I don't mean with a penchant for children, because he wouldn't go there, none of us did, but for other things."

He swept his hand down the soft thickness of her hair. There was comfort in that simple movement when the days and nights of his childhood were too close.

"Honey, I know this is hard for you. I didn't realize, because I had no way of knowing about the terrible things you had to endure as children, but . . ."

"Zane is our son, Breezy. Ours together. We made him, from you and me. The club views him as theirs as well. We're all family. Family takes care of family no matter how bad it is or what the cost to us personally is. If you belonged to Savage, and Zane was his child, I'd be right here, and so would everyone else. That's what we do. We're Torpedo Ink, and that *is* Torpedo Ink."

Steele knew that Breezy's fear of clubs was so ingrained in her that she would have to have that affirmation over and over again. He didn't mind reassuring her often, now that he was aware of her issue. She had to reassure him that she loved him, so much so that she was willing to let him have photographs of them when he fucked her . . . That brought him up short. He didn't "fuck" Breezy. It had never been that for him. He hadn't known what it was, but it wasn't that. He hoped she felt the difference just the way he did whenever he touched her.

She rubbed the back of her head against his chest. "Maestro and Keys watch over you the way Reaper and Savage have always watched over Czar. I noticed it even then, when you all rode with the Swords. They were never far from you. Most of the time, the members were close. Bridges used to be angry that he couldn't be in the little 'pussy clique,' as he referred to you. He said you were pussy magnets and everyone considered all of you badass and were afraid of you. He wanted into that circle."

Steele had known that about Bridges. All of them knew it. Steele had maintained a distant but friendly relationship with the man because he'd wanted Breezy and he had a plan to get her. He'd maneuvered Bridges into a position of offering her. He hadn't wanted Bridges to know he was gone on her, that would have given the man too much power. As it was, in the year before Bridges had made the offer, Steele had beat the shit out of thirty-seven of the club members just for thinking about going there. Word had gotten around, that although Steele didn't go near her, he used his fists on anyone who approached Bridges about her.

"Maestro is like Reaper in a lot of ways, yet where Reaper is rough, Maestro is gentle. That doesn't make him any less lethal. He's faster than you can imagine and has no qualms about slitting a throat if he thinks it's justified. Keys matches that. He's a little less laid-back than Maestro, but the two work very well together. They know what the other one is going to do in any given situation and they just take care of business."

"I like that they protect you."

"I don't." He didn't. He didn't want anyone else dying for him. He wasn't going to lose someone because they put his life before theirs. "They can protect you and Zane now."

He slid his hand from under her breast, up over the curve to her throat. He loved to feel her heartbeat. More, he loved that she never flinched when he wrapped his very large hand around her throat. She did trust him, she always had. His thumb brushed her chin. All the while his gaze stayed glued to the house, the one where most likely his son was being held prisoner.

"I want a daughter, Breezy. One like you. One that has your sweetness and your ability to love and feel for others. You wanted to know why I wanted such a big house. I want to fill it with children." He did. He wanted their children to have the childhood the ones who had died in that dark, cold dungeon didn't have. He wanted to do right by them.

"At the same time, I want the freedom to fuck your brains out in every single room without you being nervous our kids are going to walk in on us. I wouldn't give a shit because I think sex is natural and they should know their father wants their mother with every breath he takes. But you aren't going to like that. So, lots of rooms and cameras. They'll be taught to let us know when they're coming to us."

He made that a statement. A decree. He was going to have her at any time, in any of the rooms they had. Outside by the pool. Hell, *anywhere.*

Her reaction was typical Breezy. She laughed softly. He felt the sound in the palm of his hand. Felt her pulse. Was damn grateful she took him back and was capable of accepting him the way he was. He'd try like hell to learn. To be better for her, but he loved that she took him the way he was, a fucked-up mess with so many flaws they couldn't be counted.

She turned back toward the house and pressed the back of her head into his chest. "If no one ever comes out to confirm he's there, is there another way to find out?"

Her voice shook, and he glanced down sharply. His woman had been holding it together, pretending she wasn't so anxious she wanted to scream. The tremor he felt running through her body told him it was all she could do not to run over there and bang on the front door of that beautiful, serene mansion.

"We'll find out, but we'll have to wait until nightfall, baby. We can't go in blind. We don't know where he is or how close they are to him. If he's in one room and they're in another, we're golden, but if someone has their hand" — in his mind an image of a knife rose and his stomach lurched — "on him, then we have to be more careful. I know it's difficult to wait. You've been a trouper through this, but we're in the home stretch. I have a gut feeling about this, and I'm usually not wrong. The others feel the same way. In a couple of hours, Lana's going to change her appearance and go out on the boat. She should be able to get close enough to see what's happening from that angle."

"Has Code gotten back to you with any more information?" She pushed at her hair and looked over her shoulder at him again. "It's strange to think he looks like he does and he's all about computers. He's so good on them, but he looks as lethal as any of you."

Steele remembered Code as a little boy, thin and small for his age. He wasn't thin and small now. He had never gained the six feet he wanted to be, but that didn't matter, he was close, and he'd filled out, all defined muscle, not an ounce of fat on him. He kept his dark blond hair closely cropped. His whiskey-colored eyes were intense. He wore a short beard, more like scruff really, and the same with his barely there mustache.

"He was trained as an assassin just like the rest of us." Deliberately he kept away from their sexual training. He didn't want Breezy reminded of that. He knew it made people uncomfortable to think about the way adults had used them or how they were in such control of their bodies. He didn't want her to ever think he'd seduced her to get his way — and he had. He'd have to admit that to her if she asked.

"Code works out every day and still trains

like we all do. He's very, very good on a computer. That's his weapon of choice, but he's no less lethal with any other kind of weapon." He was glad she'd followed her question with something he could divert her attention with because so far, Code hadn't responded to any of their queries that morning, and it wasn't like him. That was worrisome.

Waiting was always the most difficult part. He'd learned patience in a hard school. They all had. They could stay still for hours. They could go without sleep. They could endure torture and lack of food. He'd had years of that shit and his body was used to it. All Breezy could think about was her child, whereas he knew how to distract his mind.

"All of you are different ages. I'm a little surprised by the fact that you're the vice president when several are older than you by a few years."

"We had to learn to work together when we were children. We each had different strengths and we pooled our resources. Czar was the one who pulled us together. He'd been in that hellhole the longest of the eighteen of us. There were others who had been there longer when he arrived and were far older, but they didn't try to get out. They had lost all hope. There were others who believed if they curried favor by turning on the rest of us and ratting us out, any little thing we did or rule we broke, they'd eventually get out. Of course that wasn't so."

"What did you do to make it out when so many others didn't? How were you able to turn the tables on them?"

"Czar. In one word, Czar. He got sick of all the dying children and he realized none of us would get out. He decided to fight back. He recruited Reaper and Savage first. They were younger, just around four or five, I think. I wasn't there yet. Czar put together a plan to take out the worst of the instructors, the ones who were so cruel there was no hope of a child surviving the time spent with them. Reaper crawled through the vents and killed his first one while the man slept. Slit his fucking throat and then washed up in the man's bathroom before crawling through the vents back down to the dungeon."

That had been one of the first stories ever told to him by Czar when he was trying to convince Steele there was hope.

"Czar was careful which of the children he recruited. They couldn't afford to be caught or betrayed. Czar, by the way, was only a boy himself. We're not talking a teen. He was a boy. He had to watch any child brought in carefully because once we began to fight back, even though we made the kills look like another adult was doing it, Sorbacov suspected and sent in plants."

"That would have been terrifying," Breezy said. "How could Czar know and still risk it?"

"There was no way *not* to risk it, not if we wanted a chance to get out of there alive. We saw dead or dying children monthly." Just saying it brought the images into his mind and the smell into his nostrils. He could taste the filth of the dungeon in his mouth. His stomach reacted, churning violently.

A shudder went through his body and Breezy immediately turned back to him and framed his face in between her palms. "Honey, we don't have to talk about this."

She knew how sickened his past made him and there was no hint that she thought he couldn't handle it, just that she didn't like him upset.

"No, it's good to remember, Breezy, and to tell you. I want you to know what kind of a man Czar is. He hates trafficking so much, he gave up five years of his life, five *years,* in order to bring that ring down."

"I'm beginning to see." She pressed her lips to his throat, just a brush, but it felt like a velvet stroke over his skin, chasing away demons. He inhaled to take in the scent of her hair, fresh from the shower. Her skin smelled like wildflowers, further distancing him from the horror of his childhood.

"Czar risked his marriage to the only woman who ever meant anything to him. Blythe is his only, the way you're mine. Our bodies don't react the same as other men's. I told you that. They made certain of that. Some of us are really fucked up in sexual ways — like Reaper and Savage and Ice and Storm, Maestro and Keys . . . Okay, all of us. And then there's me and a few of the others who are just plain crazy . . ."

"No, you're not. Don't say that. You can't believe that."

"Even if I do, I'm not letting you out of your word."

He bent his head to capture her mouth with his. She tasted like fire every time. Sweet, sweet fire, burning him clean when he was so dirty he hadn't thought anything could do that. He kissed her over and over because once he started kissing her, there was no stopping. He took a step, pushing her back against the window, trapping her there while his mouth explored hers.

He had been too close to those nightmare years of living in the dungeon with the others. He hadn't realized how close he'd been to falling into the abyss until her mouth and soft body pushed it all behind a door somewhere in his mind and he was able to close it. He needed chains and locks to hold it closed, but she helped him get it there.

Steele wanted to tell her. He needed to tell someone, and who could an assassin go to? *Yeah, I've killed hundreds of people. Started when I was a kid. Still doing it. It's my first, go-to thought when people fuck up and piss me off.* That would not go over well. But Breezy . . . There was no judgment. She didn't seem to judge anyone. Even the idiots who'd looked down on her when she'd been part of the Swords.

He pressed his forehead to hers. "Any new kid coming in was so traumatized there was no talking to them, sometimes for months. That was difficult. Czar could only try to ease their suffering. He was the one to organize us all, making certain everyone got equal shares of food and water. Sometimes Sorbacov would favor someone and give them baskets of food. It didn't matter if they didn't want to share, Czar made certain they did."

"That would be fair."

"Fair and necessary. After I got there, I was big into hygiene and Czar helped me implement what we could. We didn't have a lot to work with." He flashed a quick half smile at her. "We even made all the kids brush their teeth, sometimes without water. We had to steal toothbrushes and paste and hide them from Sorbacov's guards. In the other schools, they were given every kind of skill to blend with society, but we weren't expected to live. They trained us, but they really didn't believe we'd ever make it out of there for a kill. At least not for a long time."

His gaze jumped from her face to over her head, so he could see the sprawling estate next door. There was still no movement and it was heading toward noon. He didn't know if that was a good thing or not, but little boys at the age of two tended to get up and want to run and play. He needed to keep distracting his woman so she didn't freak out on him.

He could tell, looking down at her, that she was thinking about their son. Her upturned expression held sorrow. Catching her chin between his thumb and finger, he tilted her face up to his. "Baby, you have to look around you at the men, and Lana, here with you. They have one purpose for being here — to get Zane back. To put him in your arms. To bring him home. That's the purpose. We know what we're doing."

"I'm holding on to that. I did think it would take a long time to track him, so if he's here, we're already way ahead of schedule, but it's so difficult to think he might be right there. Right in front of me, scared and helpless with my father . . . He'll hit him if he cries," she explained.

It was all Steele could do to tell her hitting wasn't the worst Bridges could be doing to Zane. Not just Bridges. There was Donk, Riddle and Favor. And Boone. Who knew what Boone was like, other than the fact that he was ugly to everyone and in and out of prison. He'd made a lifetime of moving in and out of the prison system.

"Lana's heading out any minute. She had to wait until noon, at least, to make it look normal. She's taking the boat, wearing nearly nothing and getting in close to their backyard. She'll have equipment on board that will allow her to hear what's going on in the house. It's very sensitive. Mechanic cooked it up for her. He'll be down in the cabin of the craft where no one can see him. It will look as if Lana took the boat out alone on the lake."

"Is that safe?"

He gave her a brief grin, mostly teeth. "Babe, Lana is as good as any one of us when it comes to taking out the enemy. Don't ever underestimate her. What you saw earlier at your apartment was nothing. Had you not been there, she would have disarmed him and probably killed him, at least incapacitated him in seconds without the help of you throwing the blanket. She's lethal as hell. We call her 'Widow' because she's made so many. Don't think for a minute she can't take care of herself, or you or Zane for that matter."

She nodded. "She's very beautiful and confident-looking. I used to look at her and Alena and I was so intimidated, not because I thought they would hurt me but because I couldn't measure up to them."

That surprised him. He tried to think back to the days she'd ridden with him as his old lady. "Were the girls not nice to you?"

Had they been nice? Lana and Alena had been aloof because, like the rest of them, they really didn't know the rules of society. They fit better in the motorcycle club world than anywhere else, and even there, they sometimes didn't know exactly what was expected of them. They learned fast and adapted when they had to. Mostly, they stuck to themselves because it was safer.

Riding with the Swords had been a mission every one of them eventually joined. They were there to kill as many as possible without causing suspicion. They disrupted shipments, and every time a chapter acquired new young girls, a team went out under either Czar or Steele and freed the girls, killed the Swords running the portable brothels and disappeared before anyone could identify them. It was what they were good at.

Meanwhile Code went after the books of each chapter, not the ones anyone could find but the real ones reported to the international president. That was what he was good at. He managed to transfer all the money to their accounts. Then he went after the Greek shipping magnate, Evan Shackler-Gratsos, who had inherited from his brother. It just so happened he was the main target and the international president of the Swords. Code managed to get that money into their accounts as well.

Torpedo Ink was set up financially for life. Every member had access to money. Code managed the paperwork, so anytime they ran into a problem, he could set it right. He did all the things necessary, like making it so Steele was able to practice medicine in the United States, even do surgery legally if he desired. Code was the one who sorted out adoptions if they brought children to Blythe and Czar. Gun permits. Concealed gun permits. Whatever paperwork was needed at any time, Code could easily provide it for them.

"Babe." He said it as a warning.

Her tongue touched her lower lip. "They weren't mean."

He groaned. What the hell was wrong with him? He hadn't told the others Breezy was the one for him back then. He'd had his reasons for being careful, but he should have asked that the girls befriend her.

"I'm sorry, Bree, that's on me. Czar wouldn't have let me stay if he'd known how I felt about you, and poor decision or not, I made my choice to stay. I should have noticed that you could have used friends. We were careful all the time. Lana and Alena had to be careful. No one could know that Alena was Czar's 'sister' and not his old lady, or that Lana and Ice weren't really a couple. That said, there's no excuse for my oversight."

"It was three years ago, Steele. I think I'm over it. I had to be careful as well. Anything I told any of the girls in the club would get back to Bridges. If they didn't tell him, he would beat them. I tried to protect you at all times."

He stiffened, something in her voice telling him there were things he didn't know. "What do you mean?"

She tried to step back, but the wall was behind her. Her head was against the window. It was low and long, giving them a good view of the lake and the backyard next door. Even from a distance, it was easy to see how beautiful it was. It never ceased to amaze him how he could be surrounded by beauty and yet evil was still present.

Steele put both hands on either side of her head, holding her captive, looking down into her eyes. He could get lost there. He did every time he looked into that vivid green. She couldn't hide what she was. All her compassion was centered there. Her capacity to love. He couldn't have chosen a better woman to be the mother of his children — or his wife.

"It doesn't matter now."

"Yeah, baby, it does. It matters to me." A sudden memory came at him out of nowhere. Walking into their room, that tiny place she always kept immaculate, and finding her eyes red, her face swollen from crying. She was rocking back and forth on the bed, holding her stomach. She'd told him she had cramps and that sometimes they were really bad.

Steele had gotten a heating pad and laid down beside her, holding her while she curled up into a ball, the pad on her stomach. She kept adjusting the pad, and when he wanted to examine her, she'd shaken her head. When he tried to talk to her, she just said it was cramps and they'd always been like that. He let it go, but he shouldn't have. He knew at the time he shouldn't have.

"That bastard hit you, even when you were mine, didn't he? He wanted information about me, and you didn't give it to him. Was that it, Bree? Did he do that?" The monster in him opened his eyes, tasted ice-cold rage. Wanted vengeance. Needed it.

She nodded, her gaze sliding from his. She knew he wouldn't like her answers. "He wanted me to convince you to let him close to Czar. You were friendly, all of you were, but at a distance. He had a lot of clout in the club. I was afraid if you knew what he was doing, you'd go after him and he'd get you hurt. A man couldn't put his woman before his brothers. You know that wasn't done. It was never done. If you did, they'd all go after you."

He had to fight to maintain his composure, so much so that he stepped away from her and paced across the room. He would have killed Bridges then if he'd known the man had hit his old lady.

"How many times?" His voice was low. Velvet soft. Scary.

"Steele."

She pressed herself against the wall, going very still in that way that pissed him off because she was making herself into the frozen mouse. He knew he was scaring her, but right at that moment, it didn't matter. He had to know. Bridges might be right across the way, within reach, and Steele was racking up every sin the man had made against Steele's family.

"Fucking tell me, Bree. I'm not going to ask again."

"Every month. At the end of the month he demanded a meet with me."

"And you kept that from me?"

She nodded. "I didn't want them to hurt you."

"So, you took that man punching you to keep me from being hurt?"

She shivered. "Don't be angry. It was a long time ago. And he was afraid of bruising me, so he didn't hit full force like he did when I was without you."

He was going to slice Bridges up, make it so the man suffered a thousand deaths before he actually died. He glanced up, into the doorway, and saw Savage looking at him. Clearly, he'd overheard. Their eyes met in complete understanding.

"You do something like that again, Breezy, and you won't sit down for months. Anyone threatens you for any reason you come to your man, do you understand me? You were my woman then and you are now. A man or woman wrongs you, slights you, does anything to upset you, you come to me. That's for me to take care of. It's club business if they put a hand on you. Say you understand. And you'd better mean it."

She looked stricken. Hurt. She remained pressed against the wall, her fingers tight against her mouth as she nodded at him.

"I do. I'm sorry. I do understand."

Abruptly, Steele turned and stalked out. Savage threw her a glance, radiating the same ice-cold rage. Bridges deserved their anger, and he was about to find out what it meant to hurt the families of Torpedo Ink.

Fifteen

"How's she holdin' up?" Savage asked as he walked with Steele around to the back of the house. "She's quite a woman, Steele. She stood for you. I know that pisses you off. It would me too, but she stood for you. She took Bridges's fist for you."

"I ought to turn her over my knee for that. Fuck, Savage. That bastard punched her in the stomach, so I wouldn't see it on her face. What the hell kind of doctor am I, let alone her man? I should have known it was going on." He hadn't been paying attention to her the way he should have. This was on him. He should have known. Damn him to hell for being such a fucking selfish bastard.

"Difference is, she was mine, she would already by sportin' a red bottom. On the other hand, I've got nothin' but respect for that woman." Those ice-blue eyes slid over Steele. "She gonna hold when this goes down?"

"Depends on how it goes down. If something goes wrong, watch her for me."

Savage shook his head. "Somethin' goes wrong, I'm going to be right there with you, Steele, taking those fuckers apart. That little boy is one of us. We're not going to let this happen. Nothing going wrong on our side. They're the ones who had better look out."

He leapt up and caught the edge of the eaves, somersaulted up onto the roof and climbed in a casual display of strength. Steele watched him for a moment, getting his emotions under control. The thought of Zane in the hands of anyone close to those who had brutalized him or any of his brothers and sisters was almost more than he could endure.

He wasn't alone in this, Savage had made that clear. His boy was one of them. Torpedo Ink. He leapt up, caught the eaves and performed the same maneuver Savage had. With his strength, it was easy enough, and balance wasn't an issue for any of them.

Preacher had been up since dawn, stretched out on the gabled roof. That type of roof could be problematic in a hurricane if not properly supported, but it was a beautifully constructed home and the roof added to the beauty of it. He walked with ease in spite of the sharp pitch, crossing to the front where he could lower his body down beside Savage.

Ink was there as well. He sat tailor fashion, paying no attention to them. He looked up at the sky. Somewhere in the distance a hawk let out an eerie cry. Ink didn't move. He kept his eyes on the sky and his hands over his knees.

"Lana's in the water," Preacher reported.

The tension went up significantly. If there were any men at the estate next door, they wouldn't be able to resist a beautiful woman in a thong bikini and very little string for a top. The material barely covered Lana's full breasts. Her body was sculpted with curves and sleek lines. She looked like a model for bathing suits. Her hair was long, a blazing red that went with her pale skin. Even so, there was always the possibility that if any of the Swords were at that estate, they would recognize her in spite of her disguise.

Lana took the boat out onto the lake easily, evidently confident in her driving. She went slow as she passed the houses but picked up speed once she was on the lake. She hadn't looked at the estate as she glided past, merely glanced at the beauty of the oasis created by the builders, but Steele knew that one glance was enough for her to mark every point of entry from the lake side.

She went on past, sweeping out in a big arc, going across the water at a much higher rate of speed. The weather was perfect. Humid, and hot already. It was going to be a good day, with the sun blinding on the water. Anyone would want to be out, which only added to the normalcy of Lana taking the boat out on her vacation.

Steele used binoculars to study every inch of the estate he could see. There were no child's toys. No animals. The yard was pristine, clearly kept up by a landscaping crew. No one came out of either the main house or the smaller cottage. He studied the trucks. Information was crucial when planning any assassination or rescue. The more information, the smoother and safer the operation.

A hawk circled above them and then drifted on the wind to the estate next door. He circled the structures and then settled in a tree overlooking the front yard. A flock of sparrows approached, the group larger than normal with more birds joining as they got closer to the vacation rental. In the sky, the dissimulation looked like a dark, twisting shadow, coming fast, suddenly veering away and rolling into a strange-looking apparition.

The flock of birds changed direction in

midair, looking as if they came to a standstill almost directly above Ink. He didn't move, as still as a statue, his face a mask of concentration. The birds wheeled and dipped, moving back toward the neighboring estate.

"Any of those vehicles look familiar?" Steele asked.

Transporter shook his head. "None. They seem fairly new, all but the one in front of the guest cabin. That's several years old, but even from here, you can see it's in good condition." He indicated the smaller pickup. "My guess? It's a road rocket. Someone put some money into that baby. Swords put their money into their bikes."

Steele didn't change expression, although his heart dropped. He wanted his son to be close. If he wasn't here, they had three other places they knew to look. This had been their best shot at finding him fast. With the information Steele had gotten from Bruiser and Scalp, as well as what was collected on their phones, it looked as if this estate was a sure thing. He wanted it to be. Every minute in the hands of Bridges meant Zane's life was more at risk.

Transporter had noted the Swords liked adding speed to their rides. He used to shake his head when he saw them pay so much money and get practically nothing back. He never offered to help them though. None of the Torpedo Ink crew had given away any of their abilities to the Swords. If someone had fixed up the little pickup, it most likely hadn't been a Swords member — or at least one from the New Orleans chapter.

Steele had learned patience, and this was still nerve-wracking, so he didn't want to think too much about Breezy and how she would be taking this. "I shouldn't have gotten so angry with her," he told Savage. "About Bridges. That was three years ago, and she's going through some heavy shit right now. She did something amazing for me and I wasn't very nice about it."

He'd probably hurt her. How did Czar maneuver through his relationship with Blythe? He wanted Breezy safe and reliant on him. She must want the same thing for him. "Fuck." His hissed the word through clenched teeth. "I just fucked up again. I should have been more understanding."

Savage shook his head. "The bigger picture is you make sure she's safe at all times. From anyone. From everyone. She has to know that. You don't make a point now, she might hide things from you again. Better to let her know you won't put up with that kind of shit."

It didn't surprise Steele that Savage was hard-core about what he expected of his woman.

"A man hits my woman, that's a dead man. If she kept it from me and I found out after the fact, ten hours, ten days or weeks or years, she would be a very unhappy woman for a long time. I would make my point, Steele, the first time, so I never had to make it again."

"I get that. But I could have chosen a different way to make my point. Breezy isn't the type of woman to do things just to piss me off. She thought she was doing right."

Savage shrugged his broad shoulders. "Doesn't matter, her motivation. She put herself in danger and didn't tell you. That's not ever going to be okay, and you know it. Hell, Steele, I want to go down there and shake some sense into your woman. She's ours. Torpedo Ink's. The minute she became your old lady, he had no right to touch her. Pisses me off."

Savage turned away but continued talking. "We have a code we all live by. It's what keeps us all alive and safe. We bring a woman in, she lives by that same code. She doesn't, she endangers all of us as well as herself. You have to shut that shit down fast."

Savage didn't look pissed off. He looked scary as hell. Overhearing the conversation, Preacher took his eyes from the binoculars and turned to look at them. Transporter did the same. Even Ink blinked and glanced their way.

"What the hell did Breezy do? Who touched her?" Transporter demanded. "And how?"

Maestro had come up on the roof behind them, handing water to Preacher. He raised an eyebrow at Steele. "Someone hurt our girl?"

Steele nodded. "Back when we rode with the Swords. Breezy told me Bridges beat her every month because she wasn't doing what he wanted, getting him in good with us. She didn't tell me because she was afraid for me. Hit her in the stomach so I wouldn't see the marks on her. She'd say it was cramps." But he would have known better if he'd taken the time with her that he should have. That was on him.

There was a shocked silence. He didn't know if they were all shocked because Breezy had hidden it from him or because Bridges was that reckless and stupid — or because he hadn't known. Steele would have killed her father had he known. All of them knew that with certainty.

His jaw hardened. A muscle ticked there. He was getting fired up all over again, feeling the gathering rage pouring off the others that someone dared lay a hand on one of their women.

"She hid it from you?" Maestro echoed, as if he couldn't quite believe it.

Steele nodded. "Yeah. Pissed me off but made me all the prouder of her."

"The woman never lacked for courage," Transporter said. "Everyone knew that. Never could understand what was wrong with the men in that club. I guess when you traffic women you lose sight of what's important because you rot from the inside out."

"She know never to do that shit again?" Ink asked, his gaze back to the sky, following the path of the birds until the hawk chose a tree at the back of the house to settle in.

"She does," Steele assured.

"Hope you reinforced that with a good lesson in what a man does when his woman fucks up," Maestro said, anger shimmering in his voice.

"He's pussy whipped," Savage stated.

"Can't deny it," Steele admitted, in no

way offended. His woman probably needed him right now to go down to her and wrap his arms around her. He was torn by that. It would only take a moment or two to reassure her and maybe apologize. Maybe he'd scared her. But wasn't that the point? Hell. He was going to have to ask Blythe what he should have done.

Preacher grinned at him and settled back onto the roof. "I like your woman, Steele. She's got courage." He took a slow drink of water and put the binoculars back to his eyes. "Lana's making her circle, coming back around toward the target. She'll slow the boat some distance away, drop anchor and sunbathe. Mechanic will listen in for us, see if he can catch anyone talking."

"Who's on Breezy?" Steele asked Maestro immediately.

"Keys is with her. She's in the kitchen fixing food. She fixes any more food and we're going to have to roll ourselves to the bikes to get home."

"You could actually skip a meal," Transporter said. "Leave more for the rest of us."

"I'm eating for Ice and Storm," Maestro pointed out. "Someone has to do it when they aren't around." He toed Steele. "Your woman is nearly as good a cook as Alena, and that's saying something."

Steele nodded. "She is. She likes cooking. I was thinking I'd get a chef for us, but she seems to like to have the kitchen to herself, and it's one less outsider. Don't want to shock the poor bastard by eating her out on the counter in front of him."

"Smart," Transporter said. "Knowing you, a stranger looked too long at your woman, you'd slit his throat."

Steele sighed. "Yeah, I don't think I've evolved very far. I'd hate to kill the chef. It might become a habit. After losing a few of them, Harrington and Deveau would show up asking questions. They still coming to the bar, Preacher? Asking about those bikers and hit men disappearing?"

"Not for a couple of weeks, but they're keeping an eye on the place," Preacher answered, but most of his attention was directed at the backyard pool and cabana area as well as the boat that had dropped anchor a good distance away.

"Czar was going to talk with Deveau," Steele told the others. "He wanted to make certain Jackson was warned the Swords were making another play."

"They aren't going to stop coming at him," Maestro said. "Or us. We just have to hit them hard every time and keep them weak."

"That's a good argument to patch over this other club," Steele said, "then we've got twice the firepower against the Swords and any other enemy. They still don't know who we are or where we are, but if Breezy found us through process of elimination, the Swords could. By now, Code has all kinds of dope on the chapter. Gavriil did an investigation before he brought us the idea. I'd like to know we've got more brothers watching out for those scumbags."

"The Swords are used to their women doing their dirty work," Transporter pointed out, contempt dripping from his voice. "They think it makes them stronger to have their women prostitute for them and carry their drugs, but in the end, it weakens them. What the fuck do they do all day? Sit around the clubhouse drinking, doing drugs and getting a beer belly."

"You talking about me?" Maestro demanded, patting his flat washboard stomach.

"You're eating twice as much as the rest of us," Transporter shot back.

"I'm taller than all of you. I've got more to fill up just from sheer size alone," Maestro pointed out.

Steele shook his head. They were all crazy, but it was a good crazy.

"I'm with you, Steele," Savage said suddenly. "I like the idea of bringing others on board. Gavriil was talking to Czar the other day, and he pointed out that there were four schools. We had it the worst, but the others had it bad as well and they were trained in the art of assassination, using every means possible. They had to go through similar trials. There are quite a few of our brethren out there. Men who survived the training and the missions and, later, Sorbacov's purging when he tried to kill every single one of us and sweep us under the rug. The more men we have that we can count on, the stronger we're going to be."

Steele nodded. "I agree. I think we need to bring them in slow though. The Diamondbacks are definitely going to protest if they see our numbers growing, especially if it's done too fast."

"Lana's making her show," Preacher announced. "She's laid out her towel and pulled off her suit and she's pinning up her hair, making certain if anyone in that house is looking, they're seeing something worth getting a closer look." His rifle was inches from his hand. He was fast, and more importantly, he didn't miss. He was all business with a rifle.

Immediately the attention went to the

lake, and then to the backyard of the Abernathy estate. Lana stood in the boat, body swaying with waves, making a show of smearing suntan lotion over her skin. She paid a lot of attention to her breasts, rubbing in the lotion and then placing one foot up on the cab so she could spread it over her leg. She concentrated on making certain every inch of her front was covered before she lay down on the towel and put her sunglasses on to cover her eyes.

"Nice, Lana," Maestro said. "You're going to get skin cancer."

"Not in the half hour it will take to get this done," Transporter objected.

"How do you know? It could happen in the first few minutes of exposure," Maestro informed him knowledgeably.

"You're so full of shit," Transporter said. "I read a book on that —"

Maestro cut him off. "You've read a book on everything, but if whoever wrote the fuckin' book didn't really know shit, then quoting them makes you look bad."

"I've got movement," Preacher said.

Every eye went to the glass back door. A man stepped out, scratching his crotch as he walked to the other side of the wide patio and spit over the wrought-iron railing. His eyes were on the boat anchored between the two properties, but more toward the estate.

"Donk," Preacher identified. "We hit the mother lode first time out. Nice hunting, Steele. All that work you did paid off."

Elation burst through him, but Steele held it in check. They had yet to see Zane. Until they did, they had no way of knowing if he was alive, dead or sold to some pedophile. If Donk was there, for certain Bridges was as well.

"Mechanic," Steele spoke into the radio. "Donk has eyes on Lana. Tell her to keep him occupied. When he starts to turn away, we'll let her know. In the meantime, you try to pick up sound. We need to know as close to the real number how many are in that house." He hesitated. It hurt like hell to even express his worry, but it had to be said. "Or if Zane is there."

Zane. His son. He wouldn't be able to face Breezy or himself if he couldn't get his boy out of the situation. He wasn't leaving the child behind.

"Steele."

Savage's voice was low, but it brought him up short. Steele looked around at the others on the roof. The building trembled. Just a little. "I'm good," he managed, and picked up the binoculars to sweep the area.

Ink hadn't moved. He was so still he could have been a carving. Steele knew he was concentrating on reading the impressions the wildlife surrounding the house was giving him. It had been Ink who had drawn out the original tree that represented Czar in their colors. That sturdy trunk with the many roots. The seventeen branches represented the survivors. In the original drawing there had been eighteen branches. The crows were the children they had tried so hard to save — Steele had tried so hard to save. The skulls rolling in the roots represented the men and women they had killed in order to survive — or the ones they had killed to exact vengeance for those children who had never left their prison.

Steele felt the weight of that sacred ink on his back. It was there for a reason, to remind all of them they were stronger together. They were now. They moved in complete sync, each knowing what the other would do, what he — or she — was capable of. They had counted on one another since they were very young children. Now, grown, having run countless missions alone and together, they didn't make mistakes and knew with absolute certainty that their brothers — or sisters — would be there when they needed them.

He didn't take his gaze from Donk. The big man gripped the wrought-iron railing and leaned forward as if that would give him a better view of the woman tanning herself on the boat. He turned and called out something over his shoulder.

"You get that?" Steele asked.

"He asked for binoculars," Mechanic reported from his position on the boat.

"Nice," Transporter said. "Lana is an absolute work of art."

"You know I am," Lana said softly.

"Where's the music coming from? You have a radio on board? Or an iPod? Are you using a radio so she can communicate?" Steele asked.

"She doesn't need a radio on board," Mechanic explained. *"I didn't want to take a chance of it slipping into the water, or if they had really good binoculars, they'd see it. We have her player on so Lana can sing if she thinks any of them notice her talking. Having her iPod would seem more normal."*

"Don't talk," Steele advised. "I don't want him making you."

"Sweetheart, he isn't going to be thinking about your Lana, not when he has a hot redhead just a few yards away. He's going to be thinking how he can get to me," Lana said with absolute confidence. *"I like being a*

redhead. I think it suits me."

The door opened, and Favor trotted out. He had two pairs of binoculars and he rushed to the railing, handing Donk a pair, already putting his to his face. He nudged Donk several times.

"They're on you," Preacher reported. "Stay still, Lana. I'll tell you when to move."

The two men watched her for some time, then put their glasses down and faced each other. Across the distance it was impossible to hear them, or read their lips, but Mechanic could pick up not only what they were saying but other sounds in the house.

"At least three other male adults," Mechanic said. *"Two upstairs talking. One downstairs heading toward Donk and Favor. I'm betting Riddle. Donk told Favor to get him a drink and Favor said no way he was leaving so Donk could have the bitch to himself."*

"That's you, Lana," Transporter said. "The bitch."

"So happy someone finally noticed," she replied, and then sang a few words to the song on her playlist. *"I've worked at perfecting my bitchiness, but none of you seem to get it. So disappointing."* She sang those words to the melody of the song.

Steele waited for Mechanic to tell him he heard a child's voice, but it didn't happen, and the silence seemed to stretch out endlessly. He knew the others were feeling it as well, because they were not slinging their usual banter around as much as normal. The air was fraught with tension, so much so it felt like a breaking point.

Donk suddenly shoved Favor, slamming a meaty palm into him, rocking his friend.

"Donk's pissed because he wants a drink," Mechanic reported.

Steele's gut tightened. He'd seen Donk like that a few times. Wound up. He liked to hurt things smaller than him. He had taken advantage of every girl they brought into their trafficking ring, volunteering to train them. He was brutal about it. That was the man Bridges had given his daughter to when she was fourteen.

The members of Torpedo Ink had refused to take part in any kidnapping or training of girls for the prostitution ring, or ones they sold to the ships. They'd tried to disrupt the various chapters, but they'd never managed to catch Donk and kill him. They'd had to be careful not to hit their own chapter repeatedly.

If Donk couldn't beat on his girls and fuck them repeatedly, he got nastier and progressively antagonistic, looking for a fight. Favor recognized the signs and stepped back, away from his friend. He turned toward the house just as Riddle emerged.

"Favor's calling to Riddle to get them beers. Riddle's giving him shit."

Riddle was clearly shaking his head and taking steps toward them. Donk spun around and all but roared at the man. His arms waved up and down and he lowered his head as if he might charge like a bull. Riddle hastily turned and headed back inside.

"You're doing great, Lana," Steele said. "Don't fall asleep on us."

"No worries. It's a little too hot here for me. I like our coastal weather. I'm never going to complain about the fog again."

Keeping his eyes on Donk, Steele tried distracting her. It wasn't fun to lie out alone right in front of the enemy, particularly if he might be able to identify you. It was what they did, and Lana was a pro, so maybe his guilt was still weighing heavy on his mind.

"Lana, Breezy told me that Bridges used to beat her once a month during the time she was riding with me. When she belonged to me. She was afraid for me because she knew I'd go after Bridges." It occurred to him that Breezy was smart enough to time those beatings with her monthly period just so she had evidence in case Steele had noticed, but he never had, because he was a selfish bastard. Damn him. Why had he reacted like an idiot? Why hadn't he pulled her into his arms and held her? Thanked her for having his back.

There was complete silence. Mechanic was clearly absorbing what he had said. The others waited for Lana to weigh in. It took a couple of minutes.

"She knew the Swords would expect you to be okay with Bridges beating the shit out of his daughter," she mused finally. *"If you retaliated, she thought they'd hurt you. Maybe even kill you."*

"I would have killed him," Steele conceded. "She probably knew that."

"Most likely," Lana agreed. *"And then the others would have gone after you."*

"But she should have told me," Steele reaffirmed. He believed that wholeheartedly. She *should* have told him. His head hurt from trying to understand what was the right way to handle Breezy's reticence. He could plan a battle against an enemy whose numbers were far more than his team's, carry it out and never so much as blink, but knowing the right thing to do with a woman he loved, that was completely different — and much more difficult.

"Yes," Lana agreed, *"she should have."*

They all waited for Lana's take on it. No one spoke. Living in a society other than their own was difficult when they didn't know the basics. They had been children making up their own rules for survival. They'd kept those codes because they'd worked all those years under the worst possible conditions.

The instructors at the other three schools may have been brutal but they'd taught the inmates how to fit in because it had been helpful when they'd been sent on missions. No member of Torpedo Ink had been expected to live. They'd been sent out on straight seduce-and-kill missions. How to use a fork at an upscale restaurant had been deemed useless to them.

"Were you angry with her?" Lana asked.

"Yes. He could have done any number of things to her and . . ." He trailed off, the sneaking suspicion coming to him. He didn't want to voice it.

Lana did it for him. *"Mostly, she should have trusted you."*

The others were nodding, but Steele knew it was more than that. So, evidently, did Lana. He could tell by her voice. Breezy should have trusted him, and it angered him that she hadn't. He thought she was all his, but she wasn't. In Torpedo Ink's world, they trusted one another to have their backs. They talked things out. They didn't keep secrets . . . He pulled himself up short. That wasn't true.

He hadn't told the others that Breezy was his one. His only. Reaper had kept secrets, and it had nearly blown up in his face. Everyone had secrets, even them. He closed his eyes for a moment, anger stirring. He'd had a shit childhood. His teenage years hadn't been so hot. His early twenties hadn't been anything to write home about. Now he was blowing his one chance because he didn't know shit. Not one fucking thing about relationships. Relationships were a minefield, far more dangerous than any battle he'd ever been in.

"This is a difficult call, Steele," Lana said. *"I've spent a lot of time with Blythe. She seems to navigate this stuff so smoothly. I would have been angry at my man if he'd done it, but her reasons were to protect you. You wouldn't have told her and you would have taken the beatings if you thought it would save her from harm in some way. I would have done it. Any one of us would have."*

That was the truth. Steele's eyes met Savage's. Simultaneously, they both shook their heads, rejecting the idea of it. "It isn't," Steele said. "It's not the same thing at all."

"Nope," Maestro weighed in. "Not at all."

"Why? Because she's the female? I'm a woman. I have the right to protect my man if he has the right to protect me."

"That's different and you know it, Lana," Transporter said. "Breezy doesn't have our background. She's . . . I don't know. Not supposed to get hit. If a man hit you, you'd have him for breakfast and not in a good way."

"Thanks for clarifying," Lana sang to the melody on her playlist. There was a hint of laughter in her voice. *"What did you do, Steele? How did you react?"*

Steele hesitated, but he really wanted Lana's input. He needed to know how to deal with problems of trust that came up between Breezy and him. "I wanted to turn her over my knee and I made that very clear." A part of him still wanted to go back into the house and do just that. Another part of him recognized the hurt on Breezy's face and wanted to pull her into his arms and comfort her.

The others nodded, deeming that an appropriate response. Lana took so long to respond that Steele thought she might not.

"So, you threatened to hurt her because someone else hurt her and she didn't tell you.

I'm not altogether certain that makes sense, Steele."

"It's not the same thing," Steele muttered, no longer sure if it was or not.

"You're wrong, Lana," Maestro said. "It's not at all the same thing. If a man's woman goes rogue on him and puts herself in danger, he has to make absolutely certain she won't make that mistake again."

"There are probably better ways to make the point," Lana sang.

During the entire exchange, Mechanic was relating the conversation between the three Swords members.

"What better ways?" Steele asked immediately. That was what he was looking for. An answer. A better way. Something to make Breezy want to stay with him always. There had to be a way to make a point without hurting her.

Again, there was a long silence. *"I don't know,"* Lana finally admitted. She sounded frustrated. *"You should ask Blythe,"* she reiterated.

"Blythe doesn't know how dangerous the world is," Savage contributed unexpectedly. "She doesn't have the experience to judge when something is potentially life-threatening."

"Breezy withheld important information

from her man," Transporter added.

"From the club," Preacher put in his two cents. "Lana, they're getting antsy. Put on a little show to grab their attention. I've got them now. One bullet for each, take me three seconds."

"Don't," Steele cautioned. "We don't know where Zane is."

His anxiety level was going through the roof, when he was always the calmest man. He found it was far different experiencing trauma as the father. When it was his own child. They went after pedophiles as a rule, planning out the rescue of children, both boys and girls. He had never had his heart pound, or his lungs feel raw from lack of air.

Lana rose up to her knees, her red hair a sheet of pure fire. She tossed her head back and her hair went flying, drawing attention. The men at the railing who had begun talking among themselves turned back, gazes riveted to the woman on the boat. She stood slowly, pulled her glasses off and walked toward the side of the boat, looking at the water.

Preacher had his eye to the scope of his rifle. His hands were rock steady. The first target was Donk. The big man had always been unpredictable. He would be the first to go. Ink didn't so much as blink, his gaze in the air rather than on the water or the three men, but his concentration was utterly focused. Maestro had dropped flat, lying in a prone position, a rifle to his shoulder, his aim not on any of the three men but on the door of the house. The others trained their binoculars on the backyard of the estate, that beautiful oasis the Abernathys had created, only to have their son take it over whenever he was released from prison.

Lana dove into the water, swam around the boat and caught at the ladder to climb right back out. She was naked, beautiful, the water running off her, first in sheets and then drops as she once more climbed on board, mesmerizing her audience. All three Swords members had their binoculars to their eyes, their attention once again riveted on Lana.

"I hear a female voice," Mechanic reported.

Steele held his breath. His son had to be there. He had to be. His stomach was in knots. How many times had he crawled through the ventilation system at their prison when he was a child, stealing medical supplies and sometimes killing one of the adults. He'd never so much as flinched. He had nerves of steel. It was an often-told joke. He didn't feel that way now. He didn't want to exercise caution. He wanted to run to the house and search it, room by room, taking apart those inside until he found his boy.

"A child's voice." Mechanic's usually steady tone cracked. He cleared his throat. *"Definitely a very young child inside. Second floor. On the move with the female. She's talking low to him and cautioning him not to speak until they're outside. I don't think she's aware that Donk or the others are out there."*

Steele was grateful he was sitting down. He knew his legs would have given out in sheer relief. *"Keys."* He spoke into his radio. *"Tell Breezy he's there. Inside the house. We've found him. Don't let her do anything crazy, like run over there."* That was exactly what he wanted to do — get to the house and take his son back.

He kept his binoculars focused on that back door. Breezy had shown him pictures of his son, and now he had them on his own phone. He wanted to see his son in flesh and blood. Alive. The relief was overwhelming.

"Pickup on the move, the small little rocket that was parked in front of the guesthouse. Lizard is driving," Ink said. His voice was pitched low, but it carried over the rooftop so all of them could hear. He sounded as if he might be in a trance, talking while hypnotized. "He's making his way to the main house."

Steele didn't allow that information to divert his attention from the entrance. The door opened, and a woman stepped through. She was leaning down slightly and talking. He could see that it was Candy, although she seemed grown up in comparison to the young girl she'd been three years earlier.

She was laughing, and she reached down. He could see a little hand going into hers. Together they stepped through the door. They walked along the patio and rounded the corner where the flowers formed a small barrier.

His son. Steele focused the high-powered binoculars on the child. He had a wild mop of tawny hair. His heart ached. Beat uncontrollably. The boy was thin. There was a bruise on his face. Very distinctive. Very dark. Rage burst through him and the monster inside roared.

Candy's smile faded, and both of them came to a halt. She leaned down and whispered something to the boy.

"He's beautiful," Lana said.

"Looks like you, Steele," Transporter said.

"She's reminding him to stay close to her and away from any of the men. Not to make a lot of noise or cry. Especially not to cry," Mechanic reported. *"She told him they would swim later, that they needed to get back inside."*

Steele knew Candy was aware Donk liked to hurt smaller creatures. The girl straightened and started to turn.

"Candy," Donk roared. "Get your ass over here and suck my cock."

"Mine too," Riddle said.

Favor just opened his jeans.

Candy pushed the child behind her and indicated the door to the house. "I'm supposed to be watching him." She took a step to try to get back to the safety of the house.

Donk started toward her, his strides long, arms swinging angrily, reminding Steele of a gorilla. "You do what I say," he snapped. "Get your ass over here and bring that little pissant with you. I'll drown the little mongrel."

Candy held up her hand to placate him. "I'll blow you, Donk. No problem."

Steele focused on the boy. He was looking at Donk with fear, but also with open distaste. He didn't turn and run as Candy had instructed him to do.

Donk reached Candy and grabbed her by

the hair, twisting her head, clearly prepared to shove her to her knees. A startled cry of pain came from Candy, and both hands went to Donk's arm to try to ease his hold on her.

Zane exploded into action. "Don't hurt her!" he yelled and flung himself at Donk.

The big man swung his fist at Zane. Candy stepped in front of the child, so the blow took her just above the elbow. She screamed and sank down onto the patio, cradling her arm.

"What the fuck, Donk?" Lizard yelled as he ran to his daughter, leaving the gate open wide behind him. He leaned down to examine her arm. She kept crying, rocking back and forth. Lizard straightened slowly, glaring at Donk.

"Stop whining, you little bitch. This is your fault. Open your mouth and I'll give you something to do besides cry like the whiny little bitch you are. You've always spoiled her, Lizard. She doesn't do anything she's told."

Lizard glared at him. "You broke her fuckin' arm." He got Candy to her feet. "I'm taking her to the hospital."

Candy indicated the little boy. Zane started toward her, but Lizard shook his head. "Can't take him, Candy. Bridges would never allow it. Let's go." Lizard all but forced her around to the gate that led to the front drive where he'd parked his vehicle.

Donk wrapped his fist around his cock and then roared. His gaze dropped to the little boy. Furious, he took a step toward him. "I'm going to drown you, you little fucker."

Sixteen

Steele heard Breezy's frantic cry and knew she and Keys had been watching closely from the wide window in the house. Birds took to the air, all the sparrows, lifting off the branches of the tree they'd been resting in so that the air turned black. As one unit they flew like a dark shadow to insert themselves between Zane and Donk.

Everyone was on the move with the exception of Preacher. He squeezed the trigger, and Donk's head exploded. Immediately he shifted his aim and shot Riddle right between the eyes.

Transporter's rifle also sounded, and Favor dropped to the ground. Steele, Maestro and Savage leapt from the roof, landing in a crouch as Breezy burst from the house, Keys on her heels.

A truck was already in the front yard, everyone leaping into it, Player at the wheel. Keys tackled Breezy, stopping her.

"Go, go," Steele ordered, and Player stepped on the gas.

Keys could handle Breezy. Steele wasn't going to allow his woman anywhere near this mess. He had no idea how many men were still inside. Mechanic had confirmed at least five, but there was likely to be more. Any one of the Swords was capable of shooting Zane from a distance, even if Torpedo Ink could keep the boy from entering the house.

Player had mapped out the quickest route to the estate, covering the distance in record time, but it was the longest few minutes Steele could ever remember. Dirt rose in clouds around the vehicle. The birds shrieked, and the hawk darted in the air. Steele caught glimpses of it diving as if attacking something and then rising sharply, only to go back, talons extended, wicked beak in play.

They hit the ground running, spreading out, some going in through the various entrances, the layout of the house and grounds already completely familiar to them. Steele went to the backyard, Maestro and Savage beside him.

Donk's body lay only feet from Zane. The child stood in a pool of blood, tears streaking down his face. The door to the house was open. A wall of birds spun in circles between Zane and the door, making it nearly impossible for the little boy to move.

"Get in here," Junk snarled. "I'll beat your ass if you don't get in here, Zane," he called to the child.

Zane turned toward the sound of Junk's voice, and Junk stuck his head around the door to give him another order. The hawk dropped from the sky and ripped its talons across Junk's face, digging deep, leaving long furrows over his cheeks, one eye and forehead. His high-pitched scream matched that of the hawk as the bird rose into the air. Junk staggered and fell. The bullet tore into the doorframe where his head had been. He scrambled backward and kicked the door closed, leaving Zane alone with the three dead men and all the birds.

Zane put his arms into the air, trying to shoo the birds away. Steele hurried across the patio, staying low, Maestro running with him. From inside, guns spat. Glass shattered, and bullets zinged past both men. Steele, heart in his throat, kept moving toward his son, terrified that Bridges or Junk would shoot the boy out of pure spite before he could get to him. More windows shattered, proving the two men weren't alone in the house.

Zane put both hands over his ears and walked backward away from the house, leaving a bloody trail of footprints. He was getting dangerously close to the pool. The dark cloud of sparrows circled him continuously, making it difficult to see him through the spinning shadow of birds. The noise was horrendous with all the birds making a riotous racket.

The boat came at the pier fast, Lana at the wheel, Mechanic training guns on the estate. Steele threw caution to the wind and sprinted toward his son. Maestro ran with him, his body a solid wall between Steele and the house. Ordinarily, the moment he realized Maestro was in danger, Steele would have stopped his reckless behavior, but this was Zane. His son. Breezy's son. He kept going, hoping the universe would be understanding and Maestro wouldn't get hit.

He reached Zane just as the little boy realized he wasn't alone out there. When he spotted Steele rushing toward him, he turned and started to run, heading right for the pool. Steele renewed his efforts, trying to put on more speed. He reached the boy just as Zane had one foot over the edge. Wrapping his arm around him, he dragged him to his chest, whirled around toward the lake and kept sprinting fast, heading for the boat, Lana and Mechanic.

Bullets hit all around them, and then Preacher and Transporter were answering, returning fire, hosing the house back and forth across the windows so that whoever was firing at Steele and Maestro had to hit the floor to keep from getting killed. Preacher had switched weapons but was no less lethal.

Zane struggled, trying to get free. "I've got you," Steele whispered. His heart felt like it would explode in his chest any minute. He had his boy. His son. Safe. Relatively safe, he qualified, as he raced along the pier toward the boat. He was more exposed than ever now, right out in the open, his feet pounding on the wooden pier as he got closer to the boat, although the birds were forming another dark wall between Maestro, him and the house.

He had Zane wrapped up tightly, so nothing could hurt the boy. "We're taking you to your mommy. She's waiting for you," he assured, over and over, as he ran.

The boy stopped struggling as they reached the boat. Lana had pulled on a long shirt that covered her body as she drove the boat. She had the powerful craft alongside the pier and she reached for Zane as Mechanic steadied it. Steele transferred his son to his "sister." She took him, immediately bringing him in close to her.

"Mommy's going to be so happy to see you," Lana said, and there were tears of happiness in her voice. "Look at him, Steele. He's you. He's Breezy."

Steele dropped his hand on top of Zane's head, just for one brief moment, and then he turned back to face the house. All softness drained from him, leaving behind pure rage. He glanced at Maestro. Maestro nodded. Behind him, he heard the powerful engine of the boat as Mechanic took Lana and Zane out onto the lake, away from the Abernathy estate.

"We know how many yet?" Steele asked, all business. They moved fast, in perfect sync as they'd been doing for years. Both used the landscape and layout of the house as cover as they moved back to the firefight.

He wanted to see the reunion between Breezy and her son, but this was far more important. He had to remove the threat to her, to his family, once and for all. The Swords, as a club, would keep trying for them, but Torpedo Ink was keeping them weak, draining all their money from them. They continued to keep them from making new money using old methods. As Code found it, they provided evidence against club members to law enforcement, anonymously, of course, but the evidence was too solid to ignore. There was no way the new problems the club faced could be traced back to Torpedo Ink. They were completely off the club's radar and hopefully would remain so. They intended to destroy the Swords using every means possible.

"Seven shooters left in the house," Maestro reported. "The others took out four. Three live upstairs, four down. Bridges and Junk are both downstairs. Preacher caught a glimpse of them. He could have taken out Junk a couple of times but figured you would prefer to do that."

"He's right. Anyone else is fair game. What about Boone?"

"He's upstairs in the room with the big balcony overlooking the backyard. Preacher kept him away from the window. He aimed at Zane, not at anyone else. Definitely wanted to take out your son."

They were moving into the danger zone, so Steele halted and then signaled that he was going up. The balcony overlooking the backyard was very long and deep, most likely associated with the master bedroom. It curved in places, which was helpful, because the twisting, dark railing made it harder for someone looking through the French doors to see now that the glass was shattered.

Steele went up the side of the building fast, using his strength. Boone would think he was safe because he was up high and the outside walls, although brick, didn't seem as if they could be climbed without equipment. Those very shallow cracks between bricks were all Steele and Maestro needed to make their way up.

Steele waited until Maestro was in position. Maestro had climbed the building from the opposite side of the master bedroom. They ignored the gunfire erupting from various spots around the house. All that mattered was to do their job. They would take out all shooters on the top floor and clear every room, so when they went downstairs in search of Bridges and Junk, no one would be left behind to retaliate.

Steele crept into position, going high, up on the overhanging roof. It protected anyone on the balcony from sun or rain as they sat outside enjoying the view of the lake. He crept along the edge of the roof until he was almost over the spot where he was certain Boone was crouched behind something solid he'd overturned.

Steele lowered his head until he could see

into the room. Boone had crawled away from the window and was dragging a very large end table over to the window. He placed it behind him, making certain that it was set up to protect his back from anyone who might try to sneak up on him.

While Steele watched, Boone stabbed his finger onto a button on the landline. "Bridges. Where the fuck are you?"

"We're taking heavy fire down here, Boone," Bridges told his father. "That fucking Steele. I told you about him and his friends. He's here. He got the kid out of here. Breezy must be close by."

"Send someone to pick her and the kid up. You have them and he's going to back off."

There was silence. Bridges cleared his throat. "Not Steele, Boone. It won't matter. He won't stop. None of these men ever stop."

The voice was tinny coming from the phone's speaker through the intercom system.

"Then you give that little bastard to me. I'll skin him alive in front of the man. That doesn't work, I'll do the same to Breezy."

"Boone." Bridges's voice was cautionary.

That surprised Steele and told him something at the same time. Bridges was afraid of his father. He believed the man was capable of doing just what he threatened.

"Kill the son of a bitch then, just do it fast." Boone slammed down the receiver, picked up his gun and once more moved into position, pressing close to the window, his body behind the heavy table, the barrel of his gun on top of the edge to steady his hand.

Steele maneuvered along the roof until he was just overhead of where Boone had set up his fortress. Once in place, Steele signaled to Maestro to let him know he was ready. *In position. Need him to turn toward you.*

On it. Maestro slid his steel-toed boot along the outside of the glass. A high-pitched shriek erupted from the glass. He kicked hard at the last second, breaking more of the glass out of the window.

Steele swung down, driving right into Boone's face as the man lifted up, gun in hand, slightly turned in order to shoot Maestro. Steele's motorcycle boots slammed into Boone's nose and both eyes so hard there was a crunch of bones as the nose was crushed. He'd targeted the orbital socket, deliberately fracturing both the upper and lower. He swung on into the room, letting go with his fingertips, following Boone down to the ground and kicking his gun away.

Boone tried to sit up and Steele kicked him in the head, crushing his cheekbone on the left side. Boone howled for help. Maestro followed Steele in, picking up Boone's gun as he hurried across the room to the closed door. He stood to one side of it and listened while Steele proceeded to beat Boone, using just his boots. He never so much as bent down or got out of breath.

"Shouldn't have threatened my son or my woman," Steele said. "You're going to die slow and hard." He continued kicking, going for maximum pain, breaking bones and smashing internal organs. He stopped when there was no possible way for the man to move. He was done for. He would lie there suffering until his heart gave out or he bled to death internally.

Steele crouched down and stared into his eyes. "I'm killing your son and your grandson, so you won't be going alone to hell. I'll give that to you as a present." He stood up and signaled to Maestro he was ready.

"Eyes or ears on second floor," Maestro asked. *"Ink? Can you tell us where the shooters are and what's around them?"*

The others were keeping everyone pinned down in the house. On the off chance that anyone managed to slip through the guard outside, every vehicle had been disabled.

They heard the sound of wings as the birds flew in a mass through the broken windows. The noise was much like a wind gusting at a high rate of speed. The sound of flesh hitting wood was loud to their left, as if someone had tried to club at the birds. If they did, the blows went through the flock as if they were insubstantial, nothing more than shadows. The wind howled as it retreated. Steele saw the huge flock of birds change shape in the air, looking for a moment like an hourglass with time running out, and then the birds were back in the tree.

"Single shooter in third window to your left. Looks like a sitting room of some sort. Couches and chairs. The shooter is right at the window. Box of ammo next to him. He's ready for war," Ink said.

Someone screamed downstairs and a gun went off. More screams — this time the same voice was agonized. Savage was at work, cleaning out the enemy. There were two more upstairs of no consequence, and two downstairs that didn't matter. Savage was taking out the two downstairs. He'd leave Junk and Bridges until Steele joined him.

"Can you check the entire floor, Ink?" Maestro asked.

"Give me a minute."

They all knew it wasn't easy on Ink, controlling wildlife. He could do it, and practiced daily, but keeping an entire flock of birds close and sending them between a child and adults as well as into a house would take its toll. Preacher and Transporter couldn't assist him if he grew weak because they needed their rifles for insurance.

Steele's fingers tapped on his thigh. He was aware of seconds and then minutes slipping by. Downstairs, the screams had faded to sobs and pleas. No one, evidently, had come to the man's aid. Most likely, Bridges and Junk were cowering together, trying to figure out how to sneak away, leaving behind their brethren to face the enemy.

The sound of the birds' wings was loud as they once more entered the building like the howl of the wind. They moved through the hallway, feathers brushing the walls and ceiling. They were gone and then came back, entering each room they could through broken windows. The windows had been shot out or broken by someone inside, so they could aim at the Torpedo Ink members firing at them. Most of the time when those inside shot, they were shooting at shadows, not an actual target. It was frustrating and wearing on the nerves. It seemed forever before the wind retreated and it was quiet again.

"Second shooter in the last room facing the pool. It's a bathroom. Tub to the left as you walk in. The toilet is all the way to the back of the room. Sink by window. He's there, using the sink to give him height. It's a tighter space than it looks. A couple of the birds almost didn't make it out and when they came in through the window, they hit him repeatedly in the face. He covered up fast."

"Thanks," Maestro whispered. He opened the door cautiously. "The one to our left? In the sitting room?"

Steele nodded. He didn't like any of the members of the Swords, but as far as he knew, they'd come to help protect a brother, which he understood. They weren't there to hit his son or kill him. If he knew any differently, with a certainty, he would kill the bastards slowly. Instead, when Maestro pulled open the door, Steele stepped in and shot the Swords member three times, all kill shots.

Downstairs, another high-pitched scream told Steele that Savage had found another shooter and was taking care of him. The wail was cut off abruptly and then started again, a jagged piercing cry of agony.

"Shut up. Shut up. Shut up." Junk's voice was raised. Shouting. Trembling. Fearful.

"Distraction," Maestro said into his radio as they crept down the hall and positioned themselves on either side of the bathroom door.

At once a barrage of bullets tore through the window of the bathroom. Maestro and Steele counted. Five seconds later, Maestro tore open the door and Steele stepped into the bathroom and shot the Swords member three times, just as he had the one in the sitting room.

Steele reloaded as he made his way down the staircase to the main floor. He knew Junk and Bridges were at the back of the house, pinned down by heavy fire coming from Torpedo Ink members outside. Savage was in the house, killing the others who had been with the two men, and making certain neither Junk nor Bridges moved from that spot. They were all waiting for Steele.

Steele walked right up to the door of the kitchen and peered in. Bridges faced outward toward the pool. Most of the glass had been shattered, or shot out, but one big slab hung like a death trap, waiting for an unwary visitor. It swung macabrely, as if it were a living thing. Bridges occasionally lifted his gaze to it. When he did, he shuffled back involuntarily and then looked back over his shoulder to see if his son had witnessed his display of nerves.

Junk faced the open kitchen door. The door hung on two of the three hinges and looked as if someone had repeatedly kicked it in a fit of rage. Junk was hunkered down behind a table, gun in his hand, trembling so bad the gun shook. The more the man Savage had taken screamed, the more Junk closed his eyes, wincing.

Steele stepped right into the room and calmly shot Junk in the shoulder and, as Bridges was turning, did the same to him. Junk dropped his gun. Bridges somehow held on to his weapon. Bullets hit all around the man from behind as Torpedo Ink opened fire.

Bridges cried out, a hoarse shout of protest, and lifted his arms to cover his face. He still maintained possession of his gun, but it was in his hand, almost forgotten. Steele smashed the barrel of his gun against Junk's head as he swept past. Maestro picked up Junk's gun. Steele kept moving straight to Bridges, disregarding the barrage of bullets.

"Cease fire, cease fire," Maestro instructed.

Steele brutally kicked the gun out of Bridges's hand. "You think you can hit my woman and get away with it, you piece of shit?"

He had marked every bruise on Breezy's body and he proceeded to use his steel-toed boots and his enormous strength to map every bruise right back on Bridges's body. He did it fast and hard, giving the big man little time to react. He was careful to make it as painful as possible without letting him off the hook by killing him too soon.

"You took my son, Bridges. That was really stupid. You knew I'd come after you. You had to know that. You just stay right there while I have a talk with junior. Your father is dead. Boone wasn't all that good of a man, so I doubt many will mourn. Certainly not his family. You won't have time."

He caught Junk by his hair and yanked him to his knees. Junk screamed as the movement wrenched his shoulder. "I didn't do anything to Breezy," Junk denied. "I didn't do anything."

Steele stared down into his eyes. It was the monster staring at Junk, not Steele, and he was grateful for that monster. "No, you didn't do a thing to Breezy, not to help her. You stood a few feet away while your father hit and kicked the shit out of her. You watched, didn't you?"

Junk didn't answer, and Steele drove the toe of his boot into Junk's bloody shoulder. Junk went sailing sideways, screaming to rival whatever was going on in the other room. Steele waited until Junk's voice was dying down and the man was attempting to crawl toward the door before he caught him by the hair and lifted him back to his knees.

"I asked you a question, Junk." As always, Steele's voice was low. Mild. In complete contrast to the steady, wicked blows he'd visited on Bridges and the kick to Junk's shoulder. "You watched your father beat your sister up, didn't you?"

Junk nodded. "Yes. Yes, I watched," he said, desperation in the pitch of his voice.

"What were you doing while your father punched and kicked your sister?"

Junk's eyes widened in terror. He began shaking his head wildly. "I kept the boy safe. I held the boy."

"*How* were you holding my son, Junk? Like this?"

Steele released the vicious grip he had on Junk's hair and walked behind him. Junk fell forward to his hands and knees. Again, he let out an agonized scream as his hand touched the floor, jarring his shoulder.

Steele caught him from behind, wrapping his hand around his nose and mouth, his arm around his neck, cutting off all air.

"Is this what you did to my son, Junk?" Steele asked in the same mild tone. "Bridges? You recognize this hold? You teach him this is what you do to your own flesh and blood?"

He ignored Junk's wild thrashing, keeping his eyes on Bridges. His hands never wavered. He had completely cut off Junk's air supply. His enormous strength allowed him to hold the man there while he stared at Bridges.

Bridges shook his head and tried to get up. He was too broken and fell back down, but he didn't look away. "Let him go," he ordered hoarsely.

"It's not going to happen, Bridges," Steele said. "I don't feel in the least bit sympathetic. Not at all. The two of you hurt Breezy. Not just physically, but with the things you did to her. You would have sold my boy or killed him. Same with her. This piece of shit doesn't deserve to live, and neither do you. The problem you have isn't how you're going to die, it's when you're going to die. Because both of you are going to die right here, today."

His tone suggested a conversation, nothing more, nothing controversial. He was merely explaining facts to Bridges. He waited until Junk quit fighting and went limp before he released him. Junk fell forward onto his face, gasping, wheezing and choking. Steele walked around him and then kicked him hard in the ribs. Junk shrieked.

"It isn't over for you, Junk," Steele said. "You made her suffer. Both of you. I'm not okay with that." He looked at Bridges. "Did you think I would be? Did you really think I wouldn't come after you?"

Bridges tried to spit. Blood and spittle trickled down his chin. "Thought I could get her to kill you."

"You were wrong. Breezy's got more loyalty in her than the entire Swords chapter you belonged to. You chose your son because he was male. He's weak."

Very casually, Steele walked right up to Bridges and started on him a second time, beating him, this time attacking his internal organs. He was thorough and systematic.

"You're going to get tired a hell of a long time before I am," Steele said.

A few minutes later, he left Bridges sobbing on the floor and started back over to Junk. Savage appeared in the frame of the broken door. "Thought I'd join the main event. The house is cleared. All cameras are removed, inside and out of the house."

Savage walked right up to Bridges, who was moaning and writhing on the floor. "Nice to see you again, Bridges," Savage said.

He crouched down beside him, caught him by his hair and turned his head to face him. "Steele was nice enough to allow me to join the party. He doesn't mind beating the shit out of you, but he can take it or leave it. Me? I love that fucking shit. I love to hurt bullshit men like you. Pussies. Crybabies. You kidnap little kids and sell them to perverts and you rape and beat young girls. I take that into consideration when I'm planning the proper retaliation. I like to see you suffer. It gets me off, you know. I'm already high as a kite from hackin' Obe in the other room to pieces." He took out his knife and slowly, one by one, flicked the buttons off the shirt Bridges was wearing. "Hold still. This blade is sharp. Wouldn't want to cut you too soon."

Bridges shook his head in horror. Steele had always been the steady one. Savage was unpredictable. And he liked to hurt people. Everyone knew that. He wasn't kidding when he said he was high from it. He got off on that shit. Steele was bad enough, with his dead eyes and ice-cold rage. Savage was a demon from hell.

Bridges's entire body shuddered. "Just kill me, you bastard. Get it over with."

"Where's the fuckin' fun in that?" Savage demanded.

Steele was standing over Junk again, watching him dispassionately as he tried to crawl away. He reached down fast, yanked Junk to his knees, arm a bar across his throat, nearly crushing it with his strength, hand once again over his mouth and nose to cut off his airway. Junk's body thrashed wildly.

Savage walked over, leaned down and shoved his knife deep and then ran it up Junk's belly like a zipper, opening him from groin to ribs. Intestines spilled out and slithered across the floor like snakes, straight at Bridges.

The smirk disappeared from Savage's face, leaving Bridges facing the devil. "Breezy is Torpedo Ink. She was always Torpedo Ink. She belongs to Steele. Zane is Torpedo Ink, and he belongs to all of us. You never should have messed with either of them."

"Fuck you!" Bridges screamed. "Fuck you both!"

Steele dropped Junk right in the middle

of what were formerly his insides and stalked to Bridges. He rolled him over and held out his hand. Savage tossed him the bloody knife. Steele tore the man's jeans into strips, ripping them away, so that some of the rags hung from the cut waistband, but leaving Bridges's bare skin and genitals exposed.

"That can be arranged, you sick pervert," Steele said. "You think I don't know about what you did to the kids the chapter kidnapped? Boys and girls? You're a sick fuck. You always were." There was an edge to Steele now, as if his thin veneer of civilization was beginning to crack. "Everyone knew what you did." Code had uncovered quite a bit about Bridges Simmons.

"We don't like your kind, Bridges," Savage added. "You're a pedophile. You like children. You know why? Because you're so weak you can't handle a real relationship. You have to rape children to get off."

Bridges shook his head violently back and forth. He was helpless, lying on his back, his body exposed to both men. They looked at him with utter contempt. Not as though he was human, but as if he were the worst piece of dirt on the planet.

"You know those stories you told Donk and the others about the little boys and girls you raped? What you did to them? Got news for you, you fuck. You're going to experience every detail," Savage said.

Steele stood up, went back to Junk and cut his throat. Bridges howled his need of revenge and sorrow. Neither man so much as blinked. Savage was laying out their tools to make certain Bridges experienced the things he'd done to kids. He had already been beaten until he couldn't move or stand.

They spent nearly two more hours with Bridges, making a point to the Swords, to every pedophile who might know Bridges. His screams and curses fell on deaf ears, as did his pleas and sobs when they got down to work with knives, making him very aware he would never be able to harm another child or woman. He had to watch and feel, but neither showed mercy, their faces grim and purposeful.

As always, the Torpedo Ink members stripped after, down by the lake, the clothing and gloves going in a bag to burn. They washed off in the lake and then dressed again in the clothes Player provided before heading back to the vacation rental. The guns were broken down and would be disposed of on the way home, across several states. They had been careful in the house not to wear their own fingerprints. The key to the vacation rental had been mailed to them. The owner never saw Phil McBride, the man he'd rented to, and the key was to be left for the cleaning crew beneath the mat by the front door.

Steele walked into the house, shocked that his hands were shaking. Not just his hands, his entire body. He hadn't been in the least affected by what he'd done to Bridges and Junk, or the others, but knowing he was going to be meeting his son for the first time threw him. Torpedo Ink members were loading the truck and bikes, giving him a few minutes alone with his woman and son before they wiped down the house with their cleaner and put as many miles as possible between Lake Pontchartrain and them.

Breezy sat in the rocking chair, Zane in her arms, eyes closed, humming as she rocked. The boy had his head buried in her neck, his little arms wrapped tightly around her neck. Steele stood just inside the doorway, his heart pounding and then settling to a rhythm he hadn't felt in a long while. Contentment. Joy. He had experienced both those foreign emotions when he'd been with his woman.

"Thank you, Steele." Her voice came out of the gathering shadows. "You said you'd bring him back to me and you did. I don't have the right words to tell you what it means to me. There is no greater thing that you could have done for me. No better gift."

Steele was silent for a long moment, drinking her in. Those green eyes. Vivid. Overbright. She'd been crying, but this time they were tears of joy and relief. She was looking at him as if he were someone special. Someone she looked up to. Adored. That adoration she'd given him before was back.

"Baby, he's our son. Mine too. There was no question I would get him back for us." He tried for matter-of-fact. He didn't want her thinking he was some kind of hero — and yet, perversely, he did. He loved that particular look on her face, the one that told him she believed there was no other man like him or as good as him.

She smiled serenely. "I love you, Steele." She brushed kisses over the top of Zane's head and then began to ease him away from her, so she could turn him around. For a moment the boy resisted, his little arms tight around her neck, nearly strangling her.

"It's okay, baby," Steele assured her.

Breezy insisted, turning Zane in her arms so he faced his father. She wrapped the boy tightly in her arms. "This is your daddy.

Remember I told you all those stories about him? How brave he is? How he will always look out for you? Your daddy took you away from the bad men. They'll never be able to get to you again." She kissed the side of the boy's face several times.

All the while his son — his *son* — stared at him curiously. He recognized those eyes. He looked into the mirror daily and saw them. There was no denying Zane was his child. He had his jawline. The eyes. Breezy's wild mop of thick tawny-colored hair. It wasn't like his own dark hair wasn't thick and wild as well. Most of the time he didn't bother to try to tame it. He might cut the sides shorter, but the top of his hair was always left longer, and it went every which way, just as Breezy's did. Their son inherited from both. Double the thickness, her color and thick curls and waves everywhere. Zane was so beautiful, Steele wanted to weep.

The two stared at each other. Steele let him look his fill. The little boy reached out a hand, and Steele leaned down, so he could touch his hair. Evidently, they were thinking the same thing. "Did they hurt you, buddy?" he asked.

Zane nodded, his eyes narrowing a little as if the memory made him angrier than scared. "The bad man hit me. Mommy said don't hit."

That little voice turned Steele's heart over.

"He has bruises all over him," Breezy said. There were tears in her voice, and she buried her face in the mop of curls on the top of Zane's head.

Steele's gut tightened and the monster in him roared. Bridges had paid for his crimes. Junk had as well. They wouldn't be coming back to threaten or harm Steele's family, and there was satisfaction in that.

"Come here, little buddy," Steele said gently. "Let me hold you for a minute. I want to see how big you've gotten. Mommy gave me lots of pictures of you, but you're so much bigger than those pictures." He wanted to lay his hands on every bruise and try to ease any pain.

Zane's eyes lit up. "Pictures aren't big."

The boy didn't pull back when Steele brushed his hair out of his eyes. Very slowly, so as not to startle him, and extremely gently, just in case he put his hands on a bruise, Steele lifted his son from Breezy's arms. His entire body reacted. Every cell. Every organ. This was his child. The meaning of that slipped, for the first time, all the way into his mind. Before, he'd been careful not to think too much about it, because that way led to disaster. Now that Zane was safe and with them, Steele could let the reality slide into his brain. He'd never been more emotional.

This was his son. He'd made him with Breezy. He might not be good at telling her he loved her, but it was the stark, raw truth. Having a child with her was nothing short of miraculous. He wanted to crush the boy to him, absorb him through his skin the way he wanted to with Breezy.

Zane put both little hands on his jaw, reminiscent of the way Breezy sometimes framed his face. He knew she must do that to their son.

"So your mama told you I was brave, did she?" Steele's gaze jumped to Breezy's face. Slow color slid up her neck. She shrugged and tried to look away, but he didn't let her. "She told you stories about me?"

"Steele." Her voice held embarrassment.

"Baby, I fuckin' love that you did that." He moved his hand gently over the boy's body, feeling the heat he generated reaching into his son.

She frowned at him. Narrowed her eyes. "There is no need to teach him foul language."

"Got it. No more saying *fuck* in front of the boy."

She rolled her eyes and he grinned at her.

Teasing her. She smiled back and shook her head, pretending to be exasperated. He loved that she got that he was teasing her and shared the moment with him. His woman. Not giving him a rash of shit when it wasn't needed.

"Let's go home, baby. Can't wait to get him back where he belongs." He turned his attention to his son, finishing with his arms and legs and that bruise on his face. He was so little, it didn't take long. "You'll love your new home. We've got a swimming pool, and I can see you were very fond of swimming. Ours is warm."

Breezy shook her head. "I've got to go to the hospital and see Candy. She took that hit for our son," she added when he shook his head. "I can't just leave her behind, Steele."

"Lizard is with her. He didn't see any of us. He can't know you found us."

"I'll go into the hospital alone, honey. Lizard won't try to keep me there and if he did, I could yell for help or tell him there's a gun on him."

"I don't like it, Bree. We're out right now. Free and clear. No one saw us and there's no trace of us left behind. We even cleaned up the baby's DNA."

"You saw what happened. She stepped in

front of him and took the hit. I have to at least ask her."

"Do it over the phone."

Breezy shook her head. "I need a face-to-face with her. If nothing else, I can thank her for taking care of Zane. I know you can keep me safe. You'll have our son with you, and no matter which way it goes with Candy, we'll be ready to leave immediately."

"She's no longer in the hospital. We've got eyes on her and Lizard. Her father put her up in a motel. He hasn't gone back to the estate, but he did get pizza. They're both there now."

She reached out and caught his hand. "I need you to make this happen for me."

What the fuck was he supposed to do when she gave him those emerald eyes and it made sense? Candy had risked herself to save Zane. He just didn't want to trust her around Breezy and Zane. He wanted to wrap them up in a cocoon and keep them safe from every possible threat.

Seventeen

The motel looked as if it had seen better days. Breezy approached from the other side of the street. She wasn't to go near the room unless given the signal that everything was clear. Torpedo Ink didn't want any other Swords member close by. They would have preferred that Lizard was gone as well, but they didn't have the time to wait him out. For one thing, someone was bound to discover the gruesome scene at the estate very soon. They wanted to be long gone from Slidell when that happened.

She glanced up and down the street warily. She knew Steele's main concern with her going into the motel room with Lizard was another Swords member showing up. This was their territory. They might be weak from the loss of members and money, but they had held this territory for a very long time. They had allies.

"Slow down." The tiny radio in her ear was

easily heard. She didn't like wearing it just in case Lizard spotted it, although with her hair, it might be difficult. She was wearing it down to hide her ears and the radio. Who knew something that powerful could be so small? Mechanic had made them for the team.

"I want Preacher in place in the front and Transporter in the back." Steele's voice brooked no argument. He was in charge, and if she didn't do exactly what he said when he said, he'd take her out of there.

She knew him, she knew he'd kill both Lizard and Candy to protect his family. Already she could see what he'd been talking about when he'd told her he would probably hold on too tight. He'd turned into a dictator the moment he'd given in to her. She hadn't dared go against him, and she wouldn't. He would pull the plug on the operation immediately, and she wanted to give Candy a chance.

She took a breath and paused, looking down at her phone as if she got a message. There was nothing on that phone. She could type in anything, gibberish, and the Torpedo Ink club would come running. Out of the corner of her eye, she saw an older-looking woman dressed in a miniskirt with her arm around a man's neck. They walked up to one of the rooms. She pushed her key in the door and the two disappeared inside.

Breezy blinked several times trying to register what she'd seen. She hadn't recognized the woman, but she was definitely a prostitute. The man was older, and he looked hard, like a biker, but he wasn't wearing colors. Could this be one of the places the Swords club used their women to bring in money for them? Wherever the new location was — and they often changed it — they would also do drug deals as well as arms deals. This wouldn't be a trafficking location, all the women would belong to the club.

She stepped back farther into the shadows. "Is this one of the Swords motels?"

"Looks like it, baby. That means get in and get out fast. You don't want Lizard calling for backup. It would turn into a bloodbath. Consider aborting."

It would be the intelligent thing to do, but she couldn't forget the sight of Candy taking the hit that would have knocked her son into the water, and probably knocked him out. That blow had been hard enough to break a grown woman's arm. Candy was a couple of years younger than she was, and Breezy wanted her to have a chance at life the way she had. Steele and the club could help her, set her up in a house, find her a job. They could be friends . . .

"I have to try to help her, Steele," she said softly, hoping he understood.

She knew why he was giving her this concession. He didn't want her to do this. Now that he had Zane, he wanted to get both of them home, where he was certain he could keep them safe. He was upset with his reaction when he'd learned that Bridges had hit her every month when she rode with Steele as his old lady. She had seen it on his face when he'd stormed out the door with Savage. He hadn't been happy with himself and he was trying to make up for it by giving her something he didn't want but knew she did.

Her man. Steele. He didn't realize some things didn't matter that much to her. She'd been momentarily hurt by his reaction, but after she saw the look on his face and knew he hadn't liked his reaction any more than she had, it was all right. Breezy had learned, practically from birth, to let things go. If they weren't big and didn't threaten to swallow her whole, she dismissed them from her mind. If she really needed to deal with something, she thought about it carefully, formulated a plan and then carried it out.

"Everyone's in place, Bree." Steele's voice

was in her ear.

She swallowed down every apprehension and crossed the street. Code was back online. He'd been working on finding the little boy up for auction on the Internet. Running down leads took time, and he'd been staying up nights and eating old food. He'd given himself a very bad case of food poisoning. He was back on his computer, and he'd found out which room Lizard and Candy were in.

She went straight to the door. The paint was old and chipping off. Dirt was smeared across the cheap wood. She raised her hand and knocked, facing forward so anyone coming up behind her or on either side would have a difficult time seeing her face. She wore blue jeans, boots and a dark hoodie. The hood was drawn up over her hair and partially blocked her face on either side.

"What do you want?" Lizard growled, throwing open the door. Then he recognized her. His expression changed. "Breezy. What the hell?" He looked left and right. "You alone?"

Before she could answer, he grabbed her arm with hard fingers and jerked her inside. Slamming the door, he pushed her across the room. Candy sat on a bed, her arm in a sling, flipping through a magazine. She gasped and half stood when Breezy pushed the hoodie from her hair.

"Breezy." Candy's smile widened. "I didn't expect to see you." She glanced at her father and then lowered her voice, as if he might not be able to hear even though he was just a few feet away. "Your father is very, very angry at you."

"He's always angry," Breezy stated.

"Not like this," Candy said. "You should have kept him informed about what you were doing and where you were."

The room wasn't very big, and the two beds were nearly pushed together. There was just enough room to slide sideways between the two of them. The blankets looked filthy and the room smelled of musk and sex. Breezy had the feeling it hadn't been cleaned in years. There were coin slots to make the beds vibrate, and it looked as if the old television had seen better days. She hadn't thought there were motel rooms like this one anymore.

"Breezy, unless you killed Steele and Czar, Bridges isn't going to be happy you're here. When he's not happy, people get hurt," Lizard said. "Did you do it? Did you kill those bastards?"

"What makes you think they're to blame

for the massacre? They've disappeared too. Maybe no one was left alive," Breezy said, allowing frustration into her voice. "If the Swords couldn't find them, why would you think that I could?"

"Don't try to convince him we're dead. Just talk to Candy and get out of there." There was a bite to Steele's voice.

Breezy knew he wouldn't like it, but she wasn't passing up the opportunity to put doubt in Lizard's mind. He had quite a bit of influence with the chapter, and once it was known that Bridges was dead, he could very well be voted in as president.

"That man was crazy about you," Lizard said.

"That man threw my ass out," Breezy said. "I begged him to let me stay, and he refused. He didn't even want me around the club. He was done with me and wanted me gone. That isn't a man crazy about a woman. None of them were the type. I'm not going to say I didn't have a childish fantasy, but if you looked at them, Lizard, you had to have seen how cold they were."

"If you didn't find them, what are you doing here?"

"I was going to try to get Zane back myself. I was watching the house, but then Candy came out with him and Donk tried to hit him, and she stepped in front of him . . ." She broke off. Her voice trembled for real. That moment had been terrible. She'd been so far away, and she'd been very afraid for both Candy and Zane. She was grateful Lizard had showed up.

"I'm so sorry you got hurt, Candy. Thank you for taking care of him."

Candy shrugged. "I wasn't going to let Donk hit the kid. He was so little, and Donk's superstrong. He could have killed him. It was bad enough that Bridges kicked him around. Boone and Junk too. All three of them. I didn't like it, but there wasn't much I could do."

"Junk came out and took Zane back into the house and I could see there was no way to get Zane back, so I followed you here. I had to make certain you were all right, Candy. I was so worried about you." That was genuine enough. She had been worried. Candy had really put herself in harm's way to protect Zane.

Candy looked pleased. "No worries. He's a cute little kid. Smart too."

"You can't get him back," Lizard said. "Not without doing what Bridges wants you to do. You have to find them."

"They aren't out there," Breezy objected. She took a deep breath. "I came to talk to you, Candy. I know you love your father. He's a decent man." He wasn't. He was just as involved with trafficking as the others in the club. "I can help you get out of club life. I can find you a job and a good place to live . . ."

Candy frowned. "What are you talking about? The Swords are my life. I love what I do for them. I'm *proud* of it."

"You're proud of them whoring you out?"

"If I can bring in money for the club, then yes."

"And carrying drugs for them? Accepting all the risks while they get all the profits?"

"Of course. We all do that for them. That's our contribution. You always did whatever was needed, and you did it gladly."

Breezy shook her head. "Candy, I didn't do it gladly. Some things are wrong. The way they treat women is wrong."

Candy looked horrified. "What's happened to you? What's wrong with you, Breezy? I used to look up to you. The Swords are my life. I would never leave, and whatever they want me to do, I'm doing for them. I think you've been brainwashed."

Breezy became aware of Lizard standing between her and the door. He moved closer to it and then rested his back against it.

"I think Breezy's upset that Bridges took

her kid, Candy," Lizard said, his tone reasonable. Understanding. "Is that it, girl? You're upset that your daddy took your baby from you and gave you an impossible task?"

She was in a bad position. Candy wasn't saying those things because her father was in the room, she was saying them because she believed them. In a way, Breezy understood. She'd been terrified to leave the only community she'd ever known. She knew club rules and how to behave. It had been safe there. She'd had to do things she thought were wrong, things she hadn't liked, but she'd still known how to behave and feel comfortable in the environment. Sometimes, even after three years, she still struggled with how to behave outside the club. So, yeah, she could understand Candy's reaction.

"Wouldn't you feel that way, Lizard? He won't give him back to me. He's threatening to kill him." She let her voice waver. Tears for Candy were close. She couldn't take her out of there because Candy didn't want to go.

"He's not going to kill him, especially if it proves that Czar and Steele died in that place with everyone else."

"Why does Bridges think they're alive?" It

was another chance to try to convince Lizard that Czar and Steele were dead.

"That fuckin' Deveau is alive. Jackson Deveau. His daddy was sergeant at arms years ago. I remember him. A good brother. That was before we'd gotten so big. Before Evan took us international. Evan hated that kid. Wanted him dead. He got so that was all he could think about."

"But Deveau doesn't have anything to do with Czar or Steele, does he?" Breezy asked.

She felt like she was treading on thin ground. At least Lizard had given her an acceptable out for being upset and wanting out of the club. He still hadn't moved away from the door.

Lizard shook his head. "The connection is through Czar, from what I understand. Turns out Czar has a brother married to some famous singer. They live in that area. That singer has a sister married to Jackson Deveau."

Breezy allowed the silence to stretch out for as long as she could. "That's it, Lizard? Bridges is threatening my son because Czar is or was related in a vague, convoluted way to Deveau?" She turned back to Candy. "Does that even make sense to you?"

"Damn it, Bree, you're doing it again. Stop trying to protect me. Just get out of there. You

can't save Candy if she doesn't want to be saved. Get out now."

Breezy didn't wince at the brutal command in Steele's voice, but she wanted to. He was angry with her for even engaging with Lizard. He didn't care if the man knew he was alive. He wouldn't care if every Swords member knew. He wanted her safe. That was his first priority. Breezy hadn't known any club could be like that. Steele continually assured her that the majority of the clubs were that way and it was the Swords that was the odd club out.

Candy made a face. "Nothing Daddy said made sense to me. I couldn't even follow it."

Lizard shrugged. "I don't think they're alive, but Bridges does and that's what counts, Breezy. Go back and kill Deveau and maybe Bridges will be satisfied."

"I found Deveau, Lizard. He's a cop."

"Get the fuck out of there, Bree," Steele commanded. The bite in his words did make her wince that time. She could almost hear his teeth snap together.

She knew what Steele meant. She wanted to get out, but Lizard still stood right there at the door, preventing her from leaving. It did provide her with an opportunity to try to convince him that Steele and Czar were dead, and she wasn't going to waste her chance.

"I was scared to try to kill him, but maybe it wouldn't be that difficult. If I could get him alone somewhere . . ." She let her voice trail off speculatively.

For the first time, a smile broke out on Lizard's face. "Now you're thinking. It wouldn't be that hard for you. You look young, and if he's a cop, he'll want to go all protective on your ass. He's not going to think you're in any way a threat to him."

"If I did, do you think Bridges would let me have Zane back?"

Lizard shrugged. "I can't say for certain, but I'll try to convince him."

"I didn't find evidence of anyone left alive. He can't expect me to find ghosts when the club couldn't find them." She tried putting a little whine in her voice. She'd never been whiny, so she didn't think it sounded very authentic, but Candy whined all the time and Lizard would probably buy into it, given that both were female.

"No, but he might tell you he wants you back with him. He hasn't liked you gone, Breezy. You were always good for him, kept him mellow. You kill Deveau and tell him you want to come back. He'll let you have your son then."

Candy clapped her hands together. "Do that, Bree. We could have such good times together."

Breezy bit down hard on her lower lip to keep from agreeing. They'd have wonderful times getting beat up, used and sent out on dangerous trips as drug mules. Her father would treat her like his personal slave, and poor little Zane would be dodging slaps and kicks from his grandfather.

"Do you think he'd really give me back Zane if I agreed to come back, Lizard?"

"Of course he would. He wants you back with the club, Bree. At no time were you banned officially, even though Steele wanted that. You could have walked into any clubhouse and been taken care of, you know that. Steele made you leave, but if you'd gone to your daddy or come to me, we wouldn't have allowed that to happen."

She wasn't so certain. At the time, the club revered Czar and Steele. They had a strong chapter because of those men. If one of them wanted a woman gone, it was going to happen. All it took was one man wanting her banned and she was. A home was never secure for her in the Swords club. She was just now beginning to believe Steele when he told her that most clubs were more like Torpedo Ink than the Swords. Even the outlaw clubs.

She nodded slowly. "Maybe I could do it. Kill Deveau, I mean. I have to figure out how I could get away before the alarm was raised." She tapped her finger on her thigh and frowned, not looking at Candy or Lizard, trying to portray a woman who was contemplating killing a member of law enforcement as if it were the most natural thing in the world.

Candy beamed at her. "I can't believe you're coming back. I hope you take over the cooking for the club. I hate it."

"We all hope Breezy takes over the cooking," Lizard confirmed.

Even during the year she was with Steele, Breezy had cooked meals for those club members staying at the clubhouse. She liked cooking, and it was a habit she'd cultivated in order to stay out from under Bridges's fists.

Breezy laughed with Candy over the joke that wasn't really a joke. They would want her back, so she could make everything run smoothly again for them. If Candy was in charge, she could believe that things weren't going as well as the members would want. Candy was eighteen, nearly nineteen, and she wasn't the brightest woman Breezy knew. Likable, but not bright. Candy would try to do her best, but she wasn't organized in the least.

"Thanks so much, Lizard." Breezy poured relief into her voice. "I was so worried I couldn't think of a solution. I'll do my best to get rid of Deveau, although I'm a little scared to go after a member of law enforcement."

"He's an enemy of the Swords, Breezy," Lizard reminded. "You're always going to be Swords. Think of it as you paying your dues to get back in."

She turned and went to Candy, feeling a lump in her throat. Candy wasn't much younger than she was, but they seemed worlds apart. She hugged the girl, one of her childhood friends she had to let go of. "I hope your life is always wonderful, Candy," she murmured, unable to help herself.

"I'll look after Zane," Candy volunteered. "Don't worry at all about him."

"I won't," Breezy said sincerely. She was always going to be the one person the Swords could track. She was about to become one of their greatest enemies. They might not know who she was with, but someone had helped her get Zane back and they'd done it by killing the chapter president and several of his fellow Swords members. They would always recognize Breezy Simmons, and she would put Zane and Steele in jeopardy just by her being with them.

For a moment she considered confessing that she'd hired some mercenaries to get Zane back. She'd let Lizard take her up the chain of command, and the Swords could beat her or kill her. Because they'd lost a president and several members, they'd most likely kill her. Even with that, Steele and Zane would be safe.

"Whatever you're thinking, don't." Steele's voice was low. Persuasive. Back to a velvet caress. *"I need you, Breezy. Zane needs you. Come away from there where you can breathe again."*

How did he know? But he did. He knew her that well. He knew she would be contemplating giving up her life for the two of them.

She walked toward the door and Lizard. Her heart was pounding. She didn't know if she wanted him to step aside or to hold her right there. She tilted her head up. "Really, Lizard. I appreciate your help. I've been so confused and angry lately. I cry a lot, and I'm so scared for Zane. It's not been easy on my own. I think that's why I was desperate to have Candy go with me. I thought if she was with me, things would be so much better."

Lizard shook his head. "You need to get this done and come home to the club. I'll make sure Bridges will accept you back. You'll have Zane, and he'll be raised where he should be. If he's anything like his father was, he'll be an asset to us when he grows up."

Breezy nodded several times and took more steps toward him. Lizard stepped forward and unexpectedly put his arms around her. "You'll do good, girl. Get this done and you'll have your son back in no time. I'll see that you're taken care of."

She looked up at his face. "He beats me all the time, Lizard."

"I know he does, Breezy. There are a lot of men willing to take care of you, and they won't let him. You just have to give them the signal that you'll take them on."

He patted her head. "You've got my number and Candy's. When this is done, we'll make everything right."

She nodded and stepped out of his arms toward the door. He stepped with her and reached for the doorknob before she could grasp it. He leaned his weight there while his gaze moved over her speculatively. She wanted to scream. She knew he was testing her one last time and she couldn't break, but it was difficult.

"You understand what I'm saying? You choose wisely when you come home. Your man is going to have to have some pull with the club to override anything Bridges does."

She realized then he was talking about himself. If she gave him any kind of a signal, he'd be willing to incur Bridges's wrath. She let that realization dawn and then she smiled, but shyly, ducking her head in an effort to hide how pleased she was. Lizard caught her chin and lifted her head, looking into her eyes.

"You come back, and I'll see to you and Zane. You'll have Candy to help you."

Candy clapped her hands again. "Daddy always said maybe you'd join us, Breezy. I hope so. I want you to. We can share everything. I really like Zane. I'll help with him, no problem. We'll be sisters."

She turned to smile at Candy because she couldn't look at Lizard. He was old enough to be her father, but her age didn't matter to him. She was becoming a little suspicious of Candy and Lizard and just what their relationship was. Breezy shook her head. She had to get out of there before she accidentally said something she shouldn't.

"I'd like that, Candy. I'd better get going

before it gets much later. I like to travel at night. I think it's safer."

"Stop talking. You're going to slip up."

That had been a slip. Now Lizard knew when she traveled she drove at night and slept during the day in motels. He might not know about Steele, but when the bodies at the estate were discovered, he would be one of the angriest because of this moment — when he thought he would have her. She'd tricked him, made a fool of him, and he would never stop until he found her.

"If you don't do what Bridges and Daddy say, Breezy," Candy said in her sweetest voice, "I'll cut Zane's throat myself. No problem. We're a family. You don't just throw away family." She smiled, sugar dripping from her voice. "I've done it before. I killed every one of Jessie Barker's kids, right in front of her, for calling the cops on her old man. Then I killed her."

Steele pulled out the earpiece and shoved it carefully in his pocket. He lifted his head and looked at the others. They were all looking at him. He knew what they expected. He had no choice. None. Lizard had to go, and now, with what Candy had just said, she'd sealed her fate as well. Lizard would keep coming for Breezy, keep her alive for the Swords. Who'd want her dead. Candy just seemed fanatical. Her father had probably brainwashed her from her infancy to believe the Swords were right in all things.

"She was trying to save him again," Maestro said aloud to all of them, but he directed the statement to Lana.

"I heard." Lana sounded tired. "I'll escort her in." She turned and left the room.

Savage shook his head. "My point exactly. She's surrounded by danger, and the only thought she's got in her head is to try to cover for her man. That's definitely a pattern and it's going to get her killed. Worse, she considered giving herself up."

"We don't know that," Steele said and pushed a hand through his hair. But he did know.

Ink shifted Zane's sleeping form from one hip to the other. "We all know it, Steele. You just don't want to admit it to yourself."

"That's the problem with the bullshit rules we're supposed to learn," Savage said. "You learn it, Steele, but she isn't any safer for it."

Steele knew Savage was right, but he didn't like any of the alternatives the club came up with to deal with the problem.

Savage continued making his point. "We don't live in society, maybe side by side, but not in it. We surround ourselves with danger. That means family does as well."

"He's right," Maestro agreed. "She doesn't understand that. Blythe certainly doesn't. I don't know how much I want them to know, but at least if you try to explain it —"

"Then she isn't going to sleep at night," Ink said, rocking Zane back and forth.

"Why the hell should you have to explain anything? She trusts you, she listens to you," Savage said. "The rest is bullshit."

Steele saw both sides and neither worked for him. He was used to figuring things out easily. He found the solutions to the club's problems. He always had. His brain worked fast, compiling ideas, sorting through them and finding the ones that worked the best. Breezy seemed to have short-circuited his brain.

"Our window is closing," Steele reminded, more than happy to get off a subject that wasn't going to end anytime soon. "The moment the door was closed, Lizard was texting Bridges that she was here. He'll want credit for his plan and he'll start trying to persuade Bridges that they need Breezy back in the fold. He'll be very uneasy when he doesn't get an answer, and he'll text the others."

"I've got this," Savage said.

Steele detested that Savage would be the one to go. The more he killed, the more he edged away from all of them. Even Czar and Reaper were worried.

"Prefer you to guard Steele and his family while Keys and I take care of it," Maestro said. "It will go faster with us sweeping the room, making certain there are no cameras or recordings of Breezy. No DNA on anything. She didn't touch anything that we saw, and she didn't sit on the bed, but it's best to be safe."

Savage shrugged. "I can do that."

Steele cut him off, making the decision. "Let's put a two-man team on the motel. Get it done fast. Transporter, get the truck ready. As soon as Breezy is here, I want out. We need to distance ourselves from this place. Everyone was careful, but we still need to wipe it down. That means I'll be leaving with a skeleton crew at first. Savage, you'll be with us."

Savage didn't argue. Steele was grateful for whatever concessions he could get. He nodded toward them as Lana came into the room with Breezy. They'd broken into the building across from the motel and used the upstairs business for their point of operation. They wanted to make certain no one ever knew they were there or even suspected it.

He went right to his woman, wrapped his arm around her neck and kissed her. She tasted good. Sweet with a hint of spice, as if at any moment she could flare into heat and sin. He let himself get lost in her for a few minutes because he needed it. They had his son safe, although they needed to put distance between them and Louisiana. He'd been holding it together, worried about his child and woman, and that, at least was over. They were in his custody and the care of the club.

The bikes would filter out, only a couple accompanying the truck. They needed to get out of Swords territory as quickly as possible. Transporter would switch driving with him so they could make better time.

"You've got about three minutes. Ink's putting Zane in the car seat and then we're out of here."

Her gaze searched his face, but he gave her a little push toward the bathroom. "Don't touch anything if you can help it. We can't leave anything behind ever." He looked at Lana.

She nodded her understanding and followed Breezy right into the room. He heard Breezy's protest, but Lana didn't come back out. Everyone moved quickly. No one wanted to fill his woman in on what was necessary for her safety. She was quick, picking up on small nuances, and they all knew it. She'd trained herself from the time she was very young to get a feel for anything that might be wrong in the club, so she could fix the problem. None of them wanted that. The faster he took her out of there and had her head occupied with other things, the better it was going to be for all of them.

The moment Breezy was out of the restroom, he caught her hand and started out of the room. "Wipe it down and make certain there's no evidence of a break-in," he called over his shoulder, more for show than anything else.

Maestro and Keys waited along with Lana and Preacher until Breezy and Steele were nearly at the bottom of the staircase. "We'll catch up soon," Maestro assured.

Steele gave them the thumbs-up and opened the door that led to the street. He was cautious about it, checking for anyone that might be walking around the neighborhood. He timed it so no cars were coming. There were cameras at the motel and two on the building they were using, but none of them worked.

Transporter had the truck at the curb

directly in front of the seedy little structure that housed two businesses. He'd left the keys in the ignition and had already faded into the shadows, moving around to the back where their bikes were parked in an alleyway where Fatei stood watch over them.

Breezy went straight to the back door of the cab and pulled it open to look at her son. Steele caught her around the waist and tossed her onto the passenger seat. "He's asleep, baby, let him sleep."

"I like to look at him," she protested.

"You'll have plenty of time to look at him on the drive home." He rounded the hood and slid behind the wheel. His bike was already up on the tracks in the back, tied down. He had the truck in motion and was pulling out into traffic before Breezy could say another word. He wanted to be long gone from the state by the time the sun was up.

Breezy swiveled around in her seat to stare at their son. "He's so beautiful."

"Put your fuckin' seat belt on, baby. He's not going to want anything happening to his mother at this late date. He just got you back."

She turned slowly, her eyes on his face as she pulled the seat belt around her and snapped it in place. "Honey . . ."

"Don't. We're not talking about it right now. You were thinking of giving yourself up to them. I heard it in your voice." He'd sworn he wouldn't say a word until he had her in their home. Safe. Where he could hold her in his arms and make it very, very clear she wasn't ever to go down that path of thinking again.

"For a *second.* Just for one second."

She didn't bother to deny it, which was a good thing because Steele found he wasn't in the least bit under control — not when it came to the subject of his woman putting her life on the line for him and their child. That was his job, and he didn't give a damn if the world called him a fucking male chauvinist. He didn't know what that even was. A man who wanted to watch out for his family? A man who respected his woman enough and loved her enough to keep her safe? What the fuck did that even mean? He wasn't even certain he wanted to ask Blythe that question, mainly because he was terrified. He wasn't afraid of anything . . . but Breezy terrified him with her courage.

"I said we weren't talking about it."

Breezy turned her face away from him and looked out the window. "This relationship thing is much harder than it looks, isn't it?"

He had to agree with that. Blythe and

Czar made it look easy. Reaper didn't, but then Reaper was like a wrecking ball. He was just lucky Anya loved him enough to overlook all his craziness. Steele definitely didn't think it was crazy to be upset because Breezy had nearly blown it after they'd finally gotten their child back.

"Do you think I would have left you with them if you'd confessed?" He couldn't stop the demand, it hissed out like a coiled snake, one angry and rattling a warning.

Her gaze came back to him. "I wasn't thinking in that one second, Steele."

"I wouldn't. The answer is no, I would never have left you there. I would charge hell with a bucket of water to get you back. I'd fuckin' search hell for you, Breezy. Don't ever think you can exchange your life for mine, because it isn't going to happen. I wouldn't let it happen."

He took his eyes off the road long enough to glare at her, letting her know he expected a response. She touched the tip of her tongue to her upper lip, a little show of nerves he recognized from long ago.

"I know you wouldn't ever allow it. I do. I'm sorry, Steele, but sometimes I can't help what comes into my mind. I hate that they have a direct tie to you through me. That's all. I dismissed the idea immediately as ludicrous."

The pressure on his chest eased. He rubbed his palm over his heart. "We're going to straighten a few things out when we get home, woman. You get me?"

She nodded. "Yes. Of course. I really wouldn't have done it, Steele."

"I'm going to need fucking therapy if you keep this bullshit up, Breezy," he muttered.

She burst out laughing. "Therapy?"

"Yeah. Therapy. Haven't you ever heard of therapy?"

"Not coming out of your mouth. What kind of therapy?"

He started to tell her but decided to think that over. A smart man might see a few advantages in that question. "Let me think on that for a while."

Breezy laughed and the sound went through him the way it often did, lighting his world. She sounded bright and happy and she shed that light on him. She took him right out of the violence, the blood and death and vile world he lived in, to draw him into the sunshine with her.

He glanced in the rearview mirror so he could see their son. In the side mirror he caught a glimpse of Savage and Transporter as they rode the highway with him. In the back of the truck was his bike. His colors were tatted on his back, so even if he left his jacket home, he was complete. He had his club and his family. He was going to enjoy every single long mile going home.

EIGHTEEN

Steele nudged Breezy with his shoulder as she put away the last of the dishes she always insisted on washing even though they had a state-of-the-art dishwasher. "Will you go swimming with us?" The way her hair curled and waved in big swaths, highlighting the gold strands, always fascinated him.

Steele loved having Breezy and Zane in their home. Most of the time he couldn't sleep, getting up numerous times to stare down at his son's face or his woman's. They both slept peacefully, something that was nearly impossible for him. Breezy kept his demons at bay, giving him enough time to initially fall asleep, but within a few hours or so, they were back.

He didn't mind getting up and prowling around the house to ensure every door and window was locked and the security system was on. He'd had to get after Breezy daily because she had a tendency to go out a door and, when she came back in, forget to lock it or turn on the security system. Truthfully, that made him a little crazy, but he promised himself he'd be patient about it. Even with what happened to Zane, she didn't get that the doors needed to be locked *at all times.*

They both wanted Zane sleeping in their room with them, just grateful they had him, neither wanting to have him far from them even at night, but the little boy woke up at any noise. The third night they fixed up the sitting room off their master bedroom as a nursery. Zane went right to sleep, and as they stared at the monitor, he slept perfectly.

Breezy sang. All the time. Steele loved that. *Loved it.* She sang to Zane as she dressed him for the day. When she changed him. When she fed him. She sang as she cooked meals. Maestro and Keys sometimes came down to play instruments. He'd ordered a piano because he had enough room for one and Maestro said Zane should have it.

He noticed Breezy loved music, especially when they all got together. Zane was wild about the music, and it was clear to Steele that the boy would always want to be around it. The music sessions often deteriorated into Zane banging on pots and pans like he was playing the drums, but they all had a great time.

Zane clung a little more to Breezy than he had in the past, at least according to her, but he wasn't having nightmares. He liked all the club members when they came around. He didn't appear to be shy or in the least afraid of them. He liked that she encouraged their son to get to know everyone. She didn't hold the boy back at all. Each of the members of Torpedo Ink spent time with Zane. She watched them closely, but she gave them the opportunity, and he appreciated her even more for that.

Steele took his time getting to know his son — or rather, letting his son get to know him. Zane liked the water, and Steele's first priority was to make him water safe. He made certain Zane knew that if he wanted to swim, to come to Steele and Steele would take him in. The boy loved the water, and the pool was heated so even in the cold they could swim.

Steele took him into the water several times a day, holding him close at first and then teaching him to hold his breath and how to swim. They went in at night before bedtime, with the idea it would help Zane sleep. Steele was hoping it would help him sleep. It didn't, but he found he enjoyed the time swimming as much as Zane seemed to.

"Can't, Steele. I'm going into Sea Haven. Did Transporter ever bring my truck back? I don't want to take your truck, it's too big."

His breath stilled in his lungs. At no time had Breezy ever indicated she wanted to leave the safety of their home. He straightened slowly from where he'd been leaning against the counter, watching her do the last of the dishes. "Your truck?"

She sighed and pushed back the thick mass of her wild hair. "Yes, honey. My truck. The one I drove here all the way from Santa Fe. I know you think it's junk, but it's mine."

"It isn't safe. You know it isn't safe, and so do I." Let her fight with him over the old rusty pickup she'd driven. And the thing wasn't in her name. It was in her boss's name. It didn't matter that she had a piece of paper saying she'd bought it from the woman. The title wasn't in her name or Code would have found her a long time ago. If push came to shove, he could throw that at her — and he would.

"That's not true." She stopped. Took a breath and then nodded. "I can see why you wouldn't think it was safe, but I need my own vehicle. Transporter is good with engines. He can fix it, can't he? He's been busy, coming with us and all, but the pickup actually ran good."

"Babe." One word. That said it all. She knew better.

She waited and when he didn't speak, she went to step past him. He caught her around the waist, his arm a bar, blocking her.

"I can buy you something else." Something with armor. "We'll head down to Santa Rosa or the Bay and get you something that is safer for Zane." That was always a good move. Breezy responded to all things that had anything to do with Zane's safety.

She thought that over. "I hate that you have to buy it for me."

"Damn it, Breezy. We're . . ." He paused. Took a breath. There was that pride she'd developed and with it came stubbornness. "Let's get married. What's mine belongs to you anyway. Not the bike, but the rest of it. All of it. It's mostly got your name on it if it's worth anything."

Breezy looked shocked. "You want to get married?"

His heart skipped a beat. "Don't you? You're in love with me. You know how I feel about you. We have a son."

"Marriage is something you don't take lightly, Steele. You don't propose in order to get your way over a car."

She sounded so snippy he wanted her right there all over again. He'd taken her once on top of the dishwasher already. He could again if she gave him that voice. Made him as hard as a damned rock.

"I told you I wanted to marry you, back when we were first together I wanted to put my name on you."

"Like a brand. I'm not cattle."

He stepped deliberately into her space. "You're anything but, woman, and you know that. Yes or no? You going to marry me? You already have your name on the house and bank account. If something had happened to me, the club would have continued to try to track you down because you would have gotten it all."

He saw by her expression that was big. "Baby, I told you. I was coming after you. I bought the house for you. I want to marry you, but if you want to wait and spend more time with me, I'll be okay with that too." He shrugged his shoulders, going for casual when he was feeling anything but. He'd promised himself he'd be honest with her. "I'm well aware I need the security of marriage more than you do, but I can wait. It will happen eventually."

He despised that he couldn't quite get over wondering from one hour to the next if Breezy could really love him, but it was getting better. Slowly, but he was getting there.

"Of course I want to marry you," she said, and instantly her face changed to one of suspicion. "You don't already have some huge ring that will weigh down my entire hand, do you? Because if you do, we're taking it back."

He found himself smiling all over again. "No, we can pick that out together."

"Okay then, but I still want my truck back. I need my own ride."

He nodded. "I get that, baby. A car isn't going to break us. I don't ask a lot of you." That was a damn fucking lie, but she didn't know it. "Do it for me. Let me get rid of the truck. If you think your boss in Santa Fe needs it back, we'll get it to her. Otherwise, we'll have Transporter fix it up for Kenny or Darby. But let me get a car I think is safe for you and Zane."

He realized the moment he said Transporter could fix it up for Kenny or Darby, she would wonder why it couldn't be fixed up for her. He saw that on her face, but then, because she was Breezy, she hooked her palm around the nape of his neck.

"I will. I'll drive whatever car you want me to, but honey, you don't live your life safe. You never have. But I still, right now, need transportation. You're going to stay here and teach our son to swim, and I'm going to go into town. I guess I'll have to take the monster truck."

"You're going into town? You didn't mention that you needed anything." He kept his voice very neutral when he wanted to yank her into his arms and crush her to him.

"I knew you had another swim lesson planned with Zane and I thought I could do a little shopping. There's a new recipe I found that I wanted to try."

His heart pounded. Hard. The pressure in his chest hurt. "Baby, you want to go somewhere, you just say so. We can postpone the swim lessons. I'll drive you in."

He hated the monster truck, as she called it. Sometimes he couldn't breathe in that truck, but it was necessary when they took Zane with them. He needed the open air surrounding him. The wind in his face. He wanted Breezy behind him, so close he could feel her body as if they were locked together intimately. He needed that.

"That's silly, Steele. I can go by myself. And that's another thing. You haven't been away from here in the last week. You need to go out with Maestro and Keys and ride. All of you are getting a little crazy."

She still sounded happy. Carefree. She didn't get it. He *couldn't* leave her. He didn't want her leaving either. Unless he took her to the clubhouse. She'd be safe at the clubhouse surrounded by his brothers and sisters. He pressed his palm to his chest over his rapidly beating heart. He'd done everything he knew how to in order to ensure Breezy and Zane were safe.

It took a little arranging to find the right cleaning crew for the house, one that fit, but with the cameras everywhere, Steele relaxed enough to allow strangers in once a week. The cleaners had eyes on them all the time, but that didn't matter. Breezy insisted on cleaning their suite as well as Zane's little room right off of theirs, and Steele was okay with that — maybe even thankful.

He had an app on his phone that allowed him to check on his family whenever he needed to — which was all the time. He hadn't considered that Breezy would take it into her head to run off by herself somewhere. She was right. He needed to ride, but he hadn't figured out how to ride and keep both Breezy and Zane with him.

"I'll drive you into town and go out later

with Maestro or Keys."

Breezy turned slowly, shaking her head, resting her back against the counter, her eyes staring directly into his. Sometimes when she did that, he felt like she could see his every sin. He stepped in front of her, planting a hand on the counter on either side of her, effectively caging her in with his arms.

"You trying to get rid of me, woman?" He knew how to distract her. He kissed the side of her neck. Ran his lips up to her ear and bit down on her earlobe. He felt the little shiver that went through her and licked at the little sting.

"I want you to be you, Steele. You need to ride with your brothers. I didn't want the club life, and I'm still a little nervous about it, but you need it. You haven't been to the clubhouse since we've been back."

So much for his distraction. He was well aware that although she'd agreed, she was still leery of the lifestyle. That contributed to him getting a little crazy about leaving her alone. He might not have been physically to the clubhouse, but all his brothers — Czar included — had been to his home. They'd come, a few at a time, getting Breezy used to them being around. They'd done that for him. Most clubs wouldn't have bothered, certainly not the Swords, and he knew she appreciated it. She couldn't help being a little uneasy.

He knew Code had monitored the Swords as well as every news outlet. Speculation had it that the Swords had been involved in some war with a rival club and the other club had slaughtered the president of the local chapter and several members of his crew, both at the Abernathy estate and in town at a motel that was owned by the Swords. The other rumor was that Boone had made vicious enemies in prison and they had come to his family home to kill him, and his son and grandson had been targeted as well. The motel was considered a separate incident.

It didn't matter to Steele what the world thought, as long as no one was coming after his family. Fortunately, Bridges hadn't communicated very well with others in his club. He'd liked to play his cards close to his chest. Most hadn't known what he was up to. That worked out well as far as Steele was concerned. There was no chatter among the Swords, that Code could find, that included anything about Zane, Breezy or Steele. He hadn't given Breezy any details of the "massacre" at the estate or at the motel, and she didn't ask. He knew she didn't look at any of the news reports, and he wanted to keep it that way. He wanted his woman breathing easy.

His phone buzzed and, still holding his woman against the counter, he took it out and glanced down. Relief flooded him. "Czar needs us at the clubhouse. He's scheduled a meeting with Inez and Frank. Remember them? They own the grocery store in Sea Haven. We're trying to open a smaller version of their store here in Caspar. We figure it will help bring in the locals if Inez and Frank are partners with us and do the actual running of it the first few months."

"Why does he need us there?" Breezy asked.

"You're kidding, right?" Steele said. He eased into a full upright position, taking a step away from her. Watching her warily. This text from Czar couldn't have come at a better time. He needed to find a balance and he wasn't there yet. Czar had given him an out by requesting their appearance at the clubhouse. "You're perfect, baby. You represent everything we don't. Normal. Good. You're a mother with a beautiful baby boy. They'll fall in love with you. You don't look like an assassin."

"You don't either," she said, her palm cupping the side of his jaw.

He loved when she did that, touching him so intimately. "You're lying your pretty little ass off, baby, but I'm okay with that. We need to grab our son and get moving." As distractions went, he thought it was a good one. She might not want club life, but she'd been raised in a club. When the president said he needed you, her automatic response was to go immediately.

"He's up in his room still asleep," she said.

He knew that. He'd come downstairs after staring at Zane for twenty minutes, breathing him in, after first touching that wild hair with his fingers as if he could absorb every detail about the boy. He'd come into the kitchen determined to sit his woman on the counter and have her for a snack. She woke him up every morning, her mouth paradise and her body hot as hell, so tight she took his breath every time.

He didn't dare push his luck by saying they had time for sex. She'd give it to him, but she might decide to ask why he was keeping her a virtual prisoner. He'd hoped she wouldn't notice, but Breezy noticed everything. She was already suspicious because he wasn't riding, and he was always on his bike. She knew that about him. She'd lived with him for a year and he'd gone out every day, even when it rained. She was going to question him, and he had to come up with an answer and soon.

When he turned to go, she caught his hand. "Honey, I need a little reassurance."

His eyebrow shot up. "Reassurance?" he echoed, not reading her. What was she going to ask for? Something he couldn't give her? What if she just refused to be part of the club now that she'd gotten Zane back? Breezy was smart, very intelligent, and she wasn't above using the club to get the boy back and then . . . He cut off that way of thinking, as it could only lead to disaster. He was supposed to be evolving, becoming a better man.

"We're heading to the club and I'm feeling . . . I don't know. Like something isn't quite right between us. I don't know what I did. If you'll just tell me, I can do better." She looked around the room. "Everything's in its place. I thought you liked the meal. I said I'd get a different vehicle if that was important to you. What's wrong?"

She thought it was her. Breezy thought the fuckup in the room was her. He caught the front of her T-shirt and pulled her to him, taking her up-turned mouth. Hard. Possessive. Like he liked it. He could make love to her, be gentle, explore her body, worship her, upstairs in that bed. Down here, in any room, he took her the way he wanted. He showed her exactly what she did to him.

He kissed her over and over, devouring her. Not letting her up for air. Breathing for her. For both of them. When he lifted his head, he caught the hem of her shirt and pulled it over her head. "In the dining room."

The bitch of a dining room that was so enormous he could have the entire club over for dinner and most likely anyone they wanted to bring with them as a guest. He had plans for that table. The moment he saw it, it wasn't about feeding his brothers and sisters; it was about fucking his woman right there with that extremely expensive chandelier shining down on her body, spotlighting her soft skin for him.

Breezy walked ahead of him, and he watched her ass. God. His woman. She was a work of art. If he had his way, he would have nude pictures of her on every wall in every room. Front. Back. On her back with her legs spread. On her hands and knees, thighs and pussy glistening. Hungry for him. Her face in the moment her orgasm rushed over her. Consumed her. The look of love she reserved for him alone. He'd have those pictures on every wall because she was the most beautiful woman he'd ever seen in his life.

He loved every inch of her. He loved everything about her. The way she walked right to the table and stood waiting. He pointed to her shoes and she kicked them off while he went to the heavy blackout drapes and pulled them, covering the windows. He closed doors, not for privacy because who gave a fuck? Anyone seeing him take his woman would know she was his. Any woman wouldn't miss the point that there was only Breezy in his world and there would never be any other woman. He closed the doors so that the chandelier would shine light over her skin.

"Take off your jeans. Everything. I don't want a stitch on you."

She smiled at him. "Another fantasy?"

She was his fantasy. "Like having you any fucking way I want you, woman. I want you spread out on that table, legs over my shoulders. I'm going to take you hard, Breezy. The table was built for that. Fucking you hard."

"I thought it was built for dinners. Formal occasions." Even as she teased him, she stripped, shedding the denim and her underwear.

"This is a formal dinner. My cock is starving right now. Get your ass over here and take it out. Want your mouth. Your pussy. Your ass."

She moved to him immediately, knelt, her hands undoing his belt buckle, the one with Torpedo Ink written across it. She pulled down his zipper slowly and the relief was tremendous. "All three? Right now? While Czar's waiting?"

Her breath was on his cock. Warm. Tempting. He didn't wait. He pushed between her lips, enjoying the way his girth stretched them. She was wearing lipstick, and it made for a sexy pink circle surrounding his cock. He let her tongue lash at him and her mouth tighten and suckle, but only for a moment, just so she could get him wet with all that hot heat she generated. His hips began a fast rhythm, sliding in deeply and out again, over and over. He watched her eyes. Watched her take him. Swallow him. Give him that because he asked her to.

He'd already asked Ink to tatt him. Right above his cock, on that last ripple of ab muscles, so when she was on her knees looking at him, she would see *I love only Breezy.* He was scheduled for that next week. He had several places he planned to give that to her. But right now, when his cock was going deep, strangled in that perfect paradise, he wanted the first one right there, so she'd wake up to it every morning.

It didn't matter that he'd taken her that morning, in bed, and again, on the dishwasher, his balls were burning hot, and he had to stop before it was too late. Next time, he vowed, he'd get what he wanted. He'd take his time with her and let his body recover so he could do his favorite thing, moving from one tight place to another on her, claiming her completely.

He pulled out of her and tugged her up. Catching her around the waist, he put her on the table, right in the middle, under that chandelier. The lights instantly made her skin glow, spotlighted her breasts and, when he yanked apart her thighs, illuminated her pussy, making his cock lengthen and widen even more.

He crawled up on the wide, thick table, wedged himself between her legs and took his time getting to his goal. He kissed his way to her breasts and sucked, bit and licked until she was squirming. Both her hands cupped her breasts, offering them to him. He took his fill and then kissed his way down her body, his tongue lashing at her bare mound. He'd helped her shave it their first night home. He loved the way there was nothing between his tongue and her body. The way she tasted was his own personal aphrodisiac. He fucking loved eating her out. It was one of his favorite things to do.

He took his time before he finally knelt between her legs and lifted her bottom, slamming home without preamble. She cried out, that little low moan that always got to him, and then he was pounding into her. She felt like she was surrounding him with a tight glove of fire strangling his cock. The chandelier shone down on their joined bodies and he watched as he disappeared into her, as her body swallowed his and then he pulled back almost to the very end before slamming deep again.

The table was hard, and he pulled her legs up over his shoulders and let himself take her the way he needed. It was as perfect as it could get, and he didn't want it to ever end. Each time either of them was close, he stopped and took deep breaths, sometimes working her ass, turning it pink with his hand, feeling the wash of her liquid heat with every smack. Her little mewls and keening cries added to the volcano building in his balls.

Then he was there, unable to stop it, and he took her over the edge, using his thumb on her clit so the tidal wave took her as his cock swelled and jerked in her. He felt the splash of his hot seed triggering deeper and stronger waves through her body. He rode it out on his knees, watching her face, drinking in that look. For him. All his.

When he could breathe, he set her feet carefully on the table and leaned down to kiss her belly button. "Is that enough reassurance for you, baby?"

Eyes on his, still struggling for air, aftershocks shaking her, she nodded. "Yes, honey. Thank you."

"You need anything I'm not giving you? You'd tell me if I was fucking up again, right?"

She nodded. "I don't care about the truck that much, Steele. It isn't a big deal to me, but when something is, you'll be the first to know."

He felt the grin start somewhere around the vicinity of his cock. He fucking loved her. That was going on his body for her to read right under the tatt over his heart. *I fucking love her.* Gentle now, he helped her off the table.

The bikes were parked in a long row out in front of the clubhouse when they arrived. Breezy glanced at him but didn't say anything, and he was grateful. He didn't have the answers for her or for himself to any questions she might ask — like why he didn't ride his Harley and let her bring their son in the monster truck. Those were his issues, not hers, and he appreciated that she didn't push him. He needed time. He got Zane out of his car seat and handed him to Breezy. The boy was getting to be tall. He was going to have Steele's height.

Czar asked Steele to bring Breezy and Zane to the meeting with Inez and Frank regarding the new grocery store for a good reason. No one could resist Breezy. She had a look that told others she had joy in her. She was exactly what Czar needed to convince Inez and Frank they were just a bunch of men who loved riding motorcycles. Inez and Frank weren't born yesterday, but it was easy to see them relax around Breezy and Zane.

Inez was a beloved icon in Sea Haven. She was known by everyone, and she knew every family personally. If they could get her to front their store, even for a few months, then they would have a better chance of being accepted by the community. Already she called the Torpedo Ink members her boys. Weirdly, they all liked it. Maybe Savage was an exception, but he didn't count. No one could tell what he was thinking, and he didn't say.

Blythe was good friends with Inez, and she'd had Frank and Inez to dinner when they'd first approached them concerning the business venture. Czar felt it would be too blatant using her friendship again, but if Steele brought Breezy and Zane with him and introduced them just before the meeting, it would seem more like family had just dropped in.

Steele could see that Inez was very taken with Zane, but then who wouldn't be? After a few minutes of animated conversation, he signaled to Breezy to take the child out, so they could get down to business. Zane had worked his magic, as had his woman, showing Inez and Frank that they were a family like any other.

"What's it going to take to get you to come in with us as a partner?" Czar asked, leaning across the table.

They conducted the meeting in the common room, where their visitors would be the most comfortable. After seeing Czar and Blythe at home, they wanted Inez and Frank to be inside the clubhouse, so they could see the club wasn't hiding anything from them. As a rule, their clubhouse wasn't open to the public, not even during the parties between clubs. This was different. It was a business venture, pure and simple.

"I don't really have anything to bring to the table," Inez said, regret in her voice. "I want to help you out, Czar, I really do. Our partner, Jackson Deveau, has the money in the store. I was up front about that. He's law enforcement, you're a biker club. With regret, he can't come in on this deal."

"You did point out that we're not 1-percenters." Steele indicated his cut. "There isn't a patch anywhere on our jackets, and we've never been in trouble."

Inez nodded. "I understand. He's just very careful all the time. It's his way."

Czar nodded. Steele and Czar had already discussed their response, since they were certain Deveau would pull out. That made sense. They'd put it to a vote and the club — Savage included — had voted to bring Inez and Frank on board. Czar had a plan, and his plans had never failed. Not once.

"We've got the money for the start-up," Steele explained. "Money isn't a problem. All of us saved everything so we could put down roots. I'll be honest. We need your face. We need you to actually work the store, so the locals feel comfortable coming in. We're aware that's going to be a hardship on you."

Inez glanced at her husband. He remained silent while she spoke. "How long would you want us to work in Caspar?"

Czar tapped the table. "We thought three months, but you may have a better idea of the time it will take to get the locals comfortable with shopping here in Caspar."

"The idea isn't to take business from the store in Sea Haven," Steele reminded. "Or you. That's why we want you to have an interest in the one here. We need you more than you need us. We use the name of your store and your familiar face, you train one of our people to manage the store, and you oversee it. You're providing the labor. We're just providing money."

Inez nodded, but Frank reached out and very gently took her hand. "We would have to pay someone to work our store for us."

"We'll pay them," Czar assured. "If you're interested at all but don't like the terms, Absinthe," he indicated the third Torpedo Ink member sitting at the table, "is our attorney, and I'm certain everything is in order."

Absinthe was their negotiator for obvious reasons. He could persuade anyone to do anything and he could always compel truth. Code had given him the necessary background and schooling to become a lawyer on paper as well as on the Internet. He had the credentials, and it looked as if he'd passed the bar the first try. Like Transporter, he could read over twenty thousand words a minute and absorb the material.

"I drew up the papers for a partnership and suggest that you consult your own attorney. Have Deveau look at them as well, as he's in partnership with you in the store in Sea Haven and has to sign off on the use of the name here in Caspar."

Inez took the papers and handed them to Frank. "We really appreciate the opportunity and we'll get back to you fast. Did you have someone in mind for running the store?"

Steele fielded that one. "Lana eventually wants to have a clothing store but said she'd learn from you while she plans out her shop. Once we find someone who would like to settle here, and we feel he or she would be good, Lana can train them."

Inez nodded briskly. "I've worked with quite a few people, many that have come and gone over the years. I'm fairly good at choosing the right person. If I'm a partner, even a very junior one, I'd like to be in on the interview before you settle on someone."

"Of course, Inez. You let us know what you need to make this work," Czar said.

Alena came in, followed by Ice and Storm carrying trays. "Refreshments?" Alena set a platter of lemon-raspberry tarts on the table and added coffee for Frank and tea for Inez. "I wanted you to taste these, Inez. Frank. I would love your opinion."

Ice put coffee in front of Czar and Steele. Storm gave Absinthe coffee and put the milk and sugar on the table beside the tarts.

Alena sank into a chair beside Absinthe. "We're getting ready to open my restaurant. I'm having more trouble finding the right people to work for me than I did getting the permits for the building and business."

Inez sighed. "That's the way it is here. No one seems to want to work that much, at least not unless you can pay them money you can't afford and they're not worth."

"It's a real problem," Frank agreed.

"I really like the way you're resurrecting this beautiful place," Inez said. "It's nice to finally see businesses thriving, even if there's only a few. I see Bannister's motorcycle parked at the bar every time I drive by. He's a good man, Czar."

Czar nodded. "He's good friends with Anya. She looks after him, makes sure he eats now and then and is fine to drive home."

"His son is not a good guy," Frank spoke

up. "Watch him if he starts coming around. He gambles, and not just a little. Borrows money from everyone and then can't pay it back. Hits his father up by telling him someone's going to kill him if he won't get the money for him. Bannister sells everything and gives him the money and then his son gambles it away. It's been an ongoing cycle for a while."

Inez exchanged another look with her husband. "We're not just gossiping, Czar. If your Anya has any influence, see if she can find out if Bannister's son has moved back. We think his son has been beating on him. He's come into the store a few times with bruises. Black eyes. Said he laid down his bike, but Bannister doesn't do that. He's buying groceries for two, things he wouldn't ordinarily buy. If his son is there, it won't be the first time he's hurt that man."

"You take this to Jackson?" Czar asked.

Inez nodded. "We did. He went by Bannister's trailer and checked on him. Bannister gave him the same story, that he'd laid down his bike. Jackson checked the bike, just in passing, not making it a big thing, but there wasn't a scratch on the bike."

Czar sighed. "You know what it's like interfering in family. Bannister hasn't asked for help from us. Not sure I would know what to do if he did, but I'll give it some thought. And I'll tell Anya there's a problem. She'll keep a close eye. She has a real fondness for Bannister."

"Are the rooms above the bar being rented out?" Frank asked.

"We're in the process of renovating them," Steele answered. "They needed a little upkeep and modernization, but we don't guard any of the buildings where we have work going on, Czar. We might pay someone to sleep in one of those rooms and make certain no thieves or vandals show up in the night. Bannister might be just the man for it."

Inez beamed. She leaned over and patted Steele's hand. "You always come up with good ideas, Steele."

"I think you're snowing me, Inez, since Frank prompted me in that direction," he replied. "But I'm good with that."

"I have to say, Alena, I've never had such a fantastic dessert in my life. Not ever. You'd make a fortune selling these. If nothing else is worth eating in your restaurant, people would still come for these tarts." Inez bit the last bite and chewed it. "Heaven."

"I'm so glad you love them," Alena said. "You can take the rest if you'd like to share with your friends. Maybe they'll love them enough to come check out my place."

"Wait," Ice said. "You're giving the left-overs away?"

"There's more in the kitchen," Alena said patiently. "You know that."

There was a rush for the kitchen, every-one but Ice and Storm. She put her hands on her hips and faced her brothers. "What did you do with the tarts? You couldn't pos-sibly have eaten them all."

Steele stood up. He pulled out his phone and sent a mass text. "I know exactly where they are. Ice and Storm hid them in their rooms."

Phones dinged, and everyone looked down at their screens. Ice and Storm leapt up and took off running. Storm looked over his shoulder, glaring at Steele. "For that, we're not saving any."

Inez burst out laughing. "Those two. When they come into the store, half the female population follows them around."

"Don't point that out," Alena said. "They already know they're good-looking."

"We would love to take the tarts home and share with our friends," Inez said.

"I don't know about sharing them," Frank teased her, "but definitely take them home."

"When is your grand opening?" Inez asked.

"Hopefully next month. I'm so excited," Alena said. "It's really quite small, just what I wanted."

"You're building up quite a few businesses," Inez said. "I'm so glad to see that. Your garage appears to be thriving."

"Transporter and Mechanic are very good with motors and custom designs," Steele said. "The word's been getting out fast. They've got more orders than they can handle, but everyone pitches in to help. We've made it a policy to put all locals first, so if they bring their car in, even for an oil change, it gets into the lineup immediately."

Inez nodded. "Your tattoo parlor has a very good reputation as well. So many people have come in talking about how good he is and what a great artist he is that I considered getting a tattoo."

Frank smiled at her and took her hand. "We'd better go, honey. It was really a pleasure getting to know you. We'll have Jackson look over everything for us and get back to you as soon as we can."

Czar and Steele stood up as well. Absinthe pushed back his chair and leaned across the table to shake Frank's hand. "We appreciate you considering this. I hope you'll say yes to our proposal." He walked the couple out to their car, chatting amicably with them so that Inez's soft laughter and Frank's deeper chuckle could be heard.

Czar smiled with relief. "That's one more thing we can check off. The money's too good to pass up and Absinthe subtly worked his magic, although I think Breezy and Zane did the trick from the beginning. How are things going?"

Steele shrugged. "Don't know yet. I'm driving myself crazy and she's beginning to notice."

Czar regarded him quietly for a few minutes. He sank back into a chair and indicated Steele sit as well. Steele did. For the first time in over two weeks he was actually relaxed. He was surrounded by his brothers and sisters and they were watching his back. They were watching his family.

"Not sleeping very well. Everything's too close. This thing with Zane could have gone either way. Donk and Bridges, well . . . all of them, were fucked up on drugs. If we hadn't been there, Czar, Donk would have killed Zane. That was his intention. Even Candy was weird. They found drugs in the motel with her, quite a bit, and evidence that she and Lizard . . ." He broke off, shaking his head. "Let's just say it was a close call having my son kidnapped by fuckers that far gone."

Czar nodded. "I went over everything in detail with the others. I believe you got him out of there just in time. Does Breezy realize that?"

"She knows that it was bad, Czar, but she has no idea just what the Swords were doing to young kids, boys and girls. I don't particularly want her to know. Already, she spends time just sitting and holding him. Rocking him. She cries when she's doing it. She goes to sleep peaceful and then wakes up quite often. I think the trauma of having her child taken was enough."

"If she doesn't know, and she doesn't comprehend the enormity of what could have happened to her son, how is she going to understand that you need to hold them both a little tight right now?"

That sounded good, and maybe he could get away with it, but Steele doubted it. He shook his head. This was Czar. They could bring anything to Czar — almost anything.

"I'm not holding her a little tight. Breezy's a prisoner. The house is beautiful and includes just about anything she could want, but it's still a prison because she can't go anywhere without my knowledge or one of the others with her. She's living her life in a glass bowl. She doesn't realize that yet, but she is."

"I had the feeling you bought that house with the idea that your woman would want to spend most of her time there."

Steele nodded. "I knew I'd find her again. I had to find her again."

"You should have told me she was the one for you."

"I couldn't. You would have sent me away. In any case, I've got her and my son, and I'm not losing them again."

"There is such a thing as holding on too tight, Steele. You know you could lose her just by doing that. Women don't like a man controlling them or, for that matter, being jealous . . ."

"It's not that. It's never entered my mind, since she's been with me, that she would cheat on me. Breezy's too open. She'd tell me if she wanted to leave because of someone else. I don't want to control her just because I could — and I could. She'd let me. I have to know she's safe."

"That's an impossibility, Steele, and I think you know that. Safety is as big an illusion as control is. You're going to have to get a handle on this."

Steele nodded. "I'm very aware."

Czar switched gears. "You know that while

you were gone, I met personally with each of the men who want to join Torpedo Ink and had Absinthe talk with them. I like them. I like the idea of having others like us sticking together. We'll take a vote after you have had a chance to vet them."

"Have they given you their reasons for wanting to join us? I read everything Code had on them, and they seem to be doing well for themselves. No other club harasses them. They followed protocol. What made them decide to ask us?" Steele asked, all business.

Czar knew he was asking if individually any had differed on their reasons. "The brotherhood," Czar said simply. "They're misfits the way we are. They might have a slightly better understanding of the rules living outside the schools, but how do any of us fit anywhere? We can't. We never will entirely. If they're part of us, they have more brothers. They have a place to come to where they're welcome, brothers who understand them, places to bring their women occasionally. We'll have their backs. It adds to our strength."

Steele nodded. It made sense. Torpedo Ink was a closed community. Every member had been tortured as a child. They'd been trained to be assassins. They'd been trained in the art of seduction. They knew all kinds of ways to kill or seduce, but their rules, rules they'd made as children and lived by, weren't the same as those of everyone else in the world. Half the time they didn't even understand the way the outsiders thought. Those trained in the other schools would feel the same way, and they needed a home. A community. Brothers at their back.

"I talked to Fatei, and he wants to stay with this chapter," Steele said.

Czar nodded. "He's a good man. He'll make a good brother. We'll give him his patch before we patch over the others if the vote goes that way. They're coming Friday night with their women to party with us. Alena has the food under control. We're set, but I'd like you here. You're the only one now who hasn't signed off on them. I want you to really check them out, Steele. Your opinion matters. You see things I don't. Let Darby babysit Zane at your house or bring him to mine so you and Breezy can come."

Steele sat back in the chair, his heart doing that strange pounding again. Split them up? Zane in one place, Breezy in another? The idea of spending an evening with his brothers, relaxing with his woman, sounded like what he needed, but could he actually leave Zane somewhere else?

"I don't know, Czar," he said reluctantly. "It's probably a little too soon for Breezy to be that far from Zane, and no way is she going to like me going to a party without her, especially after the disaster when she first arrived."

Czar nodded. "I thought you might say that. Alena has a room right off the kitchen in the private wing. Darby could watch him there. It's completely closed off and protected. There's a security alarm, and all of us will be here. We could move a crib in and get it set up. You and Breezy could sleep in your room when you get tired or take Alena's room, and I'll get Darby home."

It was a perfect solution. Steele nodded. "We're in. We'll get everything and come back. I'll bring Breezy early. She's going to want to help the girls get the food ready."

Nineteen

"You're not making any sense, Steele. None." Breezy swung around and glared at him. "It's been the *best* time. We have such fun together. You. Me. Zane. Even Maestro and Keys. And then you act like this."

"I act like this because you're sneaking around —"

She cut him off. "What do you think is going to happen if I get up and go to the bathroom without waking you up and telling you first? You always wake up anyway. Do you think I'm sneaking out to meet someone?" Breezy threw her hands into the air. "Enough is enough."

Steele knew it was enough. He knew he was acting crazy. He'd woken the moment she moved. She slid from the bed, out of the protection of his arms. He'd watched her go out the door, but she hadn't headed to the bathroom.

"You didn't go into the bathroom." He

knew he sounded like a nut. He *knew* it. Still, he couldn't stop. The words kept tumbling out of his mouth no matter how hard he tried to be calm and sane. He had no idea what was happening to him, but he knew Breezy couldn't be a saint forever. She'd had more patience than any woman would have under the circumstances.

"Because I was checking on Zane. You have your app. Look at it."

"I shouldn't have to look at the fucking thing. You should tell me where you're going," he snapped. His chest hurt like hell. His skin felt clammy, but he was sweating. It had started the moment she'd slipped from the bed.

He was getting worse. The physical symptoms were becoming as bad as the mental — or emotional — ones. The monster, always so close, always so ready to protect him, opened his eyes and stared at his woman. Furious. She had no right to be upset, not when she insisted on doing the bullshit things she did.

"How the fuck do you think I know what you're doing when every time I turn around you're doing some bullshit move to protect your man?"

He watched her face, there in the moonlight. She was gorgeous standing in nothing at all but her bare skin. He loved her like that. Her breasts were round and full, high on her body so that the temptation to cup them and feed on them was always present. She'd shed the silk kimono he'd gotten her when she'd returned to their bedroom. He didn't like her sleeping in clothes, and the few times she'd tried, saying it was more convenient, he'd just stripped them off, rolled her under him and forestalled any argument.

There wasn't going to be putting this one off, and he didn't want to. She had a look on her face that told him, nearly for the first time ever, she was ready to battle with him.

Breezy jammed her fists on her hips. "What are you talking about? I thought we put that to rest. I didn't tell you about Bridges beating me and I should have. I've admitted that. Are you going to keep bringing it up every time you get upset over something stupid, so you have something else to divert attention from the fact that you're acting crazy? Because you are."

He took a step toward her. Savage was right. She wasn't getting the message no matter how much he talked to her about it. A jackhammer began pounding at his brain, a terrible thudding that wouldn't quit. "You can insult me as much as you want to, Bree.

I get that's your only defense, but you don't get a pass on this. I'm not having you stepping in front of me when you think someone's attacking me."

"Well too damn bad, Steele. In case you haven't noticed, I'm in love with you. Love to me means protecting you along with taking all the things you give me. I can't give you beautiful things, so I've given you me. All of me. That includes the way I love. Which is protective. I already admitted to you I was wrong and should have told you about Bridges. I was scared for you. And I was young, maybe too young to see you for who you really are. You were hiding yourself from everyone, including me."

"Don't you dare try to turn this on me and try to make me feel guilty."

"I wasn't doing that." She took a step toward the dresser, moving at an angle away from him. Every step sent her breasts and ass swaying. "I was stating a fact. We've already talked this over, right? I don't understand why the subject keeps coming up."

"It keeps coming up because there was no resolution. If there had been, you wouldn't have taken any chances in that motel with Lizard and Candy. But you couldn't help yourself. You just had to try to make them believe I was dead. That Czar, the others and me were all killed in the massacre with the rest of the Swords who had been there. You did, didn't you, Breezy, after we'd already had the discussion? I let it slide —"

"You let *what* slide? You didn't let anything slide, we're still talking about it. I got up in the middle of the night to check on our child and go to the bathroom. That's normal, Steele, in case you aren't aware of it. It isn't a big sin, and it isn't being sneaky."

"Don't try to change what we're talking about here." He ran both hands through his hair in agitation. Where was all his calm? Where was his ability to stay in complete control? Breezy was destroying him bit by bit. Piece by piece.

"Steele" — Breezy clearly made every effort to sound calm — "I had my own father break into my home and kidnap my child. He was taken from me. I wake up scared and have to reassure myself that he's here and he's okay. You do the same thing, so don't tell me you don't. I see you. You don't sleep for more than an hour anymore. I have trouble as well. It's that simple, so stop blowing this out of proportion."

She actually scowled, something he wouldn't have thought her capable of. He'd never seen that particular expression and it scared him. She was really upset. She was most likely thinking of leaving him, and that wasn't happening. He'd warned her. Straight up, he'd warned her.

"That's bullshit, Bree. Total bullshit." It was the absolute truth and he knew it. She had nightmares. He was worried enough that he'd put in a call to Blythe, asking her what he could do for his woman, yet he couldn't stop himself even though he knew everything he said and did was wrong. There was so much pressure on his chest he could barely breathe through the pain.

Her hands went into the air as an exclamation point. "There's no talking to you when you're like this. You don't even make sense. I have no idea what we're doing. How this even got started."

Breezy turned toward the door and he was on her, catching her up in hard arms, all but tossing her onto the bed, that monster in him surging to the surface, threatening to swallow him. "You fucking don't walk away from me when I'm talking to you."

She lay there, her eyes wide, but there was no real fear on her face. There should be. He wanted her to be afraid so she'd never walk out on him. The anger receded from her eyes and then there was only his woman looking at him. Compassionate. Knowledgeable. Seeing too much. He wanted to hide from any truth she might see. It was too dangerous. Too terrible. His heart felt as if it might explode. Sweat trickled down his body. Beads of it. He was fucked. So fucked because she saw too much every time.

"Baby." She paused, her hand cupping the side of his jaw gently. "You have to tell me what's wrong. What's really wrong. Whatever it is, I need to know. I can't say I can help you, but I want to, and maybe sharing with me will somehow ease it." Her fingers rubbed gently. Soothingly.

He caught her hand and ripped it from his face, stepping back away from the bed. His lungs burned and for a moment there was no air. The room was too hot. So hot. His skin was clammy. "Don't touch me." He pointed a finger at her and took another step back. "There's nothing to tell. Just don't fucking touch me."

To his absolute horror, his hand shook. He dropped it quickly to his side, pressing his fist against his thigh. Sweat dripped down his face, ran in beads down his chest. He had to gasp for breath. The air felt thick. His skin was clammy. He took another step back.

Breezy sat up slowly and her fingers touched the kimono she'd folded so neatly and stuck on the chair. She drew it to her, every movement slow. "Steele, do you need me to call Czar?"

His entire body jerked. Czar was the last person he wanted called. Czar couldn't know. No one could know.

"Why not? Honey, just talk to me."

He'd said it aloud. His ears hurt, the roar in them loud. Chaos reigned in his mind.

"Steele, you're a doctor. Let me call Maestro or Keys to help. I can see something is wrong. Let me help you."

"Don't call anyone. I mean it, no one." No one could see him like this. Shit. He was having a breakdown. He should have seen it coming. He was a doctor, for fuck's sake. "Stay away from me, Breezy." He gave her the warning, praying she'd obey him. He was dangerous in this state. He recognized it even if she didn't. Breezy had to be protected at any cost. He backed out of their bedroom and hurried down the hall, away from Zane's room. He couldn't take chances with their lives.

It was getting worse, not better. Steele paced from room to room, looking up at the cameras, making certain each was working. Even in his paranoid, physically-destroying-him state, he had to know Breezy and Zane were tracked and looked after.

He put his hands on the counter in the kitchen and tried to drag in air. When he couldn't, he opened the thick glass door and stepped outside, pulling air into his lungs in desperation.

"Steele?"

He didn't turn around. He closed his eyes briefly, thankful and terrified at the same time. The emotions were polar opposites. He was so grateful she cared enough to follow him, that she recognized something was really wrong. He was also aware he was dangerous, that she was treading on very thin ice.

Steele walked outside onto the spacious back patio, out toward the pool. Steam rose from the hot tub as well as from the surface of the pool. There was a sliding automatic cover for both so neither would lose heat at night, but he hadn't covered them, thinking he would swim later with his woman.

He heard her close the door to the house and knew she was outside watching him. The fog was no more than a fine mist he couldn't hide behind. Those green eyes of hers had always seen too much. She noticed the finest details, and she was looking at him when he was at his most vulnerable and at his absolute worst.

"I don't understand why you can't tell

Czar what's wrong because all of you tell him everything." She had that gentle note in her voice that always turned him inside out. "It's okay. Tell *me,* Steele. I'm your partner. You asked for my trust, and now I'm asking you for yours."

"Breezy." He pushed warning into his voice. He didn't look at her but sensed her moving toward him, and he held up his hand to stop her. He couldn't go back there for a number of reasons. He couldn't explain to her because if he did, she would leave. They all would leave him. He couldn't live with himself as it was. If he revisited that time, he would have no way out but a gun to his head.

"I'm not leaving you, Steele. Not ever. We work things out, that's what you said. I'm trying to understand your need for all this security around us, but you aren't giving me anything to work with. You know it isn't normal. You *know* that. Every time we start down this road it gets twisted into something else."

He didn't reply, holding himself very still, terrified she'd moved within striking distance. What if he hit her? What if he did something like Reaper had done to Anya? He shook his head.

"Honey." Breezy was closer. Her voice was

a soft whisper in the night. "It isn't going to go away. You're an intelligent man. You're showing classic signs of PTSD."

"How the *fuck* would you know that, Breezy?" he sneered. "You didn't even finish high school." The harsh accusation burst out of him. His chest felt so tight it might explode any moment. His heart pounded so hard he was afraid it would burst. "Don't pretend you have brains, baby. You have a killer body, just stick with what you know."

There was a long silence. His ugly retort taunted him, echoing in his ears over and over. Finally, finally, he looked at her. He had to. He had to see how much damage he'd done. He kept pushing her away, back to self-sabotaging his relationship. He'd make her leave him if he kept this up. Was that what he was trying to do? Why couldn't he stop?

Breezy's green eyes were on him. There was hurt showing on her face, but she hadn't retreated. His woman didn't retreat. She waited until his eyes met hers and then she shook her head, holding him captive just by the look on her face.

"Actually, I know quite a lot about PTSD. I got my GED. I have a son and I wanted to be a good mother to him, to help him with his homework when he needed me, so I took classes. One of them, I had to choose a subject to write on. I chose PTSD. I was a victim of abuse and finally had to acknowledge that. It wasn't just how normal people lived, it was how I was forced to live. I actually didn't realize that. Maybe that makes me stupid in your eyes, I don't know . . ."

"Breezy." He was ashamed. Felt like shit. He shoved the heel of his hand against his forehead and pressed hard, trying to stop the pounding jackhammer.

"I refused to be an ignorant mother to Zane, Steele. And I won't be afraid to speak out when I know something is wrong between us. I love you. I want us to have a good relationship, and to do that, we have to be able to talk to each other. Not only do you want me to talk to you, you *demand* it. We have a chance to be great together. To do that, you have to give me this."

"Why?" He barely managed to ask around the terrible lump in his throat. His throat burned until it was so raw it hurt like a bear.

"I have to understand your need to watch us every second. I've asked about the car a hundred times, but you avoid the conversation. I'm perfectly capable of driving. I want to visit Blythe and Anya, go to girls' night with Lana and Alena. I want to work."

The moment she said that his heart nearly

stopped. His hand pressed hard there. His head pounded, and he thought he might be sick. "You can't. Breezy, damn it. You just can't."

"I'm willing to compromise, Steele, but you have to talk to me. Trust is a two-way street. So is a relationship. I mean it when I say I love you, but I'm not a doormat to be kicked around when you're falling apart. I have a certain personality. I need to help the people I love. I have to feel I contribute to the relationship. If you refuse to allow me in, if you don't give me the same trust you demand from me, I don't see how we can ever work things out."

Breezy moved across the large polished stones that made up the patio. As she did, the kimono opened to reveal her body to him. She wasn't wearing a stitch under the silk. She was shaved, leaving her mound and lips bare. Smooth. He knew if he caught her up and laid her out on the lounger, she wouldn't stop him. She loved his mouth on her almost as much as he loved eating her out. But he couldn't. He couldn't move. Somehow, she held him immobile just with the force of her will.

He watched her come to him, his heart pounding like mad and that strange roaring in his ears. His head hurt so badly he had to clench his teeth. He found himself running his hands over the scars on his chest. So many. The knife had dug deep. It was hot. Burning. He remembered how the blade had glowed red before it sank into his flesh.

"Stop." He held up his hand and it was shaking. "I could hurt you."

It was too close. So close, the memories crowding in. He couldn't stop them now. Somehow the thick gates he held them behind had come open and he was there. Those gates had been pushing open for some time, and now it was far too late.

Twenty. So young but already too old. An accomplished killer. He almost preferred the missions where he killed when he was supposed to be a healer. A doctor. He'd taken an oath, and yet he did just the opposite of what he had sworn to do: save lives, not take them.

She halted for a moment and then she took the three stairs leading to the steaming pool. It was round, the outside bench curved, making up the seating for those not willing to sink into the heat of the hot tub. She beckoned him. "Come lie down, Steele. Put your head in my lap. I can see that you have a headache."

Even her voice was soothing. Breezy had

always recognized, almost before he did, when he was too close to the nightmare. Now he was in it. Reliving it. Caught in the web until he almost couldn't separate reality from what had happened to him. He could feel the whip flailing the skin from his back. He had to disassociate before he went out of his mind.

He shook his head, trying to save her. He actually managed to stumble away from her. "Too dangerous," he got out. "Too fucking dangerous. I'd kill myself before I hurt you." He would. He would never have struck her or paddled her ass because she didn't do what she was supposed to. That wasn't in him. He didn't know what he should do, but it wasn't that.

"Honey, just lie down and talk to me."

There was something about Breezy that had always soothed him. She was gentle. Kind. Compassionate. Everything he wasn't. Her voice had some kind of magic quality. Hearing that soft whisper stroking caresses over his skin, it was impossible to resist.

Lie down. She would watch over him. He was going to do it. Risk everything. She was risking everything without hesitating. He had hurt her over and over. Maybe not physically, but certainly emotionally. He had broken her heart when she was young and pregnant and still she had come back to him, accepting him, all the way in. Trusting him. Now she was asking for that same kind of commitment, all the way, trusting her completely. Trusting her to find a way for him, a path back to some semblance of sanity.

PTSD. He was a fucking doctor. He knew he was suffering from post-traumatic stress disorder. People threw the diagnosis around, but the ones living with it, watching their partners suffer because they were out of control, reliving the nightmares, knew how truly debilitating it could be. It wrecked marriages and tore apart families. It isolated the one enduring the illness. He had seen brain scans proving that traumatic events changed the brain itself.

He had to trust that Breezy wouldn't leave him. That she wouldn't think less of him when he thought less of himself. He wanted a partnership with her, but he hadn't given it to her. He took control and she allowed it — most of the time. That to him was the partnership. That was who he was. But she was right in this. She had rights in their relationship and would in their marriage. If he wanted her to accept his need to know where she was at all times, especially in the middle of the night, he had to man up and trust that she wouldn't leave him.

"It isn't pretty, Breezy. Nothing about my life was pretty." His voice sounded hoarse even to his own ears.

"I'm well aware of that, honey."

It was that voice that got to him. He couldn't refuse her. She looked so serene. Calm. As if in the midst of the worst chaos in his mind there was a safe haven. He had to chance it, but he was terrified of what could happen. Reluctantly, Steele stretched out on the bench, his head in her lap. Immediately her hands were in his hair, massaging his scalp, sending ripples of comfort through his rigid body.

"Czar had a plan for all of us to escape. We were going to continue working for Sorbacov, but we wanted out of the prison we were in. We were so close to getting out. We had a timetable, and we were all counting down."

He touched the worst of the scars on him, remembering how much it had hurt. "Venezuela was very important to Sorbacov. He was cultivating their friendship through a man by the name of Jose Merhi. Sorbacov had deliberately groomed him to bring out his depravity with boys, especially torture. Merhi liked to hurt the ones he fucked. Sorbacov taught him how. They went down a very dark road and Sorbacov took his time grooming him. Merhi liked to have two boys there at all times. One hurting the other often times. By having two, it ensured the cooperation of both."

He felt the heat. The rage. His monster close. The man had flayed the skin from his back. Merhi had learned from Sorbacov to threaten one while he forced the other to do whatever his sick mind came up with. Steele had to do whatever the man said in order to protect . . . Demyan.

"Absinthe had a brother, Demyan. He made it through just the way the rest of us did. We were so close to getting the hell out of there. So close. Sorbacov sent us out to meet Jose Merhi. We were to do whatever Merhi wanted. We weren't to question or hesitate. If we didn't comply, Sorbacov would kill Absinthe, and he'd do it slowly and as painfully as possible. That was always the threat."

Her fingers moved to his temples and applied pressure. It was never too much or too little. Breezy always seemed to know exactly what he needed. He turned his head more closely into her lap, inhaling her. The womanly scent of her. It helped to stop the scent of blood and burning flesh from making him crazy.

"Breathe for me, honey. Take a deep breath and feel me. You're here with me. You're not there, and that horrible man can't have you."

But he did. Jose Merhi had learned from an expert. Sorbacov had to shape Merhi into a man he could blackmail and use for his own political purposes. Once Merhi knew Sorbacov had filmed him and had him compromised, he demanded Sorbacov send him the young men he preferred. Demyan and Steele were at the top of his list.

"We followed orders. We could tell this was particularly important to Sorbacov and he would have really killed Absinthe if we didn't do exactly as ordered — at least we believed that. Merhi liked to see a back red with blood when he fucked. He'd dip his finger in the blood and write obscene poetry and read it out line by line, sometimes using his fingernails in the raw whip marks."

He was mumbling, hearing the whistle of the whip and feeling the cut as it sliced open his back. His breathing returned to ragged pants, his lips dry and hurting. Mostly, there was shame and guilt that when he knew so damned much about killing, he hadn't killed Merhi.

He knew boys and men didn't receive much sympathy from others when it came to rape and torture. The older the boy, the more they were told to sweep it under the carpet. They would say he'd allowed his attacker to do those things to his body. To violate him. To torture him. They would be correct. He'd been handcuffed, but he still could have killed Merhi. He hadn't because they had sworn to make certain all nineteen would survive. He'd kept Absinthe in his mind until he couldn't stand it and he began thinking up ways to slowly murder Merhi. When even that wasn't enough he forced his mind to go blank. He needed to disassociate.

He made himself look up at her, to see her eyes. He was afraid of condemnation, or disgust, but she only looked at him with the greatest of compassion. Tears swam in her eyes. That was what allowed him to continue.

"He heated the blade of a knife and made me say where it could go in on both of us without hitting anything vital. If I made a mistake, the death was on me. The blade cauterized the wound as he sliced into us, at least that was the theory. I had to watch him put the knife into Demyan." He touched his chest. "Into me."

Her breathing had changed, rapid and shocked, but her hands never stopped their massage. The pads of her fingers put just the right pressure on his pounding temples.

"I've never told anyone this, Bree. Not a single soul. I feel so damned guilty. Unworthy. They all look at me and think they can count on me . . ." He looked up at her. "I don't think I could take it if you stopped looking at me as if I'm your world. I couldn't, baby. I count on that look." It was why he took so many photographs of her when they made love. It was there on her face every time, and he needed that just to survive some days. "My brothers believe I'll be there for them, but . . ." He broke off, unable to hold her gaze.

She bent and pressed a kiss to the top of his head. "Everyone counts on you, Steele, and you always come through. You're the most protective man I've ever met. I know this is bad, but you need to get it out. I will never change the way I feel about you, no matter how bad this is, and whatever you tell me stays between us. You're mine. I know you share yourself with the others, but I don't share me with them. You're just mine, if that makes sense and you can figure out what I mean."

Her voice trembled, and he immediately responded to that. It helped to pull him a little further from his past. "Baby, never think you're second, or that Zane is. To Torpedo Ink, you're family and you always will be. They've taken you in and they'll always hold you close, but make no mistake, Breezy, you're mine. It's the two of us." He sent her a faint smile. "The three of us. If we're lucky, we'll add to that number and fill this house with the sound of laughter."

He needed laughter when his past threatened to consume him. It was still there, surrounding him with the smell and the heat. With Demyan. "You've seen Absinthe. He's a good-looking man. Demyan was that way. When he smiled he could charm the panties off anyone, and he did. I should have been thinking. I should have had my brain working that day, but I let the pain get to me. The humiliation. I should have been strong enough to put it aside so my brain could work."

Her fingers stroked over his temples, and then down his face. He didn't know if it was wet. He couldn't feel anything. He'd gone numb, completely numb. He wasn't certain he was in his own body. His lungs were raw and burning. He felt that. He heard blood pounding in his ears. He knew there was blood because his back was torn open from the whip and the chains Merhi had reveled in wielding. He'd set up cameras in two rooms and filmed the entire session, every detail, getting close-ups. First Demyan and then him.

"He said he had invited some friends to play. That was bad, and I knew it because it had never happened before. Any deviation was always a bad thing." His heart was pounding. Hard. Coming through his chest. Sweat broke out and trickled off his body. He couldn't lie there. He couldn't have anyone touching him.

Steele jumped up and shoved himself away from her, putting distance between them, although he could no longer see her. The fog swirled around him like coils of wire digging into his skin. They pulled tighter and tighter. The blade stabbed deep, a hot piercing that sent agony ripping through his body. He looked across the room into Demyan's eyes. As long as they could see each other, they could make it through. They gave each other the necessary courage to get through each second of torture.

The sex was nothing. A humiliation. Degradation. But they were used to that. The key was to always have another of them present in order to ensure they survived. This was beyond necessary. There was no survival without the other. They all knew that. Torture of this nature, so severe, was more than endurance of the body. It was strength of mind. Demyan got him through it. More importantly, he got Demyan through it.

He hung in those wires while they bit into his skin, nothing more than a mindless animal in pure agony. Cruel laughter surrounded him as others used his body. He didn't remember their faces, and that was worse than anything they did to him because they took Demyan out of sight. They dragged him to another room. Merhi followed. He was left alone. He had completely disassociated from the pain, and it took far too long to come back into his body. Far too long.

When the screams started, Steele fought to get the wires off. He was strong, and he had an affinity with metal. Still, it took what seemed like forever. He had no idea of time passing, but it did because Demyan's screams echoed through his entire body, shaking his bones and imprinting there. He worked frantically to get the wires, pulled tight from all his fighting, off of him.

By the time he was free, the screams had turned to animalistic moans of pain. He broke into the room to find a bloodbath. The room was red with blood, and the four men laughing and abusing Demyan's body were covered in it, as if they had bathed in him. Steele killed them. As weak and as far gone as he was himself, he destroyed them. He didn't remember how, just that he did. It wasn't pretty and it wasn't clean, and Merhi suffered before he died. That he did remember. Then he went to Demyan.

He couldn't even hold him as Demyan slipped away because it hurt him too much to be touched. He could only whisper how sorry he was that he allowed him out of his sight. He could only wish he could take his place. It had taken over an hour for Demyan's strong heart to give out. He'd been conscious the entire time, staring into Steele's eyes. Never once blaming him. He'd tried to whisper something. It had been important to him. A message for Absinthe, his younger brother, but he wasn't able to tell Steele.

Steele sank down onto the patio right at the edge of the pool, but he didn't feel the wet mist on his skin or the rougher cement under him. He was trapped there, in the past with Demyan. The nineteenth survivor. He should have lived to laugh with them. Drink beer and ride in the wind. He should have had a life. A woman of his own. Children. He shouldn't have died at the hands of madmen because Steele had taken his eyes off him.

"Honey."

A voice. Soft. Moving through his mind. Moving through his own screams of pain. His body didn't matter. The skin flailed from his back or the numerous stab wounds. None of that mattered. It was the wounds in his mind that could never be healed. He heard it again. Soft. Insistent. A distance from him. He tried to focus on it.

"Steele. Honey. You're here. Safe."

There was no safety for anyone. Those he loved were never going to be safe. He had to watch over them, keep them that way. Never take his eyes off them.

"I understand. I don't mind the cameras, honey."

Cameras. He'd destroyed those as well. He didn't want anyone to ever witness what those fuckers had done to Demyan. They had reduced him to a mindless animal, and no one was ever going to see that. Demyan's death was his alone.

"That's good, Steele. No one should see that. It's good that you did that. You need to breathe for me. Take deep breaths. That's right, honey. Just breathe."

He hadn't been able to breathe for months afterward. If he did, if he inhaled too deeply, he dragged the scent of blood into his lungs. It was on his skin. His hands. It was in his hair.

"It isn't in your hair, sweetheart," that soft voice said.

It was. It was everywhere, all over him. His blood. Demyan's blood. The blood of the men he'd slaughtered when he'd seen what they'd done. The monster had been born. He hadn't known he was capable of that kind of killing, of that kind of rage. He was a healer. He'd been given the gift of healing and he'd *slaughtered* men. Human beings . . .

"They weren't human beings, Steele. They looked human, but they were the monsters. You destroyed them because they had to be obliterated before they hurt others."

That made some sense. He shivered over and over, unable to stop. He couldn't go back and face the others. He couldn't tell Absinthe what had happened. How Demyan had died. What they'd done to him. He just couldn't face that. But he had to. He had to go back to the others and tell them. Tell Absinthe that he let his brother out of his sight and they killed him.

He found out that Sorbacov's deal with Merhi included allowing him to kill one of them. Sorbacov wanted Steele alive because he was a doctor and could get into more places than Demyan. In spite of his wounds, the terrible toll on his body, Czar and Reaper had to hold Steele back from killing Sorbacov. He told Sorbacov what he'd done, how he'd killed Merhi and the others, and how he hadn't felt a thing when he'd done it.

He told Sorbacov that he'd won, he'd finally created the monster he wanted, and if he killed Absinthe, he would tear him apart, piece by piece. His brothers and sisters, Torpedo Ink, had stood with him, guns on them, ready to die, and they backed him, echoing what he'd told Sorbacov. He gave Absinthe back to them. As always, whomever he'd had was in bad shape, but he was alive.

The others wanted to help him recover. His body was a mess. His mind was worse. He couldn't escape the image of Demyan suffering, dying right in front of him.

He should have been there with Demyan. They'd always kept eyes on one another. Always. It was Czar's rule. Their rule. Their code. Their promise to one another. It was how they survived. But he hadn't. He'd taken his eyes off Demyan and he'd died in the worst possible way.

"No one would blame you."

"I took my eyes off him. We always have eyes on one another. That's the code. That's how we stay safe. Especially when there's sex involved. We watch one another's backs. I let him down. I didn't see what they were doing to him." He repeated the rules over and over because if he'd just followed them, there would be eighteen branches on their tree, not seventeen.

"Honey, you're not thinking clearly about this."

That voice, so like the touch of her fingers. He was with her now, ashamed that he'd told her everything while he was reliving it. He had no idea what he'd said or hadn't said. He looked at her over his shoulder, drinking her in, seeing the tears running down her face, or maybe they were running down his and he couldn't see clearly. Maybe it was both.

Breezy was such a compassionate woman, she would never be able to sleep after this. He'd been selfish telling her. He'd been afraid to have her know. Ashamed. He should have known better. She was all about empathy. He hadn't slept in years — not since he'd lost Demyan. Now she would have trouble as well.

"Babe, you always get me to sleep."

He'd said that aloud too. He forced himself to press his lips together, to keep from blurting anything else out. He blinked, trying to clear the misty veil between them. To his shock, it lifted, which meant it hadn't been the fog. She was definitely crying. Breezy. His woman. He'd told her his worst nightmare. The moment his life had changed. The birth of his monster. She was still looking at him as if the sun rose and set with him.

"I'm sorry, Bree." He looked down at his hands. "You can see I'm always going to be a fucked-up mess. Always. It isn't going to go away because I talk to someone. And I wouldn't. There's no counselor for men like me. There's no fixing me. You'll be living with that the rest of your life. Me holding too tight. Eyes on you all the time. Eyes on the kids."

It was true, and she had to know it. His kind of trauma didn't just go away. He felt like he'd run a marathon, his body hurting physically. "This thing isn't going away, baby. Not ever. I wish I could tell you it will."

Breezy touched her tear-damp face, looked down at her wet fingers and shook her head. "I'm such a crier. You'll have to get used to that about me. I think, as time goes by, you'll relax a little bit, Steele."

She wasn't a crier. Breezy didn't cry, and he knew it. Tears had been beaten out of her when she was a child by her father. "Maybe. I hope. In the meantime, I need you to tell me where you're going when you leave my bed. I swear I'll try, Bree. I will, but I'll need you to cooperate when I'm losing it like this."

She nodded. "Bathroom and Zane. Whatever order, but I'll let you know if I'm going anywhere else when I get out of bed."

"You go down to the kitchen."

"If I can't sleep. Sometimes I think about taking a three A.M. swim, but I know you won't like it, so I don't."

"Tell me and I'll go with you."

"I like you to sleep."

"Breezy, I'm not sleeping if you're not in the bed with me. I'd prefer a swim anytime to lying there waiting for you. Anything I do with you is better than doing it alone. If you can get that concept, we'll be good."

"I want you to think about at least taking a ride every day. Even for an hour, Steele. Let that be the first step toward letting go a little. Please do that for me."

The idea of leaving her alone was terrifying, but he had to find a way to ease up. He needed to ride with his brothers. That was part of him, like breathing. He nodded. "I'll want you with me every other time." Just having his family separated, one at home and one with him, was already making him hyperventilate. He more than half hoped she would say no. She didn't like to be away from Zane any more than he did.

"It's a deal. Every other time. I'll ask Lana and Alena to look after him. They're always offering."

That helped, knowing both of his very lethal sisters would look after his child. He needed physical activity. His body felt as if he'd been beaten with a baseball bat. In any case, the water in the pool was warm, and the outside temperature had dropped.

He glanced at his watch. The app was there, showing him that Zane slept peacefully. Nevertheless, he texted Maestro and Keys to keep an eye on the boy. Zane hadn't been waking up since he'd been in his own crib, at least not to get up. Sometimes he woke up and played quietly in his crib before going back to sleep. Steele liked to watch him.

"Come swim with me now, Bree. I need to be in the water." Maybe all along he knew he needed a pool. He liked to be in water. It helped make him feel like there wasn't so much blood coating his skin, clinging to him in spite of all the scrubbing he did. In spite of his sterile rooms and continual cleaning.

Breezy didn't hesitate. She left her silken kimono on a lounger, neatly folded. He loved her all the more for that. Very grateful she hadn't asked him any questions about Demyan or that terrible, life-altering event, he took her hand and walked with her down the steps into the warm water. She'd let him share it his way.

"I didn't realize you were so cold, baby." He gathered her close, his arms sliding around her middle, just under her breasts. Her skin was freezing. That made him look around and really notice the weather.

The temperature on the Northern California coast could drop fast, and it had. The wind had picked up and he hadn't even noticed though he observed everything. That was how far gone he'd been, lost in his past. Breezy had been right there with him, listening to his every word, words he didn't even remember.

He tightened his hold on her. "I'm so damned lucky to have you, Bree. I know I don't tell you enough, but I feel it. I'm sorry I hurt you when I sent you away. That should never have happened." There was no way to explain how he'd felt when he'd learned her age. He didn't want to think for one moment that he was anything like the men and women who had abused the children at the school where he'd grown up.

"It actually turned out to be a good thing, Steele," she said, leaning her head back into him. "I learned how to be strong, and I needed to be. I like who I am so much more, and I know I can be a better parent to Zane."

He was proud of who she'd become. "You're a wonderful mother to our son. I hope to be as good a father to him. Just bear with me during these first few months. To know that my son was taken, whether I knew about him or not, has shaken me."

"I can understand that," she admitted. "Thank you, Steele. I know it wasn't easy sharing what you did with me. I needed to know so I could better understand."

"I'll keep trying to ease up," he assured her. He knew he needed to. He wasn't going to try to take advantage because she knew. He wanted to be better for her. For his son. For any future children they had.

"I'll race you across the pool."

"Breezy." Just her name. That said it all. There was no way she could beat him.

Her soft laughter teased his senses, made his heart just a little lighter. "You could give me a head start. To the halfway marker."

"That might be cheating just a little too

much." He knew it wasn't. "I win, I get to fuck you any way I want."

"I win, I get to do the same."

He lifted an eyebrow.

She tilted her head back, her arm sliding around his neck. The action lifted her breasts, drawing his immediate attention. "Don't be such a baby."

Steele bent his head and took her offering. She tasted like heaven. Paradise. Sin and temptation. He indulged himself, kissing her over and over because he needed to. Then he wanted to and then he just lost himself. The moment he lifted his head, she swam away, kicking strong, heading for the other end of the pool. He obliged her by waiting until she was at the halfway mark before he swam after her.

He won of course, because he wasn't missing out and he wanted to make slow love to her and make her crazy. He loved taking his time and driving her out of her mind. The little hitches in her breathing as well as her moans and soft cries were so perfect. He could listen to them all night. He kept at it until she gave him that pleading demand, his name so breathy it lit up his world. Only then did he allow her release and go with her, so that it roared through him, taking him like a tsunami might.

She looked back at him, hands and knees on the wide lounger, a smile on her face. "Who won?"

"Both of us," he conceded and rolled her over, wrapping her in a towel when he felt her shiver. "I'm wide awake."

"Go for a ride, Steele. Get on your bike and go for a ride. You need it."

"Only if you come with me." He rubbed her hip, needing to touch her. Needing that connection when his past was still too close.

"Zane." One word, but there was a hint of regret. She wanted to go.

"Keys and Maestro can watch Zane," Steele said. "It was your idea. This can be our first ride together." He brushed a kiss on top of her head. "I need you with me, baby. Come ride with me."

She glanced up toward the windows above them and then a smile lit her face. "Give me five minutes. I'll be ready."

"I'll need that same five minutes. I'm not riding naked." He stood up and pulled her up with him.

"I thought you did everything naked and I'd have something to hang on to." Her laughter was a little wicked as she ran from him.

Steele followed at a more leisurely pace, once more texting Maestro and Keys. He was lucky to have his brothers helping him watch over his family. He was more than lucky to have a son. There was a part of him that he had to fight off, the one that wanted to panic because he was actually going to leave his son with someone else, but it was an opportunity to be different and he had to take it.

Mostly, he felt he had hit the jackpot with Breezy. His woman. She was so laid-back about everything, not accusing him of being too controlling. Listening and trying to understand. Yeah, he was a lucky man, and he knew it. He silently vowed to double his efforts to make her happy and to see anything and everything that might be upsetting to her. He needed to give her as much as she gave him because he wasn't fucking up his relationship with her.

Twenty

"We've got a major dilemma we want you to weigh in on, Blythe," Maestro said, reaching around Breezy to nab a handful of chips. He stuffed several in his mouth.

Ice elbowed him out of the way. Between Ice and Storm, Breezy was nearly smashed into the counter, but Ice gallantly saved her by catching her around the waist and moving her out of the way. "Jackass," he muttered. "You could have hurt her."

"Don't pretend you moved her to save her." Storm glared at him, managing to scoop more than a handful of chips from the bowl before Blythe snatched it away from them.

"Hey," Ice protested. "Is that any way to treat a hero? Breezy, tell her how my brother was squishing you into the counter."

"I'm more interested in the major dilemma Maestro has," Blythe said. "We're working here, boys. If you aren't going to be helpful, go away."

"The other women should be here soon to help," Czar assured.

Blythe, Anya and Breezy turned to look at him. Lana and Alena turned more slowly, but they added their silence to the other three women's.

Czar backed away, holding up his hands in surrender. "I was just saying there will be extra help with the food."

"Maestro," Blythe said, still giving her husband a quelling look, "spit it out."

"We've talked this over and we all have a different idea of what should be done to handle a problem that seems to crop up every now and then. If a woman refuses to obey her man when it comes to something really important, like a matter of safety, what should he do?"

Breezy groaned and kicked him in the shins. Her face turned red. "I swear we put that to rest. Why do you insist on bringing it up?"

"It wasn't handled," Savage said, startling all of them. "Not that you're going to get a decent answer from Blythe."

"What does that mean, Savage?" Blythe challenged.

He shrugged. "You're going to say to talk to her. To explain to her. All the correct bullshit women say to one another."

Blythe frowned. "Is that what you really think we do? What we actually do is try to find ways to be of help to you, and when we don't understand something, yes, we try to talk it out with our partner in order to better understand. If something really matters to Czar, I give in because I trust that he isn't trying to be a dictator."

She continued to work, as did Breezy, but Breezy was keeping an eye on the members of Torpedo Ink. They seemed divided by the issue, even with Blythe trying to explain it to them.

She decided to try. "It isn't always easy to do what is asked of us, especially when our man might be in danger."

Maestro heaved an exaggerated sigh. "That's exactly when it's the most necessary."

Savage nodded. "It isn't even that. It's a matter of trust. Your man tells you something, you just fuckin' do it."

"Everyone is different, Savage," Blythe said. "We all have different personalities. You're always going to be in charge. Your woman will have to know that and be okay with it. Otherwise it won't work between you. I have to feel like I'm in a partnership. That's what I need in order to be happy.

On the other hand, I know Czar and what he needs. If he were to say to me, don't move from this spot because it isn't safe, I wouldn't move. For him. Because that's what he needs."

"You should do it because he fuckin' tells you it isn't safe and you trust him to know what the fuck he's saying," Savage said, and reached into the chip bowl.

"My point," Maestro said. "What does a man do when his woman doesn't give him what he needs most?"

Breezy felt her color rise, staining her cheeks. Steele moved in close to her, his body shielding hers. "We worked it out," he said, his voice conveying a warning. She wanted to kiss him.

"That's a good thing," Blythe said, "and that's what usually happens between a man and a woman. Good communication is the key."

Anya glanced over her shoulder at Reaper, who was staring out a window, obviously restless being inside. "Honey, I left the groceries on the seat of the truck. Would you get them for me, please?"

Breezy knew immediately Anya had left the groceries on purpose. She wanted Reaper to have an excuse to leave the crowded kitchen, so he could breathe easier.

He'd never been a man to stay inside much. She resolved to do similar things for Steele.

"Sure, babe," Reaper responded, and was out the door.

Anya watched him go with a small smile on her face. Breezy wondered if anyone else knew Anya had done it on purpose. The women maybe. She looked around the room at the men. Savage knew. He looked out the window and then at Anya. He sent her a small nod. Almost imperceptible.

"If communication doesn't work," Maestro persisted. "I know Steele worked it out with Breezy, but she's crazy about him and I guarantee, if he's in danger, she's going to forget all about their bullshit talk and jack up again."

"You want to step outside and have a bullshit talk with me right now?" Steele asked, his voice so low it was dangerous.

Breezy put a hand on his arm because, sadly, Maestro was probably right about her.

"We're actually trying to figure this out," Player chimed in.

"That's what you're all doing in the kitchen," Lana guessed. "I wondered. They're serious about this question, Blythe. So am I. They asked me, and I didn't know what to say."

"Talking is worthless," Savage said. "Teach

a fuckin' hard lesson once and she isn't likely to forget it." He turned and stalked out.

There was silence after he left. Blythe looked at her husband. "What does he mean by that? By a 'hard' lesson?"

Czar shrugged. "Savage isn't in a relationship, baby. He doesn't put himself in places where he'd find a woman to be in one with him."

"I plan on finding a woman," Maestro said. "And Savage makes sense to me."

"What does he mean, then?" Blythe asked.

Maestro flashed her a grin. "He means we need to communicate the importance of her obedience in a way she can understand and not forget." He made a grab at the chip bowl, missed and hurried out before he could be asked any more questions.

The others followed, leaving Breezy alone with the women. Blythe, Anya and Breezy looked to Lana and Alena. When they continued mixing the bowls of potato salad in silence, Blythe cleared her throat.

Lana glanced at her. "You won't like it or agree, Blythe."

"Maybe not, but one thing I've learned over the years, Lana, is not to judge others. Especially any member of Torpedo Ink. I don't know all their stories, and I shouldn't.

That's private between all of you and the one you want to share with."

"Savage would probably retaliate physically."

At Blythe's gasp, Lana shook her head. "Not like any of you are thinking. He wouldn't beat her, but he'd definitely react in a physical way. He's a very physical man."

"So is Reaper, but he doesn't beat me," Anya said.

"If Savage or Maestro were in a relationship," Alena said, reaching for the enormous pasta bowls, "the relationship would include some kind of dominant-submissive crap. At least with Maestro. With Savage it would include more than that."

Blythe shrugged. "As long as it was consensual, then it would be all right with me."

Lana nudged Alena. "Ice is always talking about kidnapping his woman and knocking her up. He's the one you need to talk to about the meaning of the word *consensual.*"

The two of them laughed. Blythe, Breezy and Anya couldn't help laughing with them.

"One of these days, Ice is going to fall hard," Blythe said.

"Yes, he is," Alena admitted, sobering. "He's got this capacity to love beyond measure. Totally. If any woman ever hurts him . . ." She trailed off.

"Give her a chance," Blythe advised. "If he finds someone, you have to step back for a while and let them work it out. If you threaten her, she may run."

Anya nodded. "I wanted to run when you and Lana had a little talk with me."

"That was me," Lana said. She leaned over and hugged Anya. "I still feel awful about that. You're so good for Reaper."

"You notice he isn't back with the groceries," Anya pointed out and burst out laughing. "There's no taming that man, not that I want to."

"I want to know how Breezy's doing in that house of hers," Blythe said. "Do you get lost in it?"

"Yes. I think Steele wants to fill it up with children. He also doesn't like me lifting a finger to clean it. I've insisted on cleaning the kitchen and our bedroom myself. Even with that, he wants the service to do deep cleaning in the kitchen once a week. I love the house, though. Who wouldn't? Right now, Maestro and Keys are staying there with us."

"You okay with that?" Lana asked.

Breezy nodded, suddenly realizing she was more than okay with it, even more so since Steele had told her about his past and Demyan. She was definitely looking at Absinthe with far more sympathy. "Actually, it's great having them there. It makes Steele feel better having two more pairs of eyes on Zane, especially after what happened, the kidnapping and all." She ducked her head, concentrating on cutting up cucumbers. "I sometimes can't breathe when I think about what happened, so having extra eyes on him makes me just as happy as Steele."

"I can imagine," Blythe said.

"That was so awful," Anya said. "Reaper was very torn. He wanted to watch over Czar, Blythe and the children as well as me, but also go with the others to help out."

"We were good. Everyone was so amazing. Maestro and Keys are wonderful. They look after Steele and I appreciate that. It must be how you feel, Blythe, when Reaper and Savage are with Czar."

Blythe nodded. "Absolutely."

"I can breathe easier because Maestro and Keys look after Zane too. They're a huge help. Both even change diapers, although they'd murder me for telling you that. They're helping with potty-training." She laughed. "Their ideas are rather unique, but effective. He's young to be potty-trained, especially for a boy, but he's already trying to emulate them. He'd been doing very well, not having any problems except at night, until he was kidnapped. He went backward a bit."

"That would make sense," Blythe said. "He might have other behaviors as well."

Breezy nodded. "He wakes up scared and I rock him. He likes everyone singing to him. We've ordered a piano because Maestro says we really need one for him, and I know the piano in particular is a really good instrument for children."

"How do you know all that stuff about kids?" Lana asked. "You were always good with them in the club as well. I know, because I admired you for it. It always seemed so natural."

Breezy hadn't known Lana had even watched her, and she felt a warmth spread through her at the obviously sincere compliment. "I read lots of books. I didn't want to be like my father, and none of the women he brought home were kid friendly, so I read tons. I still do. Every parenting book I can get my hands on. I'm determined I won't ever be like Bridges."

"I don't think you have to worry on that account," Alena assured.

The roar of Harleys filled the air. They'd been hearing the rumble growing louder for some time, and now they were in the yard. Several trucks accompanied the bikes. The women looked at one another. It was a party, and parties meant men and women they didn't know but welcomed all the same.

Breezy tried not to tense up. She was part of the welcoming crew. It wasn't like they had many women in their club. Heidi and Betina would be there. Both women worked as waitresses in the bar and were patch chasers. Anya was friends with them, but Breezy hadn't really been around them.

Steele claimed he wouldn't want anyone but her, not even when others threw themselves at him. She knew she should trust him, but it was hard to get that picture of him out of her mind — the one where he'd gotten up nude from under three equally naked women. A part of her wanted to run home and hide like a coward.

"Take a deep breath," Lana whispered. "He loves you. He doesn't even look at anyone else. I doubt he can see anyone but you."

Breezy was embarrassed that Lana had recognized she was struggling with the idea of going to the party because of what she'd seen. She should have the confidence to deal with parties. Steele hadn't been with her then. He had explained the three women, and she'd chosen to accept that explanation. She either trusted him or she didn't, and after demanding he trust her, she had to get over this last hurdle. She was determined she would.

"I'm just being silly." She ran a hand over the soft little spot she couldn't quite get rid of since Zane was born. "I don't look the same, no matter how much exercise I do. I swim every day, several times a day." She also had sex more than once a day and she'd lost weight, but not that little soft area she couldn't quite overcome. Okay, if she was honest, she'd had it before Zane was born, but it was nice to have pregnancy as an excuse.

Lana looked her up and down. "Breezy, you're gorgeous. The moment you go out there with the rest of them, I guarantee Steele will be glued to your side. He'll make it very plain that you're his old lady, and the women will definitely get the message along with the men."

The noise level in the compound went up several notches, although it was still somewhat muffled in the kitchen. "Czar wants Steele to talk to every man personally. All of us have," Alena said, "but him. His opinion is very important. If he nixes even one, we're not going through with it. Steele has a real feel for what people are like."

Breezy nodded. She wasn't going to panic.

She had to trust Steele. She loved him, and she believed in him. He'd insisted on putting the apps on her phone that would allow her to find him wherever he was. She had resisted looking, although she knew he had several times because he'd sent her over a dozen text messages that she hadn't answered asking her why she was still in the kitchen and to get her ass out there.

Three women were escorted into the kitchen by Preacher. He introduced them. Two were old ladies and one was a sister of an old lady. They seemed embarrassed that they were all that were offering to help. They brought food with them though, and Breezy was happy she only had to be friendly with them while she struggled to feel confident.

Steele stomped into the room. "Woman. What the fuck?"

Anya laughed aloud. Lana and Alena snickered. Blythe, always sweet, hid her smile.

Breezy sent him a look. "It's called working, honey. That's what the fuck. I'm working. There aren't that many of us to get the food ready."

"Then I'll round up some of the women and send their asses in here," Steele declared.

"We're good," Blythe said hastily. "Everything is ready. If you'll send in a couple of the prospects we can carry everything out to the tables. We're serving buffet style. Czar said the meat was ready. The pig has been roasting all day, and he barbecued dozens of chickens."

"Hyde, Glitch and Fatei are close. I'll get them," Steele said. "Miss Sassy can come with me." He held out his hand.

Breezy knew better than to ignore him. She'd been raised in the life and knew how it worked. She wasn't about to embarrass him. She dried off her hands and went to him. Steele swept her under his shoulder, walked her outside where the noise was deafening, and tipped up her face and kissed her. Hard. Possessively. Claiming her just as Lana had said he would.

"Missed you, baby. We've been together nearly every minute and then all of a sudden you weren't there. I like looking at you. Knowing you're close."

Before she could answer, he whistled to get the attention of the three prospects. He pointed to the kitchen, and all three obeyed without hesitation.

Steele kept walking her away from the picnic tables, around to the back of the building facing the ocean, where they were alone. He kissed her again and again. Melting her. She couldn't kiss him without her entire body catching fire. When he lifted his head, she had to cling to him to keep from falling, her knees were that weak.

"You okay with all this? As soon as I finish talking to everyone, we'll leave if you're uncomfortable."

"Why would you think I was uncomfortable? I like parties as well as the next person."

"Babe."

There it was. That voice reprimanding her.

"I was watching you in the kitchen. I don't mind if I never go to another one of these parties if it makes you uncomfortable."

The vice president couldn't be absent for every single one of them. She forced a smile, hoping to reassure him. "For a minute I was insecure, and only because I still have baby body. I don't think I'm ever going to get over baby body, so I'd better be okay with it." She didn't know what else to say. It was just a little humiliating that he saw she was upset. She tried to be the best old lady possible, and worrying continually about something he had explained — and she'd accepted — was wrong. She had to let it go.

"Breezy, there's no woman more beautiful than you."

He meant it. She heard the sincerity and

her heart melted. He could do that so easily. "I'm good, Steele, I promise. I just always want to be the best for you. It's my problem, not yours."

"I contributed by being an idiot. I swear, baby —"

She pressed her fingers to his mouth. "Everything is perfect, Steele. Let's just have fun. We've been cooped up in the house and we get a night off. Let's make the most of it." Truthfully, there was a part of her that was excited. She was surrounded by Torpedo Ink. They were everywhere, and when she looked at the other members, they were always watching over them. She might, for the first time, be able to relax and really have fun if she let herself.

"First, let me see the baby body you're so worried about."

There was pure seduction in his voice, and she shook her head, laughing. "You're so wrong. We have an entire club to entertain."

"I don't give a fuck about another club. I give a fuck about you. And your body." Looking into her eyes, Steele pushed her shirt up slowly.

Breezy couldn't look away. Staring into Steele's eyes was one of the sexiest things she'd ever felt, standing there, pressed against the building, his knuckles running slowly up her bare skin as he raised her shirt higher and higher. Her core pulsed with need. Hot. Coiled tight. Wet. Waiting for him. She spent half her time just waiting for him to be inside her.

"Is this what you're worried about?" He bent his head to press a kiss to that soft little area that proclaimed she'd had his baby. His teeth scraped gently and then his tongue soothed the ache. "This is my favorite spot." He pulled the shirt higher, up over her full breasts, holding the material under her chin.

"You're such a liar. You love my boobs."

He smiled, his eyes on her breasts. "You might be right about that."

Breezy wasn't wearing a bra, although she should have been, but Steele had objected. He liked the way her tight tank shaped her breasts, and she'd gone without the support just for him. Now, in the cool night air, her nipples peaked, and her breasts felt achy and hot. Waiting. Just like her sex, waiting for him.

Steele took his time, kissing his way from that soft little pooch up her rib cage to the underside of her breasts. She had to cling to his shoulders, her nails biting deep, or she might have fallen. He kissed his way over the curve of both breasts and then was sucking hard, flattening her nipple against the roof of his mouth while his hand caressed, kneaded and stroked the other breast. She gasped as sensations poured through her. He wasn't always gentle, and the contrast between rough and tender kept her off-balance. Then he worked her nipples, sending fiery arrows straight to her clit.

"Get them off."

She could barely hear him with the sound of the blood roaring in her ears. Hot blood rushed through her veins, spreading like a wildfire, until she was consumed with need. Her hands dropped obediently to the waistband of her jeans. They rode low on her hips and were fairly tight. She had to peel them from her, and he didn't stop sucking at her breast, making it even more difficult.

Her breath came in ragged pants and she wanted to arch her back, thrust her breasts into his mouth, encourage him to devour her, not bend forward to try to shimmy out of her jeans, but she did it. Fortunately, she had worn flats and she was able to kick them off, which allowed her to step on the jeans to strip them from her body. Then she was naked, the night mist lapping at her body like a thousand tongues to add to the sensual sensations overwhelming her.

He took his time, lavishing attention on

her breasts, tugging and rolling, pinching her nipples until she cried out and then lapping at them to soothe them. His marks were everywhere when he finally lifted his head. He tossed his shirt on the ground and pointed, his eyes that wild midnight color she loved so much.

She knelt immediately, her hands at his belt, swiftly opening his jeans, and then his fist was in her hair, jerking her head back, and his cock was in her mouth. The weight of it was heavy on her tongue. His girth stretched her lips. She loved the way he felt so heavy and solid, hot and perfect, steel and yet velvet. She wanted him every bit as far gone as she was. Hot and needy. Desperate for her the way she was desperate for him.

She used every skill she'd ever developed, wanting to please him. She looked up at his face, that perfect face she could spend hours staring at and never get tired of. He was hers. He loved her. She didn't know how she got so lucky, but kneeling in front of him, his cock sliding deep into her mouth and back out, over and over, fast and then slow, deep and shallow, with his fist tight in her hair, she felt like he belonged to her. He was hers, and that was everything she wanted.

She felt his cock expanding, just as his expression changed and his sac tightened. She swallowed him down, tightening her mouth, stroking with her tongue. He put pressure on her scalp, dragging her head back. She chased after his cock as he took it away from her.

"Not that way, baby. I want inside you. Stay where you are, stand up and put your hands on the wall, but head down."

She stood and turned, mostly because he didn't give her a choice. His hand went from the grip in her hair to the nape of her neck, pressing her head down with a steady pressure, so that she was bent over, nearly double.

"I don't see how I'm going to stay upright," she said and then hissed when his hand swiped across her damp, needy sex.

"I'll keep you where I want you," he assured, his fingers moving in her. Out of her. Driving her crazy.

She pushed back, trying to capture his finger as his thumb tapped her clit. Then he was flicking it, leaning in to run his tongue over it. Her breath came in ragged hitches. "Steele."

"Be still, Breezy, or we won't be joining the party. We'll spend the night right here."

She looked up at him from over her

shoulder. He looked just as needy, his cock intimidating as he fisted it, pumping up and down, his eyes on her sex. She tried hard not to move, but her body wouldn't cooperate, not when he continued to stroke and caress. He was the same way with her sex as he had been with her breasts. Keeping her off-balance with rough and then gentle. Soft little flicks that grew suddenly hard, then his tongue, then his mouth drawing out her liquid heat. Teeth that made her gasp. His hand on her buttocks hard, the sound carrying through the night along with her keening pleas.

"I'm so close." She was. Her body was coiled so tight the tension was nearly unbearable. "I have to . . ."

"*No.* Don't you dare. You hold on. I'm not done here." He accompanied the command with another nip of his teeth, and her entire body shuddered, trying to hold off the inevitable.

Steele lodged the head of his cock into her inferno, and his own breath hissed out. She was tight and like molten magma surrounding him, squeezing down, trying to pull him in deeper, trying to strangle him. It felt like heaven and hell combined. Perfection. "This what you want, baby?" She was pulsing around him. He could feel her wild heartbeat right through that broad, sensitive head. It was all he could do not to plunge deep.

"Yes. Steele." Her voice was a wail. "Hurry, honey. I need you right now."

That little wail was all he needed to hear. He gripped her hips hard, held her still and surged into her. Deep. So deep. She surrounded him with living, silken flames. Her soft cry added to the heat building in his body.

From his left, it registered that someone had come to investigate the noise, but he knew exactly where Keys and Maestro were. Maestro had already moved to casually intercept anyone from the other club who might be investigating the noise or looking for a place of privacy with their woman. Breezy was safe. He was safe. His brothers were watching his back.

Steele began to move in her, and each time he withdrew, he felt the little shudder that went through her body. That same tremor went down his spine. Shock waves walked up and down his thighs as he began to pound into her. He let himself go completely, forgetting control. Just taking her. His woman. He let himself just feel that perfect sensation. The way every cell in his body came alive. The way the flames burned over and in him. The way her pussy was so tight, clamping down on him, squeezing and massaging, the friction unbelievable.

He didn't want it to ever end. He rode her hard, twice snapping out the word *no.* How she held on, he didn't know. Only that if she didn't, she would take him with her and it would be over. He needed this monstrous release. When he was inside her, surrounded by those fiery muscles, everything else dropped away. His entire focus was right there. His cock disappearing into her, withdrawing, moist and hot. He half expected smoke to pour out with it.

A few more minutes and he knew it was going to be over. That place she took him with her body, where he left his past and every fucking mess he'd ever dealt with, was going to be gone. He renewed his efforts, determined to take every moment that he could. Then he was erupting before he'd had much warning, his seed jetting out of him, a wild, savage eruption, his cock jerking hard in her, giving her everything.

She cried out, that soft little mewl he loved, as her body clamped down hard on his. The ripples turned to quakes and then ferocious jolts until she'd milked every drop from him. He pressed kisses down her spine and waited until they both caught their breath before he straightened, helping her to stand.

"You all right, baby?" He used his T-shirt to clean between her legs.

"Better than all right." She leaned into him to run her tongue over one of his scars. She traced the tattoo Ink had put there to cover where the blade had bit deep.

He didn't pull away. She made him better. She managed to distance him from the loss of Demyan. When he was in her, Demyan and everything that had been done to both of them faded so far away, he was able to forget for a few precious moments. No one else was ever allowed to put their mouth on those tattoos. The scars were for his fallen brother. Breezy was the exception.

He pulled her tank over her head and settled it over her breasts. "Hate like hell covering these up, Bree. You're a work of art."

"Glad you think so."

"We're not finished. Before the night is through I'm going to give you at least five orgasms. Maybe more. And I'm taking you every way I want you. Everything that belongs to me." He kissed her again, because he had to. He lost himself in the fire of her mouth for some time. When he pulled back, her eyes were shining.

"Good thing I was prepared for that," Breezy said.

His woman. Of course she wouldn't say no. She stepped into her jeans and pulled them up and then slipped into her shoes while he zipped up his jeans and buckled his belt.

"I'll get you a shirt, Steele. I know you've got a few in the drawers in your room. I know you want to keep talking with the other club's members before everyone's gotten too drunk. I'll catch up with you."

He pulled on his cut. "You sure? I could go with you." He wasn't about to let her go without him watching over her. He knew her fears of clubs, and a party brought all of that out in her no matter how much she tried to overcome it.

"That's silly. I'm the VP's old lady. I know how to handle myself at a party."

She did. She always had. She was an asset to him. He had no doubt she'd circulate among the women and bring back all sorts of information to him. Still, he glanced at Keys, who nodded. He wouldn't take his eyes off the VP's old lady. She'd be safe because his brothers were there, watching, keeping their eyes on her. He'd trail after her but let his brothers keep their eyes wide open. His phone was already out, and he was sending a mass text: Eyes on my woman.

She leaned into him again, this time giving him her mouth. Steele took it. Sank into the kiss. Let himself revel in the fact that she was his. They had a son together. She loved him, and she was staying because she wanted to be with him. Right at that moment, he knew he had it all and if he was careful, he would always have it.

"I got this," Breezy lied, when Steele lifted his head, his eyes searching hers for reassurance.

Her stomach was churning, but she didn't dare press her hand there. He would notice. Steele noticed everything. She had to do this on her own. She had to know one way or the other. Pretending confidence was easy enough, she'd been doing that her entire life. Walking back into the clubhouse, head high, through a group of men she didn't know was terrifying. These were men invited to party, men Torpedo Ink were contemplating bringing into their club.

She forced herself to walk away from Steele without looking back. Her hands were shaking as she entered the common room. Sounds hit her first. Laughter. Men's voices. Women's. The smells. There was something about a party just getting started, but still, the anticipation of sex and alcohol mixed together. The music pounding out a beat adding to the eagerness in the room.

Breezy felt eyes on her. She knew the men were looking. Deliberately, she let her gaze move around the room. She was Steele's woman, responsible for making certain everything ran smoothly. One of the patch chasers, Betina, came right over.

"I'm Betina. That's Heidi." Her arm swept toward the other woman. "Is there something you want us to do?"

Breezy knew that was code for *Is there a particular man you want us to get close to?* She smiled at the woman and shook her head. "Unless Steele or Czar says differently, you have a good time." *Happy hunting,* she added silently. She hoped both women found what they were looking for. She'd been in a similar position.

Betina grinned at her and hurried back to the man she'd chosen for the night. Breezy took a deep breath and stepped farther into the room, her gaze once again sweeping around, taking in everything. She went straight to the bar to refill the wooden bowls set around the room with nuts and chips. Already beer bottles were everywhere. She started to gather them up, but Heidi was there first, taking them from her.

"I'll do this," the woman said, deference

in her voice.

"Thanks," Breezy said, working at keeping the shock from her voice.

"Hey, babe." Gavriil Prakenskii greeted her, circling her shoulders with one strong arm. He'd never done more than nod to her before. He had a woman with him, and by the way he was holding her hand, she clearly meant something to him. "Breezy, this is my wife, Lexi. It's her first time here. I was hoping you'd take her under your wing and look out for her when I'm mixing. We're just here for the barbecue."

"Hi, Lexi." The woman looked much more nervous than she was, and Breezy's heart went out to her. "The food looks great. Blythe is around here somewhere."

"I brought a variety of salads, and extra produce. Where should I put them?" Lexi asked.

"Produce in the kitchen and the salads outside on the long table," she answered immediately.

"I'll show you," Gavriil assured, his voice softening. He bent to brush a kiss on his wife's head. "Thanks, Breezy. Baby, you need anything, or you get overwhelmed, Breezy's the go-to girl. She's got this."

Lexi nodded her head, smiling, but Breezy could see she was already overwhelmed and made a mental note to keep a close watch over her. She'd taken two steps toward the hall when Casimir, another one of Czar's brothers, stopped her.

"Breezy, I want you to meet Lissa, my wife. We've brought a ton of food with us and need to know where you want it. Lissa, baby, I want you to meet Breezy. You need anything, and you can't find Blythe or me, hit Breezy up."

Breezy found herself liking Lissa, with her bright red hair and watchful gaze. She laughed, but her eyes were moving around the room, reminding Breezy of Lana and Alena. That gave her more confidence, that there was another woman watching out for all of them. She liked that. Lissa displayed an ease, being in the same room with all the men, as if she knew they didn't dare touch her if she didn't want to be touched. They chatted for a few more minutes and then headed for the kitchen.

Breezy had taken several more steps, and one of the newcomers, a tall man with a serious face and wildly long hair, intercepted her. She was forced to stop when he stepped directly in front of her. He wore his colors and his patch declared him sergeant at arms. Her heart beat wildly, and for a moment the edges of her vision went dark. She forced air through her lungs and plastered a smile on her face. As she did so, her gaze swept around the room.

Keys was there, not six feet from them and edging closer. Transporter had swiveled around on the barstool and was watching through narrowed eyes. One of the prospects, Fatei, the acting bartender, had paused in making a drink, his gaze on them. Absinthe, walking through the clubhouse, stopped dead in his tracks and turned toward them, changing directions.

Everywhere Breezy looked, there was a member of Torpedo Ink. Watching. They suddenly didn't appear as if they had no cares and were out for fun. Just the opposite. They looked every bit as lethal as she knew them to be.

She glanced toward the entrance, and it didn't surprise her to see Steele's tall frame filling the doorway. She shook her head slightly as her heart began to settle. She had to handle anything that came up on her own. She was the vice president's woman, and she'd been in the life forever. This was her domain, and she had to rule it.

"I'm Mavra. I was watching and realized you're clearly the one everyone relies on. I've brought my woman with me. Our VP and two others have women. They're new to the life and very nervous. We're going to be talking to your men and we won't be able to keep an eye on them every minute. We were hoping you'd take the time to get to know them and help them get acquainted with the other women."

Her heart lifted. Air rushed into her lungs. Another man looking out for his woman. He was from a different club. They might want to patch over to Torpedo Ink, but they still were in a club. She didn't have experience with men looking out for their women, but Gavriil and Casimir clearly were doing just that. Torpedo Ink was looking out for her. Her man was right there, waiting for a signal from her. This man and several of his brothers were looking out for their women.

"I'd be happy to. Let me get Steele a shirt and I'll be right back to meet them." She gave him a reassuring smile and glanced back at her man as Mavra moved out of her way.

Steele smiled at her, and her heart felt like it melted in her chest. She might have some anxiety when it came to the clubs and club life, especially over the parties, but it was disappearing fast.

She clearly was going to be the woman the others relied on, and that was all right with her. She had always taken the role, and it fit her. Steele was Torpedo Ink, and he was hers. He would always be her choice. Every time. She knew she was an asset to him, and it gave her every confidence. More, she was an asset to the club. Not in a demeaning way but in a way she could be proud of.

Breezy hurried down the hall to the room Steele used there in the clubhouse. She wasn't at all surprised when the door closed behind her and she turned to find him leaning against it. There was pride in his eyes. Adoration in his expression. Love. Stark. Raw. She could see it in him so easily. Her heart beat faster, the way it did whenever she looked at him.

"Want you again, woman."

"Got things to do, Steele."

His hands dropped to his belt buckle. "More important than me?"

She laughed softly, shaking her head, her eyes on his, happier than she ever thought possible. "There's nothing more important than you right now, Steele. Not one single thing."

TERMS ASSOCIATED WITH BIKER CLUBS

1%ers: This is a term often used in association with outlaw bikers, as in "99% of clubs are law abiding, but the other 1% are not." Sometimes the symbol is worn inside a diamond-shaped patch.

3-piece patch or 3-piece: This term is used for the configuration of a club's patch: the top piece, or rocker, with club name; a center patch that is the club's logo; and a bottom patch, or rocker, with the club's location, such as Sea Haven.

Biker: someone who rides a motorcycle

Biker friendly: a business that welcomes bikers

Boneyard: refers to a salvage yard

Cage: often refers to a car, van or truck (basically any vehicle that's not a motorcycle)

Chapter: the local unit of a larger club

Chase vehicle: a vehicle following riders on a run just in case of a breakdown

Chopper: customized bike

Church: club meeting

Citizen: someone who's not a biker

Club: could be any group of riders banding together (most friendly)

Colors: patches, logo, something worth fighting for because it represents who you are

Cut: vest or denim jacket with sleeves cut off and club colors on it; almost always worn, even over leather jackets

Dome: helmet

Getting patched: Moving up from prospect to full club member (you would receive the logo patch to wear with rockers). This must be earned, and is the only way to get respect from brothers.

Hang-around: anyone hanging around the club who might want to join

Hog: nickname for motorcycle, mostly associated with Harley-Davidson

Independent: a biker with no club affiliation

Ink: tattoo

Ink slinger: a tattoo artist

Nomad: club member who travels between chapters; goes where he's needed in his club

Old lady: Wife or woman who has been with a man for a long time. It is not considered disrespectful nor does it have anything to do with how old one is.

Patch holder: member of a motorcycle club

Patches: Sewn on vests or jackets, these can be many things with meanings or just for fun, even gotten from runs made.

Poser: pretend biker

Property of: a patch displayed on a jacket, vest or sometimes a tattoo, meaning the woman (usually old lady or longtime girlfriend) is with the man and his club

Prospect: someone working toward becoming a fully patched club member

ABOUT THE AUTHOR

Christine Feehan is the #1 *New York Times* bestselling author of the Carpathian series, the GhostWalker series, the Leopard series, the Shadow Riders series, and the Sea Haven novels, including the Drake Sisters series and the Sisters of the Heart series. She lives in the beautiful mountains of Lake County, California. Please visit her website at www.christinefeehan.com.

The employees of Thorndike Press hope you have enjoyed this Large Print book. All our Thorndike, Wheeler, and Kennebec Large Print titles are designed for easy reading, and all our books are made to last. Other Thorndike Press Large Print books are available at your library, through selected bookstores, or directly from us.

For information about titles, please call:
(800) 223-1244

or visit our website at:
gale.com/thorndike

To share your comments, please write:

Publisher
Thorndike Press
10 Water St., Suite 310
Waterville, ME 04901